She had fallen atop him from the ladder. He laughed good-naturedly, not in the least perturbed.

"Odious brute!" said Kate from the floor. He laughed and offered her his hand. She took it and a moment later was tightly wound in his strong embrace. His green eyes held her gray, and his mouth was very near her own. She was startled by the suddenness of his move and disconcertedly all too aware of his magnetism. She pushed ineffectually against his chest. "Unhand me, cur."

"The lady's tongue is sharp but I'll warrant her lips are sweet," said he. His mouth took her own, separating her lips, and as he took the promised honey she felt herself losing control. His kiss affected her in a way she had never dreamed possible. Here she was, in the arms of a stranger and enjoying every moment. . . .

Fawcett Crest Books
by Claudette Williams:

SPRING GAMBIT

AFTER THE STORM

SUNDAY'S CHILD

SASSY

BLADES OF PASSION

Blades
of
Passion

Claudette Williams

A FAWCETT CREST BOOK • NEW YORK

To my agent Jay Garon

BLADES OF PASSION

Published by Fawcett Crest Books, CBS Publications, the
Consumer Publishing Division of CBS, Inc.

Copyright © 1978 by Claudette Williams

ISBN: 0-449-23481-9

Printed in the United States of America

10 9 8 7 6 5 4 3 2 1

1

"Papa . . . do not say no! You must not! 'Twould be monstrous cruel of you," cried Kathleen Newbury. She was fourteen and at such an age, consents and denials take on a life and death quality.

Her father's gentle smile soothed her troubled countenance and his white soft hands took her shoulders. "Kathleen, dearest, we have already been over the matter. I thought you understood."

"No. I do not understand!" She was on the verge of tears.

He put a hand through his graying soft brown locks and turned away from her. "My dear child, you must consider the impracticalities of you accompanying me at such a time."

"But, Papa, I *do* think of practicalities. I do! It would be far more wise to have me with you, where you could keep a watchful eye upon me than to leave me to my own devices here!"

He laughed and glanced back at her earnest little face. "Nell will guard you a sight better than I."

She pouted, and her gray eyes pleaded. "Papa, please take me to England with you. Please, 'tis my home as well as yours and I would be so good."

"No, Kate." His voice was grave and unyielding.

"You . . . you *want* to leave me here," she said, her voice catching in her throat. She was of the age where change is most bewildering, and now that her one remaining parent was about to depart for England some three thousand miles away, Kate was miserable!

"Want to leave you?" repeated Sir Horace, much struck by so unthinkable a notion. "My sweet child, you have been, will always be all the love, all the good that has

5

ever happened to me." He touched her long raven curls. "Want to leave you indeed! No, child. I go to England because *I must* and cannot approve of you dropping your education and carting off poor Nell in our wake—for you know how ill the ocean makes her—simply for the few moments we can spend together. You must see that is all the time I would be able to give you. I shan't be able to remain with you at Lyndhurst Grange, for I shall be in London taking up my seat in Parliament. Between my duties there—political routs, and other obligations— well, you can see, Kate, we would not be able to spend much time together." He saw her tears begin to spill over and he sighed heavily. "Don't, Kate. Lord, you would think I was about to leave forever. I shall be back in the spring."

"You said that the last time you left for England . . . and you did not return for *two years.* Oh, Papa, *two years!"* She shook her head fitfully. "Papa, do not leave without me. Bermuda grows too small for me!"

He chuckled in spite of her distress, "Ah, naughty puss, who was it declared to me that she loved her gentle isle and would never leave it?"

"Oh, and I do. I always shall but I can remember Lynd- hurst Grange. After all, I was seven years old, not at all a babe when we left, and it was beautiful, too. It is my *real* home."

His face clouded over. "You will go home when you have come of age. Your mother's sister has often said you must, and so you shall; but not before!"

"But, Papa . . ."

"Enough, Kate. I grow weary with this," he said, and his voice was hard.

She knew the tone. His decision was final. He would allow no more discussion regarding the issue. And he did not.

That was four years ago! It was now mid-October, the year was 1804, and Sir Horace still had not returned!

The sky that topped the small coral islands known as the Bermuda Isles was gray and it hung low as though in conversation with the variegated patches of green and pink below. Clouds scudded through the air, dropping mist-like tears on the land beneath their swift route. Trees whipped dangerously into one another and argued dis-temperedly with the onrushing air. The lime-colored water of the bay had turned a dark foreboding hue. It seemed irritated by the discord above and churned angrily showing a mood that would not welcome would-be in-vaders!

Kate's cloak blew about her, protesting against her small lithe body, urging her to seek shelter. Her waist-length black hair rippled, waved, and dived in perfect harmony with the wind's cadence. Her cheeks were rosy from the cool touch of the restless air, and she stood in the force of nature, a prize of all that is beauty and youth! She had grown, and at eighteen was what her exquisite childhood had promised to the future!

Kate stood on the crest of a grassy slope. It cascaded gently into the waters of Ely's Harbor over which the Newbury estate was situated. Kate's gray eyes scanned the moving dark clouds, she was troubled by the quiet. The gulls seemed to have vanished and the uneasy silence invited the hidden threat of the swirling winds, their promise hung about, tauntingly!

The *Venture,* a merchant ship from the United States, was due into port. Nearly everyone in the house was clicking their tongues and speaking in hushed whispers. With the weather taking a black turn, the Bermudians could talk of nothing else, for a gale was expected to strike. Its obscure warnings hovered about the isle, and the good people, many of whom made an excellent living from salvaging and privateering, waited!

Kate had not been able to stand the talk any longer. She had run from the house, disgusted with the whispers, sickened by the hidden light in expectant eyes. She stood on the slope and prayed. "Please hurry. Come in safely."

The spray of rain sprinkled her face and she lifted the wide blue hood of her linen cloak and covered her head. It was beginning to come down hard and she turned, heading toward the large bright house that had been her home for more than ten years. It stood some three hundred yards away, proud and lovely and even in the gray light, warm and welcoming! Its pink sandstone and white pillared front portico was majestic against the lush green of neat gardens. Its balconies were trimmed with black iron railings whose design had been imported from the southern states of United States. The house's detail spoke of luxury, its design, of common sense. A section of the roof had been created flat, and built on it was a top reservoir which caught, held and provided the household with fresh rainwater. The windows adorning the stately home were long, wide, and diamond-paned with lead. The windows, and most of the house's furnishings, came from England.

Kate loved it, and could not remember ever having been discontented until recently. Now everything seemed to annoy or disappoint her! She hated the wreck salvaging, and she hated privateering! The fact that her father was directly involved in the questionable industry, had not softened her toward it. She had often argued the point with Sir Horace and his partner Mr. Ludlow. They were adamant and laughed at her, saying, after all she was but a girl, not able to comprehend a man's world! Yet, even then, she hadn't realized the full implications of the hushed whisperings, the strange slow smiles of the villagers whenever the winds went dour! She had been a child, and innocent enough to thrill at the sight of the big ships fighting the storm! It had been exciting to watch the seamen row out to meet the men tossed from ships that crashed into the reefs and coral traps. It had been the pride of watching a Bermudian privateer escort an enemy vessel into port, and it had been the satisfaction of thinking she was on the winning side!

Then the child began to learn. There was a thing called money! Salvaging meant money. Privateering meant money. Men made profit on men's tragedies. The kindly village people, her own father, salvaged; waited to salvage, for money. Armed privateers captured unarmed merchant ships, and she couldn't excuse it by declaring them "the enemy." She couldn't understand what sort of law, what kind of reasoning allowed one man to take another's property on the open seas! It was legalized piracy and unworthy of Englishmen. She had grown into a woman, but had yet to shed her "innocence."

A black slave girl with short frayed hair and bright dark eyes appeared at the front door and began waving her arm in welcome. She called to Kate but the sound was lost to the wind.

Kate smiled as she rushed under the protective cover of the portico and caught the expression on the parlor maid's face, "Well, Dora, whatever has you in such glory?" teased Kate.

"Lordy Miss Kate, you'll never guess, but it's that pleased you's gonna be! Miss Ellen, she wants you to come to her right away," said the girl excitedly.

Kate's smile broadened. "What's to do?"

"Tandum, he done come from Mr. Ludlow, and there be a letter . . . it's from your papa."

Kate's eyes reflected her emotions. "From Papa? Oh, silly chit, why didn't you say so at once? Where is Nell?"

The girl pouted. "She be waiting in the parlor. Said to fetch you and I did."

Kate rushed off, leaving the girl to grumble her grievances to herself. A letter . . . a letter from her father! It was the one thing for which she had been waiting. More than two months had gone by since his last. She rushed at the parlor door, forcefully flinging it open.

A woman of substantial height and girth, wearing an ivory lace cap over her short gray curls, stood by the window holding her spectacles to her eyes and scanning a crisp sheet of paper. She looked up as Kate hurled herself into the room and the smile in her soft pink face was warm. "Darling, oh dear Kathleen. You have been in the rain for your lovely cloak is soaked through. Do take it off and put it by the fire."

Kate dropped it impatiently onto a nearby stool and brought her anxious eyes to her governess's quiet expression. "Nell, is that papa's letter? Oh do give it over," she said, coming forward with her hand outstretched.

Miss Ellen Premble sighed and moved toward the cushioned sofa. She sank down heavily and patted the empty spot beside her. "Do calm yourself, love, and sit."

Kate made an irritated sound but sat on the edge of the sofa next to her governess and exclaimed, "Calm myself? I shall. Only *do* give me his letter, Nell. Really, you are a dreadful tease!"

"Hush child. I am no such thing. This letter, at any rate, was addressed to me; however, do take it and read it aloud, for I declare its contents have me spinning, and I am not sure of what I have read."

Kate frowned, and the hurt showed in her gray eyes. Not addressed to her, but to Nell. How odd. However, she took up the letter and started hesitatingly:

My dear Miss Premble,

Lady Sarah Haverly, Kathleen's maternal aunt, instructs me that it is time my daughter were presented to the *haut ton*. As her arguments are sound, I yield, and in so doing, give over to my selfish need to see my daughter again.

Kindly accept my apologies, for I am aware that you find sea travel most uncomfortable, but as I am persuaded you would not wish to be separated from Kate, I have asked Mr. Ludlow to book passage for you both as soon as possible. There will be very little other than packing for you to do as I have requested Mr. Ludlow to see to the house during our absence.

I sincerely hope you will not find the sea too unkind, and I look forward to greeting you upon your arrival, which I look to early November.

To Kate, please give my deepest love, for there was no time to jot off another sheet to her.

Horace Newbury

Kate looked up from the short strange epistle and felt her body tremble with excitement. They were going to England. Finally she would be reunited with her father! She jumped to her feet and did a tailspin, hugging herself and making a whooping sound that brought Miss Ellen's rebukes down upon her. Heedlessly, she rushed across the room, down the polished cedar floor of the central hall to its double white doors and out of the house.

"Kate! Kathleen!" called Miss Ellen starting after her. "Kathleen Newbury, where do you think you are going?" She received no response, and with a rueful twist to her thin lips she returned to the parlor thinking it a silly question. "Where *would* Kate be going but to Daniel Ludlow! She spied the discarded cloak fallen limply upon the stool and clucked her tongue. "Impetuous child," she scolded out loud.

2

Kate sped across the side lawns, unmindful of the drizzle, and found the double row of palmettos that divided Ludlow land from Newbury. She bent and wound her way through the path that she and Danny had formed years ago, coming out on Ludlow lawns and rushing across to the drive that led to the great mansion at its head. Suddenly she was pounced on from behind, "What form of wild creature is this?" rallied a young man's voice at the back of her head, as he held her steadfastly in his long lanky arms.

She laughed and attempted to free herself, but finding the effort useless, laughed again and demanded, "Daniel Ludlow, release me at once!"

"Then pay me a toll, for you have crossed my land," he replied, a tease in his voice. Daniel was a tall, thin, fair-haired pleasant-faced youth some three months younger than Kate. He had still to reach the glorious age of eighteen, but he was and always had been Kate's dearest friend and confidant.

She turned in his loosened grip, grinning up at him

hoydenishly. His yellow waves were being tossed by the damp wind and his blue eyes were still to her the eyes of a friend. She gave him a peck upon his cheek that sent a titillating thrill up the young man's spine and he pressed her closer to him. "That, m'girl, is *not* the sort of toll *I* had in mind!" It was easy to flirt with Kate, for he was totally at ease in her company. Then, too, he had recently been acquiring the knack of love-making, having learned the art from a set of willing wenches in a certain house on Front Street.

On the other hand, Kate was totally unfamiliar with such arts. She had no other close male friends, and had only once experienced the craft of dalliance. The poet Tom Moore had arrived in Bermuda just this past January. They had met at an informal dinner party and he had singled her out. His flirting was audacious and most delightful. She had been aroused and certainly dazzled by it all. However, Kate had high ideals about love and marriage and their light flirtation had gone no further than pretty words. By the time he returned to England in April, she had learned to bat her lashes and turn a remark, but she had learned little else.

She was not totally unaware of Danny's growing needs, yet she was not ready or willing to satisfy them. However, she had no objection to the adventure of exploration. "What in particular did you wish me to pay, sir?"

His lips were on hers in a minute, taking her own with the brutality of youthful frenzy. He fumbled the affair badly and Kate pulled away and laughed, "Silly boy! Have done! Now come on, I have something to tell you!"

His face took on a sulky closedness, and she laughed again, taking up his hand and pulling him along with her enthusiasm. "Let us go to the cove where we can be dry! Come on, Danny, you needn't look like a bear. I am sure if you practice you will get the hang of kissing!"

"Practice?" he asked, his eyes lighting up.

"Why yes, of course. You must, you know. That is how a man acquires the trick of it. At least *I think* that is how," said Kate, frowning over the problem.

"Very well then, let us practice!" agreed Danny amiably.

"Not with *me*, stupid! You must do so with . . ." she smiled knowingly up at him, ". . . Regina Henshaw."

He blushed and shot her an angry look. "Who told you about Regina?"

She giggled. "It does not matter. What does, is that she has not taught you quite enough."

He took umbrage. "As it happens, she has taught me a damn sight more than I have shown you!"

"I certainly hope so and if you think you are going to show me everything that little minx has taught you, you are very much mistaken, Daniel Ludlow! That, my friend, is for my future husband to teach me!"

"Then marry me, Kate. Please do."

"Danny, you cannot mean that," said Kate, startled and turning to eye him with disbelief.

"Mean it . . . you have no idea, Kate. I love being with you. I needn't worry about what I say or rush about being polite. You don't have hysterics or damned fainting spells, and I do so like the way you are formed. It half sets me to dreaming. Lord, Kate, I want you." He pulled her to him and his youthful voice was husky. "Kate, marry me . . . do!"

"Danny, why if I were silly enough to do so, you would regret it inside a month. You are but seventeen with your entire life ahead. We are the best of friends because I make no demands on you; if you were a husband 'twould be different. I don't know how I know it but I just do. We would not make good lovers, and I do think it is important for man and wife to be lovers as well."

"Why? My parents aren't, and they are most comfortable together."

"Well, I want more than comfort. Now do drop the subject or I shall go mad. I have something to tell you!"

They finished scrambling down the rocky slope to where a boot-shaped cove enclosed them with its limestone and coral walls. The beach was covered with seaweed thrown up by the angry waves, and Kate pressed herself beneath the overhang and put a hand to her wet head.

Danny regarded her with a grumbling countenance but leaned against the wall and waited.

"Danny, my father has sent for me," she blurted out all at once. "We are to leave on the next ship to England. He has asked your father to make all the arrangements!"

"Damnation!" exploded Danny, thunderstruck.

"Danny!" exclaimed Kate, stamping her foot. "You are being horrid!"

"What did you expect? Did you wish me to *want* you to go?"

"But, aren't you happy for me?" she asked, bewildered by his attitude.

He glanced at her piquant face and relented. "Lord, yes, I am glad that you will be seeing your father, because I always want you happy and I know that is what *you* want. But, Kate, how will I go on without you?"

She patted his hand. "Danny, it won't be forever."

"It will seem forever. I suppose your aunt will be having a ball for you?" he asked sourly.

"I suppose, for Aunt Sarah is to present me in London. Oh, I do wish you were coming with me. It would be so nice to have a friend in London."

He gave her a half smile. "Do you really mean that?"

She frowned at him, "Of course I do. Whatever is wrong with you, Danny? You are so bad tempered these days."

He shrugged. "Don't pay it any mind. You know, Kate. . . ." He cut himself short and listened, for the sound of his father's voice boomed through the air. "That's Father! Come on, something must be wrong!" he said, pulling her away from the enclosure and helping her up the jagged slope. They reached the flat top surface to find a tall heavy-set man wearing a dark captain's hat that covered his white-blonde locks and sitting astride a magnificent bay. The horse snorted in the wind and shook its head. He nodded to his son and touched the tip of his hat to Kate, and his voice bellowed, "Come on, lad! No time to

lose. There is the *Venture* and the damn fools are heading
for the reefs. Their mizzen is already down, and if we
are to scoop up any of those poor devils we've got to
step lively!" He turned to Kate. "You, my fair wench,
get yourself home! The storm is going to break and there
is bound to be trees coming down. I don't want any of
them taking you with them, nor do I want you blown
off this isle of ours!" He liked Kate, and had he been
a single man he would have chosen her for himself.
Choosing her for his son would have to do!

Kate put up her lovely chin and her gray eyes twinkled
and their light was warm in contrast with her tone.
"Dearest Sir, you don't really think I intend to obey such
unkind dictates. I'll come with you whether you please
or not, for I am no namby-pamby female to be left out
of such doings!" Mr. Thomas Ludlow liked her spirit,
she was a daughter of his heart.

"Namby-pamby! Ha! What you are be more than I
can say, girl! But if you are so set on getting a soaking,
then come on, for that blasted ship out there ain't about
to wait on us!"

3

He threw the reins of the roan at his back into his
son's hands. Danny steadied the horse while Kate
hoisted herself onto the flat neat saddle and adjusted the
wide skirt of her blue muslin around her. A moment
later, with Danny at her back and guiding the horse,
they were following Mr. Ludlow down the narrow road
south to the tiny drawbridge at Somerset. The wind had
picked up a sudden force and the swirling commotion
of air beat at their bodies. The crack of wood came
to their ears, as a tree, unable to cope with the wind,
fell blocking their path. Mr. Ludlow's horse reared and

its forelegs slapped at the air causing Danny's horse to whinny with fright. A moment was lost regaining control before they were able to continue on their way. Kate studied Mr. Ludlow and turned to catch the same look about his son. They were in full control, heedless of what might have been had they been caught beneath the blow of the falling tree, and unmindful of what might come!

They reached the narrow drawbridge that connected Somerset Isle with the main island and walked their horses cautiously over its wooden planks, breaking out into a canter when they reached the other side. They continued south on the main pike until they reached a slit in the dense forest where they turned sharply, making for the knoll known as Wreck's Hill. Men on horseback and some in wagons seemed to be everywhere, hurrying toward the harbor. The sound of their shouting was filled with fervor, blotting out the thoughts tumbling in Kate's mind. Then all at once there was the sea! The sharp jutting reefs seemed to have arms and hands reaching out possessively, and Kate could see the merchant yawl pitching out of control as it swung helplessly into those arms!

The mizzenmast was down and its sails flapped grotesquely in the wind. The ship seemed a veritable babe being tossed about by unfeeling, pitiless waters. The relentless waves kept up a steady rhythm, battering at the booms, cracking the gaffs, playing havoc with the shattered rudder, and the reefs beneath and before tore into the hull!

It was the sound of death and it echoed painfully, yet the sea took its payment, pleased with the victory! Kate felt Danny slide off the horse, but she remained seated, unable to take her eyes away from the heartbreaking sight. The ship's agony swept through her, for it was being taken slowly, torturously. There was a moment of awesome silence as the seamen around Kate stood on the docks and the sandy beach and watched, paying their last respects to the *Venture*. Then all at once a bustle of movements and oaths collided with the storm.

"Come on, Kate. If you are going to be of any help to those poor souls we haul in, you best keep your head and take shelter!" said Mr. Ludlow, gruffly pulling her out of the saddle and ushering her beneath a natural rock formation. He shrugged off the dark cloak he had been wearing and set it upon her shoulders, and without another word turned and left her. She watched the hardy seamen heave their galleys into the hostile waters. Three galleys went out and Kate watched as the men rowed against the current and against the gales, staying safely in the inlet, away from the reefs. The swells hid them from view almost constantly. There would be no salvaging now. Not while the tempest blew. But they would search the waters for survivors.

The yawl's mainmast gave way with an ear-splitting sound and Kate closed her eyes in a useless attempt to shut out the sight! Her mind's eye saw it all. The ship threw itself against the reefs, gnashing away at its bow, as though defying the rocks in its last proud effort! The hull split, and the thundering moan broke through Kate's body. She opened her eyes and shook her head. She hated the ocean! It was a faithless friend, capricious and unprincipled. She watched the ship take in water, knowing from past experience that 'twould be another two hours before she would be lost to sight. Only the masts speared on their deathtrap would be a landmark of the wreck . . . and then, the salvage work would begin!

She hated it! She hated all of it. There was a savageness about the sea that extended to the men that worked it. And why couldn't she see Danny and his father? These ragings went irritably through her working mind as she watched the darkly-clad seamen who had remained behind gathering blankets. Most of them were known to Kate. Some were fishermen and others worked for her father and Mr. Ludlow. All at once she saw a sailor in wide dark slops jump and make a bugle of his hands!

He shouted a welcome to an incoming galley and Kate went forward hopefully. It wasn't the Ludlow galley and Danny was still out of sight. The men were straining at the oars, yet their countenances expressed their pleasure.

Three men, soaked and half conscious were carried and laid out on the soft creamy sand and Kate exclaimed pitifully as she knelt beside them, "Oh dear, poor things are half drowned. Where is Doctor Wilton?"

"He be delivering the Starkes' baby," answered a sailor handing her a blanket.

"Of all times!" exclaimed Kate impatiently.

The same sailor laughed. "Babies don't wait on gales and their like, Miss Newbury."

She said nothing to this but continued to attend the injured crew of the *Venture*. One of the crewmen, an older fellow with blood pouring from a wound gashed across his bald head, attempted to sit up and called out for someone named Jake. Kate attempted to quiet him, gently pushing him back onto the sand, but he would have none of it. She dabbed at the blood streaming over his temple with the clean linens that had been brought, and she tried to calm him. "Now, don't worry, your friend Jake will be here. All the boats have not returned yet."

However, as she was speaking the second galley was rowed in. The downcast looks of the men told its own story. They had brought no human catch. The Ludlow galley had not returned yet, and Kate scanned the dark rolling waves. Where was Danny? Oh God, let them be safe, please let them be safe. Suddenly she heard a whoop of hurrah shoot through the men on shore. She saw their woolen caps fly into the air and her heart began beating again. She stared hard, trying to find what they had already spotted and she caught sight of Danny and his father, their faces triumphant because they had not returned with empty hands!

Their galley was pulled on shore and surrounded before Kate was given five more battered crewmen to nurse. She had to take a moment to find Danny and pinched his chin proudly. "What a wonder you Ludlows are! I knew you would do it!"

He blushed but seemed pleased enough. " 'Twas nought! The poor devils we fished out had sense enough to ride the wreckage! That's what saved them you know, floated right to us."

Kate sighed and went back to her job, but she was soon called away by the sailor whose head injury she had tended earlier. He had seen the new arrivals and put up his head calling again, "Jake, Jake?"

Kate frowned and called for Danny as she went to him. "Do lie still, sir. You will open up your wound and begin bleeding again. You will see your friend, for soon the wagons will take you to a local tavern where you will be fed and sheltered."

He sobbed into his hands, "My son, my son Jake."

Kate watched him and was struck with pity. Danny arrived and frowned. "What's to do?"

"His son. He is worried about his son."

Danny closed his eyes, for there was little hope for any man who had not yet been brought in. He put his hand on the old man's shoulder and patted it, and Kate felt a sudden urge to cry. Oh God, death was terrible to the ones it did not take!

Mr. Ludlow appeared suddenly and took Kate's hand, leading her firmly away. "Now then, Kathleen, up you go," he said, lifting her up and seating her like some baggage atop Danny's roan. "There be nought for you to do now. We will be taking the men to the Boar's Head and, if I'm not to catch it from Miss Ellen, you'd better hurry home!"

Suddenly Kate felt drained, but she looked directly into his eyes, needing to know. "How many men died today, Mr. Ludlow?"

"You don't ask that, Kate darlin'. 'Tain't how many died, it's how many lived. Eleven men survived that wreck!"

"Damn the winds!" said Kate harshly, heedless of her tongue. "Why didn't the *Venture* stay in open waters? Why did she try to make harbor in such a gale?"

"Hush, Kate. Why don't matter anymore. Go home," he said gravely. She acquiesced. She was tired and could do no more. She'd wanted a miracle. Oh God, she did believe in miracles, but it hadn't come about. She had wanted to see the *Venture* sail safely past the reefs and into port. She'd wanted that old man's son to be alive, and she discovered that she was powerless! It left her empty. Wishes were for children and power belonged to the gods!

Danny waved as she rode his horse past them all and made her way up the slope. The rain had soaked through Mr. Ludlow's cloak, and she felt wet and miserable, yet when Danny's eyes had found her, he had laughed and shouted out that she looked like a wet kitten. His voice stroked her and it was a good clean sensation.

She knew that she would always think of Danny as her closest friend, but never as a lover. Ah, but he, young fellow, suffered as all youths suffer when met with a bout of infatuation! She chose to ignore it, hoping the problem would go away.

The windows of the Newbury house were alight with glowing tapers. The light threw itself eerily on the bending palms and the dark sky thundered. A black slave came running out of the stables and Kate jumped off the roan, putting the reins into the boy's hands.

"Wipe him down, Jude; he has had a rough time of it."

"Jest as ya say, Miss Kate," he said smiling, "but yous better hurry up to the house, for they be in a real fret about ya."

She smiled and ran up to the front portico to find the door flung open for her. Dora was frowning and her eyes were wide open. "Lordy, Miss Kate, how ya can go off in such a terrible storm. Why, Miss Ellen be that fitful . . ."

"Hush, Dora, for I am back and shall set her at ease," said Kate, making for the parlor door.

Dora shook her head, displeased with her mistress's

carefree manner, and returned to the kitchen quarters.

Miss Ellen looked up from the tapestry she was working on and her hazel eyes were reproachful. "So, young lady, you have decided to return home."

Kate recognized the tone and grimaced, for it usually meant a severe lecture would follow. "Now Nell, love, don't be put out with me. You know that the doctor was at the Starkes', delivering their baby, and Nell, the *Venture* went down!"

Miss Ellen's brows drew together. "Oh, those poor men. Those poor wretched men."

"A few I think . . . were not found," said Kate in a whisper.

Miss Ellen clucked her tongue but turned a grave expression on her charge, "That is of course quite dreadful, but it does not excuse your going out in a hurricane!"

" 'Twas not a hurricane, Nell. Only a wee gale," said Kate, picking up a sweet.

Miss Ellen reached out and swooped the sweet out of her charge's hand. "Not before dinner, and don't offer me such fustian! 'Twas a tempest and well you know it! It is exactly as Shakespeare described in his play *The Tempest* when those poor strange people became shipwrecked in Bermuda."

"Ah, but how do you know 'twas Bermuda? For *that* Isle had all sorts of monsters dwelling there, and *we* do not!" laughed Kate banteringly.

"Do not change the subject!" said Miss Ellen, not to be put off. "Was it a *little wind* that took that poor ship?"

"That, Nell, is underhanded," returned Kate, putting up a brow.

"So it is, love, but *I must* make you see. Your hoydenish manners may do very well for these heathenish islands, but it will not serve amongst the ton of England!"

"Oh Nell, don't pucker up so. I shall do very well in London, for I doubt they have our gales!"

"Look at you! Your gown is soaked through, your hands are brown from the sun, for you are too stubborn to wear gloves. Oh, Kathleen, you have no idea the sort of snubs you will incur if you continue your care-free antics! Once in London you must adhere to the proprieties!"

"And so I shall. Now . . ."—Kate started to brush the matter aside—"you are quite right, Nell, my gown is wet through and I will catch my death standing here listening to you prose on. I shall go upstairs and change before dinner, for I am famished." Spying her governess's dissatisfied expression she stopped and patted her cheek. "Dearest Nell, mother of my heart, I shall contrive to make you proud. Why, in no time I shall be *strutting* like a lady."

"Strut!" ejaculated Miss Ellen, cutting her off sharply. "Oh, child, never say so. A lady strolls demurely."

"Stroll then—dash it, Nell!"

"Dash it! What sort of an expression is that for a lady?" scolded her governess.

Kathleen Newbury put up her hands and decided 'twas best to leave Nell to herself. Something was picking at the governess, something that had little to do with Kate being out in the storm.

Indeed, in this thought Kate was correct. Miss Ellen was in a most disturbing pucker. Ten years ago she had hoped they would not leave England. The thought of leaving Lyndhurst Grange and going across the ocean to some outlandish island had terrified her. The sea voyage had made her ill and the early months in Bermuda left her pining for home. However, she had come to love the coral isles with their slow, gentle society. She had thrown herself into the refurbishing of the estate. Her friends were numerous and her life with Kate delightfully sheltered. Leaving here would be a sad undertaking, but even this was not the root of her disturbed state of mind! It was another concern, a far more serious concern. Taking Kathleen whom she loved as her own, taking her sweet innocent to England would be like taking a drop of snow to a torrid land. There were *truths,* the very truths Sir Horace had brought Kate to Bermuda to escape, the truths he had shielded her from all these years would be there waiting! And how was she to protect her charge from their discovery?

4

Kate drew the mauve damask draperies and tied them back with their dark brown ropings. She pulled open the glass door, unlatched and threw the shutters wide, breaking one of her nails in the process, for they had been bolted tightly against the storm. Controlling an urge to swear, she examined the damaged nail and sighed.

The morning was too lovely, too bright to be spoiled by such a thing. She rushed onto her small balcony and leaned over the iron railing surveying her familiar world. Everything glowed. One could hardly remember that only hours ago winds had ravaged the islands. But the telltale signs lay strewn about for inspection. An up-rooted cedar and the battered fronds of palmettos had fallen on the lawn, their leaves sadly sighing their story in the breeze. The estate was already buzzing with life as black slaves set about putting the gardens to rights. Kate listened to their early morning humming with a smile. Their song was sweetness to her ears . . . yet they were slaves! She had often wondered how they could sing as they so often did. More often than not she was struck by their capacity to endure the unendurable, to smile when life demanded their tears!

Kate sighed and turned off such thoughts. England lay ahead of her! She would go into Hamilton today for there were a few purchases that must be made. It would be November when they arrived in England and unlike the gentle warmth of Bermuda, her motherland would be cold! She had not the proper garments!

Dora knocked and came lightly into the bedroom car-

rying a tray laden with coffee and biscuits and jabbering
easy nonsense as she went about her business. Kate instructed her to lay out her riding habit and proceeded
to wash before drinking her coffee.

At length she stood before the looking glass for final
inspection. She wore a velvet riding habit of pale blue,
over a yellow high necked organza blouse. As she had
not yet come out, her long black hair hung down her
back, brushed and tied with a blue ribbon at the nape
of her neck. Black curls fringed her forehead and a
modish hat of the same blue velvet as her riding habit
was set naughtily upon her head. Her gray eyes were
sparkles of warmth and her complexion an enviable
attribute!

"It's that pretty yous be, Miss Kate," said Dora approvingly.

She smiled at her maid, well pleased with the compliment, and made her unhurried way downstairs. She
peeked into the morning room where she found Miss
Ellen enjoying a hearty breakfast.

"Good morning, Nell," said Kate, picking up a piece of
toast and munching happily.

"Wherever are you off to? Do sit down and eat breakfast, darling," replied Nell.

"No time, and besides I'm not really hungry," answered Kate amiably.

Miss Ellen eyed her. "For a girl who is not hungry,
you are doing rather a thorough job of downing my
breakfast," said Nell, as Kate swallowed a piece of
bacon.

Kate laughed, wiped her fingers and drew on her blue
kid gloves. "You are such a love, Nell," she said, giving
her governess a hug. "I shall be back for luncheon."

"But where are you going?" demanded Miss Ellen,
frowning.

"To Hamilton. We have nothing suitable to wear on
our sea voyage, you know."

"But darling, you will want to purchase your gowns

for your coming out ball in London from a modiste of the first stare."

Kate laughed and eyed her governess. *"Modiste of the first stare?* To be sure, Nell, love, so I shall, but in the interim we must be clothed and neither of us have anything warm enough."

"Very well, but don't bother your head about me, I shall uncover something from my trunks, no doubt."

"No doubt, but dearest Nell, you have grown so beautifully in the last ten years, I am sure they might not fit you." She giggled at Miss Ellen's expression, hugged her once again and merrily made her way out of the house.

A few moments later she was astride her mare, trotting down the drive to the main road. Sidesaddle was a thing she had detested and given up long ago. She quickly learned the knack of adjusting her skirts to accommodate her unorthodox, masculine seat. The mare champed at her bit, anxious for a run. Kate smiled and whispered soothingly into the horse's ears, but at length gave the mare her head. They cantered easily, at one with each other and the glory of morning. The exhilaration of the ride was in harmony with her mood but Kate reined in gently. "There now, love, you don't want to be doing too much too soon. We have a bit of a ride yet."

She guided the mare into a paced trot over the road and reached Somerset Drawbridge quickly. Here she held her mare in check, because the planking of the bridge had been raised to allow a small sailboat to pass through. She was taken with the picturesqueness of the masted fishing galley sailing through the bridge's opening. The colors of the bay were once again lime hued and the sea was quiet, apparently tired from its earlier unrest! Only the encrustations, seaweed, and broken-legged crabs strewn about on the sandy beaches hinted of the night's gale and the *Venture's* wreckage . . . but *that* was hidden from her view!

The drawbridge was lowered and she crossed to the main isle, taking the pike road. This wound through mangroves of fanlike palmettos, thickly clustered, though frayed by the previous evening's winds. There were slaves working in the fields, chanting.

She passed brightly clad, barefooted slave girls, whose wooden yokes dangled milk buckets. For her it was an everyday scene, but she still marveled at their strength, for she had once tried to manage such a thing and found it difficult indeed! They smiled at her and she returned the pleasantry with her eyes as well as her lips.

Kate took her time walking her horse over the narrow road on the way to a point she loved best—Horseshoe Cove, where Danny and she had so often frolicked. Her gray eyes were alive, reflecting the cerulean color of the sea. Hills ascended and dipped, oscillating with their green artistry, and she was conscious of the beauty surrounding her. Hamilton Harbor, a safe, boot-shaped inlet, was reached after a sharp bend in the road. It was a village whose growth had been so sudden that there was talk of making it the capital. St. George, the present capital, was at the very tip of the islands, and the spread of the population westward commanded a more central port. It was inevitable, though many barked their protests, that Hamilton would soon be replacing St. George.

Hamilton's size was barely larger than its main thoroughfare, Front Street, which ended at the docks. Behind the short-clipped streets that shot off from Front Street, were but a few small cottages, wooden shacks, and mangrove fields.

In spite of the town's small size, it was a port inundated with life.

Kate smiled as she observed a few pretty shrimpers exchange ribald remarks with the sailors. She watched, fascinated, as one saucy girl, whose skirt had been hitched up and tucked into her waistband, stopped to brush her naked leg up and down a sailor's side. He grinned broadly and gave her butt a lingering pat, admiring its design.

Wide-eyed, Kate urged her horse forward, taking the length of Front Street to Main and there turning off. She tethered her horse outside Madame Winglet's shop and before long had selected the materials of her choice from the bolts the shopkeeper brought out for her inspection. Scanning the meager collection of Madame's stock, Kate discovered an olive green superfine.

"This, Madame, is perfect for Miss Ellen and will match the green silk I want for her dress."

"Indeed yes. Your choice shows excellent taste," answered Madame, and while it was true, it was also true that Kate had selected one of the most expensive materials!

"Hmmm . . . and this! I want it done up with that braiding and those buttons, and warm lining," Kate added decisively.

"Superb!" said Madame Winglet, clapping her hands.

After that, there were a few more selections and then Kate felt she and Nell's most pressing needs had been attended to. Finishing with a satisfied sigh, Kate added, ". . . and of course they must all be ready by the end of next week."

"Next week?" gasped Madame.

"Yes, though I am not sure when we shall be sailing, I expect it will be soon and I want these things ready for our journey."

"Of course, of course. I shall have my girls work on it night and day."

Kate frowned. "Oh, I see that I am putting you out. I'm very sorry, but we had so little notice ourselves. What with the packet ship being late as usual. You will, of course, charge me for the extra trouble."

"You are too kind, Miss Newbury," said Madame, very much in good humor. "I shall be very sorry to see you leave Bermuda." Indeed she should be, for she was losing one of her best customers.

Kate thought this, but refrained from commenting. The time had passed quickly and if she were to make luncheon she would have to hurry. It was past noon when she passed a group of seamen in a wagon near Wreck's Hill. They knew Kate and tipped their hats and received a smile that set them to sighing, for "Lord 'er," said one on behalf of all, "ain't she a fine piece!"

Danny shot out from a side road, suddenly, and it was obvious that he had just come from the Hill. He spied Kate and hastened his horse after her, coming abreast, his grin as carefree as his clothes. "Hello, Kate! Where you been this morning? Gad, but you look as fine as five pence!"

"Hamilton. But my, aren't you looking excited?" she asked suspiciously.

"Lord, yes, and so would you, if you had been down to the wreck this morning! They've begun salvaging and hang me if it ain't a haul! Everyone is in great spirits!"

Kate pulled a face. "And what of the poor men that *lost that haul?*"

"Now, Kate . . . don't be difficult. They'll get enough to give them return passage to the States. Lord, you'd think *we* called down the tempest on their heads!" he snorted.

"No, you did not call it down, but you are not above taking advantage of nature's whims!" she snapped unfairly.

"Kate!" said Danny reproachfully.

She sighed. "Oh, never mind, Danny. Come on, I didn't have a real breakfast this morning and I'm simply ravenous. If you like, you can accompany me home and we'll lunch together."

"Stap me if you don't have a head on your shoulders. It's half starved I am. Come on, let's have at it!" he said, leading the way. Kate smiled and urged her horse forward. It didn't take long before the two young people were laughing and racing up the road toward the Newbury Estate.

They reached the stables, breathless and in high fettle. A black lackey came running out and took charge of their horses.

"Better walk them about first before taking them in. They'll need a good rub down," said Danny, flipping a coin into the slave's hand. Kate was quick to note the exchange and smiled, well pleased with her friend. Giving a slave money was an uncommon practice. Gratuities were reserved for servants and tradesmen, and Kate inwardly applauded Danny's generous action. It was comfortable knowing there was another human being who felt and thought in a similar vein.

They entered the house laughing and Miss Ellen appeared, greeting them fondly. There was a welcome on her chubby face. "Daniel, how nice. Do you join us for luncheon?" she said, not bothering to wait for an answer as she turned and led them down the wide hall to the back of the house. Here was a glass room. It jutted out away from the house and its roof was skylighted. Citrus plants and exotic flowers covered its marble floor and hung from its beamed ceiling. In the center of the room was a large old dining table with chairs. Passion flowers, herbs, and other plants filled the room with their sweet scent and bid the guest linger.

A cold collation of meats, cheeses, fruits, and salad had been laid out, together with sweet rolls and buns. They had been arranged attractively, and as both young people were at the point of no control, they filled their plates with far more food than they were capable of devouring!

Finally, Kate pushed back her chair and groaned, "Lord, I can't move!"

"Ummm," agreed Danny.

"Really, you are no more than children! The two of you, going at your food as though you'd never have any again!" scolded Miss Ellen.

Danny gave her an open grin and Kate repeated her groan, exclaiming with a sigh, "Oh Danny, do let us take a walk! I must if I am to survive that meal!"

"Dash it, Kate! That is too bad of you. Really, you must see I am in no state to move an inch, let alone a step!" complained her bosom friend.

"Very well, brat. Stay here then. I am going for a walk," said Kate, smiling to herself.

Disgruntledly he threw down his napkin and stood up.

"Confound you, Kate. Hold there, I'm coming."

She laughed for she had never doubted he would join her, and the sound of her laughter was fresh and light. However, Miss Ellen called out hastily, detaining them. "Oh, Kate, I nearly forgot! Mr. Ludlow sent a message earlier to advise us that he has booked us passage on the *Bermudian* sailing for England in ten days!"

Kate's gray eyes lit up, and she clapped her hands wildly. "Oh, that is perfect! I love you, Nell," she said, throwing her a kiss.

Danny's light brows drew together over clouded blue eyes, but he remained silent until they were outside. They took a garden path, walking slowly, each lost to his own musings. Suddenly he broke the stillness with a sulky voice. "Papa said nothing to me. I didn't realize it would be so soon."

She stopped and looked up at him. "Danny, let's not be gloomy about our leaving. . . . It would be senseless." She patted his arm soothingly. "What we have together, well, it can't be extinguished by space or time. You will be so busy here that before you realize it, I shall be back pestering you once again."

He said nothing to this but fell in step beside her as she resumed the path. The foliage was still wet from the previous night's storm and gave off a deep bewitching scent; the colors of the blooms, still unwithered by the threat of coming winter, glistened in the sunshine. Kate kept up a steady stream of idle chatter. She wanted to assuage his feelings, brush away his confusion. "Oh Danny," she complained at length, "do smile!"

He stopped and gazed down into her piquant face and his blue eyes were clouded over with his youthful emotions. He placed his large hands on her delicate shoulders. "Smile? What? Shall you wrench it from me then, Kate? Can you be so unfeeling? 'Tis all well and good for you! Yes, you go off to a different world of new people filled with all the sort of things to make a girl forget a friend, but I . . . I am stuck here . . . on this small isle, craving after you! Smile? Take your hand then, Kate, and drag it from me. I have not the power to give it freely!"

"Danny!" she reproached, her gray eyes searching his face.

"Oh, don't make me feel the cad as well!" he snapped. "Look at me with those wide gray eyes and say me nay!" He sighed suddenly, and drew her to him. His mouth covered her own and she allowed him the moment.

Finally his lips freed hers and he gazed down into her sad eyes. There was the flicker of understanding in his, as he saw her lashes veil her eyes. Her voice came soft and warm, and her hand touched his cheek. "Danny, how you can make love after such a meal is beyond my limited capacity to comprehend. I certainly cannot . . . and will not!" The old tease was in her voice.

Color flooded his white cheeks and a shade of anger swept into his blue eyes. He withdrew his hands and stood rigidly. "I don't find you amusing!"

"Oh, don't you?" bantered Kate. "I shall strive to do better in the future, for I want nothing but to amuse you, my friend! However, you may have noticed that I have this lamentable and perhaps unforgivable habit of being me when I am with you, and being me I sometimes forget to put on a show." She ended giving him an arched look, challenging his bad humor.

He stared hard at her a moment, trying to enact the injured lover, for though he was no romantic figure, his mind was made of such. In spite of himself a rueful grin pulled at his mouth. "Doing it rather brown, ain't you?"

"Am I? Maybe so. Perhaps 'twas called for."

He sighed and put up his hands. "Very well then, Kate. If you are not going to let me seduce you, then let us go down to the sea and take my ship out. 'Tis a fine day for sailing!"

She laughed, "Seduce me . . . you wretch?" She looked heavenward as though asking the sky to bear witness. "This from a friend!" She returned her clear gray eyes to his face. "Be thankful I am so strong-willed, Daniel Ludlow, for if you did manage the thing, I might end with child and then you would have to marry me!"

"That, m'girl, is precisely what I wish."

"That is because you are but seventeen and think not of tomorrow. Come on, Danny, you would not be comfortable with a shrew of a wife, for I promise you that is what I would be! La! Get down on your knees, Danny, and give thanks."

He laughed, "To whom, you or providence?"

"To me, fool! Providence had nought to do with it!" replied Kate, tugging at his hand and leading the way.

5

Kate held her hands clasped tightly as she leaned over the bulwarks of the *Bermudian*. The wide rim of her fine straw bonnet flapped in the warm breeze, and her long black tresses swayed across her back. She was burning with nervous excitement and undid the string of the light green cloak hanging delicately from her shoulders. She took a deep breath of air, exclaiming, "Danny, I am awfully hot. Dare I chuck Nell's command and remove this burdensome thing."

"Truth is 'tis the excitement that has you feverish, Kate. Best not take off your cloak," said Danny. His top hat, blue cutaway, white frilled shirt, pale blue waistcoat, starched neckcloth, ivory-hued breeches, and gleaming black hessians had been donned in her honor, yet his eyes and face were not in keeping with such brightness!

She glanced around the ship and smiled. The *Bermudian* was a large merchant ship, armed with four guns. It accommodated a limited passenger list beneath its poop deck, and had a seaworthy crew of some twenty odd men, and it was about to convey Miss Premble and Kate to England!

Kate felt incredibly impatient and wildly restless. This was finally it! She was leaving Bermuda, though that in itself was a sadness. But she was going to England, to her papa!

Her stomach began to churn, and she put a gloved hand to her flat but active belly, wondering if she were experiencing seasickness already. Danny caught the motion of her hand and frowned. "Perhaps we had better go below. You *do* look flushed."

"What of your papa and my Nell?" she answered, casting her eyes about. "They will miss us."

"Papa is busy with the Captain and Miss Ellen is still with her friends. Come on, you can lie down a bit. Should help you to feel more yourself."

She allowed him to lead her down the quarter-deck to the poop where the companion stairway to the cabins was situated. He went ahead of her, taking her hand and helping her down the stairs. The double berthed cabin that Kate would be sharing with Miss Ellen during the journey was located immediately starboard from the stair landing, and Danny opened its undersized door for Kate to pass through. It was necessary for him to incline his head in order to follow. The small but attractive cabin was wainscoted with a deep rich brown. It was nicely furnished, and its two berths were at diagonals with the corners of the room. A large vanity spread between them and an open porthole above that. Kate found a cushioned Queen Anne chair and sank down with a sigh. "Lord, this is cramped." She then surveyed Danny's face and finding its expression one of a man who has swallowed something disagreeable, she said gently, "We shall be together again soon, Danny!"

"As man and wife?" he demanded testily.

"Oh, for gracious sake!" she exploded, impatient with him suddenly. "Do stop playing the tortured lover. It does not suit you."

He surprised her then by getting down on both knees and taking her gloved hands into his own. "Kiss me, Kate, . . . do!" he pleaded.

She laughed suddenly and threw her arms round his neck, planting an amiable peck upon his lips. "There,

Danny boy. A kiss—and do get up, for your bright breeches shall be black in a moment!"

"I don't give a hang for my breeches. Kiss me again."

"No, brat! The one I just gave you was more than you deserve!" retorted she, but the tease in her gray eyes belied the severeness of her tone.

He shot her a startled expression. "Why, what do you mean by that remark?"

She stood up and took a short quick tour of the room before coming up to face him. She gave him her hand and tugged and he got to his feet and gazed down at her expectantly. "Very well. I have it, sir, on excellent authority that you spent the better part of last evening in Elizabeth Tucker's parlor and Mr. and Mrs. Tucker were away from home!" She laughed at his ridiculous expression, and continued unmercifully, "I should think, Danny . . . you'd had enough kisses for a spell."

"Kate! Confound you, girl! Are you a witch? How could you know so soon? Come on . . . who gave you that juicy piece of news?" demanded Danny, indignant and somewhat ruffled.

She chuckled. "You needn't get yourself into a miff, old boy. If you are going to be so foolish as to allow a household of servants to observe your clandestine assignations, you had better be prepared for the tattle-mongers to wave their ugly tongues!"

"Are you jealous, Kate?" he asked, suddenly hopeful. "Lord, you needn't be. There is nothing in it. After all, I ain't a monk and you won't . . ."

"Jealous?" she ejaculated, cutting him off. "Stupid boy! If I have any feelings on such a thing 'tis nothing near to jealousy. 'Tis your own affair who you kiss, though I would caution you, for if you're not careful, Danny, you could stir up one devilish mess. No, that is not why I flapped my knowledge of your affairs before you, but I can see you still don't realize that you are not in love with me! Nevermind, in time you will find that I am right."

He sighed heavily, but refrained from further discussion

of the subject. She had removed her cloak and without its weight felt a great deal cooler. A quick pat to her hair and she was leading him back up the companion to the poop deck. He followed her silently.

The moment of departure arrived suddenly. Before Kate knew what was happening, she was taking her leave of the Ludlows and the friends that had gathered to bid them safe journey! It was a quiet, strange fantasy that engulfed her. It weaved itself around her mind, making her numb to sensation. She couldn't feel, not really! She wanted to shake herself out of her numbness and reminded her heart that she was leaving . . . really leaving. Gone would be this wondrous land . . . gone would be Danny and his father, the two men that had been an intricate part of her life, especially in these past four years when her father had been away. Yet everything floated by Kate. Words came mechanically and she lacked a sense of loss. She knew this and had no answer for it.

Hamilton Harbor blurred as the ship gouged out its path in the pale green water. She barely felt Miss Ellen at her side, and the governess, aware of Kate's mood, made no attempt at conversation. They stood beside one another, holding the bulwarks, oblivious to the ship's buzzing life, aware only of the coastline they were leaving.

After a time Miss Ellen, unable to keep still, sighed, " 'Tis wondrously lovely. Do look, Kathleen . . . the sun's rays seem to halo our small isle."

Kate giggled. "You are an incurable romantic, Nell, but you are right. It is beautiful. It puts me in mind of Tom Moore's poem, though I can remember but a few lines:

> . . . bless the little fairy isle!
> How sweetly, after all our ills,
> We saw the dewy morning smile
> Serenely o'er its fragrant hills,—
> You'd think that Nature lavished here
> Her purest wave, her softest skies,
> To make a heaven for love to sigh in,
> For bards to live and saints to die in!

She sighed with the last line and turned a wistful eye. "Do you think I shall meet Mr. Moore in London?"

Miss Ellen's face went sour. She had no liking for young Moore's erotic style of poetry. There, too, he was a bit too raffish and she had not liked his pointed interest in her Kathleen! "I certainly hope not!" came the stern response.

Kate laughed. " 'Tis odd that one with such a romantic soul as yours, Nell, should disdain a poet!"

"I do not find fault with him because of his occupation and well you know it. Mr. Moore's poetry is not fit for a maiden's ears and I must tell you, dear, that his conduct toward you was most rakish!"

"Nonsense!" exploded Kate, laughter in her eyes.

"You call it nonsense? Is it proper then for a man, at least four and twenty, to be whispering all manner of things in the ears of a girl just seventeen?"

"I was about to turn eighteen, but that does not signify. He never said one improper word to me, and Nell, he never even tried to kiss me."

"Heavens preserve us! Is that what holds him high in your esteem? How could he try and kiss you when I was forever about and made sure he knew?"

Kate laughed. "Horrid creature! Were you spying then? 'Tis not fair, Nell, I declare."

"Hush, child! The fact remains that he is not the sort who forms a lasting attachment."

"Untrue! His poetry refutes such a statement, and as to his being raffish, I find it remarkable that you should think so. Why, he is a gentleman and travels in the best of circles. In fact, the paper we had from London last month mentioned how sought-after he is amongst the ton."

"You are an innocent and see but the superficial, but do not let us banter words. My head is spinning," said Miss Ellen, putting a hand to her forehead and sending her bonnet askew.

Kate eyed her with concern. "There, Nell, let me

undo the buttons of your spencer. You are too tightly done up!"

"No, no. Perhaps if I just sit here." said Miss Ellen, moving toward the skylight bench and dropping down heavily.

Kate eyed her with misgiving. The ship was barely out a mile. The waters, though deeper in shade and marbled with veins of purple, were calm and unpeaked. If Nell were already feeling ill, whatever would she do when they met with rough seas? Waving away her governess's objections, she undid the basket buttons of Nell's dark brown spencer when the sound of a young man's voice at her back brought her face around. Until this moment she hadn't really noticed any of the seamen and in fact had not seen a sign of the other passengers.

"May I be of some assistance?" asked the first mate of the *Bermudian*.

"Oh I do hope so," said Kate at once. "My governess has a touch of the sea sickness."

"I am sorry to hear that. I believe Cook has a remedy of sorts. I'll see to it at once," he said, tipping the curled rim of his tall round dark hat and hurrying off without another word.

Kate watched him go. He wore a dark short jacket, an open-collared white shirt with a blue kerchief tied around his neck. His loose trousers were white and wide at the ankles. She had not noticed either the color of his hair or the hue of his eyes, but his dress depicted a sailor of higher rank.

Miss Ellen groaned and Kate returned her attention to the woman. "Poor Nell. There, there, dear, the nice man will bring you something."

"Oh Kate, take me to the cabin at once, for I fear I am going to be wretchedly ill," exclaimed Miss Ellen with horror.

Kate helped her to her feet and made for the companion stairway directly behind them. As they reached the cabin door, Miss Ellen made a wild dash for the room and finding the chamber pot, relieved her stomach's churnings.

She continued to do this, and with some violence, for an uncomfortable space of time, which set her to crying. Kate washed the woman's face and chin with a damp handkerchief and begged her not to fret.

A knock sounded at the cabin door and Kate opened it to find the same young sailor. His hat was tucked beneath his arm and he held a mug of steaming liquid. His hair, now bare to inspection was a pale shade of light brown and it waved across his high forehead in thick strands.

"This should help, if she can hold it down," offered the young man. His tone held concern.

"Thank you . . . Mr. . . . "

"Cooper, Paul Cooper, first mate and your obedient servant, Miss Newbury," he said, smiling and bending over Kate's extended hand. When he brought his face up, Kate noticed that his eyes were blue.

The door was closed and she returned to Miss Ellen with the mug; however the whiff of the herbal tisane brought on another raging fit and the mug was temporarily shelved. At length poor Nell slept. Kate rang for a steward who appeared shortly thereafter and gave him the chamber pot for cleaning. She looked at her sleeping governess and sighed, going across to her own berth and lying down. She was suddenly exhausted. So much had happened since her father's letter. She had seen the furniture go into Holland covers. She had bid farewell to servants she had known from childhood and she had parted from Danny. Her dear, sweet, foolish Danny. These last four years would have been unbearable without his friendship. He had always been there, always understood. Of course she had Nell, but that was different. Nell could be distant at times, and Nell was more often than not dreadfully stern-faced.

There were so many things Kate needed to know. She had often and quite innocently broached to Nell the questions plaguing her mind. However, many of these queries met with stiff rejection and Kate was left to wonder. For more and more she wanted to know about men! To be sure, she had what information was available to an only and motherless child, but it was sketchy and vague. She did what she could, turning to friends as ignorant as she and more often than not received renditions as frightening as they were fantastic in nature! Yet, Kate had pursued; hers was a questioning mind. She turned to Elizabeth Tucker, with whom she had shared only a superficial friendship, and Elizabeth would stare hard and laugh. "Silly chit, 'tis fun to let a man kiss and cuddle you! It feels wonderful!" she had informed Kate knowingly.

"Even if you do not love him?" Kate had asked wide-eyed.

"Child! What has love to do with the callings of the flesh?"

"Elizabeth! You sound a . . . a veritable tart!" exclaimed Kate genuinely shocked.

Elizabeth had laughed, "You haven't the woman in you yet."

Kate had considered this and quickly chucked it aside. She had not enjoyed being kissed by Danny, and it had not aroused her in the way Elizabeth had described. No, love *must* signify!

Kate's thoughts came homeward and oddly enough she recalled Paul Cooper's attractive face. She had liked him. She liked the look of him, though his eyes were a bit too small and his chin too rounded. She had felt a flutter tingle through her when he had brushed her hand with his light kiss, in spite of the fact that her glove had separated his lips from her skin.

A groan from Miss Ellen brought Kate to her side in an instant and such musings were put away. "Dearest Nell, do you think you could drink the tisane now? It may do you some good."

"I shall try," said Miss Ellen Premble bravely.

The brew was taken in long sips and once again Nell's head went to the pillow and before long her heavy thing could be heard. The next hour ticked by slowly and Kate watched the bright sun's rays wane. The light through the porthole had turned a misty green tint, for night was approaching. A steward knocked softly and announced that dinner would be served in thirty minutes. Kate sighed and bent over her governess. Miss Premble was resting in a deep untroubled sleep and she had not the heart to wake her. With a comforting thought that a tray could always be had later in the evening, Kate went to the vanity mirror and began setting herself to rights. She washed, then brushed her black thick hair into luxurious waves, tying it with a green silk ribbon. She stood and smoothed the straight line of her simple country green silk. The light from the flame in the whale-oil lantern against the wall flickered across her lovely face and she examined herself and felt well satisfied.

"You look lovely, dear," came a gentle voice, and Kate spun round and smiled.

"Oh Nell, you are awake. Are you feeling better? Can I help you wash for dinner?" exclaimed Kate hopefully.

"Oh my goodness no, no food just now. I do feel much better, though I would like to just lie here and rest. You go in and don't worry about me."

"But Nell, if you are better, perhaps you should eat. I could bring you a tray."

"No love, the thought of food is repugnant at the moment. Do go into dinner; you must not keep them waiting, and please do make my apologies."

"Are you sure you will be all right?" asked Kate frowning.

"My dear, as the dining galley is but ten feet from our cabin door, I trust we will both be quite comfortable about the other," said Miss Ellen, attempting to smile.

"Nell, you are the dearest thing," said Kate, giving her a fierce hug before leaving the cabin.

6

The *Bermudian* ran its course smoothly, unaware
that some distance ahead the *Gypsy* ran purposefully
through the deep indigo blue! The wind was fair and
the *Gypsy* was built for its pleasure. Her men worked
the decks easily but their ministrations were underlined
with excitement. It would be soon. Their captain was
never wrong and he had promised it would be soon; so
they waited for their prey! For the *Gypsy* was a British
privateer!

Captain Branwell's thick black hair blew with the
wind and glistened in spite of the fading sun. His profile
was a study of control; only his bright green eyes un-
veiled his anticipation. The long black spy glass was
brought up once again. He peered through its telescopic
lens and his deep voice underlined with triumph was
carried by the wind.

"A merchant vessel, Mr. Hatch! Stap me if she ain't
Spanish!" He threw the long spy glass into his first mate's
open hands and turned his attention to the forecastle. His
fist shook the air. "Look alive, lads! All hands ahoy!"

The activity that resulted was tumultuous and yet
streamlined in purpose. The *Gypsy* carried eight cannons,
but her figure was lean and built for the speed her fore
and aft square rigging could give her. *Gypsy's* crew was
proud to sail her, proud to be captained by the man
shouting orders at their heads, proud of the sixteen ships
they had captured in the last four months. And they were
sure of the immediate outcome of this encounter!

The Spanish vessel spotted the *Gypsy* with its British
flag. Theirs was but a yawl, privately owned and unarmed. They were on their way home, had, in fact, been
at sea less than a week. Their captain and owner, a

41

Spaniard of considerable property, had hoped that his small vessel would attract no undue attention either from England, with whom they were at war, or from the French, by whom they were dominated. He had discovered and closed a unique deal in the South Americas that had made him a chest of gold and jewels which was secreted in his quarters below. If the French were to discover it there was no telling how much would be confiscated in the name of taxes, and if found by the English 'twould be lost.

His watch called to him, advising him that another ship had been spotted making its way at them. The Spanish captain raised his own glass and saw the British flag. "Privateers," he breathed out loud and proceeded to cross himself. There were tales of how English privateers would cannon a Spanish ship and leave its crew for the sharks! His ship was unarmed, he could put up no resistance, and though he was himself no fighting man, there was no telling what he might have done had he but one cannon. However, he had no such weapon and the English ship was already tacking. He could see four of her eight cannons leveled at his hull! Both honor and wealth would soon be lost, but, perhaps, he could yet save the lives of his crew and himself. He motioned to his man to put up the white flag!

The *Gypsy* drew close, and her men, boarding axes in hand, knives and pistols ready lest the Spaniards think twice of their surrender, began their move. But the men of the *Bahia* were not fighters and stood about hoping for mercy.

When Captain Branwell appeared on the quarter-deck of the *Bahia* some ten minutes after boarding her, he found its crew already gathered and awaiting his orders. He perched himself on the quarter-deck rail, his pistol idly clasped in his strong hand, and surveyed his catch. "Take them to our brig and make them as comfortable as possible," he ordered his men before turning to eye the *Bahia's* captain. One of Captain Branwell's well-defined black brows went upward upon finding the

Spaniard resplendently attired in full-dress garb and standing rigidly awaiting his fate.

Captain Branwell was himself dressed in an open-necked white shirt whose sleeves billowed in the wind. His tight buff-colored breeches seemed molded to his athletic legs, and he sat at ease, swinging his booted foot and grinning broadly. "My compliments, captain. You made the only wise decision possible under the circumstances."

"English pig! *Perro!*" hissed the Spaniard, showing his teeth.

"Really, sir. I cannot be both a pig and a dog. You must decide which and then I shall answer you," returned Captain Branwell amicably.

"Pirate! You have attacked an unarmed ship!" spit the Spaniard.

"Pirate! Much better adjective and one I shall not at the moment quarrel with, though I do beg to differ with you on one point. We did not attack you. Indeed, not one shot was fired. We merely suggested that you surrender and you very wisely did so."

"Base! We are but a poor merchant ship."

"Poor? I would not define your cargo as poor. Indeed you give the appearance of a small ship carrying only spices and some silks, but upon closer scrutiny one discovers the error of such hasty appraisal. Though it pained me to do so, I did search your cabin and am accounted quite efficient in such undertakings. Though I am certain Napoleon's men would have allowed your excellently designed compartment to go undetected, it was not passed over by me! It is remarkable that you would carry such a treasure without the benefit of cannons to shoo away such creatures as myself!"

"Damn you! I had hoped we would go by untroubled. My ship was not built for cannons," snapped the Spaniard. Then putting his head up, "Very well. May I ask what you mean to do with my ship and my men?"

"You may. Your ship and its cargo will make an excellent prize for my king. Your men and yourself . . ."

he glanced over the Spanish man with a frown, ". . . will not. However, we are privateers, not warriors! You will be set adrift when we are within sight of Spanish waters, with enough provisions to enable you to reach help."

"If you are not taken by one of our war ships first!" snapped the outraged Spaniard.

"Do not mistake, sir. We are privateers yes, and we take what the sea offers whether it be armed or no, but we are well able to fight those who will it! Prepare yourself, you have the honor to be boarding the *Gypsy!*" He motioned for Master Hatch to escort the Spanish captain away and turned to his men who were still working the *Bahia*.

Captain Branwell remained on board the Spanish vessel only long enough to see her securely in tow before nimbly taking the shrouds and making his way up and over into his own ship. His voice came from his poop deck and it roared, sharp and gay, "Vast there lads! Well done! Unfurl those sails and get your clean shirts ready, for we are bound for England!"

Master Hatch rubbed his whiskered chin and gave his captain a long admiring look before nudging the men to hurry with their labor. His captain and his ship had not acquired their "thunder 'n lightning" reputation without earning it. Lord, he thought with the glimmer of a smile, Capt'n Branwell, the fifth Earl of Mannering, was quite a man!

It is interesting to note that just about this time, though many miles behind the *Gypsy,* Kate had timidly entered the dining galley of the *Bermudian.* This was a long wide room whose dark wainscoting was well polished and relieved with various ship parts, serving as ornaments. There were a few superb paintings of the sea hanging on the walls; intended one supposes to enliven what otherwise would have been somewhat dismal surroundings. A long table with chairs were centrally positioned and faced the companionway at one end, while the serving board and pantry headed the other. A stove occupied one corner beside the serving board and a delectable aroma was now filling the air. The galley was squared by the various staterooms whose only means of entrance were the doors opening from the galley. There were six rooms in all: the captain's quarters, the one shared by Kate and Miss Ellen with a room housing a bath in-between, two small single-berthed cabins, and one double-berthed cabin.

Kate moved into the well-lit dining galley and was immediately greeted by the round-faced captain she had met earlier that day.

"Ah, Miss Newbury," beamed Captain Palmer, his light eyes watery from drink, "but where is Miss Premble? Never say Cook's brew did not fix the poor woman's ills right and tight."

"As a matter of fact, sir, she is feeling a vast deal better, thank you; however she prefers sleep to food, and under the circumstances I am persuaded she is correct in her decision."

"Of course, to be sure, poor woman," sympathized the captain, nodding his head so that its graying dark locks fell forward across his forehead. "Never mind that now; you must come and meet your fellow travelers," he said, taking her arm a bit too tightly and bringing her face to face with a woman who upon first glance struck Kate as the most sophisticated female she had ever clapped eyes on!

Lady Susan Medwin had been a London belle in her day. Neither her ten years of marriage, nor her two and thirty years of age had dampened her style. The inexperienced eye saw only the beauty of golden brown locks, cut in the prevailing mode, curled around her delicate forehead and dangling over her small ears. A sapphire egret clasped a frond of curls over one ear and picked up its own light in the sapphire collar around her neck. On her tall thin body hung a gown whose transparent silver sarcenet glistened over the thinnest of pale blue silk, and the lowness of the scooped bodice brought the blush to Kate's cheeks.

They were introduced, but Kate's spontaneously warm smile faded when met with Lady Medwin's disinterest.

The woman's coldness bordered the road of undisguised rudeness, and Kate's instinct told her here was no friend with whom she could wile away the journey's hours!

Kate's arm was gently tugged by the captain and she brought her clear gray eyes around to find Sir John Medwin awaiting an introduction. He was of average height and some ten years his wife's senior. His brown drab hair was curled à la Brutus around a pleasant face. He was impeccably attired in a brown velvet waist-length coat with rounded tails, an embroidered buff silk waistcoat, buff-colored knee breeches, white stockings, and gold buckled shoes. Kate found his hazel eyes and they seemed to twinkle, so she smiled.

"I am charmed, Miss Newbury," he said quietly before releasing her hand.

"And of course you have met my first mate. Fine lad, Paul, excellent seaman," said the captain, taking another swig of his brandy.

Master Cooper broke off his idle conversation with Lady Medwin and came forward, making a slight bow to Kate's easy acknowledgment. They were passing a few words when one of the cabin doors opened and emitted the last of the passengers.

"Ah, Mr. Walepole," said the captain, and Kate looked around, for there was something in the captain's tone that caught her curiosity. When her eyes focused on Mr. Walepole, she knew what that "something" had signified. Her introduction to Mr. Jack Walepole sent a recoiling sensation through her! It was more than his appearance, which poor fellow, did him little good. The man was but five feet in height and neither nature's whims, nor his own choice of clothes had come to aid his lack of inches. His head was set upon his shoulders without the benefit of a neck to ease the transition, reminding Kate somehow of a toad. This same head, a rather pointed pinnacle with a triangular base, held an unruly shock of black hair. Two swatches of blackness served him as eyebrows, and, beneath these, two pinpoints of darkness claimed to be eyes. However it was not his physical deficiencies that sent a shiver through Kate. No, for it was Kate that would take the crippled hunter for pet, and nurse the broken-winged bird and befriend the friendless. No, pity was withheld and replaced by revulsion when she looked into his eyes, those pin-like eyes, for though his purple lips smiled, his eyes were unable to veil his soul, and his soul twitched with years of demented agony!

Years of taunts, rejections, and all the baseness and petty cruelties of man upon deformed man had served, and Mr. Walepole had not survived! Hate had etched itself deep in his mind and as all children seem to see truth in spite of their innocence, Kate saw and knew.

Mr. Walepole's dark eyes rolled and took in every line of Kate's exquisite proportions. "Lovely, quite lovely, my dear. Your move is most inspired! You should give yourself to England! Such beauty is wasted in the Islands."

"Give myself to England? I do not understand your meaning, sir," said Kate frowning.

His eyes went to her full bosom. She felt them tear at her bodice and her cheeks became as hot as their color. "Of course you don't, my dear," he continued, and his tone seemed to mock her. "Nonetheless, you will find your way to London and *London will take you!* That city swallows young pretties such as yourself whether you shall will it or no."

"I find your conversation both distasteful and full of hidden implications which I am persuaded are most . . . irregular," answered Kate, unsure as to how she should deal with the odious man. She looked around, but found that Master Cooper had moved out of range and was occupied with the cook. Further inquiry brought her eyes to those of Sir John's. There was no mistaking the call of help in her glance and he was not backward in his offering. He was before her almost at once, and putting a cool glass of lemonade into her hands. "Thank you, Sir John," she said gratefully.

"Ah, I believe we may take our seats now, Mr. Walepole," he said, leading Kate to the table.

"You are most kind, Sir John, for I am afraid Mr.

Walepole's mode of conversation was above my head. But where is Lady Medwin?" said Kate in a half-whisper as she allowed him to seat her and take a chair at her side.

"She was a trifle unhappy with some frippery or other in our compartment and insisted on Captain Palmer's having a look at the plaguey thing. Ah, there she is now," he said, standing up as his lady floated to the table. She seated herself opposite Kate. Captain Palmer took the head of the table and congratulated himself merrily on having a beauty on either side of him. Master Cooper sat opposite Sir John and Mr. Walepole beside him.

Dinner proved, for the most part, to be an enlightening period for Kate. She was all too aware that while she sipped lemonade, Lady Medwin took wine. And her gown! Gracious, how could she have thought herself elegant, she scolded herself. She was nought but a countrified school girl. Telling herself that Lady Medwin had the advantage of years and experience seemed an inadequate balm. Kate suddenly felt out of place and shy with her fellow man and the sensation was a new one!

Sir John attempted to bring his dinner companion out of herself and smiled warmly. "How marvelous for you, Miss Newbury, to have lived most of your life in Bermuda. I imagine leaving the island was a sad trial."

"Yes, indeed, Sir John, but you see my father has been in England these past four years and I am afraid the thought of being reunited with him rather shut out all else," answered Kate, once again animated. Her eyes found those of Paul Cooper's and she quickly and shyly lowered them to her plate.

"Ah, of course, and I expect you are most anxious to get into the hub of things in London?" continued Sir John.

"Oh, sir, can you ask? I have dreamed of London, longed for it. Why, it shall be the most exciting thing I have ever done with papa."

"Yes, for a time London can be most enjoyable. I, for one, prefer my island plantation to all the routs and hells of the city," he said wistfully.

"Oh, you own a plantation? Surely not in Bermuda. I would have heard of you and your wife," she began with incredulity.

He laughed, "Indeed, but, no, you are quite right. Our plantation lies in the West Indies. We are returning from a six-month sojourn there. It had been my intention to remain another six months, but my wife detests the climate and pines for England. So, we return." His tone told a story, and it was not lost on Kate, who was ever sensitive to such things.

"Oh, I am sorry," she said, involuntarily glancing at Lady Medwin, who was vivaciously conversing with Captain Palmer. Sir John seemed quiet after that, and Kate was given time to observe his lady.

Lady Susan flirted with her eyes, with the movements of her head, and the tilt of her fingers, and she flirted indiscriminately first with the captain and then with the young man at her side. Kate watched with wide eyes and felt a twinge of annoyance when Lady Medwin's ungloved fingers strayed beneath Paul Cooper's chin. Kate sent a hurried glance at Sir John and was unsure whether or not he had noticed, for his face was an enigma.

Later that night when she undressed in the quiet stillness of her cabin and slipped between the covers, her mind was a tumble of mixed thoughts. Captain Palmer seemed merry enough, though she was certain he drank more than was good for him. Lady Susan Medwin was lovely of face but not very friendly; however she had decided the lady's flirting was a superficial thing. Sir John was a dear, Paul Cooper a very sweet and attractive young man, and Mr. Jack Walepole a fellow to be avoided. Her verdicts in, Kate closed her eyes and fell into an untroubled sleep.

7

The *Bermudian* had been at sea nearly three weeks, and early November was proving to be a mischievous month. Harsh rains and unfriendly winds were the season's emissaries. Their force had brought an anxious time to the crew and passengers.

It had started with a clear day, the wind mild against Kate's bright cheeks, when the watch began their sudden cry. "Master Cooper!" they yelled frantically, "Master Cooper!"

He had been closeted alone with Kate against the companionway door and he moved to answer their call. His reply was sharp when he called in response. However, the watch changed his expression of irritation to concern with their hurried, "To starboard, sir!"

Master Cooper's blue eyes narrowed and he hurried down the poop into the waist, taking up his spyglass. Kate, her curiosity aroused, followed without invitation. Kate heard him curse softly before he turned to find her at his back. "Miss Newbury, I must ask you to go to your cabin at once. I am afraid it is going to be rough and quite soon!"

"What is?" inquired Kate, startled.

"The squawl," he answered, and his tone was grave.

"A squawl? But there is barely a cloud . . ."

He took up her arm and pulled her forward gently, putting the spyglass to her eye. She sucked in her breath, for there was a gathering mist covering the sea, and it gave every appearance of a living creature on the attack! "Faith!" exclaimed Kate, "Shouldn't we call the captain?" A sneer distorted Paul Cooper's mouth. "Unfortunately, the captain is indisposed . . . again."

Kate had learned some time ago what that meant, and replied simply, "Oh."

"Now do go below. I couldn't possibly do what I shall have to with you up here. I should be constantly worrying lest a spar fall in your way. Go below, Kathleen," he said, taking up her gloved hand and kissing the palm with more fervor than etiquette.

She withdrew her hand, shyly, feeling as though her cheeks were on fire, and decided it best to obey his instructions. Miss Ellen would need her!

Soon after they were hit with it! Miss Ellen cried that 'twas the devil himself reaching out for them, and wailed until her seasickness returned. Kate patiently attended her, soothed her and massaged her into slumber. The ship grappled with the elements and its occupants were tossed heedlessly during the quarrel. Kate was frightened and excited by it all. She wrapped her warmest cloak around her shoulders and braced herself with her arms against the walls as she made her way up the stairs to the quarter-deck. She had to see for herself and know what they were up against. She needed to look into the heart of the storm and know of the future!

The crew had already taken in the topgallant studding sails and were now working the lower and topmast sails. She heard Paul Cooper's voice sing through the growling wind, "Haul 'em down, you slugs! Clew up! Come on, damn you, clew 'em up!"

She frowned, thinking him harsh, and then saw the mist. It swirled and blanketed the air, stretching itself between sky and sea. It seemed almost to grin wickedly as it ate everything in its path, gathering up the spoils, delighted with the opportunity to call war on the *Bermudian!*

Kate felt spellbound by its gray, eerie light. She stared into its labyrinth and knew a quiet fear. She tore herself away from the horror to observe the men working the sails. A wave of pity clouded her eyes as she watched them furling up the cloths. Their thin garments were wet through, and she knew the cold must be beating them torturously. At last, she heard Paul Cooper call to them to leave the fore and main topgallant sails up a while, and they gathered in the forecastle awaiting further instructions.

Paul Cooper looked them over disdainfully. "What in hell are you waiting for, you stupid lubbers? Get below, damn you, and get dried, you'll have little time! Hell, but do you think it is over? Get some coffee and food into your guts and be quick about it or half of you will be dead by morning, and I need a full crew!"

They were slow in moving, tired and half frozen, and one of the men received a vicious kick to rearward from Master Cooper. "Vast there, mate! I said be quick about it!" shouted Cooper.

Kate felt a sting of surprise. She had never seen Paul Cooper so harsh, and was sure she did not like it in him. However, she excused him presently, telling herself he was under strain. After all, he had done it all himself— the captaining of this ship—while Palmer lay in a drunken stupor below!

Paul Cooper turned and saw Kate standing beneath the quarter-deck overhang. His expression softened instantly. He was wet, he was cold, and he was tired, but Kate's soft beauty tantalized him, even now. The water dripped down his face and she reached out, wiping the streams away. He put his hands on her shoulders, surprising her with the boldness of the act. "Kathleen, darling, you will catch your death of cold up here. You must not come up during the storm, please."

Kate moved gently out of his grasp and smiled as though in apology for moving. "Oh, I don't mind the rain, and I wanted to see how the ship is worked."

"You mean you wanted to see what straits we were in with me at the helm," said Cooper, showing some irritation.

"Of course not," she returned at once. "I was never in doubt of your ability to pull us through this. I merely wanted to observe the machinations of the storm."

"You will observe them very well from your cabin,

but at least there you will not get in the way, and you will not get hurt. Now will you please go below or do you mean to get washed off deck!" he said, taking her around the shoulder and leading her back to the poop deck companion stairs. Before releasing her, he gave her forehead a fond kiss, and she looked at him a moment before going below. Blushing hotly, she hurried to her cabin. The storm seemed to have stilled itself in the last few moments and she made her way without difficulty. However, as she opened her cabin door, the ship pitched violently and she was sent flying across her cabin and landed with a forceful thud against her vanity. The first blast of the squawl had hit!

The next few hours would be there in Kate's memory always. To a land lover, the sea is at its best a lovely mystery, an exotic and capricious beauty that whispers of romance. But to a true seaman, the sea is a dangerous, quixotic companion, never to be called friend, and yet always to be loved!

There were times when the vessel lay nearly over upon her beam ends, causing Miss Ellen to renew her earlier woeful prophecies.

"Lord preserve us, the sea will take us yet!" cried Nell fretfully.

"Now Nell, 'tis but a mild wind rushing about trying to blow itself out. We'll ride it until it's finished playing and then we'll be on our way. You must not worry, really," said Kate gently. She smiled and tried to gain a smile in return. But Nell would hear nothing good.

"The sea hates me, it's always hated me. I'll never live to see England. Oh, I feel so ill," cried Nell.

At length Kate lost patience and snapped testily that she was beginning to wonder who was the child and who the governess. This, not because she considered herself child, never. Kate thought herself quite mature, but she knew what was needed to bring her governess around!

This hit its mark, and far better than had all the earlier words of gentle soothing. Miss Ellen's countenance, though cowered, was most contrite and as the remark mulled around in her mind, she began to foresee the possibility of altogether losing Kathleen's respect. As she had attained this after many years of praiseworthy behavior, Miss Ellen felt inclined to get a hold on her nerves.

On deck, the seamen met rain and sleet and winds enough to make the toughest man amongst them breathless and weary! Sir John ventured above only once and a sharp command returned him to his frightened wife. Mr. Walepole, tucked in his cabin, sought no one. As the crew worked the rigging, there was a thunder of cracking wood, as the rigging and spars surrendered to the relentless beating. The topgallant mast, thick and sturdy though it was, gave over like a whipstick in the wind and the crew of the *Bermudian* eyed its swaying with a heavy heart.

"Clew up, you lubbers!" shouted Paul Cooper, moving forward. "Get the fore and main topgallant cloths furled. Now, damn you!"

The ship sliced water as though it were a discharged bullet, and its bow seemed choked with foam. The men worked through it all, some frantically at the reef tackles, others at the frozen yards. They were soaked through, stiff with cold, their fingers slow with numbness, and still they worked!

Brandied coffee was brought up by the cook and placed into Master Cooper's hands. In between sips, he shouted orders, before standing back to observe the results of his commands. Such amenities were given to the captain and officers only, 'twas the law of the sea . . . and the time.

One of the men, his hand torn from frozen ropings and his face swollen to twice its normal size, stared hard at the first mate and turned to his friend working beside him. "Lord, my tooth is paining me something fierce. It's near driving me mad! Lookee there, the Master be sipping like a god, while we Jacks who stand through everything—working in this wet and cold—we get nought for our blood!"

"Aye! But he be not 'alf as bad as the old man! He sleeps 'alf the day he does, in his cups all night. Word has it he is so foxed, he don't even know we be in trouble!"

"Devil! But I tell ye, I'm gonna ask the Master for some rice instead of pork jerky. I ain't been able to eat with m'mouth like this!"

His friend grunted, "If ye applies to him I'll wager ye a pony he won't 'ave it. He'll let ye starve and damn your soul for the asking!"

Paul Cooper moved their way and gave the wretch with a toothache a nasty kick into his rear. "What in hell are you jabbering about! Get those lengths tied!"

The men worked into the night and when they had weathered the storm, those not on watch went below the forecastle to their narrow berths and began the process of wringing out their wet clothes. As there was no way to dry them without the sun, they paired off, each partner taking one end of the garment and twisting it until most of the water was out of it. Then it was hung about the walls. In the morning they would select the least wet article of clothing to wear for the day's work!

The morning came and it brought a gentler sky. The sails were once again flapping in the air, and the air, though cold, seemed at peace. Kate and Miss Ellen, arms linked and faces bright, walked around the quarter-deck watching the busy activity. The crew seemed in excellent spirits, congratulating themselves on their victory over the storm and well pleased to be repairing the damage.

Sir John, hands clasped behind his back, caught sight of the two ladies and smiled, making his way up the quarter-deck stairs.

"Good morning," he said, tipping his curly brimmed top hat, "I am very pleased to find you both looking so well. I was somewhat concerned when neither of you made an appearance at breakfast."

"We took coffee and biscuits in our cabin," answered Kate. "How is Lady Medwin?"

"I am afraid she was terrified by the storm. I managed to calm her, but she, too, would only take some coffee in the cabin and has decided to remain there this morning and rest."

"I do hope she took no injury," said Miss Ellen. "She is so delicate, and the ship was tossing us about like so much furniture."

"Oh no, 'tis merely her nerves, but please don't concern yourselves; she will be quite the thing by evening."

He walked with them a bit, before they seated themselves on the skylight bench, where he proceeded to amuse them with a series of personal anecdotes. Miss Ellen's shivering caught Kate's eye and she immediately suggested fetching her governess a blanket. This suggestion was readily accepted, and Kate hastily made her way to the companionway.

She scurried down the companionway stairs, rushed into her cabin, pulled out an extra blanket from the cupboard and laid it across her arm. She was crossing through the galley when the scent of fresh coffee caught her attention. The urging of her stomach pulled her toward the sideboard, and the hypnotic scent. Resting the blanket across the back of a chair, Kate poured herself a cup of black brew.

A muffled noise issuing from the captain's quarters at her side sent a sinking feeling through her. Impulsively she slipped into the pantry room next to the stove and waited. This childish action stemmed from her reluctance to encounter the captain while she was alone. She had recently discovered that his drinking clouded his sense of the proprieties and set him in a mood that was overly demonstrative. Miss Ellen had set him down as lecherous and wagging a finger at Kate admonished her strongly to avoid him. However, until a few days ago Kate had discounted such renditions on Captain Palmer's character, herself thinking him a rather silly older man. But Captain Palmer had quickly lent his support to Miss Ellen's warnings by overstepping in a manner that left no doubt in Kate's mind regarding his nature. She had found herself alone with him at lunch one afternoon, and while they waited for the others he began a tale of one of his adventures at sea. This became rather burlesque in tone and as he laughed heartily his hand strayed up Kate's arm. Once there it proceeded to caress in a manner that could no longer be thought fatherly, and Kate attempted to disengage herself. He would have none of it and heartily took her to him in a strong clasp around her waist and a gusty laugh, during which time he advised her that he thought her a fine red-blooded wench.

Paul chose this particular moment to appear fresh from a wash in his cabin. As he was within sight and hearing range of the scene he was unable to contain his anger. He took strong exception, and only the captain's refusal to take insult saw them through a difficult moment. It had ended well enough, but the incident had left Kate acutely embarrassed and shy of further contact with Captain Palmer.

Thus it was that when she heard signs of his possible emergence into the galley, she thought it expedient to dart into the pantry room. There were several wide cracks between the wood planking of the pantry door, and Kate peered through, hoping for an early escape from her self-made prison. She could see the captain at his cabin door, and he wore only a brocade dressing gown. She couldn't see his face, for he was looking into his room and saying something in a low, hushed voice. This piqued Kate's curiosity and her fine brows drew together in a puzzled frown. Then she saw, and the frown was replaced by round-eyed shock!

"Hurry, my pet, there is no one about," said the Captain in a tone that indicated he had been in his cups, but was still able to function with lucidity.

Lady Susan Medwin, dressed in a satin wrapper and slippers, appeared at his open door, and her fingers touched the captain's mouth as she brushed up against him. She whispered something that Kate could not hear, and was certain she should not, when the captain suddenly moved. He pulled Lady Medwin back to him and plunged his hand into her satin wrapper. It fell away, exposing her nakedness, and before Kate could close her astonished gray eyes, she had seen the man bring down his mouth to the white breast he fondled in his heavy hand!

Oh God! thought Kate, putting her hand to her stomach and holding her forehead with the other. "Lady Medwin and Captain Palmer? 'Tis absurd . . . unthinkable . . . yet, there they are!"

Kate was the, flower of a sheltered environment in a society that chose to spare its chaste young maids from intimate knowledge of the intrigues of men and women! She had never witnessed such things!

Lady Medwin's outrageous flirting all these weeks had raised Kate's brow and widened her gray eyes. She put the woman down as roguish, though not seriously so. After all, her husband seemed not to mind. She had never thought the woman's flirting went beyond words. She still found this scene too incredible to believe.

Lady Medwin drawled, "La, darling . . . I think I hear someone about. Let me go!" With which she swished across the galley into her own room.

Susan Medwin glanced about hurriedly as she opened her door, taking one last look at the man she had just bedded. Oh God! her mind cried, why was her body still in heat? Why did not the ache leave her loins? She still throbbed, and she squeezed her thighs together in an effort to cease such burnings. She had just given vent to her needs, she had found her momentary exultation in a drunken man's bed, yet she knew herself in need of more! A sickening upheaval tore through her belly. Please, she begged silently, when will it end? How many men? How many times? Let my aching end. How can I go on always wanting . . . always finding, and still wanting more? How many men will it take to still the craving of my body? A small groan shattered in her throat as she flung herself onto her bed, but there were no tears. They had ended long ago.

Kate peered into the empty galley, opening the pantry

door slowly. She snatched up the blanket quickly, left the coffee behind and dashed down the length of the room to the companionway. She had to get out, she thought wildly, scampering up the stairs. In her haste she never noticed Jack Walepole standing in his cabin doorway watching her!

She reached the skylight bench and attempted a smile as she spread the wool blanket over Miss Premble's knees. She was careful to avoid Sir John's eye, only half listening to his amusing chatter. There was a pounding in her mind. For no reason at all she felt herself betrayed! She had to think, and made a lame excuse and returned to her cabin alone. Moving about restlessly, she attempted to assemble her thoughts. Yet they jumbled about, refusing to make sense. Confound the woman! thought Kate. Why the deuce would Lady Medwin prefer Captain Palmer to her own sweet husband? The captain was neither handsome nor witty, and certainly older than Sir John! Why did Lady Medwin sneak about in such a detestable manner, making a cuckold of the man she had vowed to honor and to love? The obvious answer that came to Kate's romantic mind was that the woman must be in love with Captain Palmer. Somehow, this did not fit. She could not believe the woman was in love with Palmer, but she must be to risk hurting Sir John. Yet she did not hurt Sir John, for he apparently had no inkling of his wife's clandestine activities. Yet, here too, Kate balked. She could not excuse such skulking about by saying the woman was attempting to spare her husband pain! Such was stuff and nonsense to Kate. Lady Medwin apparently wanted to avoid scandal. Kate reasoned that if the lady was unfaithful, 'twas because she had fallen madly in love with Captain Palmer. Unthinkable as that notion might be, apparently love was blind! Such dishonesty irked young Kate. She thought 'twould be better for the woman to own up to her passion or to forego it. Such was the way of the true heroine. Lady Medwin was weak. Then she thought once again of sweet, unsuspecting Sir

John, and put the woman down as wicked, decadent, and horrid!

Now while she thought Lady Medwin should be honest with Sir John, she did not think it right for anyone else to bring such sad offerings. No, on no account should such hurt be wrought on his head. Perhaps Lady Medwin would forget, or give up this passion of hers, and Sir John need never know. At any rate, she could think no longer, and with the final decision that Sir John was not to hear of his horrid wife's activities from herself, Kate put the matter away.

8

The repairs to the ship had kept Paul Cooper busy and inaccessible to Kate all that day. Miss Ellen lost Sir John to his afternoon nap, and took up a Miss Radcliffe novel. As she situated herself on her berth and prepared to read, she received some lively jibes from her charge. "What have you there, Nell? Romance? La, Nell, how many you gobble up. 'Tis a wonder you never married, and there is no use telling me no one ever offered for you, with those pippin cheeks of yours. I'd never believe such a round tale!"

Miss Ellen wagged her finger at Kate. "Naughty puss! But I do so love a novel, and as to giving you round tales . . . such terms, my darling, are not fit for young ladies!"

"Well then, tell me true, Nell. Did you ever have a beau?" asked Kate curiously.

Miss Ellen's eyes looked ahead, but their light was in the past, and her voice strange. "I had a beau, but you were a wee thing, much in need, and he had no prospects. I let it go!"

"Oh, Nell, you gave up a chance at love and marriage

for me?" asked Kate, feeling suddenly guilty.

"Oh, no, my darling. It wasn't right. It would not have worked, and having you . . . well, it helped me over a bad time." She wished it away with her hand. "Now enough of such nonsense. Let me read."

Kate sighed and proceeded to while away the tedium with a letter to Danny. It was her first since they had sailed, and she filled it with an exact accounting of her days at sea. It stretched over those first exciting days, into the endlessly lazy days and nights of growing boredom. She carefully avoided excessive mention of Paul Cooper, and proceeded to set down with much dramatic description the storm they had battled and won. At last her pen hesitated. She was unable to discuss her morning's discovery with Nell. Lord, Nell would be in a wild state if she heard what the captain and Lady Medwin were about and then there would be no living with her until they were off the ship! To write such a thing to Danny might sound like gossip, yet, she reasoned, had Danny been here, she would have discussed it with him. Thus it was she set her newly acquired knowledge and opinions to paper, requested his immediate thoughts on such "goings-on" and signed her name. Satisfied, she sealed and put away the letter for mailing when they would reach England.

The afternoon strolled into evening, which proved to be equally mundane. The food, due to spoilage, was beginning to be less appetizing. Then, too, conversation that night proved to be a difficult task, and both Miss Ellen and Kate retired early.

Sometime late into the night, try as she might, Kate could not sleep. She lit her lamp and sat up in her berth. Fumbling about, she discovered a book and tried to read it. It availed not! A cup of warm milk was the thought that presented itself as a solution. Perhaps! So she donned her silk wrapper, found her slippers, and quietly made her way to the pantry. Here she found a container half full with milk and congratulated the cow in the hull for not going dry! A few moments saw the milk heated, and

Kate was returning to her cabin when a small dark figure moved toward her. Startled, Kate jumped, spilling some of the milk. Taking her hand away from her mouth, she exclaimed with some annoyance, "Mr. Walepole . . . you frightened me!"

"Miss Newbury," he drawled, and his pin-like eyes glinted in the dim light of the galley. "I am indeed fortunate to find you at last alone. There is something . . . a matter of some urgency . . . that we must discuss," he said, and though he smiled it was belied by the look flickering in his eyes.

"Really? I don't see why we must discuss anything alone. Perhaps in the morning, sir," she said, beginning to move away.

He detained her by reaching out and catching her elbow. She looked at his hand, but even the raising of her brow did not cause him to remove his grip. She pulled her arm roughly out of his hand and it sent her cup with its contents flying across the room. She regarded him out of gray stormy eyes. "How dare you? Stand aside, Mr. Walepole, and allow me to pass!" She was angry, and though a prickle of fear haunted her, her logic told her she was being foolish. What could he do, here, closeted by occupied cabins all around?

"Very well," he said, moving slightly. As she proceeded to pass he gave a weary sigh. "I suppose then it will be up to me to advise Sir John . . ."

Kate stopped and spun around. "What do you mean? Advise Sir John about what?" She felt her heart beating at an extraordinary rate.

"Why, you know very well, Miss Newbury. Did we not both observe Lady Medwin's movements this morning? To be sure, I have known these past few days and more, but I had no collaborator."

"You have none now, you horrid man!" snapped Kate, incensed, thinking him less than a toad.

"I horrid? My dear child, how is that so? 'Tis Lady Medwin with her many lovers that is horrid. Not I! She makes a cuckold of Sir John—not with one, but two."

"Stop it! You are talking filth at me and I won't have it!"

"I see I have wasted my time by attempting to discuss the matter with you. I thought you would best know how to break the news to Sir John. However, I suppose I shall have to deal with it as best I am able," he said roughly, crossing to his cabin door and opening it wide.

This was terrible, thought Kate immediately. She had to stop the insensible toad. Such hurtful knowledge should not come to Sir John from a third party! That was cruel, as cruel as Lady Medwin's unfaithfulness. It was for his wife to tell, not anyone else . . . and especially not any-one like Mr. Walepole. She rushed at Mr. Walepole in an attempt to get him to listen to reason. "Please, sir, do but reconsider . . ."

She had no time in which to utter another word. Suddenly she was dragged brutally into the room, and before she could open her mouth to scream, he had his hand over her mouth. She was pinned to the wall and as he stuffed her mouth with a ball of linen, he chuckled wickedly. "Damn your wide eyes, you haughty bitch! I've seen you looking down your nose at me. Thought me ugly, thought I had no right eyeing you. Well, I'm going to have you, and in a way you'll probably never get taken again. I have my own sort of playfulness! I could have had Lady Medwin, you know. Yes that's right, even ugly little me. It's a sickness with her. She's bedded the captain and your handsome Paul. She's with Paul Cooper right now. That's right, wide-eyes. She's with your Paul, but I didn't want *her!* I have a need for fresh young things. Virgins . . . you are a virgin, ain't you? Well, we shall soon find out." His voice was guttural, hoarse and profane. She felt sick at his touch and as he flung her hard upon the floor, she thought she wanted to kill him. He straddled her, holding her wrists over her head and began placing his hot, wet kisses over her face. She jerked away from him and discovered the stainwood table beside her. If only she could topple it, perhaps it might make noise enough to rouse someone. She felt herself gagging with the handkerchief in her mouth, and the more she tried to scream the more she gagged. His hands fumbled with her wrapper, tearing it across her full bosom, exposing the thin nightgown beneath. As he worked, he talked, his voice as frenzied as his movements. "You're wondering how I dare, stupid chit! They shan't do anything to me. 'Tis not my first rape! I told you I have a propensity for virgins, and virgins don't offer themselves to me easily. So I take them! No, they won't do anything to me. Fear for your name; if people knew you had been taken by such as me 'twould ruin you! No, my pretty, it will be hushed up. I'll have you and there won't be none that will touch me!"

There! Her ankle linked the leg of the table and it went over with a resounding crash as the china pitcher and basin hit the floor and splattered! A corner of the table hit Walepole's back and he brought his hand crashing across Kate's face. But it had worked; she could hear Miss Ellen's voice in the galley and someone else's as well. A knock sounded at Walepole's door and Sir John's voice came through clearly. "I say . . . everything all right in there, Mr. Walepole?"

Walepole turned his hoary head, loosening his grip unconsciously as he moved. "Yes, it seems I knocked over a pitcher in my sleep. Now go away and let me get some rest."

Kate had suddenly surprised him by ripping her hand out of his clasp. She pulled at the gag in her mouth and managed a muffled sound before he caught her. Sir John's brow went up and Miss Ellen could be heard behind him asking what had happened, for surely was that not a cup of spilled milk on the floor, and where was her Kathleen?

Kate brought up her knees and attempted a valiant push that did in fact wobble him. Once again she loosed her grip and tore the handkerchief from her mouth. "Sir John!" she screamed.

The door was immediately pounded upon. "Open this

door at once, Mr. Walepole. Good God, sir, have you gone mad?"

Mr. Walepole released Kate and stood up hissing, "I'll open it now, my bird, but 'tis not over between us." He moved to the door and flung it open, whereupon Kate ran across past Sir John and into Miss Ellen's embrace.

"My God!" exclaimed Sir John, "What is the meaning of this?"

"Damn you, what do you think it is? You have interrupted a tête-à-tête!" said Walepole leering.

"How dare you!" scolded Miss Ellen, "You evil man, you should be locked behind bars like the animal that you are!"

"He forced me in there, Nell, and he was going to . . ." cried Kate.

"Hush there, my lamb. Hush there, my angel. He will never touch you again."

Sir John turned on Mr. Walepole, "What in hell do you think you were about, forcing Miss Newbury into your room?"

The captain had joined them by now and frowned at the assembled gathering. "What the deuce are you all about, shouting out here. Can't a man drink in peace?" His eyes were vague, his steps unsteady.

Sir John ignored this remark and pursued the subject at hand. "Mr. Walepole, you will answer me, one way or another."

"Who are you to question me? She came into my room willingly enough; 'twas only when you all came down around us that she scurried off with such a tale. How else did I get her out of her cabin and into mine!"

"It is obvious that Miss Newbury was in the galley preparing milk. And the cup with its contents on the floor are an indication that she did not go willingly with you," replied Sir John, looking the man over with disgust.

"That is the chit's story. It ain't mine! Who do you think people will believe? How could I drag her across the room into mine without her making a stir? Truth is . . ."

"Shut your filthy mouth, you swine, scoundrel! I could break your neck!" shouted Sir John, much incensed. "Don't you ever cast your ugly eyes in Miss Newbury's direction ever again, for I swear I'll have them out for the trouble!"

"Will you? Should I tremble before you?" answered the toad, showing his false pride. "Think I don't know why? Think I don't know you want her for yourself . . . have wanted her from the first day she set her dainty feet on board, and why not? With a harlot for a wife, it would be nice to have something clean and fresh beneath you. Who is to blame you, or me, for that matter?"

He received a blow in the face for his rendition, and it sent him flying backward into his cabin. Sir John stood, fists clenched at his side, prepared to dole out a bit more of the same; however, when Walepole rose, it was to rush across the room and slam the door shut against his foe.

Sir John ran a hand through his disarrayed hair and turned to Miss Ellen. "You had better take her to her room."

"But shouldn't Walepole be locked in his room?" asked Miss Ellen fearfully.

"I shall see that his room is bolted from the outside tonight, and from here on in," said Sir John.

Kate, her tears still in her eyes, reached out a hand. "Sir John, thank you."

He took up her hand and placed it to his lips, his eyes full on her face. "Get some rest, Miss Newbury. No one shall harm you."

He turned to the captain. "Please order a steward here at once, and have him set about putting a latch on Mr. Walepole's door."

"Good notion," said Palmer blinking, and moving to the bell rope.

As Miss Ellen led her to their cabin, Kate glanced around, acutely aware that all the commotion had not served to stir either Paul Cooper or Lady Medwin from their chambers.

Sir John stayed only long enough to see his orders carried through, before returning to his cabin, a cabin where he knew his wife did not await him.

9

The next morning, November 3, 1804, was unusually bright and unseasonably warm. The ship cut through the dark blue swiftly and Kate, alone on the poop deck, looked down into the waters' depths. She was glad she had ended and sealed the letter to Danny before last night. She would need time before she could tell him of that particular experience. One of the most frightening moments was when she knew herself virtually helpless to escape. For a toad of a man, he had been surprisingly agile and astoundingly strong.

She was annoyed with Nell. She wanted to bring charges against Mr. Walepole. Hadn't he tried to ravish her, hadn't he boasted of the evil deeds he had accomplished with other poor young girls? She had been fortunate, but what of others in England, were they to be left exposed to such an animal? He should be brought to justice. But Ellen would hear none of it. " 'Twould bring scandal to your name, and there would be those who would say you had invited the attack upon yourself!" Nell had said.

There was more fretting at Kate's mind. Walepole had accused Paul of being Lady Medwin's lover; he had said she had two, the captain and Paul. She didn't want to believe it and yet it answered much that had always puzzled her. Kate was not in love with Paul Cooper, and yet it hurt to think a man who had indicated a strong attachment for her was making love to another woman. A voice at her shoulder brought her around sharply. "Sir John, good morning."

"It is a good one, and you look charming. You always do in that shade of blue."

"Thank you. I had liked this cloak when I had it made for this voyage, but after observing your wife's fashionable things I realize it is far from being all the crack!" chuckled Kate.

"You are far more charming in your simplicity than she could ever be in all her finery," said Sir John, and his voice had a tinge of bitterness.

"Oh, please don't say such a thing, Sir John. You must not be affected by what that horrid man said last night," said Kate, reaching her hand toward him with concern.

"Walepole? Did you think he told me anything I am not aware of? My sweet lovely, you are an innocent! I have known about my wife from the day we were married, perhaps before. She attempts to be discreet, but it has always been impossible. There are too many lovers, they tumble over one another. There is for us no chance at the normal way of life. She has an illness, and it leaves our marriage devoid of love."

"Oh, Sir John, please. You mustn't tell me this. I am so sorry," said Kate, much distressed by his confession.

He looked at her strangely. "Ah, I see that you are, and indeed I have been a fool. Walepole was right, you know. I have wanted you."

"Please, Sir John, stop!" cried Kate, standing away from him.

"My dearest child. You have nothing to fear from me. I assure you, not all men take what they want, and I certainly have no intention of attempting it. Had I been free, I would have tried to win your heart, but I am not free to do so, and refrain from such efforts. Our journey draws to an end and I felt there were things I had to tell you."

"Oh, there is Paul." She began waving to Master Cooper, hoping for an interruption, but Master Cooper's attention was elsewhere.

"He is not for you, Kathleen. He is shallow and he is

one of my wife's lovers, has been since we sailed from the Indies."

"Stop it, do you hear? I won't listen anymore; it is enough!" cried Kate, backing away. Disillusionment shakes the mind, wobbles the soul and leaves a gentle spirit broken. Kate felt as though her world had gone astray. Where was she, who were these people, what manner of creatures were they? She had to get away from them before they broke her heart! She had to get home to her papa, where things were in their proper place.

"Ship ahoy!" shouted Master Cooper from the forecastle. "Take in sails, men; it's the *Gypsy* and I mean to salute her, for she has a Spanish vessel in tow!"

Kate looked round, momentarily diverted, and there just ahead of them to the starboard was one of the sleekest most beautiful schooners she had ever seen. At its stern was a lumbersome Spanish yawl, very much in tow. The *Bermudian* was fast gaining on it, and she could see that the crew of both vessels were excited at the prospect of greeting one another.

A skeleton crew worked the riggings of the *Bahia*, making her fall into line astern the *Gypsy*, and Kate watched them all, wide-eyed and pleased with something new to break up the tensions of the journey.

They had seen neither sail nor land since they left port and there was much commotion buzzing round the *Bermudian* as they took in sail. Master Cooper seemed as excited as his men as he shouted to his crew to heave to! He scaled the distance through the waist, jumping the steps to the raised quarter-deck and nearly collided with the captain as he emerged from the companionway.

" 'Tis the *Gypsy* herself, Captain Palmer. We've had her in our sights and were fast gaining, but we only just discovered who she is and what manner of prize she leads to England!" glowed Master Cooper, much animated.

The captain moved forward, resting his arm on the binnacle and shaded the sun with his roughened hand. "Aye, I've been wanting a look at her. Heard tell she's brought more into English ports than any privateer on the waters. I understand why—just look at her lines!"

They had by this time drawn up abreast of the *Gypsy* and the sailors of both ships were hurling greetings, congratulations, and jests at one another. Some rather ribald remarks came to Kate's ears and she blushed hotly. Sir John touched her arm gently. "Perhaps, Miss Newbury, you would be more comfortable in your cabin?"

"Oh, no, Sir John. I don't mind their jokes, and I do want to see what is afoot."

He said nothing to this and Kate continued to look on, smiling at the men's pleasure, herself somewhat thrilled by it all. Paul Cooper tipped his hat and came up beside her, so that she felt surrounded by gentlemen. As his attention was still taken by the privateer, she ventured a question. "Is the *Gypsy* one of our war vessels?" she asked innocently.

"War vessel?" he laughed incredulously. "Lord, no! You have the honor of looking on the finest privateering ship beneath the English flag!"

"A privateer?" repeated Kate, dismayed. She returned her eyes to the *Gypsy* and there found its captain. He had moved to the ship's port side and had one booted foot upon its bulwarks. He wore no captain's hat; indeed, his neck-length black hair blew in dark thick clouds about his handsome head. His cloak was negligently tied at his throat, from which the collar of his white linen shirt protruded. His dark knit breeches were tight fitting, yet moved when he did. There was nothing to label him captain, yet all on board the *Bermudian* who looked on him knew him to be so. He grinned at his men, calling out to many by name and then, bending onto his raised knee, looked upon the *Bermudian* and its passengers!

He discovered there a woman, and his boyish grin slipped into a subtle smile. Kate stood leaning onto the rails, her long glistening hair framing her exquisite face. Her blue cloak hid much of her figure, but her movements gave her grace away. Bright green eyes looked into gray ones and she felt shaken. Kate met his gaze, blushed rosily, and looked away. However, when she glanced his way next, he swept her a gallant bow and she felt like running for shelter.

Both Sir John and Master Cooper suggested that she go below, but unwilling to comply with what she knew the proprieties obliged her to do, and unable to find excuse for it, she moved away from them and lapsed into watchful silence.

"Here is a drink to you, captain," shouted Palmer, suddenly raising the glass that he had been holding.

Captain Branwell grinned, and his white teeth gleamed. "Thank you, sir."

"Would you do us the honor of having a light lunch on board my ship?" asked Captain Palmer jovially.

Captain Branwell was still smiling. "I thank you, no, sir. As you see the ship we have in tow slows us a bit more than we are used to traveling. It is my plan to reach England by the end of this week. I'd like to keep full sail as long as I can."

"Aye. Got the prisoners below or did you feed them to the sharks?" asked Palmer curiously.

"The crew of the *Bahia* were put in its long boat off the coast of Spain." Captain Branwell smiled, looking again at Kate and thinking his six weeks at sea were causing him to see more than was there. No woman could look as enticing as she seemed to; it had to be his forced celibacy. He was half inclined to chuck his intentions to the winds and take lunch on board the *Bermudian,* just to get closer to the pretty. However, he put such selfish thoughts aside, with the consoling thought that she would probably prove to be inaccessable. She had the eyes of an innocent, and as a rule he avoided innocents.

"Set them off the coast of Spain?" ejaculated Master Cooper unbelievingly. "You could have been sighted!"

"Aye, but we weren't."

"But what made you take such a risk?" asked Captain Palmer.

"The poor devils had to get home. We took what we wanted. Now, I'm sorry, my friends. I am afraid we'll have to say good-bye." said Captain Branwell suddenly, nonchalantly giving them his back and returning to his men.

The *Bermudian* slowly passed with much hand-waving, hoots, howls, and merry jibs. Kate sighed and found Sir John silent and stony-faced. She attempted to bring him out of his doldrums. " 'Tis a handsome vessel, in spite of its vile work!"

"Vile work?" frowned Sir John, "I don't understand . . ."

"Don't understand? Why how can you not? Just look at it: 'tis heavily armed but the ship it hauls in tow is not! 'Tis nothing more than legalized piracy, and its Captain is nothing more than a pirate!"

"My dear child, I have my own reasons for disliking Captain Branwell, but you mistake. He does our country a service. He risks his ship, which I assure you cost him a handsome sum, and himself by going on the high seas, where you must realize he is prey for French warships, and they are far better armed than he . . . for what? He does it for England. Every month, French privateers comb the waters and interfere with our trade and they do not always set our sailors safely into a long boat. We retaliate, and he does a fine job of it as well!"

"It is still vile, taking an unarmed ship. He would do better to chase after the French and prevent them from attacking our merchants."

"Our navy must do that."

"I still cannot like it, but, you called him Captain Branwell. You must know him then, for no one said his name. Yet you did not greet one another?" asked Kate, changing the subject.

"We are not acquainted, though I know his face. He and my wife were friends last spring, when we were residing in London."

"Oh," said Kate, finding one more fault with the captain of the *Gypsy,* and marveling at Lady Medwin's many accomplishments.

She excused herself shortly thereafter and went below to look in on Nell. For no reason at all the face of the captain of the *Gypsy* flashed into her thoughts. His green, speaking eyes glowed arrogantly at her as though to say, had he wanted her, he could have had her. She put up her chin, combat in her demeanor. Not I, she thought, the swaggering blackguard! I certainly would not be taken in by his handsome visage. Yet, even as she announced this to her palpitating heart, his smile danced upon her mind. Stupid girl, she chided herself, to be thinking of such a man! He is nought but an adventurer, the sort who always goes about breaking foolish women's hearts!

That evening her eyes strayed to Paul Cooper. She knew she didn't love him, but she was honest enough with herself to admit she had been attracted to him. Walepole's accusation had stirred an irritation in her. Walepole, confined to quarters, was not present to witness her agitation. She watched Lady Medwin flirting with Paul and noted the strange slyness of their gazes, and she knew the truth. The first dawning had sent a wave of anger through her. She asked herself why, and knew it was anger at herself. She had always prided herself on being a good judge of character and it was pinching to find once more that she had been wrong!

Her anger ebbed. She excused him; he was but a man and hadn't Lizzie who knew much more about these things, hadn't she said that men can't help themselves. After all, Lady Medwin was obviously available. She rose and sighed, making her way to the poop deck, when Paul's soft voice was heard at her ear. "Kathleen?"

She turned around, surprised by its tone. "Oh, Paul."

He was looking at her face in a way that brought the blush to her cheeks and she backed away, for she was not sure she liked it. "I heard about Walepole, and insisted he be kept in his quarters during meals. When I first heard of it I wanted to kill him. I would have killed him had he touched you," he said, reaching out and taking her by the arms, pulling her to him. Suddenly his mouth was on hers, wildly, hungrily, and he was saying her name. She pulled out of his embrace. "Stop it! Paul, stop it!"

"I can't stop. Kate, let me; you want me too. I've seen the way you've watched me; you want me as much as I want you," he said, wrapping his arms around her again. His mouth was on hers again, sucking in her breath, and she began to feel her head swim. There was a dizzy, overwhelming sensation clouding her mind, for his was a man's kiss and it was not without its power. It set her on another plane and she felt her heart beat at a stupendous rate. She felt her body aroused, but then, suddenly, clearly her mind and heart agreed, she wasn't in love with Paul Cooper and the thought cooled her. His kiss no longer affected her, and she yanked away from him.

He persisted. "Lord, but you are soft," he whispered, trying to catch her to him again. "Let me, Kate. I could teach you all about pleasure."

She hated the sound of his words. They were cheap and ugly. "Keep your degrading offers for Lady Medwin. She may appreciate them. I assure you, sir, I do not!"

He stood back as though a bucket of cold water had been splashed over him. He was off balance and repeated idiotically, "Lady Medwin?"

"I . . . I am sorry. I should not have said such an ill-natured thing. But you did take a liberty. If you will excuse me . . ." Kate attempted to step away.

He cut off her path. "No, Kathleen, you can't go like that. You must let me explain."

"Why?"

"Because I won't have you think badly of me."

"Who would you have me think ill of then?" asked Kate sweetly.

"But Kate, it was not my fault. She sought me out. She comes to me, to the captain . . . she's a slut."

"How very chivalrous of you, Mr. Cooper," said Kate with contempt. "You have held that woman in your arms and yet you stand here and malign her to me! I like you far less now that you have explained!"

"Kate!" he called after her.

She vanished from his view. Her heart and mind was as hard as a highlander's heelpiece for the likes of Paul

Cooper. How could she have ever thought him a nice sort of fellow?

Master Cooper watched her go. Kathleen had been a work of art he longed to explore. A beautiful alluring female. He had wanted her from the first, though truth has it, he was not in love with her. Very few men with Master Cooper's nature ever do fall in love. However, he was taken with her. He had watched over and cared for Paul Cooper too many years to begin thinking of anyone outside himself. Kate was, in her innocence, easy prey. He had charmed, wooed, and now he had thought he would seduce her. It was safe enough. For she would be on land, and he would return to the sea.

It would appear that his game was at an end. It was a passing sorrow. He had lost many times in his youthful career and knew well the method of recovery, that being to immediately replace the loss! He pondered this philosophy a moment or so within the night's cool air and then made his way below. There he found Lady Medwin sipping sherry and flirting with the captain. Apparently, her husband had retired with his usual good book! The captain had imbibed enough to put a lesser fellow under the table and was not quick to note the gleam in Lady Medwin's eye, but Paul understood.

He took Lady Medwin's soft hand and put it to his lips. "Later, sweetbun?"

"Now," she said, sliding her hand up his chest.

He sent a look to his captain and turned to him. "Sir, I have the log prepared; if you would care to step into your quarters I should be glad to show it to you."

"Log?" said Captain Palmer, blinking. "Damn the log, but help me to m'quarters. . . to lie down."

Master Cooper sent Lady Medwin a meaningful look as he hunched the captain's arm over his shoulder. A few moments later he entered his own small cabin to find one whale-oil lamp lit and Susan Medwin standing near his bed, free of her clothes. Her figure was slim, and there was a lithe beauty to her form. Her breasts were small, her nipples dark, protruding at him. He watched her as he threw off his clothes. She licked her bottom lip, lingeringly biting into it, waiting for him to touch her, and when he did, she threw back her head with ecstasy. Without a word he pulled her down on the bed. Without a word, without the foreplay of lovers, he mounted her.

She was wide open, juicy, and in no need of foreplay. It had all taken place in her mind. But she wanted him to paw at her body. She wanted rough usage and she clawed at him begging for it, and he did her bidding, excited by her demands. He reached his peak before her, but she held him still, refusing to let him go, begging him to take her again, to finish the job.

"Satisfy me, Paul, satisfy me," she pleaded, biting his ear.

He looked at her oddly, and though their bodies had met his own needs, his thoughts went to Kate and he wondered what it would be like with Kate in his arms. He wanted Susan Medwin out of his bed. She was an impossible woman to satisfy and she made him feel somehow inadequate. But he played with her breasts and allowed himself to rub his reduced muscle against her buttocks. She was all over him, pushing his knee between her thighs, pumping herself against its hardness, crying for him to take her, and he felt his manhood grow at her sensual display. Soon he was entering her again, and this time he was able to control himself long enough to give her what she craved. At its end, they turned their backs upon one another, not wishing to touch, not wishing to look, and without another word, Susan Medwin donned her clothes and left his cabin.

10

It was Sunday, November 5, 1804, when the *Bermudian* sailed into safe harbor at Southampton, England.

The habitually active port was notably quiet, as was the custom on Sunday, yet even so the *Bermudian*'s arrival caused quite a stir. It was but one week overdue, yet the townspeople had begun to despair its arrival. The news that it was here sent up a cheerful cry. Shouts of joy went through the streets, for there was many a shopkeeper who awaited its stores from the West Indies! She was safe and her valuable cargo, mostly sugar, had not fallen into French hands.

Kate and Miss Ellen stood upon the poop, tightly wrapped in their warm cloaks, the brisk wind lapping at them. Neither spoke, for each had thoughts preying in her mind. Kate saw the clean, bright harbor with its aged wooden dock planking and its rows of meat shops, many of which sported the brown Tudor stripes she loved so well. It was so different from Bermuda. There were some that might have called it bleak in comparison, but not she. Not Kate, she loved its lines. It held a special beauty, one of history and varied architecture, and it held her father!

Miss Premble looked into the harbor town that had been her home until she had gone a few miles farther west to be Lady Newbury's companion, and then, after her ladyship's death, Kate's governess! It had been for her a long, frightening, nerve-racking voyage.

She had been sorry to leave Bermuda, but, now that she was seeing English soil, her own beloved English soil, she was overcome with a quiet exuberance. The only thought that struck against her grain was that Kate was now in danger.

"I don't see Papa anywhere, Nell. Where can he be?" exclaimed Kate with some concern.

"Bless you, child! I heard tell we are a week overdue. He has no doubt been sending someone to check on our arrival every day. Depend upon it, he has had the news and will be here any moment!" soothed Nell.

"But the Grange is not so very far from Southampton. I remember," argued Kate.

"You remember? You were just a wee thing. But you

are right, the Grange is not so very far, and if I am not mistaken that is your family crest glinting in the sun," said Nell, pointing to a coach that had just turned down the wharf. "I must say, child, he has come for you in proper style, outriders and all!" There was an underlining to her tone that Kate could not help but notice. She knew that her beloved Nell did not like Sir Horace, though Nell had never said so. Yet Kate knew it, and had never understood why. They were certainly civil to one another, and Papa had always seemed to like Nell, but now was no time to bother with such thoughts for she could see her father and he was waving. Kate set up shouts and jumps enough to bring the blush to Miss Premble's cheeks on her behalf. "Really, Kate, you are behaving like a veritable hoyden. It won't do!"

Kate had no care for the proprieties at such a moment. The woman in her had vanished, making way for the child and she called, "Papa," until she was nearly hoarse.

The gangplank had not yet been set into place, and Miss Premble called Kate to attention. "Kathleen, I believe you have not made your farewells to Sir John and Lady Medwin, and he had been eyeing you these past ten minutes."

Kate turned impatiently. "I said good-by to everyone earlier this morning, but if you think I should say good-by to Sir John again?"

"Indeed, he was most kind, and we owe him that much for his handling of that creature Walepole."

Kate glanced around fearfully. She had scarcely seen Walepole since that night and had managed to put him from her mind, but the thought of him now drained her cheeks of color. Nell saw this and chided herself for reminding Kate of him. "Go on, love, make your farewells."

Kate traversed the length of the poop where Sir John sat with a book, and he quickly rose to his feet. Hesitatingly she offered her hand. "Farewell, Sir John, and do extend my apologies to your wife, for my father has arrived and I am unable to take my leave of her."

"It is of no consequence. Fare thee well, Miss Newbury. May God go with you, child," said Sir John, clutching her gloved hand and putting it to his feverish lips. She represented his lost youth, and beauty in its pure form. She represented his dream of the ideal woman. She moved away gently and he watched her go with a sigh. She saw Paul Cooper standing in the waist and he was gazing hungrily at her, but she turned her head against him.

It occurred to her as she followed Nell down the gangplank that she had never before met another human being whom she wished never to meet again. Yet she had managed to feel that way about each and every individual she had gotten to know on board the *Bermudian*. It was a sad and disquieting reflection. But what had she to do with such things for long? Was she not youth, and was she not diving into the arms of an adoring parent?

She buried herself in her father's loving embrace, and there found her world and its stability. She felt fresh, bright, and once again, she felt whole. Balance had been restored, sanity maintained. "Papa, Papa," she cried joyfully and stood back to have a better look. "But, oh Papa, you have grown so thin," she said with a note of concern.

"Very good of you to notice, exactly what one hopes for when one has been torturing himself with exercise and diet." He smiled, and she saw herself reflected in his light eyes. It sent her back into his embrace and she clung, never, ever wanting to be parted again. Miss Premble watched them silently, a flicker of thought creasing her brow.

Sir Horace put his daughter from him gently, though he kept his arm around her dainty shoulder. Extending his hand to Miss Premble he said amiably, "Well, Miss Ellen, I am relieved to see you looking as well as ever. I hope the voyage did not prove as harrowing as the last I imposed upon you."

She dropped a quick curtsey and forced a smile for, indeed, at times it was easy to forget what she knew about him. Such was his charm, and it had won Kate's mother. "Thank you, Sir Horace; it was but a wee bit uncomfortable, but I shall do."

"Well then, come along, come along. I shall send the livery boys for your luggage later in the day. No sense our waiting out here in the cold," he said, ushering them into the coach and seeing their laps spread over with a rug before settling down himself. He coughed during the motion, but seemed determined to ignore it; however, at length he was overtaken with a spasm of fitful coughs that caused a cloud to cover Kate's eyes. "Papa, Papa, are you ill?" cried Kate when he had managed to control himself.

"Ill . . . I? Never a day." He grinned at her.

"But you cough so?" persisted Kate.

"And so would you if you had been handling these dusty rugs," countered her father.

Kate eyed him suspiciously but said nothing to this, for he was already pinching her rosy cheeks. "Now my kitten, I have a surprise for you. Your Aunt Sarah has invited you to London. She shall be there—it seems she is now visiting at Oatlands—but expects to be home in a day or so, at which time I shall send you and Nell to join her."

"What of you, Papa?" said Kate, dismayed.

"Good Lord, it won't be any fun for me. This is a shopping expedition. For females only! Sarah advises me that you will need clothes and more clothes for your debut into society and it is her intention to spend me blunt on an entire wardrobe for the occasion."

"But Papa, I do not wish to go without you," pleaded Kate.

"Nonsense. I should only be in the way amongst all the finery and fripperies you shall find . . . and I have some work at the Grange that must be completed before we leave for London together at the end of the month."

"We will be going together, later?"

"Indeed, for your ball, you know." He grinned.

"Do you hear, Nell? Isn't it exciting?" demanded Kate

of her silent and prudish-looking governess, who smiled her assent.

Her father laughed. "Lord, Kate! You may be a woman grown, but you have the manners of an imp. English misses do not jump about in such a fashion. They are very shy, reserved, and elegant."

"I am elegant, Papa, for while I admit to jumping, I never fall. Does that not make me graceful? And being graceful is being elegant."

"Your reasoning is most assuredly that of a woman's!" her parent replied. "I left a child and am presented with a woman. 'Tis a wonder surely. It is not, Miss Ellen?" he requested cheerfully, pleased with himself over the feat.

"She has all the promise, sir." said Miss Ellen quietly.

"Indeed yes. She has her mother's beauty, though she has a fire in her that her mother surely never had. Her mother was soft ivory. Kate is of a far more daring hue!" He grew silent with this reflection, going back in space and time until he heard Miss Ellen exclaim, "Oh, Kate, love, we approach the New Forest!"

He perked up once again. He adored the New Forest. The Grange situated in its midst had gone from father to son for more than a century. He was the last of the line. When his wife had produced a girl and then died it had been his duty to remarry and beget a male heir, but he had been unable to find it in his heart to carry out his obligation to his name. He sighed, for though the estate would go to Kate, time would change her name.

The land was flat, winding, and sandy. Densely wooded patches skirted the road, their lines changing subtly as elms were replaced with evergreens and oaks. They passed the village of Buckler's Hard, where the oaks from the New Forest were used to provide timber for the construction of warships. Much of Admiral Nelson's fleet had been built in the small New Forest Harbor.

They passed Beaulieu Abbey, and Kate oohed over the old abbey's beauty. Its stone walls were half hidden by the dense forest. It was like a dream. She felt free, as free as she had in Bermuda, yet here was excitement, the excitement that Bermuda had never really held for her. Here the land offered romance of a different nature. In Bermuda one dreamed of a gentle poetic Adonis, beautiful but vulnerable. Here in England her romantic fancy brought her a charging gallant, hard, handsome and well able to slay a dragon! Then Kate saw them and exclaimed with something of glee in her voice, "Look!" Her father smiled, for the sight of the wild ponies of the New Forest was a common sight to him. Kate's face was glued to the coach window. They were wild, free, and ineffably beautiful. They rippled through the forest, and Kate could see the waltz of their colors through the trees. Their ancestors had roamed here unhampered for centuries, and they were as much a part of the land as was the soil. Their winter coats were shaggy, and Kate giggled over their short legs. One adventurous fellow sauntered up to the coach and turned his head to inspect her, and she cooed with utter delight. "Oh Papa, I want to stop and feed them." He pulled a face. "Now, you mustn't do that. You shall have to remember that they *are* wild and known to nip!"

"Oh, but Papa . . ."

"Never mind now," he ordered. "They have food enough." He frowned suddenly. "Had a few tragedies recently. We had a good nut season. Chestnuts came down in hordes, and before we could get most of 'em up and stored the stupid ponies started eating at them. Lost a few. They can't digest them for some odd reason or other. Most sad, most sad."

"Oh Papa, that is terrible," cried Kate. "Why do they eat them if it isn't good for them?"

"Don't know, suppose for the same reason a man drinks port, drinks himself to death or into the gout— and a man is considered to have intelligence."

She sighed, "Oh!" She returned her attention to the window, and found yet another wild pony. He glanced up from his nibbling and his eyes met Kate's in understanding. It was as if he spoke to her saying, "Look upon me, human. Am I not beautiful? 'Tis because I am free to wander over my home. I am my own master. Look upon me, but do not touch."

She smiled and respected his right, understanding it suddenly. It was not enough to say you love a thing, you must love it enough not to destroy it. To paw at a wild thing was to threaten its freedom. There could be nothing lasting with a thing made for wandering.

Her father brought her out of her reverie. "Kate, our servants will be assembled to greet you, and while you will not remember any of them, most of them will most certainly remember you, for you lived here seven years beneath their eyes and were a most engaging minx. I know I have no need to instruct you how to behave."

"Of course not, Papa," said Kate, putting up her chin. "I am not a child. Nor am I a dunce!"

He laughed. "Of course not. Do accept my apology."

She laughed in turn. "It has been duly noted and accepted."

"I don't think that I wrote to you about my house guest. A young lad I met a few years ago in London and trained to be my secretary. He is most efficient and has recently been helping me with my research for my manuscript. I think you will like him. His name is Peregrine Banyon."

Miss Premble stared at Sir Horace with disbelief, and he found her glance disconcerting. He blushed beet red and this was followed by another series of coughing. Kate's interest in the flat heaths was now lost to contemplation of her father. He was too thin, his complexion was not good, and this cough of his—she had no liking for it.

Then Lyndhurst Grange came into view! Her father pointed it out, and the pride was in his eyes as well as his voice. It stood at the end of the drive, parted from them by a small wooden bridge overlooking a shallow stream. The house's broadside faced the road, its pillared façade faced the woods. There was a span of neatly trimmed lawn from the roadside to the garden beds which surrounded the Gothic-styled stone mansion, and only a few scattered trees broke the view. It was home, and it was beautiful.

Later, much later, Kate lay back against her pillows. It was night, she was home and all was well . . . or was it? Her father was ill. He said it was nought, but his cough worried her. She had asked Mr. Banyon whether a doctor was attending Sir Horace, and he had said that her father cared not for the leeches and rarely called the doctor, but he too had no liking for Sir Horace's cough!

She thought of Perry Banyon, remembering her reaction when she had first seen him. She had been stunned into silent admiration. He was tall, slim, fashionably dressed and quite, quite handsome. He had a flash of yellow hair, streaked with lighter shades of flaxen hues and it waved and curled around his head like that of a cherub's, but his face was not a cherub's. His cheekbones were well defined, his nose straight, his chin ever so slightly rounded, his lips thin, and his eyes blue beneath pale gold brows. His manners were meticulous and his address charming enough to leave her shy. Yet she had learned on board the *Bermudian* to be wary of strangers. They were not always what they seemed. Still, by the end of the evening, she thought she might like Peregrine Banyon very well indeed!

11

Branwell Mannering, fifth Earl of the house of Mannering, lay with his arm resting beneath his head. He stared thoughtfully up at the shrouded pink canopy of Lady Claire's four-poster bed.

The lady beside him sighed as though to draw attention to herself. Finding him unresponsive to subtlety she began caressing the dark curling hair on the Earl's bare chest. "Bran, darling, what is it? What are you thinking?

Was I not good?" She believed she was, but she wanted to draw him out.

He brought his green glinting eyes to her lovely face and looked into her light brown eyes. They hid her thoughts. "What could be wrong, after such a performance? You were as ever perfect." That in itself was part of the problem. He felt always that she was performing for an end!

She brushed his body with her firm young breasts, swinging one leg over his. She felt his manhood stir beneath her thigh and reveled in the knowledge, pleased with her power. His arm went round her as he turned to meet her and he pulled her buttock with his large hand, bringing it to him. "Take me again, Bran," she whispered. His mouth took hers and as his tongue found its way, so did the pulsating hardness in his groin. There was no need to ready her, no need to caress her into acquiescence and Branwell Mannering wasted none of these efforts. He had been at sea six weeks and he had driven into London without having had a woman. Lady Claire's waiting invitation was discovered on his desk, and Branwell Mannering had lost no time picking up where they had left off before his departure.

He worked himself deep into the groaning female clutched against him, taking her wildly, aware that she had already climaxed. She writhed in his arms, yet tried to keep her purpose in mind. She wanted his child. She had been trying to trap Lord Mannering into marriage these six months. She was already twenty-one and he was the best of her suitors, except that he was in reality *not* one of them at all! She had given her virginity when she was scarcely sixteen. It had gone to a stableboy, but she had too much of a head to lose her heart. She wanted more. She proceeded to learn the machinations and arts of love-making, miraculously getting with child only once when she was nineteen. She had been staying with an aunt who quickly and without hysterics taught her how to lose such a burden. Her father had never known!

Branwell Mannering was a marriage prize, and one

she meant to have. If she could get herself with child, his child, the earl's hand would be forced! Getting Branwell to her bed had been no difficult task. Getting him to seed her was a thing she found entirely impossible! She had never had such a man before. She had believed she knew everything about such matters, until he had taught her one thing more! He was a most unusual man. She had at first been shocked and fascinated when she discovered the meaning of his hasty withdrawal. They had been making love, she had reached her peak and he was about to reach his when suddenly he pulled himself out of her. She had frowned and asked him what he was doing, and he had laughed. "Upon my soul, Claire, never say there is something you haven't yet experienced. I am, my dear, keeping you free of child by giving my seed to your linens."

To this night, she still had been unable to get him to change such methods. He was good—oh God, she thought, he was better than any other man she had ever had—and she wanted him, his name and his money! She felt him getting ready to climax, felt him begin to haunch himself away and she attempted to foil his retreat by wrapping her legs around and pulling him back toward her. However, a moment later she was free of him, despite her efforts. She made an irritated sound and rolled over, away from him. "I hate when you do that!" she snapped testily.

He laughed amicably. "Would you rather get yourself with child and walk about London with a swollen belly? I assure you, Claire, you would not enjoy such a turn."

"I have managed to keep myself from such a state. Besides, darling, I have a method which would enable me to lose the child, should I want to."

He frowned suddenly, sitting up and regarding her with a look of contempt. "We share little more than this bed, Claire. You have no notion what I am about! I have no intention of allowing any child created by my doing to be—how did you put it?—*lost*. And as I do not want such a decision left to *you*, I think I shall continue to be ruler of my own sport."

She sat up and put herself against his back, but his irritation with her governed him now. He shook her off and proceeded to pull on his breeches. "Bran, don't go! I wouldn't lose any child of yours! Bran . . ."

He turned on her then. "I made it clear to you from the start, before I realized I was not your first, marriage is out of the question. We don't love each other, Claire."

"We have just loved each other quite thoroughly, Branwell!" snapped the lady, flinging her honey-colored hair away from her face. She sat on her knees upon the bed, glaring at him. The dark nipples of her white breasts were taut and they teased him to return. He looked her over and felt little more than disgust. "You play an excellent game, but 'tis time it ended." He turned and proceeded to don his white linen shirt.

"Bran, don't go like that. Forget what I said," pleaded the lady, realizing she had gone too far. She scrambled off the bed and rushed up against him, hugging him around his waist. "Please, darling, do not call an end to it. There is no need."

He made no attempt to touch her but his grin had returned. "Claire, can it be that you think you are dealing with a boy? You attack and retreat, for what purpose? It will come to parting, you know that it will. Why leave it to its last dregs? Let's not claw at one another."

"You are a bastard!" she hissed.

"If I were you would not be trying to get my name." He pulled on his waistcoat of blue silk and began working its buttons.

"Wretch!" exploded the lady.

"Ah, precisely what I have been trying to convey to you. I am, am I not?" agreed his lordship, much pleased with her description.

A pillow was discovered and flung at his merry head. He dodged it, allowing it to go waywardly onto the floor, and laughed, "*tch, tch,* Claire. You ask for my heart, and then try to bludgeon me. Untrustworthy female!"

She once again ran to him, shivering slightly, for they were now some distance from the fireplace. "Bran, darling, do you not care for me, a little?"

"As much as you care for me, darling," he answered, still smiling.

"Then, I will see you again?"

"If you behave," he said lightly.

She reached around and pulled his face to hers, but as she brushed his lips, she felt herself scooped up into his arms and carried to the bed, whereupon he dropped her onto the mattress. As she watched him take his leave she shouted at his back, "Blackguard!"

He ran lightly down the front staircase, shrugging on his elegantly cut coat of dark blue superfine. His neck-cloth had been tied somewhat indifferently in his haste to depart, but this, though it would most certainly draw a rebuke from his intimates, seemed not to weigh heavily on his Lordship's mind.

A phlegmatic-faced butler came forward and Lord Branwell eyed him, wondering how much Claire paid him to keep their affair from her father's ears. He was helped into his many-caped greatcoat, given his top hat, gloves, and walking stick, and relieved of a sizable gratuity before the front doors of the Viscount Rath-borne's elegant town house were opened for him to pass through into the crisp night.

The cold air hit him like a slap, but he seemed pleased enough with its curtness. He walked the length of Berkeley Square and made his leisurely way toward his own lodgings. Lady Claire and their clandestine affair was to be reflected upon! He would have to see less of this particular female. She was, though no virgin, the daughter of a powerful viscount. She was discreet enough to keep her activities away from her father and most of the ton. If the viscount were to get wind of their affair there would be the devil to pay!

He rounded the corner and made his way down to 38 Mount Street, where his own town house was situated. It was an old mellowed brick building of three stories. It had been in the family for many generations, though it boasted the new bow window, which had only recently been introduced and approved by Beau Brummell. The steep steps were taken in twos, his double doors reached and a key produced, whereupon he let himself in. The hall was well lit and ready to receive him, though his butler had already retired, having had instructions not to wait up!

He dropped his greatcoat onto a chair against the richly wainscoted wall. His hat and gloves were given to the stainwood oval table in the center of the marbled hall, and his cane stuck into the pot of a growing palm beside the stained glass panel beside the front doors.

With a weary sigh he made his way across the hall to his study, for he had no urgings to sleep. A low fire was burning in the huge grate and several candles had burned themselves nearly out. He lit a table lamp and moved across to his desk where he put it down and poured himself a brandy. He sipped his drink and felt its warm fluid ease his body, and with a sigh sat heavily upon the Oriental chair at his desk. There he scanned the desk top and one black peaked brow went up with surprise. If he was not mistaken that was his aunt's notepaper lying there, and where the devil did it come from? It wasn't there earlier that afternoon! His hand reached for it, then stopped when he reminded himself that this was a late hour to attempt to decipher his Aunt Sarah's penmanship.

He turned away. Finding he needed more resolution, he picked himself up and crossed to his sofa facing the fire and attempted to hypnotize himself with the flames. At length, he gave such efforts up and returned to his desk and picked up the envelope. His Aunt Sarah had a very special claim to his heart. She was the wife of his late uncle, brother to his mother, long lost to him, and though his uncle had never instilled any great devotion in him during his youth, it was quite different with Aunt Sarah. He adored her. However, she had a knack of always embroiling him in affairs that he'd rather be well out of.

With resignation, he unfolded the notepaper. "Very well, Aunt Sarah . . . have at me!"

The letter began:

Dearest Bran,

Best of my nephews—indeed, all my other nephews are quite horrid as well you know, excepting dearest Matthew who by the way tells me he is quite contented to be at Cambridge, in spite of the fact that he originally wanted to attend Oxford. It doesn't signify though, does it, for you went to Cambridge and being brothers I rather thought it would turn out that way! But I digress.

I have returned to London, though I daresay you had not realized I had left, for you neglected to drop by my home before *you* sailed and there is no need excusing yourself for I don't approve of your privateering which is what you will say you were at! However, I have returned and have with me, my dearest . . . indeed my only niece! I believe I may have mentioned something about her to you, but if I haven't no matter.

You will pay us a morning call tomorrow promptly at nine, for you must know that I intend to take her shopping quite soon after that. As you will be escorting us to Vauxhall (now Bran, don't balk) I do so want you two to become acquainted before we go into public. It would be far more comfortable for her to know someone of consequence before she is set upon by the ton!

There is no use trying to fob me off, Bran darling, for I have been more than a mother to you these eight years and one does not fob off one's mother!

Your loving and affectionate,
Sarah

He read and reread the note before allowing himself to swear. He drank his brandy down and perused the letter once again, swore, and sank onto his desk chair. He thought of his flighty aunt and her demands. He thought of the evening he had planned to spend with the Beau and some of his intimates, and then he thought again of Sarah! With a low growing chuckle he decided to take himself off to bed if he was to rise early enough to obey Aunt Sarah's wishes!

12

Kate was looking beautiful! Her black hair flowed cascadingly down the back of her gown, reaching her waist, and swaying as she moved. Her gown was a low-cut brown jumper over a yellow organza transparency, gathered at the neck with a brown velvet ribbon. Its billowing sleeves were banded in the same manner as was the high waist. The sleek day gown fell in a straight line to her dainty ankles, where brown slippers covered her pointing toes!

Kate stood on these attractive toes of hers, atop a high, leggy stool in Lady Haverly's library, making a concerted effort to reach an old volume of Tom Moore's poetry.

Lord Mannering, himself looking very smart in his cutaway of green superfine, had entered his aunt's home, refused to have himself announced, and made his way to the library, which he had been informed was presently occupied by his aunt. He reached its wide open doors to find his aunt absent, and, instead, a very alluring female quite handsomely displayed upon a pedestal!

Lord Mannering folded his arms and leaned his broad shoulders against the doorjamb, with every wicked intention of appraising his aunt's house guest. Kate continued her exertions, giving his lordship a rather pleasant and thorough view of her many charms! He allowed his eye to cover her profile, noting the enchantingly pert nose and her full sweet lips. From such well defined scenery he followed the line of her dainty shoulders and noted with appreciation the fullness of her swelling breasts and the smallness of her hidden waist. His experiences counseled him to further investigation. After all, one must endure, if one is to learn. He allowed himself to suffer the thrill of her alluring curves, her legs quite available to his green eyes because of the height upon which she stood and her many reaching movements. Inevitably his praiseworthy occupation made him uncomfortable, for his tight-fitting breeches were not made to house his growing virility!

Totally ignorant of his Lordship's presence, Kate, much vexed, exclaimed, "Confound the odious thing, why would anyone put up a shelf so high? 'Tis a silly thing to do, and then to stick Tom Moore on the very top. Why?"

A slow smile had curved Branwell Mannering's sensuous mouth, and he came forward leisurely, interrupting her. "I heartily agree with you. However, my late uncle was not especially keen on Moore, called him an erotic minstrel, if I recall correctly."

Kate turned on her low heel, a rather unwise course considering the height and unsteadiness of the structure upon which she balanced herself. What happened next may be thought by some to be most romantic, but did in fact obliterate all chance of early romancing!

Kate was startled to be so approached, but she was not without wit. She felt her stool wobble and knew this called for immediate action. She put out her hand and held to the nearest shelf within her reach, but alas, this was to no avail! With a screech born of the sure knowledge that she was about to fall, Kate and several volumes of various authors came tumbling down to earth.

Now, think not that the perpetrator of the above harrowing event stood unconcernedly by and allowed poor Kate no protection. Ah no, much shocked that his idle words should have imposed such a state of affairs, he immediately perceived that help was needed to set things to rights. Rushing with strong arms willingly extended to receive the pretty, he arrived in time to catch her fall. However, the pretty came with surprising force, one that sent them both to the floor!

The new oilcloth rug was little cushion between the victims and the oak flooring. They landed with a thud as painful as it sounded. Upon closer scrutiny one may note that the lady did indeed seem to have the more comfortable position, being quite nearly fully atop the man. She lay heavily across his chest, looking full into the gentleman's green eyes. His expression doubled the mirth that sprung to her mind. She bubbled with laughter as lovely to look upon as it was to hear. However, his Lordship, somewhat disarrayed, discomposed, and awkward, saw nothing to laugh at! Though the gurgling sound of her voice tingled his senses most delightfully, he shrugged such wayward stimulus off and pulled himself out of his circumstances.

This was done with more alacrity than care, which resulted in the lady's taking a further tumble to the floor. She bumped rather thuddingly and ejaculated, "Oh!" Putting a hand to her derrière with an expressive wince she glared, gray eyes darkening. "Of all the horrid . . . ungentlemanly things to do! Don't you think making me fall off the stool was enough for one morning's work? Did you feel it incumbent upon yourself to complete the deed by pushing me the remainder of the way?"

He laughed good-naturedly, not in the least perturbed. "Make you fall? Don't blame *me* for your clumsiness, love," said he, proceeding to brush off the dust from his buff-colored breeches.

"Odious brute!" flung Kate from the floor. He laughed and offered her his hand. She took it and a moment later was tightly wound in his strong embrace. His green eyes held her gray ones and his mouth was very near her own. She was startled by the suddenness of his move and disconcertedly all too aware of his magnetism. She pushed ineffectually against his chest. "Unhand me, cur!"

"The lady's tongue is sharp, but I'll warrant her lips are sweet," said he. His mouth took her own, separating her lips, and as he took the promised honey she felt herself losing control. His kiss affected her in a way she had never dreamed possible. Here she was, in the arms of a stranger, and enjoying every moment. He was aroused by her struggling body and her unwilling response, but reminded himself who she was and where they were. All at once he released her. She felt suddenly at sea. Her body burned, yet she was surrounded by cold nothingness. She sought relief. One small hand made its stinging path across his cheek!

He threw his head back and gave over to a hearty laugh and then swept her a bow. When he brought his head back, black locks waved across his forehead and green eyes glinted. His laugh had brought a memory to life and she stared at his arrogant face for a moment. Suddenly, she took a step backward, hand flying to her mouth as she exclaimed, "It's you!" She accused with disbelief.

One brow went up and he pulled himself back into his green superfine with a shrug peculiar to himself. "I should hope so, love. I would rather dislike discovering at this point of my life that I am not after all me!"

"Scoundrel, villain, usurper, what are you doing here?" demanded Kate, "Oh faith! When I think of what you are . . . you are nought but a proud, puffed-up bully!"

The Earl surveyed the beauty with some amusement. When he had first allowed himself the treat of appraising her figure, he had enjoyed the notion of a future mild flirtation. The fact that the girl was his aunt's protégée eliminated the immediate possibility of a more substantial affair. However, he had been too intrigued and was too much the adventurer not to take her in his arms when the situation had presented itself. Her immediate reaction was not totally unexpected. A slap was the very least a chaste female might dole out to an aggressor. He might very well find himself called out by an irate father. However, he knew Sir Horace and much doubted this possibility! Her insults seemed a bit strenuous though. Usurper? He thought with puzzlement. This was a bad start, and certainly seemed to preclude his earlier hopes of an enjoyable relationship! "Do you know, sweet fondling, that

I did not expect gratitude for my inadequate rescue. But really, madam, usurper?"

"Rescue? Indeed, sir, you caused my fall, sneaking up on me in such a manner! Then, then your odious insult to my person. But, I shall not spend the time quibbling with you. No, sir, the thought of standing here in the same room with you is repugnant to me!"

"Really?" said the Earl, his patience ebbing and his ego on the defensive. "May I know why?"

"Of course, though I perceive your lack of understanding to be as enormous as your rudeness! You, sir, are nought but a pirate! You make your living by preying on helpless merchant ships!" spit Kate.

"Pirate? *Hold!*" ejaculated the Earl, a light coming into his green eyes. He stared hard at Kate before slapping his leg. "Devil a bit! You are the one . . . the girl on board the *Bermudian!*" He moved forward imperceptibly as he spoke, so that he was once again towering above her dainty frame. He reached out and found one of her long black locks and touched the textured silk lingeringly. She tossed her head, removing the lock from his objectionable embrace.

"It is pleasing to find that you remember me," said the Earl softly, and his eyes found her lips in a way that made the blood tingle in her veins. Even now, hating him for his forced attentions, his mode of occupation, his arrogance, she found his smile strangely unsettling.

"Remember you? Faith, how could I not, sir! When I observed you on board your ship, the arrogant hero towing in a poor unarmed Spanish vessel!" She spit sarcastically.

The muscles in his cheek worked and she caught the movement and knew he was angry. His amusement had vanished, leaving his green eyes cold. They were but two opaque stones. "You draw pretty conclusions of your fellow Englishmen. Do you draw them from fact?"

"I draw them from what I have seen with my own eyes," she returned waspishly.

"And your eyes, such lovely eyes, do they never err?"

he asked, watching her face. He had no intention of defending himself to this child, yet he would know her mind.

"Err? How could they? They see what is there!" she said, frowning over his question.

"More child you," he said, softly hinting of his own superiority.

"La, my darlings! You have met!" exclaimed a bright-eyed fashionable lady in red velvet. Lady Haverly, auburn curls seasonally tinted with silver and wound round her head, beamed as she came forward to take Lord Branwell Mannering into her motherly embrace.

Aunt Sarah was considered by most of the beau monde to be a tall, regal matron of fashion. She towered over most of her kind and over many a man. In her nephew's arms, she seemed a veritable sprite. Kate, somewhat dimly aware of this observation, stood open-mouthed and staring hard, conscious now that the man she had been flinging insults at was the cousin whom her aunt had been raving about all the previous day!

Aunt Sarah stood back and took the Earl's hand, reaching out to take up Kate's hand as well. She held them to her tightly and her smile was as wide as it was genuine. Her eyes were filled with the pride of one who has accomplished the first in a long list of hopes!

"La, darlings, you can't imagine how pleased I am. To have my children about me, filling this large empty house. Why, it makes me feel quite light-headed!"

Lord Mannering's eyes twinkled. Kate found their light and quickly looked away, reminding herself who and what he really was.

"Faith!" continued Aunt Sarah, obviously quite beside herself. "How I wish my own dear Jeoffrey were here. He would be even more excited than I! Why he would be in a tither!"

"Really, Sarah, I can certainly imagine what sort of a *tither* our presence would arouse," teased the Earl.

"Horrid boy. You never understood your uncle. None of his nephews understood him. 'Twas because we never had children of our own. But never mind all that now.

You and Kate are here and it pleases me greatly."

"Kate?" inquired the Earl, lifting a brow. "What an enchanting name."

"What? Never say you have not introduced yourself, Branwell?" queried his aunt, obviously much surprised. "Naughty boy. What can you have been thinking of?"

"I can't imagine, Sarah, but you are quite right, and it was remiss of me."

Kate blushed hotly, realizing she had given him little opportunity, and feeling she should not allow him to take all the blame to himself, yet unable to utter a word.

Her aunt rattled off the Earl's title, but as Kate began a curtsey her aunt stopped her midway, pulling her up with a laugh. "Nay, child, no formalities. I won't have it. You will call him Cousin Branwell. 'Tis your right, though truth has it there is no blood relation at all. No matter." She turned to her nephew. "And you, love . . ."

"Will most assuredly address Miss Newbury as Cousin Kate. 'Twill be my pleasure to do so," supplied the Earl, his eyes alight with a secret smile. Kate knew not where to cast her glance and was heartily relieved when her aunt linked her arm and began leading them out of the room, her voice full of spirit. "Come along, darlings. We will breakfast together, and then, Branwell, you will take yourself off, for Kate and I have a dozen shops we must visit!"

13

Vauxhall, it was the epitome of all Kate's fancies. She had read about it, fashioned its design in her mind, heard her father speak of it, and dreamt of being placed there, even if but for one hour. Now here she was at Vauxhall! She gazed silently in wonder. Was she really here in London, and at Vauxhall Gardens? Surely even the way she had arrived had been all too dreamlike. The Earl had come for them in his handsome carriage and Kate sat on its rich upholstery in her new velvet finery, feeling every bit a queen! He sought to be charming, pointing out various monuments and parks along the way. His smile was light, his words witty, quick and easy, but Kate was wary, for there was the mock in his eye and he chose not to veil it!

Aunt Sarah was a dear and so very different than her Nell. She was lively, full of frivolous talk and startling gossip and Kate found herself growing fond already of the flighty woman. Ah Nell, she thought fleetingly, poor grave Nell! She could see that her governess was torn between the pleasure of seeing her Kathleen going out into society, and dismay at losing her charge . . . her child! She would have to do something for Nell, something to ease her pain, but now, now there was Vauxhall!

The Earl dismissed his carriage with instructions to return for them promptly at midnight, before leading the ladies into the park. Vauxhall was acres upon acres of spacious gardens, deliciously spiced with graveled paths leading to grottoes, groves, and temples. Rows of evergreen trees and bushes made walls separating one area from another, giving seclusion to those who willed it. They traveled past pillared statues, rotundas, and green lawns still rich in their color, challenging the coming of winter. The Earl escorted them through covered porticos housing many of the works of the artists of the day and he displayed his extensive knowledge with a flippancy that brought Kate's eyes upon him. What manner of man was he? A pirate, a scholar, a rake?

Lamps filled the sky! A profusion of illuminated lamps kept Kate's eyes wide. There were some created in the figure of the sun, while others took the shapes of stars and various constellations. Kate had never before seen their like. She was silent during most of this tour, allowing Aunt Sarah's easy chatter to return the Earl's kindly attention. The fashionable men and women that passed before Kate were as awe-inspiring as the gardens' trumpery. Their laughter filled the many different lodges as they supped on lobster salad, thinly sliced ham and wine. The air swelled with the mass of mirth and animated humor, and the music's revelry was as raucous as the merrymakers'!

Everyone at Vauxhall seemed determined to be gay. Kate's attention was caught by them all, for there were so many different sorts. Ruffians ran across the lawns chasing laughing vulgar women, and when Kate's eye discovered a bright-eyed brute, he tipped his beaten hat to her and mumbled something that brought the Earl's eyes up with a flash. Spying his lordship's disapproval the burly fellow retreated with some speed, exclaiming that he sought no trouble.

"I think," said the Earl, turning his hard eyes to Kate, " 'tis time I showed you ladies to our seats, for the concert is due to begin momentarily."

Sarah had not been attending him, for her attention was all for a set of brightly clad fashionables waving to her from a nearby pavilion. She turned to her nephew. "You go on, love, there is Lady Cowper and I declare 'tis been an age since I have seen her. I shall join you presently," she said, floating away without another word.

A frown flitted across the Earl's countenance. He could not be sure, for one could never be certain what Lady Haverly's motives were, but he did not like playing nurse-maid to a chit who had no liking for him! It appeared to him that his Aunt Sarah seemed bent on flinging her niece into his arms, for what ulterior purpose he could well suppose. This irritated him, though truth had it, she had never interfered with his amatory pursuits. He frowned darkly over this new problem and Kate, whose eyes flew to his suddenly silent form, discovered there a shade of irritation upon his brow. Kate, ever sensitive, was on the defensive. So, she thought, feeling a whiff of indignation, the bully shows his true colors again! He does not appreciate being left to attend me. Horrid man! All his exertions at being charming tonight were but for his aunt's benefit! I should have known at once. She moved away from his side, her mouth as dour as her gray eyes.

He felt her departure and brought his attention to her again. Watching her stroll away from him, black velvet cloak hiding her provocative form, he felt a sudden stirring in his breast and chided himself for a fool. There will be none of her in your bed, so careful, man, he told himself, picking up his step and reaching her side. She had a perpetual freshness about her, the scent of spring, and it tingled his senses, irritating him further.

However, he caught the sour expression on her piquant face and his brow went up inquiringly. "How quickly we become accustomed. Vauxhall no longer pleases you, Cousin Kate?"

"It pleases," said Kate curtly.

"But you are no longer dumbfounded by its rich designs?" he mocked.

"Dumbfounded?" exploded Kate. The gall of the conceited fellow. What did he think her, some country bumpkin to be scorned? Her eyes flashed. "How so? By flamboyancy? No. Vauxhall is amusing, and as you pointed out to us earlier, it is most dazzling. While I may have been silent during my appraisal, 'twas not because its exuberance had struck me dumb! Its constellations, its grottos—why, even its music are but the products of man. What are they after the natural beauty of Bermuda? The stars that tease my island's nights are alive. Their brightness needs not the lift of man's imperfect strokes. The grottos and caves that glisten with my island's natural colors are not rivaled by man's design. And music? Listen to that band, my lord; they bang out sounds, but what are those sounds when compared to the tempo of ocean waves rapping against pink coral in total harmony with the wind's cadence through the palms? No, my lord, Vauxhall does not strike me dumb!"

He had stopped to watch her face, startled by the depth of her feeling, intrigued by the sincerity and the sweetness of her tones. But yet he would banter further. "Yet, Cousin, you left your earthly paradise for England's baubles!"

She bit her lip for there was some truth in his statement. She liked not its sound and rushed to her own defense. "I left Bermuda because my papa is here, as is my home!"

"Ah, poor child. So you are sacrificed to filial loyalty. Brave girl. I do hope all these imperfect amusements you have been dragged into won't prove too disheartening!" His green eyes as well as his tone pinched at her.

She found such nips infuriating. Her chin went up. "You mistake, my lord. I did not say, nor did I wish to imply, that I do not find such baubles entertaining. Indeed I do. I am not so narrowly formed that I must only smile at one scene. How foolish that would be. I came most willingly to England. Why should I not? 'Tis my home. I was born at Lyndhurst Grange, my mother's grave lies there, and I am most pleased to be here again." Feeling that she had defended herself with aplomb, she sought to finish the matter by moving away from him. However, she had not gone more than a few feet down the lane when she was suddenly stilled!

Two burly young men, dressed in the manner of laborers, swerved before Kate, blocking her path. Thus confronted, the younger and more adventurous of the two males focused his hazy sight onto Kate's face and found there much to applaud. He swung his tankard of ale, indicating to his friend that he had discovered something noteworthy, before he began to express himself. "Gawd . . . stop me if you ain't a prime Nancy!" His arm went around Kate's delicate shoulders, whereby his ale went flowing to the ground.

"Watch it!" cried his friend, much aghast at such a fate for good ale.

"Let me go!" demanded Kate, much shocked, and even more so that such daring was taking place in public.

"Aw, now love, don't take on so. All I want is . . ." started the young ruffian. He was never allowed to express his wants, for he suddenly found himself flung backward with a power that sent him onto the back of his heels. He lost all balance, threw his hands up, and gave himself over to the sparkling fountain immediately at his back. Kate giggled and turned to the Earl. He was not amused. His green eyes were set hard beneath taut brows. His mouth was contemptuous and his fists were clenched at his side as he faced the second offender!

"Gawd gov'nor," cried the man, "we didn't mean no trouble. Jest 'aving a bit of a time . . . din't know she was your mort!" said he, inching away from the Earl and reaching a hand to his drowning comrade.

The Earl made no reply, but picked up Kate's arm from beneath the folds of her velvet cloak and silently led her away from the scene. She was still inclined to chuckle, for the sight of the poor fellow floundering about in the icy cold water still tickled her mind. A gurgle escaped her and the Earl's frown found her dancing eyes. "I see nothing to laugh at. We could have had a healthy little scandal on our hands."

"Scandal?" she said, much surprised. "Over what?"

"Over such a scene. London thrives on gossip. Where there is none, some must be supplied! Had we lingered, there is no saying what a chance observer might have rightly or wrongly deduced, repeated, and sent on its way to the tattle-mongers. Our family names are amongst the best of the ton. I would have them remain so!"

"How very stiff you sound. So, you care very little for the fact that had I been unattended such men would have been allowed to accost me?"

"You were not unattended, though you chose to give such an impression. Most unwise of you, and in the future, my dear, I expect you will know better!"

"I think you are odious. Still my lord, what of the poor woman who wishes to attend a concert at Vauxhall but has no escort?"

"She finds an escort or submits to such things."

"It's not fair."

"That does not change the facts."

"If the place was properly patrolled. . ."

"But it is not!"

"It should be. Why . . . really, my lord. Just cast your

eyes about. Even your 'so-called' gentlemen are more than a trifle foxed."

"Foxed?" he quizzed her, a smile lighting up his features. "Wherever did you pick up such a term? I understand from Sarah that you have no brothers?"

She smiled warmly, thinking of Danny. "No I do not. I have a very dear friend. He has taught me a great deal that would surprise you."

The Earl's brow went up and he eyed her speculatively. "Ah, did he, Cousin Kate? No doubt he is a part of your island?"

"Yes," she answered quietly, a wistful look creeping into her eyes.

The Earl said nothing to this, as they had reached the concert pavilion. He led her to their box and helped her remove her cloak. As he draped it over her chair, he glanced over her figure. She wore the peacock blue velvet she had bought that very afternoon. It had been made for another who had not paid for the gown. A slight alteration to its waist, a few inches tacked up at its full-skirted hem, and it fit Kate to perfection. Its bodice was scooped lower than Kate was wont to wear and she was a bit self-conscious, aware that the fulness of her breasts swelled above the confines of the gown. She felt the Earl's eyes glow as he traveled his gaze from the top of her high Grecian curls over her profile and brought them to rest on her heaving bosom.

His hand reached out gently and took up her own gloved one and he raised it to his lips, sliding the cloth away as he pressed his mouth to her wrist. She felt her heart beat furiously within her, and her mind ordered a halt to such unquiet sensations. She pulled her hand away and raised her eyes to find that he was laughing at her!

"Such a frightened child," he said lightly.

"I am not frightened, just particular!" returned she, her eyes snapping.

"Faith!" exclaimed Sarah stepping into her box, pulling an older well-dressed gentleman along with her. "Did you give me up for lost?" She then proceeded to introduce the plump smiling man as Sir Francis to Kate. He bowed graciously before turning his attention to the Earl. "Branwell, my boy! Dash it, lad, but you are a charmer; just look at you! They can't stop blabbering about you down at the Horse Guards and the Admiralty! That was a plump treasure you brought in!"

"Nonsense. You are far too good, Sir Francis," said the Earl, smiling.

"Eh, modest? But now that I have you . . . seem to recall that I was specifically requested to give you a message tonight."

"Sit down, darling. They are about to start the concert," said Sarah.

"Eh, to be sure. . . ." said Sir Francis, taking his seat.

Kate watched him with growing amusement, thinking that Sarah's friends were for the most part the most delightful people.

"Have it!" exploded Sir Francis, bringing down many '*shhsss*'s from the audience.

He lowered his voice and leaned into the Earl. "Remembered! It's the Admiral . . . Nelson. Wants a word with you. Said it was important but didn't want to make it official."

The Earl nodded and settled back in his seat where he allowed his eyes to wander once again to his Cousin Kate seated beside him.

14

Kate sat back in her father's lumbersome barouche and gave a hearty sigh. "Oh Nell, this has been a wondrous week!"

"Indeed it has," agreed Miss Premble, her eyes lighting

up with a spark of animation Kate had never seen there before.

Kate studied her a moment, but continued along the same vein, "My aunt is the best of dear women."

"That she is, child. A most gracious hostess. She showed me every kindness and consideration and I was most pleased with her affection for you," said Miss Premble, reaching for her embroidery.

"Is she much like my mother was?" asked Kate, suddenly frowning.

"Well, as to that, I'm not the one to say really, not knowing your mama more than a month or so, but, no, your mama was a wee thing. A small gentle creature. You have something of her face."

"Hmmm. Papa said Aunt Sarah was flighty and scatterbrained, but I do like her so."

"Oh yes, indeed. I would rather say she has a gift for enjoying life. Would that you could continue beneath her roof!"

"Nell!" Kate objected, with surprise. "What a very odd thing to say to me. Anyone would suppose you to mean you did not wish me to reside with Papa!"

"You mistake, Kathleen. I only meant that, perhaps, with your aunt you would find more companionship, and going into society would be more comfortable," said Nell quickly, frowning over her slip of tongue.

"But, Papa is a perfect companion, and when we take up residence in London for my ball, Aunt Sarah will be at hand. At any rate everyone makes too much of London and all its lures! I am well pleased to be returning to Lyndhurst Grange."

"Oh?" bantered Miss Ellen. "I rather thought you were quite taken with all London had to offer . . . including a certain young earl!"

"Horrid Nell! The Earl of Mannering disgusts me. I have good reason to dislike him!" protested Kate a mite too vehemently.

"Hmmm," responded Miss Premble.

"Well I do . . . so don't scoff!"

"What then might it be? The Earl seemed very charming," chided Miss Premble, whom his Lordship had won over quite early in his game.

"Never mind," said Kate, turning to stare out the window. She couldn't tell Nell. It would shock her so, and it might go to Papa, and then the Earl's company would be forbidden and for some unfathomable reason she did not want the Earl forbidden to her. She had fast learned his consequence on the London scene and 'twould not do to shun him. There, too, her aunt Sarah was overly fond of him, and she had no wish to be the cause of any rift between them. She would have to keep yesterday's memory to herself!

It had been a glorious week. That is what she would think on. It had been a whirlwind of shopping. Gowns of blue, red, green, and yellow. Riding habits, morning gowns, bonnets, feathers, slippers, and trinkets lay packed in evidence atop the barouche. She smiled to herself, sure that even her generous father would wince when presented with the bills!

She had loved Vauxhall, but never would she forget her evening at the theater. Richard Sheen had played Hamlet. He *was* Hamlet! The theater roared for ten minutes after the curtain. *Bravo!* seemed not enough, though the crowd shouted their applause with their bodies as well as the shattering crescendo of their voices. Kate had loved every minute.

There had been two "at home" dinner parties with only a small assemblage of Sarah's intimates. Kate found them wildly witty and vastly entertaining; only one among them stood out to rub Kate's nerves raw! The Earl of Mannering. To be sure, the gentleman was most polite and quite attentive, if one discounts the frost around the fringes. His morning calls, though curt and always brief, were most regular. His escort was freely given, his conversation lively, and his eyes coldly aloof. He seemed to give Kate little notice, and what nibbled at her mind was the fact that he seemed to like her as little as she did him!

This should have pleased the lady, who after all, found him in all ways objectionable! It did not! Alas, the contrary female heart. It irked Kate into a state of extreme agitation. She speculated on this circumstance, being a young woman who considered herself logical, and came up with what she felt was a most reasonable explanation. That being, the Earl had no conceivable cause to take her into aversion! She felt that he should have been smitten with guilt over his crimes. She felt that he should recognize her qualities and attempt to find a place in her esteem. Yet he seemed not to care for her good opinion. Then he quite took her by surprise yesterday afternoon!

The Earl drove his open phaeton down the clean and fashionable Bond Street, past the shops with their tempting wares. He nodded absently at passersby and smiled mechanically at the ladies, for he was in deep conversation with Master Hatch, who sat beside him. That seaworthy gentleman's watery dark eyes were veiled as he listened to his captain. He was twice the Earl's age, yet the younger man was his master, had been these past four years, and he wouldn't have it otherwise!

"I don't expect to be too long with my aunt, Hatch, and I did want you with me when we visit the Admiral. You've got a store of good judgment and I want you to hear what he has to say directly."

"Aye Capt'n, 'tis proud I am ye thinks such of me," said Hatch, gruffly.

The Earl laughed and pulled up before his aunt's house. Jumping to the curb with a natural grace, the Earl slipped the reins into a young groom's hand and wagged a gloved finger. "Walk 'em, lad, but stay within calling distance." He then turned to his first mate. "Look here, Hatch, there is no need for you to shuffle about out here. Go pass the time of day with Mrs. Travis in the kitchen and I'll send Travis down to you to say hello."

"Thankee, Capt'n. I'd like that real well," said Hatch, following him to the curb. He watched the Earl mount the stairs to the front door before going around to the

back and taking the stairs to the kitchen door. He gave
it a friendly rap and waited.

Miss Premble put down her teacup and looked toward
the door, for Mrs. Travis was busy at the stove. "Shall
I get that? You quite have your hands full."

Mrs. Travis was a woman of wide girth and a merry
disposition. She turned with a ready smile. "Lord love ye
for a good woman! Ye jest sit and sip yer tea," she said,
ambling toward the door and pulling it open wide. "Bless
me, as I live and breathe! Master Hatch! Why ye be a
sight. It fair sets m'old 'eart a trippin' to see ye looking so
fit. Come in, come in!" she called, taking his arm and
pulling him into the room with a gusty laugh.

He hunched his shoulders and cocked a smile at her.
"Ahoy there, good lady. Thought I'd set a spell with
ye and that rare man of yers."

"I daresay he's got wind of yer being 'ere and should
be coming through that door jest about . . ." At that moment a well groomed, tall, somewhat heavy-set man of uncertain age stepped into the kitchen. Travis was the
butler and had been these past twenty years. His manners
above stairs were sedate, aloof, and stately. He greeted
his friend with a hearty handshake. "So you've come, have
you? You old seadog!"

"Aye, though truth is sad, I don't think I've got much
time."

"You set down, my covey. I mean you to stay a goodish
while!" ordered Travis, pulling Hatch toward the kitchen
table where Miss Premble sat, her cheeks somewhat
flushed.

"Mrs., we'll be having tea, and drop a bit of fire in it,
love," called the butler. His wife chuckled and went
about the business, while Hatch's eyes discovered Miss
Premble. One brow went up, for she looked a fine,
healthy wench. Travis caught the look and hurriedly
apologized to Miss Premble for his oversight and went
through a warm introduction.

"Now, Hatch, I want all the details," said Travis, pulling up a chair between his friend and Miss Premble.

Hatch grinned and began a tale that kept his audience spellbound. Miss Premble, who had come from the sea swearing never to go near it again, found herself trembling at the thought of its beauty, such was his tale. His voice was moving enough to carry the song of adventure. Miss Premble listened to him wide-eyed, and when his admiring eye fell over her, she felt her cheeks glow beneath his scrutiny. She felt suddenly shy, but met his look squarely. Lord, she thought chaffingly, she was forty-seven, yet she felt as though she were a school girl meeting a beau for the first time!

The Earl had given his greatcoat, hat, and gloves to Travis. He was in a strange mood these days, vacillating between happiness and misery! The only thing he was certain of was his restlessness. "Travis, thank you," he said, shrugging himself into shape. "Where may I find her ladyship?"

"Out, my lord," said Travis.

The butler was eyed somewhat intolerantly. "Out where, my fellow?"

"I couldn't say, my lord," said Travis, beginning to feel uncomfortable, for he was familiar with this particular mood of the Earl's.

"Damnation!" said the Earl.

Wanting to please, Travis ventured a confidence. "If your Lordship cares to wait, I noticed that Miss Newbury went into the library a few moments ago."

Suddenly the Earl was grinning. "Thank you, Travis. That is a prodigiously good notion you have . . . and Travis, I nearly forgot. Hatch is in the kitchen, if you care to see him."

The butler's eyes betrayed him. "Thank you," he said, just barely containing his smile.

Miss Newbury had found her bath too hot. She was, herself, unusually restless. With her habitual firmness of decision, she thought there was no harm in going down to the library and scooping up some paper with which to write a letter to Danny. She didn't bother to do more than don a silk wrapper which she tied loosely around her before scurrying below. Finding the paper and a blazing hearth she settled on the rug and began her letter.

The Earl entered the library to find Miss Newbury stretched out on her belly, pen in hand, black hair trailing over a thin pink silk wrapper, under which it was most obvious to his experienced eye that she wore nothing. As she scribbled, one bare leg bent upward, foot circling the air and toes wriggling happily at some communication she had just jotted down.

The Earl, thoroughly enchanted, stood for a silent moment, unable to move. However, sound judgment came to mind and he decided it would serve him better to make his presence known.

"Cousin Kate, how comfortable you look. 'Tis a shame to disturb you."

Miss Newbury jumped with surprise, and a hand went to the open neckline of her wrapper. Finding that it was, indeed, the Earl, she hurriedly got to her feet, allowing the floor-length silk to fall askew about her. She saw that her earlier position had allowed it to separate down the center and before she had it pulled back in place, his lordship had an excellent view of her lovely legs. She saw his glance and her cheeks went hot, "Do you never have yourself announced, my lord?" she snapped. "Or do you have a purpose for always sneaking up on me?"

"Absurd chit!" answered his lordship, irritated with her hostility. "If I wanted to sneak up on you, I could have, and mind I would have when you were sprawled out in that most delectable position on the floor!"

"Oh, you are impossible!" the lady returned, stepping away from him, tripping and finding herself in his arms. She had no need to pull herself away, for he set her on her feet, apart from him. Somehow, this kindled her fire further. "If you will excuse me, my lord. I was about to take my bath," said the lady, moving away.

"Will you not keep me company until Sarah returns?"

asked he, suddenly giving her a charming smile.

She couldn't believe his perverseness. One moment he was taunting her and the next asking her to stay. "Do you think I would stay a moment longer in your company than I have to?"

"No. You have already given me reason to believe you find me loathsome," he said, looking the unwanted child.

Her heart took a quick pinch; he seemed genuinely hurt. "Oh, as to that, my lord, 'tis not that I dislike you, only that you have a habit of getting me in a miff."

He moved toward her suddenly, his eyes alight. "Do you always say things you don't mean?"

"Only when I am angry, but I meant what I said to you," she said, feeling herself strangely cornered.

He was nearly an inch away now and his hand went out for her arm. This caused her to fling her arm out of his reach and the letter she had been crushing in her hand went into the air and landed in the grating. With an exclamation she dove at it, burning the top of her finger in the process. She made a pretty cry of pain, which brought the Earl upon her immediately. This time his concern was genuine. "Here, child, let me see that," he said, reaching for the injured extremity.

Angrily, she pulled away. He stepped forward, accidently catching the hem of her wrapper beneath his boot whilst she was still moving backward. The loosely tied ribbon around her waist yielded and the silk fell apart. The Earl found himself gazing at the perfection of naked flesh. Large pink-tipped breasts swelled tauntingly before his avid eyes. Their full whiteness bounced with Kate's movement. She gasped, but before she could pull the material over herself, his large hands had taken her waist and pulled her to him. The touch of her small waist drove him wild and her fists beating at his chest and shoulders were scarcely felt as an urgency grew within him. His mouth took hers roughly, hungrily, parting her lips, demanding submission. He was beyond reason. He wanted her. He had been wanting her from that first moment, from that first kiss. She felt his hand stray from her waist and take firm hold of her breast. His mouth left hers, taking its journey to the fullness in his hand. His tongue fingered her nipple before he returned to her mouth, taking her, bending her to his will.

She was on fire. His body was made of iron, for she was sure her fists pounding on him were feeling more pain than was his chest. She felt crushed beneath his embrace, frightened by the fierceness of his kiss. She was sure she should scream, but hoped she could make him stop. All the while her body raged and she knew herself aroused! She fought it. On principle she fought it. Because he dared, she fought it! Because she told herself she was a lady, she fought it. Her mind won over and she brought her hand walloping across his cheek. "You cur! Animal!" she hissed at him. She had won, for he released her immediately, almost flinging her from him. As she pulled her wayward covering around her nakedness, she knew another part of her had awakened into being.

"You are not fit for the noble title you bear," she flung at him.

"What did you expect? Lord, girl, the moment I entered this room and you knew of my presence you should have taken yourself off! No, you pranced about in bare feet, your sweet nipples playing through the silk. You wanted that to happen! But take heed, girl, show a man as much as that and next time 'tis more than his kisses you'll have to endure!"

"I hate you!" she screamed before running from the room. Danny's letter, more than half burned, lay crumpled upon the floor, and as he watched her go a corner of his eye found its contents. "I miss you, Danny love . . . " he read before picking it up and flinging it angrily into the flames!

Kate plunged into her bath and tried to forget. But all she could do was remember. He had seen her naked to the waist, he had touched her. Oh God! She had been touched by a man! The thought brought shame pouring through her. Her cheeks and forehead felt aflame. How could she face anyone ever again? How could she face him? He had said she wanted him to kiss her and she was not one to be dishonest with herself. Yes, she knew that she had not really wanted to quit his company. She had felt a tingle of excitement when his eyes wandered over her, she had not wanted that feeling to end, but she had not meant for him to see her bared. She had not meant for him to touch her. Yet, accident or no, his kisses had aroused her in a way she had never experienced before. She was all too aware that her body had responded. Even now with only memory touching her, her body was responding. Stop it, she thought; what am I, at odds with myself?

That was yesterday, she thought putting it away. Yesterday is gone. She had not seen the Earl again. She had not to face him, and her thoughts were many as the coach rumbled on.

The Earl of Mannering had stood in stony silence while he waited for his aunt. Fool! he berated himself silently, stupid fool! What the deuce is wrong with you? You've never attempted to seduce a chaste wench before, and now you plow in with as much grace as a hamhanded youth! Lord, but when her naked flesh had glowed before him, 'twas all he could do to keep from taking her, making her his!

Aunt Sarah swept into the room, crashing in upon his thoughts. "La, Branwell. Travis said you were here. Goodness, dear, whatever is the matter? You look a veritable dragon!"

He smiled ruefully and sank upon a sofa. "Chastise me, Sarah! You have good cause. I have just nearly raped your niece!"

"What?" shrieked his aunt.

He laughed at her expression, "I said nearly, not quite."

She stamped her foot angrily. "Stop your teasing and tell me at once what you mean. What has occurred?" She was most distressed. She had been pining to herself that the match of the century was not taking, for neither of her beloveds seemed well pleased with the other. And *this* certainly was *not* what she had intended.

"Don't pucker up, love. It's not as bad as it will sound. I came upon the chit whilst she was at some task on the floor—and really, Sarah, I would have thought you would instruct her as to the proprieties! Anyone could have popped in on her. Why, all sorts of cavalier devils are forever calling on you. Had anyone else come across her in such a state, 'twould have been all over the town by now!"

She clasped her hands together and sent her eyes heavenward, saying, "I shall go mad!" Returning her biting glance to her nephew, she cried, "What would be over town? Tell me at once, Branwell, or I swear I shall run you through!"

"Easy, Sarah, and you shall have it. As I was saying, the chit was sprawled out most enchantingly before the fire in nothing more than a silk, loosely tied wrapper. We exchanged a bevy of unamiable words, she lost her letter to the fire, went after it and burned her finger. I merely tried to give her aid when she yanked herself away. Her wrapper caught beneath my foot and voilà! I behaved the cad!"

"What?" screamed Sarah, falling beside him on the couch. "What did you do?"

"You would have the details?" asked his Lordship, his brow up.

"No . . . yes . . . "

"I kissed her much against her will," said the Earl quietly.

"Oh, Branwell. How could you—with all your finesse —go charging at the innocent like a bull in a cowfield?"

"Well, 'twas more than my flesh and blood could bear. She is a beauty, but as to being an innocent, Aunt Sarah, you romanticize. She may be a virgin—that is yet to be seen—but she is no innocent. No woman is."

"You are wrong," said Sarah quietly.

"Am I? I do not think so," said he, remembering the

feel of her in his arms. Remembering her fists beating in-effectually, but beating nonetheless, and her body, pliable, strangely submissive in its unwillingness. "At any rate . . . I did not come here to discuss your niece's innocence, though if you would have her remain so, you had better teach her not to go about so scantily clad when below-stairs!"

"Stop it, Branwell! I am quite out of patience with you," ordered his aunt, pulling a petulant face.

He smiled winningly. "Lord that won't do! Especially when I have come to beg a boon."

"A favor? When you have by your own confession behaved the cad?"

"Yes," said he unflinchingly.

"Scamp. What is it?"

"Have you come across that Venetian twosome—the Count Mirabel and his sister Lady Moravia?"

"No, I have not met them. They are at Claridge's still, though I have heard talk they mean to take lodgings near Duke Street."

"I want you to invite them to dinner, with a select group of your intimates. Pitt wants to be there, and we want it select."

"What is toward?"

"You have seen the lady?" said he inquiringly.

"Why yes, but . . ."

"I want to find favor in her eyes. She is very beauti-ful, don't you think?"

"Yes, but Branwell, what are you intriguing?"

"An affair of the heart."

"Fiendish liar! What are you about? The Austrians are our allies, and Venice is under their protection."

"Of course they are, love, and Napoleon threatens them at their door. Will you arrange it?"

"I cannot until the Prince's dinner party next Thursday. They have not been officially received, though I am told the Prince has paid the lady several visits already."

He stood up and took his aunt's hand in a firm clasp, placing a kiss to her fingertips and tempting her smile with his wink. Then he was gone, calling for his carriage and sending a lackey for Hatch.

His huge first mate came hurrying toward him and hopped into the phaeton to take up his seat beside the Earl. "Sorry, Capt'n, didn't mind the time," said Hatch, his mind's eye filled with Nell's quiet smile.

"Nor did I, Hatch," said the Earl. He urged his team forward, saying softly, "We'd best hurry. Nelson awaits."

15

Kate strained at her window. It had been a long tedious journey, and Nell had been strangely quiet. She herself had not felt inclined to conversation. But now, anticipation welled within her and she felt whole and once again secure. The open road with its span of uncluttered heaths was left behind as they turned onto the Newbury drive. The coach lumbered thuddingly over the flat wood bridge spanning the stream bed. They were home at last! Kate sighed. What was London? Nought without her papa! Now she would parade herself in all her new finery and show him what a fine lady she had become, and he would be so proud!

The coach moved too languidly for Kate's comfort, taking the long straight path slowly to the house. It stopped in the stone-paved courtyard, but Kate did not wait for the footman who came forward to open her door. She was out and across the stone yard and at the front doors in a thrice. Gibbens stood aside at the edge of the open doors, which was fortunate, as her tumbling entrance might certainly have bowled him over. She was such a whirlwind that it was difficult to distinguish anything more than the sight of flying clothes.

"Papa! Papa!" she exclaimed gaily, turning with offhanded grace to her butler. "Hello, Gibbens, how nice you look. Have you trimmed your hair?"

Gibbens was flattered that she noticed, and a smile melted his shocked expression, "Thank you, Miss Kathleen."

"But Papa? Where is he?" asked Kate, casting her eyes about.

Gibbens made an evasive cough, "I regret, Miss . . ."

Mr. Banyon entered the central hall from the small study flanking its western front in time to hear both Miss Newbury's question and Gibbens' hesitation. He interrupted, "Miss Newbury, how good it is to have you home. We were not expecting you until after dinner."

"Oh, as to that, we decided to leave earlier this morning, but Mr. Banyon, where is my father?"

"Above stairs. Do come into the study. Gibbens, will you have tea brought for Miss Newbury."

Nell had entered the hall by this time and Perry Banyon smiled his welcome at her. "Gibbens, tea for Miss Premble too, please," he added.

"Perhaps later, Mr. Banyon. Now I should like to go up and see Papa," said Kate, starting toward the stairs.

"Please do not," he said quickly.

His tone halted her and she spun round wide-eyed. "But, why not?"

"He is resting." He smiled again, encompassing both women. "And I am quite certain *you* are in need of refreshment."

"Indeed, Kathleen, you had complained the last hour that your throat was dry," said Nell. "Do let your father continue with his rest."

"Very well," said Kate, leading the way, but stopping as she saw Nell hesitate. "Do you not come, Nell?"

"No, I think not. If you don't mind, love. I think I'll just go lie down for a bit," said Nell absently.

Kate sighed and entered the study. It was a small square room, cluttered with books and dominated by a huge desk overlooking the courtyard. Kate threw off her cloak and plopped beside the fire. Mr. Banyon followed her into the room, carefully keeping the door to the hall ajar, and took up a chair opposite her. "There now,

Miss Newbury, you must tell me all about your expedition," he said smiling, and she was aware of his extreme fair looks and gentle charm.

"Oh, I shouldn't dream of boring you with such nonsense, but I did enjoy London."

His eyes scanned her figure, which was encased in a fashionable gown of brown satin striping and banding on brown velvet. A brown velvet ribbon collared her dainty throat from which a blue cameo hung elegantly. The long velvet sleeves were tight-fitting, showing to a nicety the slender arms they contained, and the low heart-shaped bodice allowed the observer an excellent view of her full ripe breasts.

"When did you have time? For I am sure if the remainder of your new wardrobe is anything like this"—he motioned with a nod of his head—"you must have spent the entire length of your stay in Bond Street."

She laughed. "Indeed, my Aunt Sarah took me to Bond and a few other more out-of-the-way modistes, all of which she assured me were houses of the first stare, and there, Mr. Banyon, we did spend interminable intervals. But the evenings, there was Vauxhall, and the theater, and Aunt Sarah has some of the most interesting people I have ever met for her intimate friends. But tell me, Mr. Banyon, why does Papa rest at such an hour?"

He hesitated. "I suppose you will have to know, though, in truth, I know not how to inform you."

"Straight out," said Kate, sitting up, her cheeks suddenly losing their color.

"I fear Sir Horace is gravely ill," he said, watching her intently.

She stared hard at him a moment as this soaked through her mind, making the required stops before racing to her heart. She stood up, and started for the door, nearly colliding with the lackey who arrived with the tea tray.

Perry Banyon had risen to take a step after her. "Miss Newbury . . . please, do not go up to him."

She turned, ignoring the lackey's startled expression as he hastily placed the tray on the table before the fire and scurried out of the room, evidently in the belief that this was no time for him to be about. "How dare you issue such an order to me. I am his daughter!"

"It is not an order. You misunderstand; indeed, it is a plea."

"But why, why?" cried Kate, much distressed.

"He did not sleep well, he has not been sleeping well these weeks and more. He takes a bit of laudanum in the afternoon, at least whenever I can convince him to it."

"My God! What is wrong? Where is the doctor?" cried Kate, now feeling suddenly helpless.

"He has only just left a short while before you arrived, but I must tell you that the doctor's hopes for your father are not great," said Perry sadly, quietly.

"I . . . I don't believe it! He had a cough, just a cough. He told me it was nought!"

"He told you but a half truth, to spare you. Miss Newbury, I think he does you an injustice. I think you are strong enough to know, and in knowing be able to give him some of your strength."

"Know what? Know what?" demanded Kate, feeling as though she were in a dark lonely pit.

"Your father wastes . . . from consumption!"

"No! No! and no again! Do you hear me? I won't believe it! He is my father. Wastes . . . consumption . . . 'tis not true . . . he would not!" said Kate irrationally. He was her father; are not fathers indestructible?

"What is this? I thought I heard your goose's honking!" said a gentle voice from the open doorway.

Kate spun around, tears in her eyes, and dove at the soft-spoken man who had created and maintained her fairy-tale world. "Papa . . . Oh, Papa!"

He stroked her head, looking over it at Mr. Banyon, and though he frowned at the lad, his eyes held another expression. He kissed his daughter's head. "Tears? My daughter returns from what should have been the most exciting trip of her life, and all the thanks I get are salty wetness on my dressing gown! Fie on you, Kathleen," he teased.

Oh, how she loved him. He was so good. In every way he was so good. And he had come when she needed him. For a moment ago, she had needed him. She wanted Perry's words burned from the air. Had he not burned them with his appearance?

"Sir Horace, I thought I left you sleeping. I took you at your word; you said you would have your tea," said Perry reproachfully.

"And so I did. I simply did not remember to take my medicine. Did you really think I would when I knew Kate would be arriving today?"

Kate stepped back and out of his embrace, but he held her shoulders fondly. She surveyed his face and what she found made her want to weep again. He had lost more weight and there were dark lined circles beneath his eyes, and his eyes seemed almost sunken. "Papa . . . you are ill," she said as a statement, not a question any longer.

"So they would have me believe." He chuckled. "I intend to outwit them all and live another hundred years!"

"Oh, I wish you may. Please, Papa, do whatever the doctor says and get better, do," said Kate, once more a child handing him a doll to repair.

"I shall most certainly try. Now your tea grows cold. Let us sit and have some, for I am certain that I have often been told that there is nothing like tea to restore the soul!"

She watched him pulling up a chair next to the table, near her by the fire, and she watched the manner in which he fell into it and it occurred to her that he had not been able to stand a moment longer. He was ill. Her father was ill. She said it to herself, trying to make it sink in, trying to make it real, real enough to deal with, but all she could think was, yes he is ill but he is Papa and he will get better. See if he doesn't.

She poured the tea and placed it before Sir Horace

and as she poured for Perry she noted that her father seemed lost to another world. She watched him. She saw Perry watching him, and she noted the concern on Perry's face. Mr. Banyon loves Papa, she thought. He really cares. She found herself warming to him.

"Black canyons, Perry, black canyons! They swell with horrors unknown. I would not have *you* face them, yet I brought you to them," said her father in a strange voice. It came from afar and he seemed not to realize that they were with him, although he addressed Mr. Banyon.

"Hush, sir, you have nought to fear," said Perry soothingly. "Look, your daughter has poured your tea."

"My daughter," said Sir Horace, back from his distant world. He looked at Kate and sighed, "You have grown, and I am aged."

"Papa, tell me true. What illness is it that strikes at you?" demanded Kate, going to her knees beside him, taking his hand.

He frowned, "Very well, child, I have had an attack of apoplexy, or epilepsy—the physicians have not exactly decided which, but no matter, my constitution remains suspended between the two opinions. This leaves me free to reject both. Perry here has his own diagnosis; he thinks me consumptive. Utter nonsense. All but myself believe that I should be bled, which I have been most suitably nearly every day this week, leaving me inclined to think 'tis m'blood they are after." He saw that his jesting had not brought a smile to her face, and he patted her hand. "Never mind, child. I take the proper physic most of the time, and presently I shall recover." He smiled. "Does that uncover your sun, my babe?"

"My sun? 'Tis *you*, Papa," she said, softly kissing his hand. But when next she looked at his face, she saw there a twitch in his cheek and the corners of his mouth were being pulled by some invisible force. She glanced across questioningly at Mr. Banyon and his face was grave. "Sir Horace, may I see you upstairs?"

"Stop plaguing me!" shouted Sir Horace in a tone unlike any she had ever heard from him before.

"Would you rather your daughter witness your discomfort?" persisted Mr. Banyon.

"My daughter?" asked Sir Horace; once again, evidently, he had forgotten her presence. He recalled it now. "My daughter, no, forgive me, Perry. You are right. I must rest."

Kate could say nothing as she watched Perry help her parent out of the room. She had never before seen her father laid so low. She was still sitting on the floor when Mr. Banyon returned some twenty minutes later and he approached her with some surprise. "Miss Newbury?"

She looked up at him and got to her feet. "He said he had an attack." She threw it at him.

"He has had an attack, and he continues to have them."

"What exactly do you mean?"

"He suffers much, Miss Newbury. Sometimes his convulsions are quiet, at other times he raves."

"About what?" she asked, a note of despair in her voice.

"About his fears . . . His . . . It doesn't matter."

"But . . . what can be done?" asked Kate, pounding her brain for an answer.

"All that can be will be," he answered quietly.

Much later, Kate lay in her bed. She had tossed, sat up, walked about, and returned to bed, still unable to sleep. She was exhausted in mind as well as body. A cure, she must find a cure. This was her papa. In the morning she would write to her Aunt Sarah and they would get the best doctor in the country! She would consult the medical text herself. She could and she would. Her thoughts were full because she was young and she was one that hopes, believes, and finds the alternative to this . . . unthinkable!

Suddenly the air was rent with the sound of her father's voice. It was a scream and such that she had never heard. She pulled her wrapper around herself and ran from her room to his own, flinging his door wide open. She stopped, terrified by the sight of him standing at the open window. His back was to her as were his arms, as though he were begging some unseen force to come fetch him. "Papa," Kate cried, "Papa, come away from the window. The wind is enough to blow out your fire. Please, let me close it," said Kate going forward, forcing the fear from her heart. This was her father. He was ill, but no stranger! He turned his face and watched her glide toward him. He watched her close the window and his voice filled the air with a reverberating pitch. It was the deranged cackle of an unknown man. "Such things . . . aaah . . . . such things have I seen lurking . . . for me. They want my flesh! *Aaaah* . . . the devils, those evil hours, all for the evil hours." He shook his fist at the window. "Begone, begone! You'll have none of me!"

Kate stared at him with disbelief. This is what Perry had tried to tell her! Then Perry was there. She saw Perry Banyon's eyes close as he steeled his face and came into the room, but her father's ranting went on. "'Tis the devil's minion . . . *aaah* . . . treading my soul!" he groaned, and the sound of his pain pierced through Kate. She couldn't move, she couldn't think what to do. She stood transfixed in horror as he cried, "Passion! It haunts me still. Crimes in hot passion!"

Kate sought Mr. Banyon's aid. "He sees us not. Oh God, what can we do?"

He had heard her. Sir Horace heard her cry to God and his laugh tore through the room. "God? No, 'tis not God that calls me. He wants none of me!"

"Sir Horace, come to bed," said Perry Banyon, holding Sir Horace's flagging arms.

"My child . . . my child," said Sir Horace suddenly as Perry came near. "Oh death, death awaits."

"Hush now, please Papa . . . rest," cried Kate, the tears streaming down her cheeks. She was by his side, taking his hand, calling to him, cooing to him, and he heard her notes through the torturous buzzing in his brain. It snapped the drilling in his ears, leaving his mind clear, returning his sight. "Kathleen," he said softly.

She saw him fall asleep after Perry had given him laudanum. But when she returned to her own bed, she felt wretched with fear, and her heart held less hope.

16

Two days had ebbed away into oblivion since Kate had returned to Lyndhurst Grange. Her father's condition had steadily degenerated. His moments of lucidity were rare and brief, and Kate's emotions were on the verge of collapse. His nightmares were terrifying. In them his fears were all of the devil and the unnamed crimes of his imagination. Each time she left him she would be drained and confused by his rantings. Today it had all started so innocently. He had been quietly watching her arrange the hothouse flowers in a vase over the fireplace in his room when he called her to his side. She had gone happily, pleased to hear her name upon his lips.

"Kathleen, you reminded me much of your mama. She was wont to move about quietly, gently giving me beauty. Your face has her loveliness." Then suddenly his eyes took on that look she had learned to know, learned to dread, and his voice filled with sorrow. "Julia, my gentle bride . . . the only woman of my heart. You would have been proud of our daughter. Julia, forgive me, my heart withered. It withers still before your tears. *Oh God, I have sinned!* Unhappy heart, wicked thirsting heart, unhallowed yearnings. They did kill me! Yet still I crave, for I was early smitten."

Kate sobbed with him, unable to hear anymore, her tears mixed with his, but he would continue. "My thirsts called all vouchers in. They would be quenched, and quenched they were! May death take me!"

"No, Papa! No, Papa. Stop, please stop. *For me . . .* please, for me," cried Kate.

But he would not, he could not. He no longer heard her. Miss Ellen came in upon them and gasped to hear him so, and she cried to see what state her Kate had been reduced to. She sent for the doctor, and Mr. Banyon, too, was called.

Sir Horace ceased his ravings suddenly, as his eyes focused in upon Perry's youthful and distraught countenance. "Perry," he said gently, "how you must hate me!"

"Say not such things to me!" cried Mr. Banyon, his eyes bright with unshed tears. "You have been good to me. It is but the fever that burns your mind, alters your thoughts."

"Fever?" Sir Horace balked at the word. "Fever? 'Tis life. Life is nought but an endless fever. I would that it would burn itself out." His hand swept his brow, covering his eyes. He was weary with the effort of survival. His voice was pained. "Unhappy heart," he muttered, " 'tis filled with my crimes!"

"Speak not of crimes!" shouted Kate angrily. "You are not now in a delirium. You are not now overtaken with the fever. Speak not of crime! You are a good man, whose life is spent in goodly ways. You have loved, you taught me to love. Why, Papa, do you torture yourself with things untrue?"

"Kate?" said Sir Horace, seeing her suddenly. "I . . . I did not know you were here. I am aging, girl. Think not on what I prattle; 'tis that I am tired." His eyes glossed over again but he remained silent. The doctor arrived and shooed them all out of the room. Kate waited now to be called. She waited to be told some new tisane had cleansed his veins and that he was resting comfortably.

Kate was called! Nell came, as did Mr. Banyon. Each standing a little apart, each waiting. She could see Perry Banyon's eyes were wet and his face haggard. He stood leaning into the fireplace mantel, his fist clenched to his mouth. And Nell . . . Nell stood sadly to one side. Kate heard her father muttering incoherently, and she looked at the doctor and what she saw on his face spun her heart around. It was a cold webbing enmeshing her spirit and its frigid net left her short of breath. She moved to her father's side and as she approached he cried out against some evil force, falling into a paroxysm of convulsive coughing, and then, suddenly, spastically, he was still. Kate's eyes flew to the doctor's face and what met her inquiry scattered her voice in her raw-lined throat. "Papa?"

"I am sorry, Miss Newbury," said the doctor, and he seemed a useless figure. For what had he come, what was he doing here? She wanted to beat at him! She trembled as one white small fist flew to her mouth. She stepped backward as though to run from the truth and Nell's heart felt splintered as the sight of Kate's face. "Oh my child, my poor child," she said coming forward.

Kate jerked away, stepping farther into the dark recesses of the room. "NO!" And it was a cry of agony. "NO!"

" 'Twas God's will, child. You mustn't take it so," tried Nell.

"God?" shrieked Kate, bending over in pain, a fist beating at her chest as though to punish her betrayed heart for believing. "Where is God?"

"No, no, child. You know not what you say," cried Nell, coming closer.

Kate screamed her anguish, stepping away from Nell, but she caught sight of her father's still form and stopped short, pointing her trembling hand at him. "He was God! He was *my* God . . . and now my God is dead!"

Miss Ellen released a sob for she saw Kate's open wound, saw the blood gush from its clean sweep and could do nought to ease her pain.

Kate ran past her. She saw blankness all around, for her mind was dark with her loss and the ache was caught in the canyon of her throat. Her chest heaved with her sobs, for it was the "wail above the dead" and she ran down the stairs and through the wide long hall, flinging the doors open to meet the night's wind!

She raced against the hurt, thinking to outrun it. Her legs carried her across the stone yard and onto the lawns. She stopped on the crest of the sloped lawn and looked into the dark sky. The wind slapped at her pitilessly, and she challenged the heavens.

"God!" she called. "Do you see? Was that your will? And why—do, please, do tell me why? Am I so wicked that you in your almightiness must needs take from me yet another parent? Was not my mother enough?" The tears stormed her face and were carried by the wind. Her voice jagged with each word. "Is this your notion of justice? Why not me? Why couldn't it have been me?"

A firm male voice broke in on her pain. "Because you are young and strong and far more able to cope with his death than he would have been with yours!"

She spun around to find Peregrine Banyon standing before her. His blue eyes were watery and there was the evidence of strain on his face, but she didn't want him here! Her grief was her own; she could not share it. "Please go away; you mean well but you don't understand," she cried, her voice breaking.

"But I do, Kate." He had taken her shaking shoulders in his hands, but he was gentle and his eyes cosseted her. "This is wrong. Think on it. You are but pitying yourself. That is what grief is; it is for yourself, not him. Kate, his body was in pain. Would you have had him endure more suffering simply to provide you with the pleasure of his being? I think you are not so selfish!"

"Then you think wrong!" Each word was wrenched from her heart. "I would have him endure and endure and endure until I could have found a way to ease his pain and banish it, without giving him to the soil! I love him. He is my papa." She broke then, for her father was dead. The horror of such finality scraped its hooked claws through her soul, leaving it bloody and raw. Her heart had scattered in her bosom, each morsel beating at her chest, and she knew not how to regain control. She could only think, her papa was dead, and such a thought was renewal of her agony! She was Prometheus chained, waiting for the vulture to peck at the burdensome liver, enduring its unspeakable torture, only to have the horrendous act repeated and repeated and repeated yet again! She sobbed and Perry took her trembling body into his arms, rocking her gently, feeling for her, crying with her until he felt her go limp. She had a safety valve. It had said, enough! I can stand no more. He collected her into his arms and carried her back into the house!

17

"You are most kind, Mr. Hatch," said Miss Premble, feeling comforted by his enormous frame and gentle glance. "But in truth, there is no reason to be concerned on my behalf. If I am sorely these days, 'tis for Miss Kathleen."

He nodded, waiting for her to seat herself at the kitchen table, before easing himself onto a wooden chair beside her. "Aye, I could see the poor wee thing was taking it hard. She'll come out of her dismals. See if she don't. 'Tis the way of the young."

Miss Ellen shot him a thoughtful look and smiled. "You've got a deal of wisdom, Mr. Hatch." She poured the tea and pushed the cup toward him, watching as he took a long sip.

The gentle brew sent a mawkish sensation through him which in turn pulled at the corners of his mouth. He controlled the grimace and averted his face from Miss Ellen's eye.

A chuckle transformed Nell's solemn face, "Would you like a bit of brandy in your tea, sir? To stave off this cold weather?"

He grinned broadly. "Ye be a fine woman, Miss Ellen. A drop of firewater 'tis just what this brew be needing!" He watched her move over to the cupboard and produce a bottle, noting that he found the sway of her ample hips much to his liking. As she poured the dark liquid into his cup, he rubbed his hands together approvingly. Leveling his bright eyes upon her over his cup, he watched her face as she returned to her seat. He sipped long and hard, and when he put down his cup he looked at her squarely. "Would ye be taking offense, Miss Ellen, if I was to tell ye that you're a fine figure of a woman?"

She opened her eyes wide, somewhat shocked at his forwardness. This was moving too fast. She had been too long unapproached and fantasies had not prepared her. "Why . . . why, no. I would not take offense," she answered hesitatingly, concerned lest she mistakenly give him leave to proceed. "But I would have you remember, sir, that I . . . "

"Aw now, Miss Ellen, you've no need to raise your brow at me. Did ye think I meant to turn yer head and take ye under the table?" cried Mr. Hatch boldly.

Miss Ellen opened her mouth, but found that nothing emitted. Indeed, nothing formed in her mind to put into words. She could but stare at him. He laughed and chucked her beneath her chin. "There's a love! I'll be setting out to sea with the Capt'n in the morning, but when I gets back, I'd like to come calling."

"Mr. Hatch, we have only just met," faltered Miss Ellen, excited in spite of herself.

"Aye, thank the Lord! I'm fifty years old, ma'am. Think on it. M' youth was spent on too many ships and with too many women. Never found a one that touched m'eart, such as it is. So I ask ye straight out without the fineries, do ye forbid it?"

Thus faced, Miss Ellen felt trapped. Yet she *did* want to see him again. At least, the thought of not seeing him again brought a sigh to her lips. "I make you no promises, sir, but I do not forbid it," she said quietly.

Kate sat rigidly upon a wooden backed chair in the parlor. Her dark dress intensified the paleness of her cheeks. Her long black hair had been drawn tightly away from her face and tied at the nape of her neck. Only the wayward curls at her forehead bubbled in relief to the severeness of her appearance.

Mr. Peregrine Banyon, flaxen locks neatly brushed, and sweeping his pale forehead with style, sat donned in black and gravity at Kate's side.

Mr. Hansen, Kate's family solicitor stood behind the window desk and looked sternly over his spectacles at Lady Haverly. "You, ma'am, are not on my list! The will is explicit . . . only those named were to be present!" He then cast his eyes over a young man with black silky billowing hair and bright green eyes beneath his brows, and he made a clicking sound with his lips. "Nor is that gentleman listed!"

Aunt Sarah threw up her hands in exasperation, looking back upon her nephew. The Earl's green eyes twinkled, much in contrast with the quiet solemnity of the room. He sat at his ease, clothed in sombre gray and mute observation of the proceedings.

"You, sir, are a fool! I am Kathleen's aunt and need no invitation from you to remain at her side during this ordeal. The gentleman you refer to is my nephew and, therefore, part of the family! Now do get on with it; can't you see what a strain this has put on my niece?"

Mr. Hansen's face turned beet red in hue. "My lady, these things cannot be rushed. Your nephew's name does not appear on my list, nor does yours, for that matter!"

"Mushroom! I am here and so I shall stay. The Earl remains as well," retorted Aunt Sarah, beginning to show evidence of her temper.

The lawyer made as if to retort, but Kate interrupted him. A flush had stolen onto her cheeks and her chin was set in a hard line. "My dear sir, no doubt you mean well, but you have overstepped. List or no, my aunt is here because I wish it. The Earl, because *she* wishes it; and in this house such wishes are respected!"

"Very well, though 'twas not stipulated in the will. However, never mind, never mind. Be seated, be seated," he said, looking pointedly at Aunt Sarah. She moved away and took up a chair on Kate's other side, glancing over Mr. Banyon without favor.

Mr. Hansen took up a chair behind the desk and shuffled the papers a moment before he began the reading of the will. It was to be seen that the bulk of all that had been Sir Horace's went to his daughter, ending with but a slight deviation:

" . . . and as I have brought my daughter to a woman wise, I trust she will pension those servants whose retirements fall due after my demise," read Hansen, turning the page. "Now, to Peregrine Banyon. Mr. Banyon has been a trusted secretary, and though I have to this date not completed my manuscript, what I do have would not have been without his superior efforts. I owe him much; only he knows just how much. I bequeath to him the Dower House, which he so often praised. In addition, a living of one hundred pounds annually is to be allocated to him. I may now rest easy, knowing the two loves I leave behind will not want."

Kate's head had dropped into her hands, but she made no sound. Mr. Banyon's hand went to her arm. "Miss Newbury, Kathleen . . . "

She did not look up for she could not bear to be seen so weak. Her aunt's arm went around her, but she broke away, suddenly, getting up and running from the room. Sarah's eyes went to the Earl's, but a moment later she was hurrying after her niece.

Mr. Banyon watched helplessly and turned to find the Earl's green eyes upon him. "Congratulations," said the Earl quietly.

Mr. Banyon frowned and his blue eyes looked doubtful. "I have just seen someone dear to me put with the dust, and you say congratulations?"

"Bravo!" mocked the Earl. "No fool have I here." He watched Mr. Banyon stalk out of the room, thinking the lad had his wits about him!

Sometime afterwards, the Earl stood before the fire watching its sparks and sipping the ruby port in his hand, while he awaited his aunt's return. He looked up as she floated into the room, brushing the wayward strands of her auburn curls from her forehead and sighing as she came to sink upon the sofa. "Oh Branwell, that poor child. She is simply wretched over his death!"

"Yes, I can see that and I am heartily sorry for it. But she will survive," he said, and his tone was hard.

She sent him a searching look. "You were much the same, but you did not face your parents' death as well as Matthew did."

"Did I not? Well, 'tis been eight years since then. My twentieth year went hard for me. I was a man and not supposed to cry!"

"Ah Branwell, so bitter?"

"He caused her death, and having deprived us of her took his own. And I loved them both," said Branwell, a strange catch to his voice.

"No! It was not so simple, Branwell. You would never hear me out. Perhaps you will now. Your parents loved one another, and it was good what they had. You and your brother gained by their love. But your mama was not brought up to accept the idea of infidelity. There came a time when your father strayed. It didn't matter that his one indiscretion was meaningless to him. He had been unfaithful, and she couldn't bear it! She didn't know about it until it was over and she learned it from him. He was overjoyed when it ended, for it filled him with new purpose. He told me how he would tell her, and didn't think I was right when I cautioned him against it. She was ever a wild-tempered love, as you are. You have your temper from her, you know. She went mad with jealousy. She ran from the house, unmindful of the street. She never saw and never awoke from the accident. Your father drank himself to death because he saw her killed before his eyes," said Sarah sadly, the tears rolling down her cheeks.

The Earl's jaw worked and his brows were drawn, his looks dark. "I never quite saw it in that light, but he didn't just drink himself to death, Sarah. We both know that he poisoned himself."

"But you don't fully understand why, Branwell. You and he were always worlds apart. He was a cavorter, never serious, but you, even when you jest, there is a gravity in you . . . a sincerity that he never really knew. He had been idle and he was reaching that age when men need something more. He thought it was another woman. When he found that she did not serve, he was delighted. He felt his love for your mother cemented and was wildly elevated with this new-found devotion . . . and went to her with it. He had no way of knowing that his confession would send her flying. Can you understand now, Branwell? It was just too much for him."

"Why do you bother telling me all this now?" he asked, suddenly coming to sit beside her.

She looked into his eyes. "Because, Bran, I see a change in you. A softening. And because, Bran, we have a truth hitting at us and cannot face it, if we are burdened with a lie."

"*Hmmm*, you mean Banyon," he said thoughtfully.

"Yes. What will people say when they hear Sir Horace has left the Dower House to him?"

"Many things. People always do."

"Yes, but what of Kate?" she asked anxiously. "I don't want her hurt."

"At this point, what they will say will shock, perhaps, if she believes. It won't hurt."

"But if the entire truth is suspected?"

"Sir Horace was discreet. I doubt that the issue will come up, and at any rate the Dower House is Banyon's. Odd name he chose for himself," he said thoughtfully. Then getting up he took his aunt's hand and kissed it lovingly. "You will make my farewells to your niece. If I'm to be off in the morning, I had better collect my man and ride to Southampton."

"Oh no, Branwell, won't you stay to dinner?" cried his aunt.

"No. I'll dine on board the *Gypsy*. This house and its air of gloom depresses me," he said amicably, making off.

"Wretch!" called his aunt after him.

18

March crept in secretly, somewhat forgetful of its promise to lion in and lamb out. And Kate had learned in the four years her father had been away to manage without his physical presence. In Bermuda, she had learned to rely on memory, and it had helped her through some lonely hours. Her will to survive, subconscious, yet ever there, returned her to such ways.

"Oh miss, you look grand, you do," exclaimed Eliza, appraising Kate in her green velvet day gown. " 'Tis made for a body such as yours. I'd look a stick in such a sleek gown."

Kate laughed and twirled around before her mirror. "You don't think enough of yourself, Eliza. You have a charming figure."

Eliza's short straight hair framed her oval face. Her tresses were partially concealed by a white mop cap, but their amber color attracted the eye in spite of their limpness. She flipped them now and pulled a look of disbelief. "M'curves . . . charming? No, bless ye, miss; why, m'hair be nought but a swish of strings, and m'body? Gawd . . . only m'darlin' John thinks it wondrous and that only because he be besotted. Which don't 'ave nought to do wit looks."

Kate considered this a moment and shook her head. "Now . . . he wouldn't be besotted if there was nought there to love!"

The girl's hand wandered over her thin body. "I'm not full bosomed like you, miss, but I have a way to keeps him loving me," she said, smiling secretively.

Eliza was Kate's personal maid. She had been assigned to her from Kate's first day on the Grange, but it had not been until after Sir Horace's death that a friendship had been struck up. As of late, they were often together, and in spite of their class difference, they found enough to share. They were of similar age and Kate found someone with whom she could speak without restraint. Christmas had been a sad time with Sir Horace in the grave, and January had raged into February, making the two windy months gray, dull, and sad. Kate had come through, somewhat quieter for her loss, but nonetheless whole. She had fond memories, and they were good!

"What sort of things are you talking about, Eliza? What way do you have to keep him loving you?" asked Kate curiously.

"There's some things, miss, I can't tell you. It wouldn't be decent," teased Eliza.

"Odious creature! Why not?"

"Because if I was to teach ye what I knows on how to please yer covey, Miss Ellen would go off into convulsions!" she laughed.

"And what makes you think I would trouble Nell with such information?" countered Kate, her curiosity eating at her. "Fie, Eliza, I am no dunce."

"Then how comes you be the one doing the asking and me the teaching?"

"Because you have the beau and I have not!"

Eliza peacocked about the room, much pleased with this mode of conversation. Kate pulled her by the hand and laughed. "Tell me, you wretched girl!"

Eliza lowered her voice and whispered a tale into Kate's ears. The enormity of her disclosure kept Kate's gray eyes wide for some time afterward and several times she looked doubtfully at Eliza and said, "Really . . . and you are not afraid? I mean . . . "

"No, and what's more . . . " started Eliza, cutting herself short when Miss Ellen peeped her head around the door.

"Oh, Nell," said Kate, warning Eliza with her eyes.

"Well, miss . . . I'll jest go get these linens done then . . ." said Eliza making good her escape.

Kate halted her. "Eliza, would you tell Mr. Banyon

I shall join him for that walk I promised. Tell him I will be but a few moments."

Eliza bobbed, smiled, and vanished in a thrice, and Miss Ellen pulled a face. "That is a very saucy wench."

"Yes, and she is also a love," said Kate on a challenging note.

"I don't doubt it, though her ways are a bit too free and easy for her place."

"Nell, snobbery from you?" cried Kate admonishingly.

Miss Premble frowned. "Not snobbery, Kate, but do you think it wise to carry on such a loose friendship with your maid?"

"Wise? I never questioned the wisdom of it, only the pleasure," said Kate, raising a brow. Really, Nell was getting to be impossible these days. If she wasn't criticizing Mr. Banyon, it was Eliza. All she seemed to want was for Kate to go to London to visit her aunt, and while Kate adored her Aunt Sarah, she didn't want to leave the Grange, not yet.

"At any rate, we will drop this friendship for the moment, but Kate, sending messages to Mr. Banyon in such a hurly-burly way, it simply will not do. It is most unseemly. There will be talk, and many will say that your fondness for Mr. Banyon is growing out of proportion."

"I don't know who would say so, and don't care whether they do or not," said Kate, growing impatient.

"Kate? 'Tis impossible. Never say you are growing too fond of Mr. Banyon, not in a romantic way!"

"But if I were? Why should it trouble you so, Nell?"

"There are reasons, Kate. Oh my, I do wish the Dower House were ready to receive him. It will not do for him to continue beneath our roof."

"Why not, Nell? Papa had no objections to having Perry housed under the same roof with me," said Kate testily.

"Your papa had no notion that you would take to Mr. Banyon. Had he known that knave would serve him so traitorously, he would have killed him with his own hand!"

"Nell! How can you say such a thing? Papa loved Mr.

Banyon. You know that; he was a father to him, and well you know!"

"That may be," said Nell, retreating suddenly, "but he would not have approved of your attraction to the man!"

"My attraction?" asked Kate, her tone dangerous. "Then you have decided I find him attractive?"

"You certainly give the impression that you do," said Nell, feeling she was losing ground.

"If I were attracted, and I am not saying either way, 'twould be a matter for my heart and my mind, no others. Not even yours, Nell," said Kate, pride swooping away consideration for Nell's feelings.

Miss Premble felt a pinch and indeed a wounded look crept into her eyes, disarming Kate at once. "Oh, Nell, I did not mean that. You know how dear you are to me, and so are all your thoughts. I simply meant to say that some things, such as my friendship with Perry, are not disputable."

"Perry is it? How long has it been Perry?" demanded Nell, finding a better line of attack.

"Oh, Nell!" exclaimed Kate exasperatedly. "How you do fuss. Don't pucker so, love." She turned and picked up her fur-lined cloak, throwing it over her shoulders. "I am just going for a walk about the grounds, and Nell . . . I do love you."

She made her way down the corridor to the balconied stairway, and her thoughts were full with Perry! Three years her senior was not so very much older, yet he seemed centuries more mature. His fair face was at times absurdly youthful when caught off guard at something he enjoyed! Those moments took her to Danny, for in many ways they looked like one another, both lean and blond, both youthful. Still, Peregrine Banyon was no Daniel Ludlow, and well she knew that! Perry's world-wise aspect hid a deeper being and his shell was as yet impenetrable.

She had fallen into a comfortable relationship with Perry after her father's death. They had shared her moment of grief, dispelling all her reserve. She enjoyed his company, though she knew 'twas not because he was a playmate as Danny had been, as Danny was still. Her letters continued to flow to her old friend, and they were full with Perry's name!

Kate's womanhood had awakened many months ago. With a frown she remembered that it was Branwell Mannering who had first stirred such awareness! However, it was Perry Banyon who worked the embers. She was drawn to his deep blue eyes and his handsome features. His gentle courting, barely perceptible, was just what she felt was proper, and she could find no cause for Nell's concern.

Upstairs, Miss Ellen sank onto the white coverlet of Kate's pretty bed. She was frightened. Things were far worse than she had imagined. She wished that Lady Haverly was present to lend her aid to the problem, but the indomitable woman had left for London the day after the funeral. Oh God! Poor unsuspecting Kate . . . how could that scoundrel pursue her? 'Twas not to be thought of, and certainly not to be allowed to continue. She would write to Lady Haverly at once!

Kate peeped at Perry sideways, moving the fur trim of her hood to look at his countenance as she giggled over her description of Nell's outrage at her use of his first name. " 'Tis antiquated, after all."

"No, Kathleen. You must not laugh at Miss Premble. She is quite correct in so advising you. People might talk to hear you refer to me so casually."

"Does it matter?" frowned Kate. "I care not for prattling tongues."

"I do," he said, stopping and looking down into her piquant face. "I have no wish to have your name bandied about by rough lips and it is too soon for me to ask you . . . to tell you . . . " he broke off and looked away.

She blushed at her own boldness but urged him on. "Perry . . . too soon to tell me what?" She had been wondering what it would be like to feel his arms go about her. She was curious about his kiss. She half hoped for it.

"Do you not already know, Kathleen? You must. My heart is in my eyes every time I look upon you," he said, taking her gloved hand and pressing it gently to his lips.

"Oh, Perry, you are so wonderful," said Kate. "Do you really care for me?"

His face seemed jubilant. "Care? I adore you. Do I have reason to think you might feel something for me?" he asked hopefully.

"I feel something for you, but I am not sure yet, Perry," she said doubtfully, shy of committing herself.

"I press you for much far too soon." Again he kissed her hand. She released a startled exclamation, suddenly pointing in the direction of the south woods. "Perry, look!"

A yellow-haired fox hobbling on three legs loomed out from beneath a straggly bush and pursued a gray hare. Around and around they went, the hare careful to zigzag between the trees until he disappeared from sight. The fox stood on all three legs for a moment, confounded, before giving up the chase and returning to his hovel.

"Oh dear, I am not certain how I feel," cried Kate distressed.

He laughed, "But why? The rabbit lives."

"But that poor fox. How will he survive? He has lost a leg!"

"He will die slowly; 'tis the lot of the deformed," he said, a strange look coming into his eyes.

"Surely he was not born that way," said Kate, much upset by the thought that he would starve to death. "He could not have survived this long, for I'd swear he has a few years beneath his pelt!"

"So he does. The old timer was quick enough to flee a second bullet, but the hunter still got in his first!"

"Oh no, Perry, never say a hunter shot off his leg?" cried Kate, much distressed by now.

"It happens," he said quietly. "Do not fret, Kate; there is naught we can do about it."

"Oh, is there not?" said she militantly. She turned and began for the house.

"What are you going to do? Where are you going?" asked Perry, hurriedly following her.

"I am going to feed that poor creature. Perhaps in time I can lure him to the back door."

"But, Kate . . . " he began to object. It was useless; she could not see pain without trying a remedy for it.

He shook his head and hastened to catch up with her.

19

April came in softly. It stroked Hampshire with its gentleness, lovingly promising the coming of spring. Crocus greens thrust through the earth, defiant, heedless of the chance that frost might still bite their buds. Skyward went the small shoots, teasing the sight with their hint of beauty.

Kate wandered aimlessly over the front lawns of the Grange. She was restless and had been so ever since she had received Aunt Sarah's feathery missive! Sarah was coming to the New Forest! That event could take place at any moment; indeed, Kate had been waiting with eager anticipation these two days and more. As usual, her aunt's letter had been full with run-on thoughts, very few of which were totally clear. One point her aunt had made was that she would not leave London without proper escort. Thus the delay, thought Kate, and who would escort her? Would Branwell Mannering be coming to the Grange? She hoped not! Her heart pained at the dreadful fancy, for she knew not how she would deal with him.

A giggle rippled through the fresh air, interrupting Kate's flowing if somewhat dark thoughts. She glanced in the direction of the south woods and there, propped against an elm, was Eliza. Johnny, the Newbury stable boy was standing over her, his forearm resting against the tree above her head. His other hand worked beneath the bodice of Eliza's gray linen as he whispered into her ear.

It was not the first time Kate had accidently come across them so huddled, and she quickly hurried out of their view, crossing the front drive and diving into the woods flanking the other side. Eliza and Johnny were betrothed and this, Kate told herself, made their rather bold behavior acceptable, though in truth it worried her to see Eliza so easy with her beau. She had often warned the girl that she might end by going too far. Eliza had only laughed. "Lordy, miss, I ain't got maggots in m'head! If I were to let him 'ave all now, why I might never talks him into giving me his name. Bless me, for I ain't no fool! I knows how to please him, keep his 'ands off the wenches and make him wild for the time he'll be calling me his own . . . without stretching meself out for him!"

"Eliza!" said Kate, choking on the coffee she had been sipping. She was, more often than not, shocked by Eliza's audacious dialogues.

The young maid laughed. "Oh, miss, we be virgins both, but you much more so! You have a virgin mind, untouched. Now I—well, I've got all kinds of thoughts rushing at me and none be those of an innocent! Lord only knows there ain't much else."

Suddenly Kate saw what Eliza meant. For Eliza and the other young serving girls in similar situations, there were not many enjoyments. They rose at dawn, worked the better part of each day, and then returned to their beds. They had nought if their life was loveless!

"Then, Eliza, is it wrong? I mean for me, not you. Is it wrong if such thoughts enter my head?" asked Kate uncertainly.

"Lordy no! 'Tis nature's way, tried and true! 'Tis wrong to deny them. What ye got to be is real. Ye've got to be whole, body and mind. Ain't right to be an animal taking every which way. No, I don't hold with that. When ye love a man, 'tis got to be real. You can't say here be m'knight in armor clad, for there ain't no sech being. You've got to love him with all his faults and know there ain't a human alive that ain't got them! If ye face his wrongs from the outset, he won't take a fall and break and neither will your heart!"

"You have a level head on your bony shoulders, Eliza," teased Kate, much struck by the girl's simple logic.

"What queers me is why it took ye so long to twig it," said the girl, grinning.

"Twig it?" returned Kate, wide-eyed.

"Lordy, miss, but ye do be a child. It means 'find out'." She laughed and went about her business, leaving Kate to finish her breakfast.

Well, thought Kate ruefully, the months were floating away and she was no closer to knowing her own heart than before. Perry and she were close. His moving into the Dower House had not changed anything; he came to visit her every day. They shared ideas and exchanged opinions. They shared the glory of the yellow fox! They had started that first day they saw the poor three-legged thing. Kate had fetched a meaty bone and taken it to the spot she had last seen him and then both she and Perry retreated into the distance. The fox, half starved and desperate, saw the food; he saw them and he panted, unsure and in need. Finally his need for food won out and he made a wild dart for the bone, running off to safety with it. It had been a triumphant moment for Kate, and Perry shared in her enthusiasm. Each day she left him food, each time bringing it closer to the house. It was always the same; the fox would dart as fast as his three legs would take him and run off with the prize. At last, just the other day, he came to the tree just outside the kitchen door. She waited anxiously, having gone some twenty feet closer to the house than the day before. The fox made wide circling motions before sniffing the ground and eyeing Kate. He growled low in his throat, but it was such a pathetic sound that Kate could not be frightened. It was the wild thing's objection to such barbarous treatment. Really, how could the human force him to such undignified lengths. However, at last, almost defiantly and with much show of pride, the fox had the meat in his jaws. He backed away, keeping his eyes on Kate, his ears twitching at the sound of her cooing voice. Her tones thrilled him and he stopped a moment to give her one long wild look. Then, as always, he hobbled off with his treasure.

This she had done, though it had been to the cook's displeasure and Nell's amazement. Perry had come and it was with excitement that she related the event, looking for his approval. He gave it freely, taking her hand and pressing it to his lips. Suddenly she wanted more. She moved closer to him and her eyes quietly asked for his embrace. His hands trembled as they wound around her waist and his lips barely brushed her own when he suddenly pulled away from her and cried in a voice filled with repressed passion, "Kate, I can't maintain arm's length with you, not when you tease me so!"

Surprised, her gray eyes widened. "I never said I wanted you at arm's length," she said. He groaned and grabbed hold of her too tightly, bruising her flesh with his intensity, but just as his mouth met hers, he flung her from him abruptly. "I am a cad to take advantage of your innocence!" Then, just as suddenly, he turned and left her standing there in the budding garden.

Nell had stood frozen in the kitchen doorway. She had overheard, and she had seen, and as he sped past her she turned to find Kate's confused gray eyes. She moved toward her charge and her face was a portrait of conflicting emotions. "Kathleen Newbury, how could you? I saw you with my own eyes fling yourself at him!"

"Oh, Nell, I only wanted him to kiss me. If I am to marry him, should I not discover whether or not I enjoy his kiss?" returned Kate, unabashed.

"Oh faith! What you are asking for is impossible! You and he can never marry one another!"

"But that is absurd. Why not? Is there something that you know and I do not?"

"Yes. You are wrong for each other," said Nell lamely.

"That is the wisdom you wish to impart to me? Forgive me, Nell, I love you, but is that all? Only that you believe us to be wrong for each other?"

"Only that," said Nell, lying. She could never tell Kate the truth.

"Then it is not enough. If I decide I want to be his wife, I shall be!" said Kate, rushing past Nell to find the privacy of her room and give way to tears she could not account for.

That had been yesterday, and Perry had not returned since. The sky was growing dark, for the afternoon was well past, and Kate turned on the path, backtracking toward her drive. The sound of approaching wheels brought a smile to Kate's lips and she rushed out onto the clearing, awaiting her aunt's coach. It was a black sleek thing, piled high with luggage. At its rear were two riders—one clothed in seaman's garb and the other a man whose top hat sat rakishly upon black billowing layers of hair, whose smile gleamed across a bronzed handsome face, and whose name she knew well. The Earl of Mannering had come to Lyndhurst Grange! Her heart quickened and when her aunt's carriage pulled to a stop, she quickly scampered into the coach and out of the Earl's path of observation!

20

Sarah swished her mauve satin skirt as she moved around the Newbury library. Her hands worked agitatedly at each other. She was upset by what Miss Premble had related to them just moments before. The thought that her niece was developing an infatuation for Mr. Banyon vexed her no end. She stopped her frenzied movements and turned to face the Earl. He stood quietly beside the fire, sipping his brandy and frowning into the grate.

"We must do something, Branwell!"

"We? Oh no, my dearest aunt, that deep I shall not go. In fact, after listening to the good Miss Premble, I am persuaded that I have been most unwise to have left my friends and my enjoyments in order to ride out here with you, for I see a Cheltenham tragedy!" he said testily.

"Branwell, you can't mean to stand by and allow my niece to throw herself away on that . . . that creature?"

"In God's name, love, what the deuce do you think *I* can do to prevent it?"

"You know very well. You are an extremely attractive man. I am well aware that you have a certain aura, magnetism that draws lovely women to you. I see no reason why Kate would not find you charming were you to exert yourself in that direction!"

"She detests me! Is that not reason enough for you," snapped the Earl.

"Oh Branwell, the scandal, it would end by involving us all," cried Sarah. "Sooner or later the truth will come out, and if Kate is actually married to him, dear God!"

"Sarah, there must be another way. I tell you the girl cannot stomach the sight of me. I represent all that is evil and lewd to the chit. *Certes!* Madam, did you not see the way she greeted me earlier? This time she had not the excuse of mourning. No, your scheme will not work."

"You are wrong. Men are ever wrong about women. I am no fool, my Branwell. I see exactly how she treats you and 'methinks the lady doth protest too much,'" said Sarah dramatically.

He laughed. "Does Shakespeare also allude to a method of weaning a female's heart?"

"Certainly, all the answers are with Shakespeare. She

behaves the shrew with you, Branwell. Treat her as such. She will come around."

Again he laughed, heartily. "Sarah, you are a delight. Shall I say, 'Kiss me, Kate' and tell her the moon is but the sun and find her in my arms? I doubt it."

"You poke fun at me, Branwell, but admit it. You would have her if you could?" said his aunt, eyeing him speculatively.

"Certes! The devil I would. She is a vixen. I want no such creature nipping at me."

"Then you will not try to catch her eye, throw confusion to her winds?" pleaded Sarah.

"Whatever for?"

"For time, my nephew. She will not consent to marry him if she is unsure of herself. Make her unsure!"

He studied his aunt for a long moment. "It won't be easy. The lad was here during her saddest moments. His manners are gentle, and she fancies herself attached to him. I have nought in my favor."

"What amazes me no end is his daring," said Sarah. "Does he believe that we are unaware of his secret?"

"Of course he thinks we don't know," scoffed the Earl. "He thinks to win her heart and gain the Grange, which he probably believes is rightfully his."

"Why won't he be satisfied with the Dower House? Oh, faith, he is greedy and cruel, for there can never be anything healthy between Kathleen and him."

"Don't pucker so, Sarah; you will end by having lines in that lovely face of yours. I shall try to be my most charming and seduce your niece as best I can," he said, grinning broadly.

She gave his hand a reproachful rap. "Horrid boy! Are you never serious?"

" 'Twould spoil my fun."

"Wretch!" She stopped suddenly. "Shh, someone comes."

Kate's heels moved down the long dark oak flooring toward the library. The room lay at the rear of the house on its first floor and as she reached its closed double doors she heard the Earl's deep voice. There was something in his sonorous notes that nearly always caused her heart to quicken its beat. She stopped before the doors a moment, trying to still her silly palpitations. Ridiculous girl, she told herself, he can't attack you in your home with your aunt as witness. She opened one of the doors and entered the cosy room, a ready smile upon her lovely lips.

The Earl watched her glide across the room to take up her aunt's hand and a murmur teased his mind. By God, she was lovely!

Her black hair was piled high upon her well-shaped head, curls forming at her forehead, over her ears and cascading over the nape of her neck. The pale pink of her silk gown hugged her trim figure and as she bent to plant a kiss upon her aunt's cheek, the fullness of her white breasts came to the Earl's eager eye. She wore no jewelry and the Earl was conscious of the fact that her beauty needed no enhancement. She looked up at the Earl from beneath her dark lashes and her gray eyes flickered at the sight of him. She was all too aware of his virile good looks and disliked the sensation he aroused within her. She caught the glint of his green eyes upon her and hurriedly glanced away.

"Come, Branwell, sit beside us," said Sarah invitingly as she pulled Kate onto the sofa. "I haven't yet heard about your latest escapades at sea." She turned to Kate. "Branwell, you know, had only just returned to London two weeks ago before I packed him up and brought him here with me."

"Oh?" said Kate sardonically, looking up into his face. "Out capturing wild merchant ships again, my lord?"

Her remark piqued him and he had an urging to box her ears. Instead, he said, "Fortunately we did manage one haul, though it was questionable for a while."

"*Tch, tch,*" said the lady. "Never say the rascals were armed?" mocked Kate.

He smiled sweetly at her. "No, they were not, but the French privateer that came upon us most certainly was!"

His words were at variance with his smile, for they were given sharply with a curt edge. He received a glare from his aunt and reminded himself that he had promised to bewitch Kate and was sorely aware that it was indeed going to be difficult. "However," he continued, "in spite of the fact that the Frogs had a ship that outnumbered our guns and our crew, we managed to rid the English waters of them and take the cargo of the merchant before she sank."

"But . . . you say you sank them?" cried Kate.

"By your tone I take it you grieve for the French. May I remind you that we are at war with them," said the Earl, out of patience.

"Yes, but was there no other way?" she asked, dimly aware that she was a bit unfair.

"As a matter of fact, we had no intention of sinking the merchant nor did we! 'Twas their own kind that put a cannon through them! The captain of the privateer seemed to feel that their merchant should go down rather than heave us their hull."

"Oh, men are so stupid," said Kate.

He ignored this. "However, my crew is most skilled, for, while under fire from the French privateer and while the merchant took in water, we transferred its hold to our own and then rid the seas of one more French privateer, and m'girl, whether you will own it or not, it was the only thing to do under the circumstances!" said the Earl on a final note.

"Well, perhaps so. I can not say I am sorry for it, for I despise such vessels, and their work, whether French or no," said Kate scathingly.

Branwell put an eye heavenward and cast an "I told you so" expression at his aunt.

She turned upon her niece. "Kate!" she admonished strongly. "You may hold such an opinion. I suppose we are all entitled to our thoughts, whether right or wrong, but 'tis not in the best of good taste to be rude to your guest, and the Earl is your guest!"

Kate's countenance took on a stricken expression, reminding the Earl of a little girl caught with her finger in the pudding.

"Never mind such stuff, Sarah. Cousin Kate may say what she likes to me. I hope she always shall. I prize honesty," said the Earl, looking directly into Kate's gray eyes.

Oh, she thought miserably, he is trying to make me feel guilty, and I won't. I shan't give him the satisfaction. She opened her mouth to retort but calmed herself and said in return, "I am certain the Earl does indeed prize honesty, and shall continue therefore to dole it out."

They exchanged glances all three, and Aunt Sarah was much relieved when the butler entered to announce dinner!

Later that evening, Eliza fussed over Kate's clothing as she put it away before coming to stand behind Kate, who sat at the vanity. She held the brush poised above Kate's black hair and studied her mistress's face in the mirror before her. Kate was more thoughtful than usual. There was much that was troubling her thoughts, sending them every way in their search for answers. She thought of dinner. It was passed comfortably enough, for her aunt's lively chatter kept her intrigued. One on-dit after another kept them chuckling, kept them pleasant and at ease. The Earl had entered the conversation and Kate was forced to admit to herself that his wit was as lively as his eyes, those wild eyes that taunted her. He had induced her to laugh in spite of her determination not to, and she knew that had she allowed her guard to wander off, she would have found herself relaxed in his company! She found that she had to remind herself that he was the same man that pirated, took what he wanted regardless of what pain it cost others. She had to remind herself he was the same man that had forced himself upon her, touched her intimately against her will! He was the same man who had evidently thought nothing of taking a married woman, for she was certain from Sir John's words that day on the *Bermudian* that Branwell had been

Lady Medwin's lover! No, she had not forgotten that. It stuck most acutely in her thoughts.

"What be puzzling ye so, miss?" asked Eliza, stroking Kate's long tresses.

"Nought," said Kate, sighing.

"Is it because young Mr. Banyon didn't come by today?" pursued Eliza, curiously.

"I suppose," said Kate, sighing again.

"Now, miss, you mustn't fret that. Lordy, jest coz he didn't have the time, 'tis no reason to go sour. Why, I knows that he were in Southampton today," said Eliza brightly.

"Southampton? How do you know that, Eliza?" asked Kate with some interest.

"M'John seen 'im when he drove Cook over to market in the wagon this afternoon. Said he saw 'em coming out of Mr. Hansen's office."

"My father's lawyer?" said Kate, surprised.

"That's the one."

Kate turned on her round, backless seat and looked full into Eliza's face. "What would Mr. Banyon be doing there?"

"Lordy, miss, fer quality ye ain't too bright," teased Eliza, and received a rap across her hand. "Bless ye, miss, what else would he be doing but signing papers and the like. Seeing as how he's got the Dower House and all now."

"Of course!" agreed Kate, satisfied. "That's what it is, and that's why he didn't come by. I thought he might be put out with me. I wouldn't want him to be angry over anything I had done," said Kate softly.

"'Tis that way wit ye then, ye'll be taking young Mr. Banyon's hand?" queried Eliza, frowning.

"Well, don't go dark on me, Eliza. Don't you like him?" asked Kate, surprised at her maid's expression.

"Oh, he be reel fine looking and a proper gent and all, but . . . "

"But what?"

"Oh, never mind me . . . 'tis nought."

"Well, of all the silly things to do, for you know now I shall always wonder what it was you had in your mind. Not that it really matters, for I am not certain I want to marry Perry," said Kate quietly.

"Well now, what's changed yer mind?" asked Eliza, interest perking up.

"I haven't changed my mind, never had it made up! I mean, well, Perry has been good to me and he was here when I needed him, but he doesn't exactly set me to quivering, and I think a man should, you know, before you marry him," said Kate, thoughtfully.

Eliza giggled. "*Hmmm* . . . methinks 'tis another set of shoulders that has you quivering," teased Eliza.

"Eliza! What do you mean by such a remark?"

"I seen enough of the Earl to make a maid swoon. Gawd, but he be a fine buck! Why, if m'eart weren't pledged to that scrawny lad of mine . . . 'tis that fast I'd jump into his lordship's bed!"

"Eliza!" cried Kate, startled by such talk. "You would not! You know you just like to shock me with your wayward words. I had heard you say often enough how you wouldn't do any such things without being in love."

"And who said I couldn't find it in me to love that handsome bucko?" bantered Eliza, enjoying herself.

"But you don't know him," objected Kate, somewhat annoyed with her maid.

"True, nor would such as I ever have the chance. He'd no more look at me than he would Cook's scanty salads. But if he did . . . " She made an expressive indication of her reaction to such a miracle and rolled her eyes. For this she got a powerful push and landed onto Kate's bed laughing.

"Horrid, faithless thing, such naughty thoughts. What if Johnny were to hear you?" rallied Kate, laughing.

This seemed to sober Eliza, at once, "*Oooh*, he'd whip me proper. Never even think such a thing. Lordy, he'd string me up by m'poor thumbs and then 'ave at me he would. Oooh lordy!"

"There now. So stop your foolishness and be off with

you. 'Tis late, Eliza, and you've unsettled my mind," smiled Kate, watching her friend go off. She climbed into bed and sank back against the pillows. It struck her that Branwell Mannering and Perry Banyon were completely different from one another, and yet each one had affected her mind and troubled her heart. In what ways they had managed this, she was unsure. She knew only that much to her vexation, both gentlemen filled her thoughts.

With their faces swimming before her and Eliza's stirring jibs still in her ears, she drifted off to sleep. It is therefore not surprising that her dreams were troubled and confused. She saw Perry and they walked. He brought the smile to her lips with his gentle spirit, and she put her arms around him, tempting him with a kiss, but his hands tightened and they were no longer his hands but those of a green-eyed devil. The Earl was holding her, touching her, ripping the clothing from off her back, and his mouth was bruising her own. She tossed in her bed, hungry from his touch, tantalized by it, and aware that it was in pleasure she received this dream! She awoke with a start, her body on fire, wet with perspiration, her nightdress clinging to her sleek form, and there was a strange aching in her loins. She moved beneath her covers and belittled herself, for she knew the meaning of such an ache. She knew that a lust had lodged itself between her legs and in her heart, and her Calvinistic principles tortured her with such digressions!

21

The sun was full in the east, foretelling a good day, and Kate took comfort in the prophecy. A wild zephyr of clean fresh air curled through the naked forest, shifting the dry leaves from their long winter's rest. The woods whispered to Kate, calling her to join their glistening glory. Was she not youth, was she not the essence of all that was spring? She wandered toward its beckoning, when a deep voice broke the melodious chain, and she turned her head to find the Earl. He came toward her, his uncovered black waves sweeping his head in a cadence all their own. His dark cloak billowed away from his tall strong body and her name was on his lips. She found his green eyes, and they smiled in tune with his sensuous mouth. She felt a nervous pinch at her heart and, agonizingly aware that she found him far too attractive, she chided herself. She waited, not trusting him, not trusting herself.

"Cousin Kate," he repeated, coming up to her, stopping and smiling full into her exquisite face. She found it difficult not to respond to his warmth, and returned his smile.

"With as many times as I have been to Southampton, I have never taken a tour of the New Forest. Its heaths and glens intrigue me. Would I be asking too much if I begged the favor of a tour?"

"No, it is a delight to walk here and about. If you like we can hike over to Buckler's Hard where they build the big ships," she said, formally aloof.

"I would like very much," he said, wondering how he was ever to break through her reserve.

She led him down a narrow wooded path, where there was just room enough for them to pass, side by side. His closeness made her feel ill at ease and she chose to veil this with her silence.

He made yet another attempt to break her ice. "History, especially our own, fascinates me," said the Earl. "I seem to remember some story or other connected with old William Rufus and the New Forest."

She smiled. "Oh, yes. 'Tis a gory one at that. That Norman king was wont to hunt here and he had gained for himself such a horde of enemies that they decided to do him in, or so the tale goes. He came here to hunt and found himself the hunted. An arrow tamed his hand and laid him to rest. Wicked Rufus . . . the church refused to give him a Christian burial."

"Poor fellow," chuckled the Earl. "Though I am certain it bothered him not, once he was dead."

"Poor fellow, indeed. He was, by all accounts, a brute," said Kate.

"Then he received what he deserved, no doubt," said the Earl, teasing her.

"No doubt," she said, suddenly smiling wide.

"It's beautiful here, but much different from your island paradise. With your father gone, I wonder at your remaining," baited the Earl.

"Do you? Both my parents are buried here. The Grange is my home. It is Nell's home. Indeed, she came to it before I did. I have no wish to leave it," said Kate quietly. She loved Bermuda. She always would . . . but England was the hope of all her romantic dreams.

"You know Sarah has such plans for you. . . . Egad, child, I almost feel sorry for you," chuckled the Earl.

"Oh? What sort of plans do you mean?" asked Kate surprised.

"For your presentation ball."

"But, that is not possible now. I am in mourning," said Kate, frowning, "I could not possibly. It would be disrespectful to Papa's memory."

"She plans it, I believe, for the spring—June," answered the Earl quickly. "And in these things you may trust Sarah. If she thinks that enough time after mourning, then rest assured if it isn't, she will make it so! She has this odd notion that youth's only obligation is to life!"

Kate smiled gently. "Aunt Sarah's philosophy usually fits her purpose."

"There is no denying that, sweetings, and there is no gainsaying the indomitable lady," he agreed ruefully, thinking of his own part in Sarah's plans.

Kate laughed. "You love her very much, don't you?"

"Yes, yes I do," he answered softly. "She was, for me and my brother Matthew, a godsend. Ever there when we needed her, and lord knows how many times we needed her."

"I didn't know you had a brother," said Kate, suddenly curious about him, about his history.

"Yes, drat the lad. A wild blade he is. Up at Cambridge in his first year," grinned the Earl, remembering his last visit with his scampish brother.

"Oh, then he is much younger than you?" asked Kate, appraising the Earl and wondering how old he was. She had never thought about it before.

"Matthew is eighteen, ten years my junior. When last I visited with him, he had a wolf-dog in his possession and was demanding to know whether I thought it fair that the dean had ordered the creature of Trinity grounds!" He barked a laugh over this memory and Kate felt suddenly conscious of a new and boyish side to his nature.

She smiled impishly. "And you told him . . . "

"That the dean was, as always, most unfair! He had treated me similarly when my pet monkey and I roomed together beneath Trinity's hallowed ceilings."

She laughed. "A monkey? Oh, never say you owned a monkey? You can not mean it; but really, my lord, that is far worse than a dog. We all have pets, but a monkey?"

He chuckled with her. "Indeed yes, and I managed the thing for nearly six months before I was discovered. A friend of mine, poor Willy, had forgotten to lock our door, and the dratted creature escaped to his freedom. The unfortunate thing was that he found himself, by what means we shall probably never know, in the dean's office. The monkey then proceeded to thoroughly demolish the place. He screeched, pulled, threw, and tore until he had brought the house down around his ears. Willy and I were sent home in disgrace for a month."

"But what happened to the monkey?" cried Kate, laughing with uncontrolled mirth.

"Drat the monkey! You see 'twas Willy and I that discovered where he had got to and 'twas we that chased him round the dean's office. When the door opened to disgorge the world about our heads, the monkey sat innocently atop a bookcase while we floundered in the squalid mess of *his* making! We gave the wretched creature back to the organ grinder from whom *I* had purchased him."

This tale tickled her sense of the ridiculous, easing away all earlier reserve. She laughed until tears wet her eyes and he stopped her, pulling out a handkerchief to wipe them away. They reached the stream that cut across the Grange woodlands, and they stood over it, listening to its trilling sound over the jutting rocks. It was clear and shallow at this point and Kate gazed into it long, feeling suddenly inexplicably shy of meeting the Earl's eyes. She had laughed away all her nervousness, only to find that the thought of meeting his glance sent an inexpressable excitement rushing through her veins. Lest he read such a hideous fancy on her countenance, she kept her face averted!

He watched her, aware that she had again withdrawn herself. He was irritated by it. What was wrong with the chit? Why was she determined to hold herself aloof? Any other female would have, by this time, offered him her lips; at least all the females he had ever pursued had done so! It wasn't innocence that kept her frosting at him. Damnation, he had wooed more than a few virgins, and though he had never taken it further than a mild flirtation, he had ruled the game. His ego was pinched! He leveled a serious glance upon her features. "Tell me, Kate, do you pine for someone?"

Her gray eyes shot up, stunned by his question. They looked at him wide and their beauty gave him cause to stare. "What a strange question, my lord. I pine for only one person, my father, as well you know."

"That is not what I meant. I lost both my parents; the loss of those that gave us birth brings on a sadness, and we do grieve, but you have yet another look about you. Do you pine for a man?" he asked boldly.

"For a man?" she repeated, taken aback. "I don't know what you mean. For what man?"

"Is your heart attached to someone?" pursued the Earl relentlessly, for he was not about to give up. He wanted to discover the extent of her infatuation for Perry Banyon.

"My heart?" She frowned. "I don't know if that is any of your business. No more than it would be mine to ask you if your heart were attached."

He smiled. "I don't begrudge the question. No, my heart remains mine."

For no earthly reason this pleased and pinched her. But she considered him a moment and then smiled gently. "Why should you ask or concern yourself, my lord, is beyond me, but, no, I am not attached to any man in any way," she said, wondering why she did not admit to her relationship with Perry. Certainly she cared for Perry Banyon. Why then not freely admit it? Yet she could not!

The Earl smiled, feeling a disproportionate sense of relief. "But what of the friend you left behind in Bermuda?"

"Danny? Oh, I shall always be attached to Danny. That is something altogether different." She thought of the dozen letters she had sent to him since her departure from Bermuda and the single one she had in return. "But Danny is more . . . "

"A brother?" he offered hopefully.

"Oh no, never a brother. He has never been that to me. In fact, poor Danny thinks he wants me for wife," she said sadly.

"Oh?" said the Earl frowning. "Then what is he to you?"

"He is Danny! I don't know if I can explain that for it is more than friendship, and yet not the ties of blood." She smiled thoughtfully over this problem.

"And then what of Mr. Banyon?" said the Earl nonchalantly. "How fares your friendship with your neighbor?"

She blushed prettily. "You are very inquisitive, my lord."

"Do I overstep?" he asked cautiously.

She smiled amicably, for he really could be charming, she thought to herself; perhaps she had misjudged him. "No, you don't overstep. It is just that I can't answer what I am myself uncertain about."

"Sarah would have it that Banyon wishes to marry you?"

"How she came by that I have no idea."

"Then it is incorrect?"

"No, it is true. However, I know not my own heart in the matter. Though certainly I am not opposed to the notion."

"I see," said the Earl, the dance vanishing from his eyes.

"Ah, this road will take us to Buckler's Hard," she said, starting forward out of the thicket.

He reached for her and took hold of her arm, pulling her close to his chest, and she felt her heart beat wildly. His eyes devoured her and his tone was almost hypnotic in its effect and intensity. "Do you give the suckling what only a man can appreciate, my sweetings?"

She was startled by his fierceness, disrupted by his touch. "You must first tell me, my lord, who is the suckling and who the man?"

"You know well my meaning. Why play words with me, Kate? Tell me! Has he taken you in his arms, this suckling who proposes and has not your opposition? Has he tasted your sweet honey?" He did not wait for her answer but pulled her roughly into his embrace, pressing her supple body against his own hard taut form.

He knew he was faulting his plan, all his good intentions, but his body and his mind burned for her. At the moment he had but one purpose, to kiss her tempting mouth. His lips found hers as she struggled within his grasp and his tongue teased itself into her cherry wine. She felt the world rock before her and vanish into blackness. The blackness exploded with red lights unsheathed in their darts. How dare he? How dare he? she thought, yet her body felt on fire, felt a need stirring within it and she had to fight herself as well as him.

Her fists beat at his iron chest, but he kissed her still. She felt dizzy from his embrace, she felt faint from the sensations conflicting within her. She felt a need for head-clearing air, but there was none to be had. His lips would not release her own, and there was no moving from him! Through her anger, through her dizziness and her fears, she felt her body come alive! She wanted to melt against his strength. She wanted him to ravish her and the thought made her rant against herself. Oh God! She mustn't think such a thing, she told herself; she couldn't think such a thing! Yet, she wanted him to assuage her scorched blood. She wanted him to trespass his will upon her and allow her body the pleasure it craved. She was a woman, her body taunted her mind with its needs, but her mind was yet the victor! No, it shouted for all to hear, No! In one final burst of strength she had wrenched her mouth and shoulders away, feeling as though she would collapse. But he held her still, held her upright and knew her weakness. "Tell me, Kate, has he taken you in just such a way? You are a hot-blooded woman-child, has he touched your embers?" said the Earl softly.

Her gray eyes flashed lightning at him, and her hand would have smarted his face had he not caught it in mid-air. "You knave . . . you beast! You walk me out here pretending concern for my welfare, pretending friendship, and *I* like a fool allow my guard to fall."

"No fool you, sweet fondling. I took you for no such ride! Nor would I. I do care, there is no pretence in that. You mistake my motives. I don't mean to seduce you, merely to instruct you. You are a beautiful woman with the naïveté of a child. The combination, though disarmingly bewitching, could result in your receiving a broken heart. Banyon is not in love with you; he could not be, for reasons you would not now understand. He is an adventurer, out to get his hands on the Grange!"

"An adventurer? Because you are so yourself you suspect it of others. You take another man's gold in the name of patriotism and condone your actions under such guise. 'Tis you that is the adventurer. Perry need not marry for money; my father has provided him with a home, with money."

"Indeed he has. Have you never wondered at it? But never mind that. I tell you Perry will not rest until the Grange is his. He is obsessed with its acquisition."

"Stop it!" stormed Kate.

"Very well, you will hear nought against him. So be it. Come, I will walk you back to the house. Buckler's Hard shall have to wait on us."

"Walk with you after . . ."

"After I honored you with the kiss of a man who finds you irresistible. Forgive me, Kate," he teased.

"Honored? Oh, you are insufferable!" she spit.

"And you are exquisitely beautiful," he countered, taking up her arm and leading her down the path. She wrenched herself free and walked silently at his side. As they reached the clearing Kate's eyes lit up, much to the Earl's irritation, for there coming down the drive, astride a gentle mare, rode Perry Banyon.

22

The Earl eased his long legs before him, resting his head idly upon his bent fingers. He sat ensconsed within the confines of a gold brocaded wing chair. The fire glowed at his side and his eyes were veiled as though sleeping. His aunt and Miss Premble sat upon the sofa flanking him. They were in bright conversation but neither he nor the two occupants at the other end of the room paid them any heed!

Kate's smile was all for Perry Banyon. It was obvious, too obvious, and the Earl was rather enjoying himself at her expense. He had not played such games these nine years and more without having learned the signs. He was quick to notice that she never laughed, never raised her voice without sending him a fleeting glance, and the more it appeared that he noticed not, the louder came her voice. However, Perry noted it not and seemed quite pleased with the maid's attention.

Aunt Sarah watched Perry's affectations with disgust. The creature must be ousted from Kate's path! Her conversation with Miss Ellen came to an abrupt end and she turned and eyed her niece with some irritation. "Kate, do you not intend to flatter me with your company tonight?"

The Earl opened one eye and sent an amused glance towards his aunt, shifting his position slightly as he watched Kate's blushing confusion.

"Oh, Auntie, I am sorry," started Kate, coming forward.

Perry moved with her, making a deprecatory bow and offering his apologies for having kept Miss Newbury from her. Aunt Sarah sniffed in response and was barely civil to the young man. The Earl's brow went up and he whispered to Sarah, "That's not in your style and it won't serve, m'darling."

"*Humph!*" responded his aunt, turning to Mr. Banyon again and casting a showy eye over his attire. He could not be faulted in this regard, as he was impeccably clothed. His neckcloth was superb without being ostentatious, his blue superfine well fitted, his embroidered pale blue silk waistcoat most elegant, and his blue pantaloons exceptional. She took to intimidation instead. "So, Mr. Banyon, I am told you have settled very comfortably into my late brother-in-law's little cottage. How does life fare for you there?"

Auntie," interrupted Kate, her tone gently reproachful, "the Dower House is now Mr. Banyon's. It should not be referred to in any other terms."

"No, no, Miss Kathleen," smiled Perry Banyon. "It is quite natural your aunt would find some difficulty in thinking in such a manner, at first." He continued to smile affably. "I find life in the country most welcome."

"Really?" Sarah said with undisguised disbelief. "I would have thought that after such an exciting life in London the country would be severely dull." There was an underlining to her words that caught Kate's attention and was not lost on Mr. Banyon. He flushed, but inclined his head as though acknowledging her challenge. "As it happens the quiet of country life is most soothing to me. When Sir Horace and I left London for the Grange it was a most welcome change of scene. I find the beauty of the New Forest stimulating and inspiring. Now I find time to-paint at my leisure, and there is much to keep my brush well occupied."

"Perry," said Kate, "I did not know you painted."

"I am sure you did not," put in her aunt with a strange laugh. "There are many things you could not possibly know about Mr. Banyon, aren't there, sir?" she said, directing him a quizzical look.

"It is that which makes life exciting, madam," said Mr. Banyon, unperturbed. "To constantly discover new things in the people we think we know."

Kate gleamed, silently applauding his adroitness and wondering at her aunt's display of cattiness.

"May I see some of your work?" asked Kate spontaneously, giving him her gray eyes and her gentle smile, making up for the coldness he received from the others.

"I should like that," he said quietly, turning once again to Sarah and the silent Miss Premble. "However, now I believe I must bid you good night." He inclined his head before allowing his eyes to stray to Kate, who had rushed out her hand in offering. He took up the gentle white fingers and put them lovingly to his lips. "Tomorrow, Kathleen."

She smiled with pleasure and watched as the Earl bade Perry a safe journey home. She could not help but note that a strange glance passed between the two men. She excused herself and went along with Perry to see him to the front door. As soon as she had left the room, Sarah's eyes found those of the Earl's and her tone was exasperated. "This gets out of hand, Branwell. Why, did you see the barefaced gall of the creature?"

"Indeed, my lady," agreed Miss Premble dolefully. "He seems most sure of himself."

"His brazen audacities are to be marveled at," said the

Earl thoughtfully. "Yet I cannot believe he would go so far as to marry her. He puts on a show for our benefit. He means to show himself a threat and thereby insure our offering him a handsome sum to prevent their marriage!"

"Then offer it and let's have done!" cried Aunt Sarah, much distressed.

"Oh yes, my lady, it pulls at my heart when I think that even now he might be putting his hands on her. Why, 'tis a sin . . . a sin!" cried Miss Premble, moving her hands agitatedly in her lap.

"He'll not touch her. Make no mistake," said the Earl with contemptuous emphasis.

Kate had seen Perry out and returned to the double doors of the library. As she touched the knob, she pulled herself up short, hearing the last of the Earl's words. They were talking about Perry, she thought with annoyance; what now were they about? She waited for more.

"Good God! What can Horace have been thinking of, bringing that creature . . . that sin of his . . ."

"He was not well, Sarah," interrupted the Earl.

"But did he not realize the danger?" cried Sarah. "Did he not see that the boy would then be thrown at Kate?"

"And if he did, he thought 'twould be as brother and sister, which is probably what he wanted in his confused state," replied the Earl.

On the other side of the door, Kate put a hand to her forehead.

Boy of sin? Brother and sister? Whatever had she stumbled upon? She would have her answer at once. This secrecy and innuendo would have to stop! She calmed herself and opened the door with a dangerous smile upon her lips. "Ah, my family, gathered about in judgment of my life and its future. Tell me, is it that you are concerned for my welfare? If so, let it extend to my peace of mind, for I mean to have some answers. You have been behaving must rudely to Mr. Banyon. He was a chosen and trusted secretary to my father and he is now my neighbor. I would know the cause of your blatant determination to tear him down in my esteem!" demanded Kate, her gray eyes flashing at them.

"Darling," soothed Sarah, immediately getting up and moving forward with extended arms, "such heat! Over what?"

"Over what? Confound it, Aunt Sarah, I love you for a dear sweet woman and a truly doting aunt, but you cannot deny that you object to Mr. Banyon's paying me court, and that objection has led you to treat him most shabbily! I would know the reasons for this."

"I have already told you, Cousin Kate," put in the Earl suddenly from his place in the wing chair. "We think Mr. Banyon to be a fortune hunter."

"But why?" said Kate, rounding on him.

"Because he is penniless," said her aunt.

She turned again with some show of exasperation. "He is not. You know very well that the income Papa has left him is quite enough to sustain him, and the Dower House is maintained by the estate."

"One hundred pounds is hardly enough to sustain a a man of fashion. And you may have noticed that *his* tastes are high!" said Aunt Sarah. "Good God, child, he has no family background; he is a skirter, attempting to enter society through an advantageous marriage to a wealthy bride of good family."

"That does not explain why you called him a boy of sin. I heard you! What meant you by such a strange remark?" pursued Kate.

Miss Premble blanched and put a hand to her white cheek. Aunt Sarah looked to the Earl, who calmly replied, "That, my dear, is due to his background. He is the child of a lady of pleasure. His name is one chosen at random, for he was born in a garret."

Kate's eyes clouded as she surveyed them. "You are then all very cruel, and heartless! You condemn someone because of things he had not the making of. You have behaved abominably to a young man my father chose to extend his home and kindness to. What matters whether he be born high or low? It is his character, not his birth, that matters to me. You have given me no reason to despise him. Rather, I hold him higher in my esteem for having risen above his poor beginnings!" With that she turned on her heel and ran from them.

The three people she left behind in the library stared at one another, grimacing respectively.

"Good lord, the child is more determined to befriend him now than she was before we began meddling," exploded the Earl.

"Faith, oh deuce take Sir Horace and his dealings!" croaked Sarah. "She will be making a hero out of that creature. Branwell, he must accept your offer."

"Leave it to me, Sarah," said the Earl. "I promise you one thing, Kate Newbury will *not* marry Perry Banyon!"

23

The Earl dropped his hat, gloves, and greatcoat into the waiting hands of the Newbury butler, startling the poor fellow with his black look. He moved down the hall toward the library in search of a stiff drink.

Sarah heard of his return and hurried down the staircase to the hall and entered the library with a flurry, her brown silk skirts rustling around her. She scanned her nephew as he downed his second mummer of brandy, noting that he looked as dashing as ever and wondering why her niece had not yet been struck by such thoughts. "Well, Branwell? What did he say?"

"I made him an offer, and to your ten thousand pounds I offered five of my own, and the devil laughed in my face!" thundered the Earl. "Damn the man's eyes, for I never wished to put a fellow out as much as I did then!"

She sank into a nearby chair. "Oh no, Branwell, he turned it down? How can he have refused? What is his reasoning? He knows he can not marry Kate. 'Tis disgusting."

"But it is not illegal, nor could we stop him with what we know, for it would ruin Sir Horace's memory and bring scandal to our family, not to mention the pain it might bring to Kate. Damn but I wanted to choke the life out of him and thereby end the thing!"

"But what is his reasoning? He can not possibly have formed any meaningful attachment for Kate."

"Well in truth, Sarah, such things have been known to occur, but he gives us no such comfort to dwell upon. No, he means to wife her, for he openly admitted to me that the Grange should have been his. He wants the Grange!"

"But that is insane," cried Sarah.

"Nevertheless, 'tis what he intends."

"And, it must mean that he is sure of himself, to turn down fifteen thousand pounds."

"It would appear that Kate has given him enough cause to believe that she will take his hand in holy wedlock," said the Earl disdainfully.

"Then we—she, poor darling—are all undone!"

"Not yet, my aunt," said the Earl angrily, remembering the interview. He did not like coming out a loser; it irked him. "You meant for me to woo Kate's heart and make it my own, so I shall! Where is she?"

"Now hold a moment, Branwell," said Sarah frowning. "I meant for you to interest Kate. Not win her heart and then leave her floundering."

He laughed. "Make up your mind, woman. She will recover from her bout with me, and it is, at this moment, Mr. Banyon or me!"

"Oh, dear . . . "

"Where is she?" he repeated.

"In the sewing room . . . but why?"

"Later, Sarah. I have dallied too long!" he said, startling his aunt by swiftly ripping off one of the brass buttons from his dark brown velvet cutaway. Just as swiftly he was gone, leaving his aunt to wonder at the wisdom of such a line of attack!

A lackey polishing the wooden floor at the top of the stairs pointed out the way to the sewing room, and the Earl strode toward it, whistling a lively tune as he entered. He moved across the room apparently totally unaware that Kate, who sat quietly mending a tear in her hem, was curled upon an old battered sofa next to the fire. He continued to whistle as he searched the sewing basket sitting atop a rather worn old desk, all this before Kate's wide gray eyes. She stretched her neck for a better view, wondering what the deuce he was about.

"Er, my lord?" said Kate at length. "Is there something that you need?"

Her voice evidently startled him, for he spun around with a surprised look. "Oh, pardon, I didn't see you here," said the gentleman, looking much like a puppy dog with his nose in the gravy. "I've popped a button and thought I'd sew it on before the plaguey thing gets misplaced. Master Hatch is the best of first mates and doubles as m'valet, but he has his head in the clouds these days. I can rarely find him about," said the Earl, giving her the half-truth, or the half-lie.

"You were going to sew it on yourself?" asked Kate incredulously, for apparently she found this remarkable.

"Is it so hard to believe?" he asked, as though he was about to take affront.

"Well, yes," said the lady honestly.

He laughed, not at all daunted. "If you will but put a needle and thread in my hand, I shall be happy to show you that I am not so unhandy."

It was her turn to laugh, and so she obliged. "Here, my lord, come sit by me. I shall do the thing in a thrice and then you may be on your way!"

He smiled gratefully and came to sit before her on the edge of the sofa. She was obliged to sit directly beneath the line of his chin in order to sew on the button, and found that her heart took on an unsteady beat. She attempted to regulate the activity of her wayward organ by putting on an exceptional show of nonchalance. The Earl felt her nearness, loving the aroma of garden freshness about her. As he sat, he watched her and came to a quick decision. He was worried about his interview with Mr. Banyon. The dratted fellow had the upper hand in this for he could now go and profess his undying love with his disdain for their bribe as evidence! This would have to be nipped, and he knew no better way than spilling out the truth his way, and being first at the thing!

"Kate" he said softly, "I have a confession."

"Oh, hadn't you better wait till I've laid my needle down," she teased.

"I give you leave to use your weapon should you so desire after I tell you what I have done," said he staunchly, fearlessly!

"My, this sounds serious. What besides your attacks on me have you done?" queried she.

"I visited Mr. Banyon this morning and offered him fifteen thousand pounds to leave off courting you," blurted the Earl purposely.

"You what?" shrieked Kate.

"I insulted the fellow," answered the Earl shamefacedly, silently praising his own magnificent acting.

"Oh, my faith! Hell and damnation!" ejaculated the lady very unladylike, bringing the roundness to the Earl's eyes. He was sincerely shocked by her lapse. "How could you? And where did you get such a sum? You must make an excellent living as a pirate!"

"Actually, most of what I make at privateering goes to the crown and my crew. I am quite wealthy you know, family money, but I can't take all the credit here. I but added my five thousand to Sarah's ten!" he said, playing the fool.

"You are without principle," said Kate.

"Indeed we . . . I . . . had the best of intentions. If he were a fortune-hunter, he would have taken the money and would bother you no more. If not he'd probably have challenged me to a duel, which I rather looked forward to, not liking the fellow overmuch. I rather fancied putting an end to him and hoped he'd choose to draw the gauntlet," sighed the Earl.

"Well?" demanded Kate.

"Well what?" returned the Earl.

"What did he say?" thundered Kate.

"Oh, he laughed. Said our fifteen thousand was rather shabby compared to the Grange!" said the Earl, allowing his voice and his eyes to change subtly with the gravity of the words.

Kate sat speechless a moment, digesting this. She had no liking for the sound of Perry's words. Indeed, she rather felt the Earl was correct in thinking Perry should have challenged him to a duel. 'Tis what she would have done were she a man insulted in such a manner.

"That is what he said?" asked Kate, and her frown stemmed from hurt pride. Much worse than that; hurt pride before the Earl was all the more painful.

"Exactly. I've decided his game is deeper than fortune hunting. Fellows of that stamp usually take the offerings from the family and leave things be. Evidently he means to have more."

Kate eyed him, angry with Perry, angry with Sarah, with them all for having created such a situation, but she was not so innocent that she could not believe the Earl was speaking the truth. "His phrasing does not mean that he does not love me," she ventured. Branwell sneered. "Loves you? You can't mean that this convinces you that the puppy, that fashion fop, has a passion for you?" said he, knowing well his aim.

Kate snapped the thread sharply and sat back against the cushion to glare at him. Whether she doubted Perry's sincerity or no, she would not have this arrogant blade behave so to her.

"I don't see that I need convince you of any such thing. It is enough that I know Perry loves me. What you think actually has no interest for me!"

"Oh, you are miffed with me," said the Earl banteringly. "I didn't mean to imply that you were incapable of inspiring passion." He lowered his voice to a penetrating throb. "You know, Kate, to what depths of desire you can drive a man, but Banyon is not in love with you!"

"You are insufferable. Swollen in your belief that you are omniscient, puffed up in your sense of self-consequence. You can not judge fairly others less fortunate than yourself. My faith, you have yourself admitted to me that Perry refused your odious bribe. Is that not proof enough that he cares for me," she blasted him, her eyes and cheeks aflame.

"Poor fondling," he offered gently. "You hurl your insults at me because I bring you such truths, but 'twill not change the situation. And I warrant you the situation needs change." Imperceptibly he had moved closer to her. "You cannot be so foolish as to think you would be happy married to that dratted fellow?" said Branwell, purposely fanning her heat.

"Oh, my God!" said she querulously, putting her hand to her forehead as though in utter disbelief of his attitude. "You are impossible! I know not how to answer you, for in truth you do not hear! This conversation grows dimwitted and intolerable," said Kate, starting to get up from her place on the sofa. He reached out expertly, catching her arm, and twisted her around to fall into his lap. He managed one arm around her shoulder, the other around her waist, firmly holding her in position. He looked into her gray eyes, his own holding her hypnotically. "No, Kate, you shan't run off and thus cover your ears. I shan't let you waste your hot blood, and mark me, fondling, it does burn—but not for such as he! He would encase you in fripperies, clothe you in gentleness and call it respect. But you were formed for more, so much more!" His lips took hers hungrily, possessively sealing his words. This time Kate's will to resist heard not its call. Each of his former embraces had been a battle against her defenses, tearing at her armor, making her aware of her body's sensual needs. She had learned to dream anew and erotically. Those dreams left her hungry and frustrated. She chided herself against such things, but there was no denying the passion his touch aroused within her breast!

Her arms defied her mind as they moved to encircle his neck, allowing him to arch her supple body against him. His hand found its way from her waist to her full round breast, cupping its pleasing form through the velvet texture of her gown. His thumb found and brushed the nipple, glorying in its taut response. She felt hot liquid spin through her veins and blot out her mind's warning call. She only knew that his touch was at this moment a fulfillment of an aching need. His lips whispered her name in her ears and she felt herself lost to him. She knew nought but that the touch of his hand was ecstasy. His lips covered her with searing kisses, burning her eyes, her mouth, her neck, and then finding and parting her mouth once more. She was in a state of fever, though her mind stormed against her weakness! She wanted to cry out against him, for there in his glinting green mirrors was a reflection of herself . . . and her state of abandonment! The sight choked out a sob. "Stop it! Stop it!" she cried, pulling away from him, realizing in that moment that he held her not against her will!

What have I done? she thought, shame clouding her eyes. Where has his kiss taken me? She bit the fullness of her lower lip, and jumped up, backing away from him. He stood up and his body firm, throbbing with desire, towered above her, wanting her. She was frightened because she no longer trusted herself. She was frightened by the glint in his eyes and the angry working of his jaw. "Tell me, fondling," he said tauntingly, "do you inspire such passion in your suckling? Does he make your body ache and burn as I have just done?"

Her fist unclenched itself at her side and found its scathing path across his cheek. He stood the blow well and a slow smile denied its sting. "Whom do you bite, my sweetings, me or yourself?" He turned and left her then, pleased with himself. He had placed the seed of doubt within her; now to watch it grow!

24

Kate swished into her room and threw herself upon her satin covered pillows, mauling them somewhat severely! This accomplished, she gave over to a bout of frenzied tears. The gall of the man. The lecherous gall. His conceit, his arrogance was beyond anything. But what was worse, far, far worse, was her own detestable reaction to his love-making!

She remembered what her friend Lizzie Tucker had so often taunted at her: "The callings of the flesh have little to do with love, Kate, little to do with love. Callings of the flesh . . ." The words rattled in her mind, jarred her battling spirits, ravishing her soul! "No! No! No!" She pounded at her fragile pillows, bludgeoning their down with her wretchedness. Yet, her imperishable need to see herself as she was came to the fore and waved its unwanted form. It bared itself before her and dared her to deny. She could not, and shame filled her gentle cheeks! She had burned beneath the Earl's touch. She hated his life style, his rakish use of her, his dominance, his devilish green eyes, yet she had wanted him!

She tried putting him from her thoughts, but even now, in the seclusion of her room, she could still feel his arms around her, and the tingling sensation perpetuated the fever burning within her. He had infuriated her with his jibs. What had he meant about Perry not loving her, not wanting her? Hadn't he admitted that Perry could not be bribed? Why then did he believe Perry had no passion for her? This pricked her ego, for she was at the point of womanhood and such things, though one rarely understands why, do fret a lovely girl. She gave over to darkening speculations.

Branwell had said Perry would clothe her in gentleness. What meant he by such a remark? Indeed, as of yet, she had not had any uncontrolled desire to melt into Perry's arms, nor had he really attempted to inspire such desire! Why? Perhaps his sense of propriety would preclude such advances on his part. Perhaps. She shrugged over this problem, and supposed that a gentleman did not attempt to seduce his future wife. Wife? She had not said she would marry Perry, and the more time that passed, the less she really wanted to. But was she sure?

Eliza sauntered into the room, a humming lilt to her voice. Her arms were laden with freshly pressed linens, and she plopped them unceremoniously upon the vanity swivel chair, sending a questioning smile to her mistress, who had immediately buried her face, avoiding her maid's eye.

"Feeling out of sorts, miss?" asked Eliza, tilting her head as she moved about putting away the various pieces of laundry.

Kate sighed to herself; she needed someone to talk to. She was too confused to sort out her own mind. She turned, giving Eliza a full view of her blurry eyes. "Yes, I am out of sorts and wretched."

Eliza immediately swung over to the bed and put a comforting arm about Kate, making Kate feel every bit the child, when she was in fact the girl's senior! "There, there, miss, whatever it be, 'twill be better soon. 'Tis the way of things."

"Not this time. I am in a devil of a state."

"About what?"

"About everything. Oh, Eliza, I know nothing about men and women. Well, very little and lately . . ."

Eliza laughed. "Nothing wrong with that. I knows what ye be feeling, miss, 'tis natural ye do. I've been hot for bedding these six months 'n' more. That's when I met m'John. But, lordy, come next week I'll be his wife and all our fretting will be ended," said Eliza with a happy sigh.

"I know, Eliza, and it's that pleased I am for you, but, well what I am trying to find out is . . . John's respect for you didn't change because . . . because . . . "

"Because I let him fondle me before our wedding day? Lordy no! John be a stud . . . lordy, thinking of him makes m'blood boil. No, he couldn't keep his hands off me . . . and I don't mind pleasing him. Keeps him from going to town for his needs . . . without taking away my virginity. He'll have that on m'wedding night and not before!"

"What keeps him from going to town?" asked Kate, opening her eyes wide.

"Lordy, miss, I shouldn't be telling ye this much. Your Miss Ellen would whop me proper!"

"Eliza, I have no one else, and there are things I must know."

Eliza looked her over and frowned. "Ye best promise me never to say nuthin' to anyone about this, miss."

"I promise!" said Kate eagerly.

Eliza plopped down beside her immediately and amidst giggles, hand gestures, and rolling eyes, began explaining some of the mysteries involved with the art of making love without becoming deflowered.

Kate felt her cheeks hot during most of the rendition, and utter disbelief at some of what she heard, but it seemed to make sense, and she sat back after its end to think it over. Eliza continued to go about her business, giggling now and then over Kate's dumbfounded condition. At last Kate sat forward again, calling Eliza's attention. "What if a man didn't seem to *want* to seduce you, yet he says he wants to marry you?"

"I heard tell how flash coves—that is, gentry—treat their intended just so, but then they goes to town and visits the ladies of pleasure, they do. Or they keeps them a fancy piece in a room the other side of town! Sometimes they do that . . . even after they be wed," said Eliza knowingly.

"Oh," said Kate in a small voice. Then with a heavy sigh, laying her vanity bare: "Perry doesn't seem to want me."

"Do ye want him?" asked Eliza, glancing thoughtfully at her.

"I don't know. He is handsome, thoughtful, charming. Perhaps I could, if he were more romantic." She pulled at her coverlet. "I just don't know how to go about making him kiss me."

"Lordy, miss, with a body like yers 'tis an easy enough thing to do," crowed Eliza with incredulity at Kate's simpleness.

"Is it? I tell you what, Eliza. I don't do a thing to encourage Lord Mannering, and yet he pursues me with his unwanted favors! But 'tis not so with Perry."

Eliza cackled. "That one don't need no urging, miss. Gawd, don't you know anything about studs? No, I can sees that ye don't. He be a buck, a rutting one at that!"

"And Perry? How could I get Perry to act romantically?"

"Are you certain you wants that?"

"If I am ever to tell whether or not Perry is the one to be my husband I think I should first find out whether or not he makes me . . . passionate," said Kate, blushing furiously.

Eliza cackled once again. "It queers me how you can want a mere lad when ye can have a man!"

"But Eliza, the Earl doesn't want to marry me, just seduce me."

"Aye, that usually be the way with such 'uns." She sighed sadly.

"So what do you think I should do . . . about Perry?" pursued Kate.

"What? Oh well, as to that, show him some bosom, miss, unwrap yeself, tease his eyes, then watch his hands stray!"

"Oh, Eliza, I don't know if I can do that. I should die to be so brazen," exclaimed Kate.

"Lordy, there ain't nought to it," Eliza said, going to the wardrobe and pulling out a lovely printed muslin. It had a false red velvet vest with tie-strings lacing it closed. Eliza pointed to its lacings. " 'Tis easy enough, miss; don't wear any small clothes, and leave the lacings undone."

"How could I? Nell would never let me out so . . . "

"Miss Ellen don't 'ave to get a glimmer of ye. Jest don yer cloak and pull it tight round ye, till ye meet him alone."

"Oh, Eliza, I don't know if I can."

" 'Tis up to ye, for in truth I prefers the Earl," said Eliza, shrugging her shoulders.

Kate jumped up from the bed. "The Earl indeed! Here, Eliza, help me undo my buttons; we'll have to hurry for 'tis close onto the hour now, and if I'm to meet Perry as arranged I must hurry!"

A few moments later, Eliza stood back and grinned. She had brushed Kate's long black hair until it hinted of stars, and Kate chose to wear it loosely hanging down her well-shaped back. The red lacings were left loosely tied from the low cut bosom to the tight-fitting waist and the voluptuousness of her well-rounded breasts taunted the eye. Kate gazed at herself in the mirror and blushed. "Oh Eliza, I look a doxy!"

"No sech thing! Why half the female gentry strut about in gowns you can see right to the flesh, but mind now, don't be flinging your cloak away or you'll startle him half to death. Ease it slow, now, while ye be talking, lean into a tree careless like, let it pull away. Be unaware . . . be . . ."

"Be cunning!" interrupted Kate sadly. "Oh, I wish it didn't have to be like this."

"Ye got to make up yer mind, miss. If ye be going to do it, ye got to be convinced it be the right thing or forego it!"

Kate threw her arms about Eliza and gave her a hug, then quickly hugging the cloak tightly about her, made her way down the rear staircase to the back door and out! She was to meet Perry where the wooded path met the brook and forked off to the east. She scurried over the path, slowing down as she sighted him in the distance, and tried to regain her breath. He saw her and came forward to meet her, her name upon his lips. He took her ungloved hand between his own and she felt him press it feverishly to his mouth, but this elicited no fire in her veins.

"Dearest," he whispered, drawing her hand through his arm and guiding her into the thicket where they could talk in private. "Your family will stop at nothing to prevent me from making you my wife." he said sadly, his tone portending much.

"I have not yet said I would marry you," said Kate quietly.

He eyed her quickly, hungrily. "But my darling, my love, I understood."

". . . that it was too soon to press me, that I had not yet made up my mind," she said, allowing her gray eyes to drink in his handsome features.

He brushed the blond fringe away from his eyes and gazed longingly into her face. "My dearest, I adore you, but how can I court you, win your heart, when your family offers me insults?"

"Yes, I know, 'tis horrid of them. The Earl told me of your meeting this morning and I most humbly beg your pardon," said Kate.

He looked startled. "The Earl told you?"

"Yes," she said, moving a bit away from him, turning to face him as she leaned back against a tall elm. The ribbon of her cloak had gone loose and the pressure of her move against the tree pulled at the velvet material, parting it down the center, and Perry had a view of her exquisite figure. She followed his eyes as he discovered her tantalizing breasts and her cheeks went hot. Oh God, she thought miserably, how could you, Kate? What are you doing? You need not resort to such things to know if you love him or not. Time will tell! But she didn't want to wait; she wanted to know now!

She wanted to know what his kiss would do to her. Would it penetrate her soul? Would his touch ignite her heart? Would he arouse her as the Earl had done? He stood gazing at her, not moving closer to her, and she frowned. "Perry, why do you want to marry me?"

"Why? Can you ask? Because I adore you. Never say they have made you doubt me!" he said coming forward, his blue eyes exploring her face, down the line of her neck, intently devouring the curve of her breasts, panting at the nearness, the possibility of more. However, his frown did not fade. He reached her and his hand took up her chin and without a word his lips pressed to hers. His kiss was gentle, loving, his caress upon her neck that of one who worships. There was a tenderness in his touch, overriding all thought of passion. She felt him tremble, felt his body arch against her own, and suddenly knew she didn't want him to go further, but before she could stop him he pulled away from her! His voice was low and hoarse and he gave her his back. "Is that what you want, Kate? My lust? You have it, bared before you. Yes, I want you, but I shan't take you till you are my wife. I love you, Kate; do you think I would do you the injustice of treating you as less than you deserve?" he asked, beating his fist into his open hand.

"But Perry . . . " said Kate, wondering at his pain.

"My darling," he said, turning to her, "I can stand it no longer being near to you, wanting you, yet taking you not. That is one of the reasons I have decided to leave for London. I go on the morrow, but when I return it will be to make you mine. I will come with a special license, and Kate, I will come with the hope that you will be ready to accept me."

"You go to London?" she asked, surprised.

"Yes, my love." He took out an envelope and placed it in her hands. "This is my direction should you wish to write me. I shan't be gone over a month."

"I see," she said slowly, a frown creasing her features, as she pocketed the paper.

He kissed her hands and suddenly she was alone, watching his retreating footsteps, sure of only one thing: his kiss had not melted her soul! No bells had rung, no lightning had struck and the earth had not wobbled beneath her feet. Only one thing had happened: she had wanted to escape his arms!

The sound of a familiar male voice made her jump with a hand to her heart and her cloak fell to the cool earth. "What a most touching scene!" mocked the Earl of Mannering, coming upon her as though through some hidden woodland door!

She stooped to pick up her cloak, but as she rose and attempted to draw it around her, she found him towering dangerously above her, his eyes ravishing her body with calculated deliberation. The next thing she knew she was pressed up against the tree, held there by the rigidness of his firm body. "Did you come here to find passion, fondling? Does it trouble you that his proprieties forbid such pleasantries? It surely must pique you after so adroit a performance! Would you care to act the harlot for me? I promise you a far better audience." There was a shade of anger in his tone, something Kate did not understand. Why should he be angry? What business was it of his?

"Stand out of my way, cur!" she snapped. "Or at least allow me to draw on my cloak. I shall catch cold!"

He moved back a step, but though she clutched the cloak with one hand, it was her intent to escape. She made a lunge for freedom and found herself held around the waist, her feet some inches from the ground. He laughed derisively, and still the sound of distemper fettered his tone. She found herself lying upon her cloak on a bed of pine needles, with a root of a tree digging into her back, and the Earl straddling her with one arm and one leg. This would seem little strapping to hold a strong lady down, yet held firm she was. She contorted in an attempt to escape his hold and the discomfort of the root pressing through the material into her back, and he laughed, "So much effort, fondling? Do you indeed wish to escape?" He nestling his nose into the fresh scent of her free-flowing hair.

"Yes, confound you! There is a branch or something threatening to sever my spine and you are as heavy as an ox!" snapped the lady, for some odd reason unafraid.

He grinned broadly, sliding her over and away from

the offensive root, situating her into the crook of his angled embrace. His hand found the loose lacings of her bodice and with a swift sharp movement the thing was snapped. The two layers of material separated exposing her lush full breasts and as she struggled, his hand fondled them. She beat at his chest and shoulder, but he slid over and mounted her partially, one strong hand catching and clasping her wrists above her head as his mouth burned her own.

He continued to hold her wrists vice-like above her head as his mouth strayed to the pleasing rosebud nipples. His tongue tortured her with its fire, teasing her tautness from her against her will. His free hand reluctantly left the supple breasts, hitching up the muslin of her gown to wander over her smooth thighs, forcing its way between their pleasing curves and finding the softness of hair pocketed therein. She gasped at his ministrations only to be silenced by his lips. He took and separated her mouth and as his tongue teased its way into its cherry opening, his finger found its way to virgin territory.

She felt a starburst explode in a canyon of blackness, and it was beyond her means to control the fire. Her body arched as he plunged his seeking finger into her honeycomb, and she knew herself lost to his passion and her own. She wanted to thow her arms about him and beg him for more, but managed still, in spite of her hungry yearning pressing body, to beat at his chest when she found her hands free. He had released her wrists to work at his breeches, nearly tearing the buttons off in his haste. He wanted her, he was going to have her, *now!* And then he heard her sob! He was on fire. Every inch of his body was in need of her. She awakened more than lust in him, much more, though he knew only that it resulted, this awakening, in an all-consuming fire. But he heard her sob. He was parting her legs with his knees, he was holding her, aiming his pulsating manhood just inches away from its goal, when he saw her frightened eyes. He halted himself, blinking as though to regain his sight, and he saw a woman-child . . . a warm, full bodied woman-child—and she was at his mercy!

Damnation, he thought, for she panted still; even in her fear she panted. He wanted her more than he had ever wanted a woman before and he was near to taking the brazen little thing. Obviously she wanted someone to take her. She was ripe for it; hadn't she come out here to that damnable fellow? But the truth of it was she was a virgin, and something caught at him. He would not marry her! Good Lord, the thought of marriage nearly sent him flying off her!

He stopped himself, rolled over and sat up to button his breeches. She lay there for a moment afraid to move, watching him as he got to his feet. He turned and leaned over, grabbing her hand and pulling her to her feet, and the closeness of her sent rivulets of exploding bubbles through his veins. He had controlled himself but he wanted to lash out. He picked her cloak up and threw it around her shoulders, tying the strings to hide her nakedness. He was in a fever, oblivious to the fact that she shook from the experience, oblivious to her shame and confusion. He was an animal crazed with conflicting emotions. "You are a hot-blooded bitch, Cousin Kate! You detest the sight of me, yet when I stroked those well-formed lines of yours, you were quite willing to give your all. Damn, how you have remained a virgin, if you are one, is more than I can fathom!" he spit.

She gasped, for his words took on bold matter, making their sharp path into her flesh, drawing blood. She had but one recourse and it came with tears. "I hate you!" she slashed, returning his blow!

He stood alone as she vanished before his eyes and he leaned back into the sturdy tree. With a sigh, a weary, miserable sigh, he did up the buttons of his greatcoat. A troubled expression lined his face and it stemmed from his heart. He knew Kate to be an innocent; something that had nought to do with logic drummed this into his senses. From the moment his hand had gone between her legs, he had known. Yet, she had wanted him to take her. He was no fool and there was no covering this choice fact. The chit had burned with acquiescence. He knew that this was due to his experienced handling, yet perversely it irritated him to find her willing. He was aware of this strange contradiction which further instilled him with cause for agitation! And, if this was not enough to tease a man's soul, there was the fact that he had followed her into the woods to discover her attempting to seduce young Perry!

He had seen her flight into the woods earlier and instinctively knew she was going to meet Banyon. He followed to make sure Banyon took no unfair advantage, only to observe the lady in the role of seductress. He watched her adept little maneuver with her cloak and had an overwhelming desire to beat Perry into a pulp when he observed him kissing her. Then Perry was gone and the Earl had wanted to teach the lady a lesson. Only it had gone further than he had intended. He had discovered he had little control over himself where Kate was concerned. Now he felt thoroughly a cad, and there was an ache in his gut. He returned to the house in her wake, his mood black and his determination bent on leaving immediately for London. He wanted away from the plaguey chit and the entire affair. He reached the library, coming in from the rear of the house, and dropped his outer garments onto a stainwood wall bench. He heard voices coming from the room and entered it, set on advising his aunt of his imminent departure.

"Branwell," called his aunt, "come in, love. I am so glad that you are here, for we have had an excellent notion, Miss Ellen and I."

"Oh?" he said, putting up one of his thick dark brows and moving toward the brandy decanter.

"Yes, we are thinking of leaving for London. Tomorrow," said Sarah, beaming wide.

He snorted, "I am leaving today!"

"What?" cried Sarah, standing up. "What is wrong?"

"Everything, pet. Look, Sarah, if the chit is determined to have the suckling fop, so be it!"

"No, oh never," cried Nell. "You are forgetting . . . their relationship!"

"Yes I am! Confound it, this thing is driving me to distraction! What does it matter anymore? Perhaps we should tell her the truth."

"No, Branwell, that would mean tearing at the memory of her father, and my sister. I couldn't do that," said Sarah.

He sighed and put a comforting arm about his aunt. "She will not be weaned if her heart is in it."

"Her heart is not in it, and you must already know that. Branwell, you must help us!" cried Sarah.

"Yes, perhaps when we are in London she will forget about Mr. Banyon," said Nell hopefully.

"Mr. Banyon goes to London, too," said the Earl, dropping a bomb.

"Oh bother!" exploded Sarah. "Then we shall remain here."

"No, my lady, I still think it would be better if we went to London. There would be the theater and some dinner parties, after all. They might take her mind away from Mr. Banyon."

"Yes, and, Branwell, you could continue to escort us about and be charming," said Sarah thoughtfully.

"Charming and seductive—is that my lot?" he teased, the laugh back in his eye.

"Oh, Branwell, you must do so; you cannot let him ruin her life," said Sarah fretfully.

"He means to have her, Sarah, for some sick reason of his own, and he is not above or beyond taking her to bed in order to achieve his goal."

"How can he? 'Tis unthinkable!" said Nell, putting a handkerchief to her eyes at such a horrendous thought.

"He means to have the Grange. 'Tis an obsession with him, and you are right, Sarah, I don't mean to let him accomplish his aim!" said the Earl, thinking suddenly of Kate's large gray eyes.

"Then you will help?" said Sarah hopefully.

Once again, Kate's sad eyes loomed before his mind,

and the feel of her body in his hands tickled his being. He wanted her, and he was not about to let any other have her!

"Yes, Sarah, I shall continue to do what I can," he answered quietly.

Kate moved away from the door, and with a sudden stabbing pain piercing her chest she ran to the staircase. She had come seeking her aunt, for she would have to tell her that she could no longer reside in the same house with Branwell, not after his usage, and then she heard them talking!

Branwell had been attempting to seduce her simply to win her affections away from Perry! The knowledge that his every move, his kisses, his touch had been but an exhibition with an aim hurt her pride and stung her heart! But what was more disturbing was what she had heard about Perry. What had they meant about telling her the truth? Tearing away at the memory of her parents? What had they meant when they talked of 'her relationship' with Perry. A sickening notion crept into her mind.

Kate had been sheltered, true; but slowly, systematically the lacy froth of life had shed itself. She knew that men could be unfaithful. Had her father been unfaithful to her mother? Was Perry his illegitimate son? Was Perry her half-brother? Oh God! The thought sent her hand through her hair and then back to her pulsating forehead. If that were true her father would have been unfaithful to her mother in their first year of marriage!

It couldn't be true. Yet what of her father's dying words, his confessions of sin, of unhallowed crimes, of her mother having to forgive him? Oh, but it couldn't be true! It was not true. Perry would never propose, he would never have kissed her today, said he wanted to marry her! She was allowing her imagination to run amuck! She would drive such idiotic thoughts away, and she did. The only thought that returned to haunt was the knowledge that the Earl's kisses had stemmed from one thing, a desire

to achieve a goal, that goal being to prevent her marriage
to Perry!

25

London beat beneath an April sky. It was in the
height of revelry. 'Twas the season for fairs, for minstrels
to rave about the oncoming spring, and, indeed, the sun
did shine. Somewhere, outside their confines, hung the
threat of Napoleon and his hints of invasion. Ah, bah!
scoffed the Londoner, invade England indeed! Somewhere, outside England, in foreign waters and foreign
lands, English soldiers fought French and Spanish. Pitt's
voice was heard in the House of Commons and at the
Admiralty. The *Post*, the *Herald*, and the *Chronicle*
printed their own comments, and the fashionable aris-
tocracy bandied talk of war, but routs and balls raged on!

Kate found herself in London, and her aunt's house
was very much a house of fashion, with notables coming
and going at all hours of the day and night! Two days
they had been here and two days found Kate deeper sunk
in melancholy.

Aunt Sarah fussed over her, coerced her, and battered
her with unfailing merry spirits, pleading her cause,
begging Kate to leave her room. But Kate's gray eyes
molded sadness, and her lips did not part in smile, and
she would not leave her room.

Nell clucked gently, then badgered with scolding, turned
to coddling and fretting over her, and Kate wanted only
to turn her face to the wall. Everything was wrong! She
felt heartsick. She wanted no food, she wanted no company. From the moment Branwell had nearly taken her
in Grange woods—no, from the moment he had stung
her with his words, "hot-blooded bitch . . . you detest the
sight of me yet . . . you were willing . . ."—she had felt

herself lost to self-reflection, and that inner seeking was beating her soul!

What shame bore down ploddingly upon her mind was the admission to herself that he was right. She had been hot-blooded, she had said she loathed him, and she had been willing to let him take her. His touch was all that had mattered!

She had run back to the house, swearing to tell her aunt, swearing never to look upon his face again, and then the sound of their voices swept that thought aside. She had heard her loved ones at their secrets. She had heard Branwell! Branwell, who pretended to want her, who tore off her clothes with a passion that had aroused her own. Branwell's purpose was not love; lord, 'twas not even desire; it was but the attempt to wean her affections from Perry! Perry . . . she didn't even want Perry! But she did want to know the truth! What were all the whispers about? What had they meant? It cluttered her thoughts. But when Branwell entered her mind, his name, his face swimming before her, her tears started again!

Branwell, he hadn't even bothered to come by these two days. She couldn't snub him if he wasn't going to give her the opportunity. He had left the Grange before them, and he hadn't bothered to even try to say goodbye. Deuce take him! How was he suppose to follow out her aunt's instructions if he wouldn't even come by?

Branwell had arrived at his London town house and found there a desk full with mail. He fingered through these to find a note from the Prime Minister. It was curt and evidently hurriedly composed. There was to be a dinner party and the Venetian couple would be there. Evidently he had arrived none too soon, as it was for the following evening.

He had gone up wearily to a hot bath, where he found himself dozing off. He fancied he felt long silken, black hair brush against his cheek and he saw Kate's face, innocently asking to be taken. His body throbbed with a sudden need for her and he rose from his bath, hungry and frustrated. He dropped off to sleep, but his dreams left him unrested, and when he rose the next morning he was out of temper. But there were things to be done.

His butler pulled open the velvet hangings on Branwell's bed, allowing the morning sun to flash unmercifully across his eyes. "Damnation, man!" thundered the Earl. "What the devil are you about?"

"Your orders were to wake you promptly at nine with fresh coffee," answered the man peevishly.

"Faith, man, did they include anything about bathing me in sunlight?" groaned the Earl, shooting him a smile to soften the words.

The butler knew better than to retort, and went about serving his lordship in silent subjugation. Some forty minutes later saw the Earl clothed and ready to depart. As he awaited his horse, he fidgeted in the hall of his majestic town house. Damn but he felt like putting his fist through a wall. What he needed was a round with Gentleman Jackson, and so he would go later that day!

He was acutely uncomfortable, for his state of mind as well as his body seemed pinpricked and he was unable to isolate the cause. He was certain of only one thing: his body ached for Kate. Odd, he thought to himself, he had often ached for a woman and then after the need made itself known, various ladies of his acquaintance would pop into his mind without any strong preference. Now he knew his body burned, but it burned for Kate. He knew that at this moment no other would still his aching for very long!

When he arrived before a fashionable-looking club, sporting a bowed window overlooking St. James, he gave his horse into the keeping of an ostler and made his way into the elegant halls of the fashionable Watiers!

His top hat was flung together with his greatcoat into the hands of a waiting lackey, and the Earl made his leisurely way to one of the club's card rooms. He looked every bit the Corinthian. The cut of his brown velvet coat was molded to his virile form, as were the buff-colored knit breeches. His waistcoat was of the finest embroidered tan silk, and his hessians shone like mirrors.

Beau Brummell raised his quizzing glass and leveled it upon the Earl's form before awarding his friend a smile. "Excellent, Bran, you may enter."

"Beau, you devil, never say you would ostracize even me if I didn't meet with your approval?" laughed the Earl, coming forward to lay a heavy but friendly hand upon the Beau's shoulder.

The Beau was the arbiter of fashion. His word was law in the kingdom of good taste, and he was well aware of his power. He took a pinch of snuff with a grace that often inspired admiration and gave the Earl a hidden smile. "Do you doubt it?"

"No, indeed I do not, you rogue," grinned the Earl. "Now, Beau, come; I would have a word with you," he said, linking his arm and drawing him away from a cluster of men. "Tell me, what know you about the Count Mirabel of Venice?"

The Beau raised a beautiful eye. "That his sister finds favor in Prinny's eye."

"Other than that."

"Should there be more?" said the Beau carefully.

"Don't play the fool with me, my friend. Lady Moravia would find favor in all our eyes."

"*Ehmmm*, and I'd like to wager Alvanley, for he'd wager on anything, that she'll be in your bed before she finds her way to Prinny's," the Beau chuckled.

"Be sure and make that bet; it may save you yet from debtor's prison. But seriously, and between us, what else do you know?"

"Very well, I don't know what your game is but there are things to stagger the mind. Such as, the count and his lovely stepsister fawn over our illustrious and foolish old prime minister just as equally as they do over Fox! Is it not odd? Fox and Pitt at each other's throats, standing for two entirely different things, and yet our Venetian visitors caress each one."

"What else?"

"They engage the oddest of all creatures as some hireling or other. He looks every bit a toad, and dresses no better than one. Comes and goes from their hotel rooms at all hours, though they don't seem to enjoy having him seen! Calls himself Walepole!"

"Anything else, Beau?"

"No. Now what is it about? Branwell, you might as well tell me; I shall find out in the end," said the Beau.

"Devil is in it that I haven't figured their game, but depend upon it they play one!" said the Earl thoughtfully. George (Beau) Brummell sent the Earl a long calculating look before he said lightly, "Had a visitor last evening."

"Oh?" said the Earl, frowning still.

"A mutual, how shall I term this, yes, a mutual lover," grinned the Beau.

The Earl glanced at him with some surprise. "Shall I bother to ask who the lovely is or do you mean to tell me in your own good time?"

The Beau smiled wickedly. "Come, let's go to the gaming room and place our bets."

"Devil a bit, George. I want to know what you're jabbering about," laughed the Earl, not at all put out.

"Luck has it that your heart ain't in it, so I've nothing to fret over, but thought it might interest you to know."

"Well then?" said the Earl, his mind roving over many of the pretties he had been intimately acquainted with these past few months.

"In my own good time," chuckled the Beau, leading him to the gaming table.

26

As the Earl's coach made the paces to 10 Downing Street that evening, his mind strayed to Kate. He had had no opportunity to pay a visit to Sarah's that day.

Had he not been weighted down with affairs of state he would have been hard put to it to keep himself away. Even now, on his way to the Prime Minister's dinner party, he had an itching to stop by, even if for a moment, to catch a glimpse of her face. Ah, *bah!* What nonsense was he at? Catch a glimpse of her face indeed! What had he to do with such youthful thoughts?

Soon he would have to take her, and in his taking of her, he would banish her torturous threads from his heart. The glowing lights of Mr. Pitt's handsome home caught his eye and he banished such flights of thought away. He must concentrate on the business at hand!

Hundreds of brilliant tapers glittered in the dining room of the Prime Minister's home. The crystal chandeliers reflected the lights and colors of the fashionable guests as they meandered about, champagne sparkling from their glasses and in their eyes.

The Earl's arrival was announced in stentorian issue as he entered the room, and he was immediately met. Lady Hester, the Prime Minister's favorite niece and hostess, came forward. She was tall, elegant, vivacious, with clear sharp eyes—enough to make one believe her beautiful. "La, Branwell, you rogue, where have you been, you wretch? For wherever it was it was sure to be exciting, while we have been wasting away here at home."

He took up her hand and put it lightly to his lips. "Whatever I have done, wherever I have been, have all been for nought as such things took me from you," he said gallantly.

She rapped his white-gloved hand with her fan. "Liar!" said she, smiling brightly.

Lady Hester led him into the room where they were joined by the Beau and the Duchess of York. The Duchess was much loved by the beau monde, and rarely to be found outside her home at Oatlands. When there, she was surrounded by some forty or fifty dogs, and she had brought with her to Prime Minister Pitts's home one of her pets. It sat crooked in her arm, and she pushed it at the Earl for his admiration. "My Poo is pleased to see you, Branwell. What news have you of Nelson?" asked the Duchess, coming right to the point.

He smiled down into her china blue eyes. "Why, what news could I have and where the devil is my host?" asked he, changing the subject.

"Closeted with Lord Elgin and Melville," said the Beau pointedly.

"Oh, how goes that?" asked the Earl.

"How do you suppose? Melville will have to resign his office in the end," answered Lady Hester. "But Branwell, do tell us of Nelson, where do you suppose he is?"

"Exactly where he should be," said the Earl, flicking her straight nose with an affectionate smile.

"My uncle knows. I'd swear to it. So you must have told him when you first returned to town last month." She turned suddenly as two newcomers entered upon the threshold. "Ah . . . I see our Venetian guests have arrived. Excuse me, darlings," said Lady Hester, going forward to welcome them.

Lord Grenville sidled over, shaking a broken hors d'oeuvre fork at the assembled little group. "Look at this! How can Pitt have such a fork as this . . . 'tis useless!"

The Beau put his quizzing glass up and inspected the objectionable utensil before allowing his intimidating eye to run over Grenville's pompous form. He neither smiled, nor appeared grave, as he replied glibly, "It has often come to my notice that our illustrious prime minister sometimes uses very slight and weak instruments to effect his ends."

Grenville snorted, adding bitterly, "You are in there, Beau. Damn, but we have not one officer to oppose our external and internal enemies."

Lady Hester had returned with the Count Alban Mirabel and his stepsister, Lady Moravia. It was notable to the gentlemen present that the lady was an eye-catching beauty. While not as tall as Lady Hester, she had an imposing figure, full and well displayed. Her complexion was creamy, her eyes dark and lit with flames, beneath long curling lashes and dark thinly arched brows. Her dark, auburn-tinted curls were cropped short around her oval face, but its lengths had been allowed to grow at the back of her head and were collected at the top in cascading ringlets. She was twenty-two and the Earl wondered again how she had managed to keep herself single.

Her stepbrother, some four years older, was tall, thin, and elegantly clothed. His dark chestnut curls fell upon his forehead Brutus-like and his dark eyes were bright and friendly. He smiled easily as Lady Hester made the introductions and hastened to put them at their ease.

"Please," he said, gesturing with his hands, "we interrupt what I am certain was to be a most delightful conversation."

"Indeed, Grenville here made a most provocative statement. He thinks we have no officer fierce enough to lead us," said the Duchess of York calculatingly.

"Ah, how so? You do not think of Admiral Nelson?" asked the Count much surprised. "His name, I assure you, carries much weight in Austria."

"And what of in Venice?" asked the Earl. "You are actually residents of Venice?"

The Count turned his dark eyes to the Earl, but his amicable grin had not faded. "To be sure, we are residents of Venice and as such are now beneath the protection of Austria."

"To answer your question," interpolated Grenville, putting a hand to his long chin, "Nelson is thought highly of, but 'tis but the sea he commands. What of our army?"

"The English army is but the laughing stock of Europe!" put in yet another young lord, joining the conversation.

They turned to find Lord Malmesbury upon them, and under their digesting eyes, he added to his previously salty statement, "Pitt's military administration is that of a driveler!"

"Is that so, my friend?" asked the Prime Minister, bearing down upon them.

They looked up into the face of a man who at forty-six had lost the youthful beauty that had marked him when he first took office some eighteen years before. His cheeks had filled out to the point of puffiness and his complexion, as well as his limping oversized foot, spoke of unmerciful gout. But for all that, he was one of the finest, most even-tempered of men, whose sole aim had been to give himself to his country. He was quite used to criticism. He greeted the Count heartily and turned to his stepsister. "So good to see you again, Lady Moravia. I hope my guests have not been boring you with our domestic squabbles?"

"Oh no, sir, I find the discussion fascinating," said the lady beneath her lashes.

"But where are Melville and Elgin?" asked Lady Hester of her uncle, and the frown tainted her features.

"I am afraid pressing business took them. But never mind, never mind. We shall do." He turned and motioned a servant to bring him some port. "It's bound to kill me in the end, but better that I shall be able to say I enjoyed the living for 'tis no use prolonging the dying," chuckled Pitt.

They had attracted to them a growing number of guests, all hanging on Pitt's words and hoping for more. A man in the company ventured, "Come on, William ole boy, where the devil is Nelson? I'd swear you know, and I've been trying to convince this idiot at my side that he is half-cocked if he thinks Nelson ain't in the thick of it!"

Pitt laughed at his oldest and best of his friends, George Ross. "Now how should I know that, George?"

Lord Grenville sniggered. "No doubt he has fallen in with yet another whore."

The Earl's face took on an angry glow as he swirled to face him. "That is beneath you, and certainly not something that should be speculated upon with ladies present!"

However, having entered upon such a line, Lord Grenville found it difficult to retract. "Damn it, Branwell, everyone knows about Nelson and Lady Hamilton. I ain't saying nought that hasn't passed through the minds of everyone here."

The room was deadly still as the two opposing forces faced each other. " 'Tis passed through the filth in your mind, perhaps, and had best be left there."

"Indeed, Lord Grenville, Admiral Nelson must always inspire admiration," interrupted Lady Hester. "Now come, Beau, I want your opinion on the marvelous snuff box I purchased this morning."

The Beau raised his brow. "I did not give you leave to take snuff, my love." His tone teased.

"Do you think it offensive for a woman to do so?" she asked, frowning slightly, for she respected the Beau.

"For any woman, yes; for you, no! You are the only female of my acquaintance who could carry the thing off with aplomb." He smiled into her eyes and allowed her to lead him off.

The Earl watched them go a moment, noting for the hundredth time that Lady Hester was the only female that caused the Beau's heart to flicker in his eyes. He returned his attention to the Count Mirabel and Lady Moravia!

Sometime later that evening the Earl meandered his way into his library. The fire had nearly burned itself out, as had most of the candles. He went to his desk and sat down, putting a hand through his black locks. Lady Moravia and her stepbrother were a close-mouthed pair. Finding out the sway of their ken was going to be a difficult job. As a weary sigh escaped him, his eyes discovered a familiar pink notepaper and absently he picked it up. 'Twas from Lady Claire. He slit the envelope and quickly perused the contents:

Dearest Branwell,

My servant advises me you have returned to town. Naughty boy, how have you kept away from me so long?

Papa will be away from home tomorrow and I shall be alone. Come promptly at two in the afternoon for

there is an urgent matter I must discuss with you
immediately.

With love,
Claire

He swore silently. Curse the female. He had no liking
for meeting her in her own home. He had arranged that
they would meet at his own lodgings in the future and
her missive irked him. There was something disrespectful about taking her in the Viscount's house. He wondered
what all the urgency was about and determined that
his meeting with her would be accomplished speedily
and without their usual love-making! This latest obligation
so irritated him that when he tried sleep, some little time
later, it was with much difficulty that he finally dropped
off. Just before he did, a pair of gray round eyes loomed
before him and he fancied the aroma of spring as he
snuggled his face into his pillow and thought it the
folds of long black hair.

27

Lady Claire's long honey-colored hair flowed negligently down her bare back. Her gown lay strewn across
the sofa's back as she stood pointing her naked breasts
at the fire glowing in her father's study!

Her butler, following her instructions, directed the Earl
to the study, but refrained from leading or announcing
him. Thus it was the Earl of Mannering let himself into
the dimly lit room. He stopped short and closed the
door at his back before turning his attention to her.

She turned to meet his gaze, hands on hips, legs spread
slightly apart and firmly planted on the hearth rug. She
was slender, her small round breasts were firm, and their
mauve blooms teased his eyes. She called his name and

swayed toward him, daring him to touch her. His eyes wandered over her hips and found the honey-colored summit at her thighs. He felt a rigidness work itself against his tight-fitting breeches as his excitement rose within. He was enthralled with her brazen movements and yet somehow, inexplicably repelled by them. Her aggressiveness irked him in some strange unfathomable way, but he went forward and took her into his strong bruising embrace. As his mouth sought hers, he remembered the feel of Kate, so totally different! He could feel Kate's gray eyes taunting his soul, whispering her charms, and the flesh that he held felt suddenly repulsive. He set Claire away from him and his eyes flitted with his inner conflict. "What is the urgency you wrote me about?" he asked hoarsely.

She laughed. "You are beholding it, my darling." She pulled at his neckcloth, laughing when he wrenched himself free. "La, darling, you can't mean to take me in full dress?" she teased, reaching up to pull off his coat.

He frowned. "Where is your father, Claire?"

"He went to hear Pitt in the House of Commons. Then he goes to dinner with the Cowpers. Come on, my darling!"

At that precise moment, the parlor door opened to emit the Viscount Rathborne, who had not yet left for the House of Commons. A triumphant look flashed across Lady Claire's face before she shrieked and went for her gown.

The Earl, his heart having steeled itself to face the Viscount, turned, feeling every bit the cad he appeared. The Viscount was an elderly man. His balding head was nearly as red as his sagging cheeks. He had always known his heart. "What is the meaning of this?" he blustered, hoped she would soon marry and put an end to his concerns. He met the awesome scene with his hand against his heart, "What is the meaning of this?" he blustered, slamming the door shut for emphasis.

The Earl found that pulling himself to his full height

didn't help, but ventured feebly, "Excuse me, sir, I know what it must appear, but do believe me . . . "

"Believe you?" shouted the older man, much distraught. "Cur! In my home, when I am abovestairs?"

The Earl shot one dangerous look at Lady Claire and marveled at the way she had managed to create tears, and how they flowed down her cheeks! "Nothing happened, sir," tried the Earl.

"You dare say that? My daughter stands there grappling with her gown and you dare offer me further insult?"

"I offer you truth, sir."

"Papa," interrupted Claire, thinking things needed a helping hand. "Oh, poor . . . poor Papa. I am so sorry, indeed. I shall never allow the Earl next or nigh me again."

Her father closed his eyes as though to shut the scene away and wondered where his prancing pretty little doll had vanished to. The Earl, watching him, found a strain of pity for the man and ventured, "My lord, if you will but believe that your arrival precluded any opportunity . . . "

"My arrival?" interjected the Viscount, turning beet red again. "My arrival stopped you, eh?"

"Indeed yes, Papa, and we shall never do what we have been . . . " put in Claire timidly, only to be interrupted again.

"Have been . . . You mean you have met like this before? Answer me, daughter, has this man deflowered you?"

Claire lowered her eyes and the Viscount's wrath turned on the Earl fullscore. "Devil!" he blasted. "You have taken my daughter. So be it! You shall honor her with your name, and the name of your father, who was my friend. For before the week is out you will make my daughter your wife!"

"I cannot do that," said the Earl, feeling weak-headed suddenly. He was in dangerous territory now and knew it.

"What mean you by such a barefaced remark? Can't

indeed! You will do it or so help me, God, I shall report this to the Queen herself. My daughter is a particular friend of the King and Queen, and they will not look kindly on such cavalier handling!"

"I have no wish to fling mud at your daughter, my lord. But, as I see I have no alternative, it is my belief that she engineered this set-to today."

"That matters not to me," snapped the Viscount.

"Nor does she love me," said the Earl slowly, gently. The old Viscount took a hasty step forward with every intention of striking the boldfaced liar who stood before him. However, Claire stepped between them and was brutally flung away by her broken-hearted father.

"Slime, it grieves me that Claire will have such a husband, but have you she shall. You will return here tonight with your aunt, Lady Haverly, and we will discuss the marriage settlements. After that, an announcement will be posted in the *Gazette* and depend upon it you will be married by the end of the week."

"And if I refuse?"

"I shall report your actions to the Queen. You will not refuse her. It is a thing I hope I will be spared, for I have no desire to flaunt my shame before all the world. I hope you will spare me that."

The Earl did some quick thinking. He needed time to find a way out. "I agree to this much. I will come with my aunt to you tonight to discuss this matter."

"You will come precisely at eight and there will be nought to discuss but the wedding settlement!" reiterated the Viscount.

The Earl inclined his head and without glancing at Claire, let himself out of the room. He went to the butler and caught the glint in the man's eye. "How much did she pay you for that little job?" asked the Earl ruefully.

"Enough, m'lord, enough."

He donned his many-caped greatcoat, set his top hat at a jaunty angle, and twirling his cane thoughtfully, walked the distance to Duke Street. Confound the wench, for he was in a devil of a bind, and saw only one way out, a way he little liked!

No. 51 Duke Street was reached, and he took the steps of the fashionable but modest town house, swept past a gentleman's gentleman in to a small, cluttered sitting room. Here he found a young man, much his own age, with a shock of sandy-colored hair, bleached bushy brows, freckles over a tipped nose, and vague blue eyes, seated in the middle of the floor and surrounded by what seemed upon first glance to be an abundance of mail. Sir Wilson Malmesy was the Earl's closest and most beloved friend, and he looked up to find Branwell towering above him and grinned.

"Hello! Back, are you? How long this time?"

The Earl dropped unceremoniously upon the floor, scattering some of the letters in his haste, and received a rebuke from his friend to be careful. "Never mind that, Willy. I'm in the devil of a mess. I've been fambled . . . caught! Lady Claire laid a trap and like a lad barely breeched I walked right in!"

"Never say so?" answered his friend, much struck by the picture this conjured up in his imaginative brain.

"The lady—and I use the term without conviction— played me dirty. She arranged for her own father to walk in on us whilst we were in a questionable state."

"No!"

"Yes, but I swear this time, Willy, nothing happened. There wasn't time!"

"Well then, if nothing happened, what's the set-to?" asked Willy reasonably, returning his attention to the mail.

"Her father thinks something did."

"Why?"

"Claire was naked, you see."

Willy opened his light eyes rather wide. "Good lord, Branwell, what do you mean nothing happened? I wouldn't believe you! Why should he?"

"Willy, look, never mind that. Claire admitted to him that I was her lover . . . and now he insists that I marry her. He threatens me with the Queen if I refuse, and there is nothing for it!"

"I don't like that," said Willy, frowning gravely over the problem.

The Earl eyed his friend with some impatience and wondered why he had come here in the first place; however, he bolstered himself and continued, "No, Willy, nor do I. However, a plan, a way out, occurred to me on my way over here."

"I don't like that either," said Willy, beginning to feel it was time for him to make his exit.

"Do shut up, ole boy, and listen. My plan is nearly perfect, but hold . . . " He took up a scrap of paper, got to his feet and rang the pull rope for a lackey. He scribbled something hastily, handed it to the servant who appeared with a coin and instructions to wait a reply. When he returned to the floor beside his friend he continued hastily, "It is a trifle underhanded . . ."

"Underhanded?" ejaculated Willy. "No, won't do anything dishonorable. Gentleman, you know, code of honor—proprieties to be upheld!"

"Willy, there is my life to be thought of first."

"Don't see that. Rather think of mine first," replied Willy.

"But Will, you have nought to fear in this!"

"Don't see that either. Whenever you set me onto one of your schemes, 'tis *I* who fear the most."

"Rest easy, yours is the smallest part to play. What I need is the Beau. We must await his arrival and his word regarding my plan."

"What, the Beau coming here? I ain't dressed. He'll throw me out, Bran, which may be a good thing. Then I can't hear your scheme, can't be expected to play my part if I don't know what it is. Very good thing, the Beau coming here."

"Willy . . . "

"Yes?"

"Nothing, Will, what have you there, anyway?" asked

the Earl, frowning over the bulk of paper at his friend's feet.

"Invitations. Can't go to all of them . . . will be in Brighton next month. Trouble is, can't go to any of them."

"Why?"

"Hadn't noticed before."

"What?"

"These are last months'! Dear me," said Willy, frowning over the problem.

The Earl stared hard a moment at his friend, shook his head, and left him to his quandary while he sought out paper and scribbled yet another note, this time to Aunt Sarah.

28

When last we left Kate, she was mooning over her problems, and wondering why the Earl had not come to call. The day dwindled away in this fashion and still she remained indoors and alone in her room.

Sarah took tea with Nell in the library and was interrupted with a note offered to her upon a silver salver by Travis. She read it, her color drained considerably, and she then retired to her room with the excuse of a headache.

Nell went abovestairs and knocked on Kate's door, only to receive a rebuff. With a sad sigh, she returned to the library. Here she received a visitor and one that nearly always put a light in her eyes.

Mr. Hatch came up behind her and plopped a peck upon her cheek. She jumped with a start and turned, hands on hips to scold him. "There now, sir, don't you be taking any liberties simply because I allow you to pay me a call now and then."

"That's not why I take m'liberties, darlin'. I takes 'em

coz I aims to wife ye, and well ye knows it."

She sighed and went into his enveloping embrace, for she needed him. He was solid and world-wise and, oh, but he could make her smile.

Kate thought of Nell and felt guilty. She had been unfair to her poor governess. Nell's world must be topsy-turvy and pouting by herself would only serve to confuse the woman more. Kate put a brush through her hair, straightened her pale pink muslin, and ventured downstairs.

She opened the parlor door, found it empty and continued her path to the library. Once again she opened a door with a ready smile on her lips and it froze and her step went rigid. There was her Nell, in the arms of a seaman whom she recognized as Master Hatch. Her Nell, being fervently, furiously kissed. If she had not been so surprised, she would have been heartily amused.

Quickly she closed the door and leaned herself against it. So, Nell had fallen in love at last! That was the immediate thought that came to her mind. Her Nell and Branwell's Hatch! Oh Lord, however would that work out?

She stood leaning against the closed door, unsure whether or not she should interrupt them, when Nell's voice came clearly to her ears.

"My poor darling child, she is the daughter I was never able to have, Hatch, and I love her as my own. I can't bear to think of her wanting that creature, that Banyon."

"No, it fair makes me skin crawl to think of them together," agreed the seaman, surprising Kate. Good gosh, she thought, whatever was there about Perry that seemed to incite universal disapprobation?

"What can I do, Hatch?" cried Nell.

"To m'way of thinking, she ought to be told."

"How can we tell her about her father? To tell Banyon's past would be to deface her father."

"Don't fret, m'darlin', there now," said Hatch.

Their voices became muffled, and Kate could hear no more. No, nor did she want to. This was all she could take. Enough, enough, she would have the truth, and if they would not give it, perhaps Perry would! She rushed down the hall, took her dark velvet cloak and flung it around her shoulders as she escaped unnoticed.

Kate paid the driver of the hackney, then stepped gingerly over the curb onto Duke Street. She felt an explosion of nerves within her stomach and she winced from the strange, dull pain and felt breathless. It was daylight still and she might be seen entering Perry's lodgings. It was an act unthinkable! A maid visiting bachelor lodgings was against all social law! It was in fact against her social law. Society would condemn her should they discover, and, oh Kate, she cried, look how far you have come! You stoop to deceit, for you would hide your actions!

She braced herself and took the front steps with determination. Everything she had heard, everything she had learned led but to one conclusion: the possibility of Perry's being her half-brother! This haunted her thoughts on the way to his rooms, but what confused her was the aching question, did he know? How could he know? He couldn't possibly know, for then, how could he have asked her to marry him? How could he have kissed her lips? He couldn't know! To know and still determine to marry her would be incestuous! The word hung about her head like a low dark cloud and it threatened.

A young man-servant opened the door, and Kate recalled having seen him at the Dower House when Perry had inherited it. The lad showed some surprise upon recognizing Kate, but he stood aside and allowed her to pass him into the narrow hall. A nervousness played with Kate's ability to command, but she controlled herself and asked austerely, "Is Mr. Banyon at home?"

"Aye," said the lad, indicating the direction with his hand. "But he left me strict orders he was not to be disturbed."

"Oh, he did not mean me, lad; he won't mind," said Kate, moving toward the door down the hall.

"Yes but, miss," said the lad uncertainly, for Mr.

Banyon had been gravely specific about his instructions. However, Kate had already reached and opened the door, so he shrugged his shoulders and sidled off.

Kate closed the door behind her, surprised by the darkness of the room. Its drapes had been drawn and the only light came from the fireplace. She wondered if Perry had dozed off and stood in front of the door, unsure what she should do, when the sound of muffled groans caught her attention. She turned her head toward the fireplace, where a sofa had been drawn up before the gentle flames, and she attempted to focus her eyes in the dark. The burning embers in the grate with their listless shoots of white light gave off an eerie glow, enveloping the sofa's occupants with their incandescence. They had been too involved with one another to hear Kate's entrance and continued their wild hungry movements, lost to one another.

Kate saw them and her eyes opened wide with total immobilizing shock. It looked to her something painted from a scene of hell! She stared, for she could do nought else; she stared, thinking the dark, the firelight, played tricks with her eyes, making her see images that were not really there. But they were there. Perry and his lover, his male lover, were there—it was not a nightmare! This fact drummed itself into her wretched mind and her fist went to her mouth in an attempt to stifle her cry. Nevertheless, it spurted out of her, gushing, demanding release! And it brought the lovers to an awareness of her presence.

"Oh, hell and damn my soul to perdition. Who the deuce is she?" cried the strange man, releasing Perry from his embrace, withdrawing his hand from Perry's breeches, buttoning his own, all in front of Kate's vision.

She saw them, heard them, and felt herself slipping into another realm. It said softly, Come Kate, what have we to do with them? Come, the palms call, the ocean laps, come. She could feel Bermuda's fresh fragrant scent fill her nostrils, fill her senses. She felt herself yearning to leave with that sweet, soothing voice, but that was not real! The voice was not real; *this*, this ugly, ugly scene was reality! She couldn't escape it in such a way, for it would always be there, in her mind, ready to battle her purer thoughts. She must meet it head on. She must beat its clawing cruelty and strike it away! So she stood, pressed against the wall, flattening herself into the corner of the cabinet at her side.

Perry was jumping to his feet, buttoning his breeches, saying something to the man, that horrid man, who was crying, "I'm ruined, Perry, ruined, unless you can trust her. But how can you? She is a woman!"

"Never mind, just go and don't worry. She can be trusted," said Perry. "I will handle her . . . somehow." And then, for the first time, she found Perry's eyes. As their glances met, she saw the color drain from his face. He had read her thoughts in her eyes and he died before them.

Suddenly the man, that awful man, was gone, and it was just she and Perry staring at one another. He swept his hand through his fair locks and cursed the fates. Life had dealt him yet another blow! Trembling before him stood the woman he had meant to marry. She was his last hope of salvation and he had thrown it away for but a moment's ecstasy! All these months he had done without his needs, his cursed perverted needs, and in one moment of madness, he had lost all. But perhaps not, he suddenly calculated, perhaps he could yet salvage something, for she had not run away. Yes, her eyes spoke of revulsion, but she stayed; did not this mean she wanted to be convinced all was still well?

He moved toward her, but she cringed from his touch and he stopped, not daring to move farther. "Kathleen," he tried, but what could he say, how could he start?

"No!" she shouted at him. "No, don't speak my name. I can't bear it. You are a sodomite! That was what they whispered about, that is what they meant. Oh God, I thought they meant you were my illegitimate half-brother, but no. There was one more sick thing I hadn't thought of. You are a sodomite!" The word echoed in her mind and she felt her heart taken by pitiless hands and squeezed until it was emptied of blood. Her chest caved in from the emptiness and she lost the ability to breathe. She gasped, suffocating within, deep within, and she felt sick and betrayed. Still she heard that gentle voice and gentle island music; it mesmerized her with its sway, it beckoned, and she almost felt herself take flight. Then she heard him say her name.

"Kathleen, let me—oh, please let me explain," he tried desperately. He was himself going through trauma. He saw himself in her eyes and needed to defend, needed to strike out the revulsion from her expression.

"Explain?" she screamed. "You are a homosexual. Oh, God, how could you have said you loved me? You spoke of adoration, of wanting me for wife." She wrung her hands and rocked herself. "How could you be so deceiving? And why me, why would you want to hurt me? You could not really marry me, you are not a man!" she hurled at him, not meaning to hurt, yet wanting to spit out her thoughts, thinking somewhere in the back of her mind: Why, Kate, why so upset? You never meant to marry him. Why, Kate? Answer, Kate! The answer was there and in spite of her indefatigable need for truth she squashed it before it rose before her eyes! Her self-protective shields stood in its path and said: Enough, enough shock for a while. She must rest!

"Not a man?" he cried. "What do you know about being a man? What do you know of life, other than the sheltered cubicle in which you have lived? You stand there disgusted with me, thinking yourself hurt by me. And your first reaction was to strike back! Have you no pity, Kate? Then take the poker there and have at me."

"How dare you? Strike at you, pity you? You have used me, for what purpose I know not. Would you have gone through with it, Perry? If I had been so stupid as to accept your proposal, would you have married me? And if so, how would you have consummated that marriage?"

Tears stained his cheeks, glistening on his face, and

for the first time Kate saw his face and knew that he was wretched.

"I would have loved you, Kate; you would not have wanted for anything. I am not incapable of making love to a woman." His voice was low, sad, withdrawn. "You are the only woman I have ever cared about. I would have cherished you."

"Why?" she screamed at him. "Why?"

"Damnation . . . couldn't you let it go? Must you have it all? Very well then, Miss Self-righteous. I wanted respectability. I am sick of eyes that follow me and wonder at what I am! I wanted a wife, a child. I wanted the Grange!" he spit at her.

"Oh, Perry, had you no thought, no compassion for me?" asked Kate.

He beat the floor as he strode across the remainder of the distance that separated them and took her shoulders, shaking her hard. She shrieked at the touch of his hand and yanked herself out of his clutch.

"You are as cruel as all your kind have ever been," said Perry, raging at her, out of control. "Compassion? What the devil do you know about compassion? You show it not!"

"For what should I show it? For your twisted, your unnatural appetite?" thundered Kate, now on the defensive.

"For the being that calls himself Perry Banyon, for the boy that grew into a man, whom you say is not a man, for the suffering the boy endured that made him what he is. Oh, Kate, my twisted ways were early taught to me!"

She frowned and sobbed, turning from him. She couldn't speak for she was lost to confusion. She was lost to her own unspeakable truths, beating them down, refusing to look at them.

"Kathleen, you must hear before you judge. I was but thirteen, living where I had always lived—in the gutters, pimping for my mother! Don't look wide-eyed. Damn, but you have seen with your own eyes; you could not have driven through London and not have seen the streets. The urchins, how do you think they live?"

She put her hands over her ears, but he yanked them down. "Damn you . . . you will hear. You turn your face away from the squalor. You throw a coin and, damn your eyes, you turn away. I could not. Then one bright day a man came along, and he didn't want my filthy mother. He wanted me! He saw a pretty yellow-haired urchin beneath the dirt, and he took me home. I went. Oh God, if I could have run all that way to his country home I would have done so! He clothed me, fed me, educated me and all I had to do was love him! It was not so very hard. A thirteen-year-old is full of energy and eager to please those who are kind to him. He was gentle, good, and for the first time in my life I felt decent and whole. Then he died. I was sixteen and his heirs came, and I was put once again onto the streets. But this time, a woman, a friend of Banyon's—that was his name; you see, I took it from him as *I* had none—well, this woman, who had been aware of our relationship, hired me. She was everything he had never been, ugly, petty, cruel, and in her hands I became impotent! So there I was, once again left to the streets, and I found myself in one dive after another, performing for men with particular tastes, until four years ago when once again a sweet gentle being found me. Do you hear what I am saying, Kate?"

She frowned. "Yes, Perry, yes I hear. How could you allow yourself to be so used? 'Tis unnatural."

"Unnatural. What is unnatural is to kill oneself . . . that was my other choice. God, Kate, love is a gift; all that matters is that it be given freely! What matters whether man loves man or man loves woman; it is still love, and love can be but one thing and that is good!"

"No. 'Tis against nature."

"Nothing that makes a being whole, that transforms him from an animal into a human, is against nature. What is against nature, what is against God, is society that condemns everything it cannot comprehend."

"No, it is sickening," cried Kate.

"Sickening? Did you feel that way about your father?" asked Perry slowly.

"What has my father to do with this?" asked Kate, feeling those protective shields slipping.

"Kate, your father was the man, the good man, who found me four years ago. Kathleen, don't you realize what I am saying? You loved your father; he was no less the man because his tastes were different. Oh, Kate, I will love you. I will please you," he said, trying to take her in his arms.

"No!" she screamed, slapping at his hands. "Never . . . I could never love you. You disgust me," she spit at him.

"As your father would disgust you if he were here today and you saw him with me instead of that poor man earlier, eh Kate?" he taunted, wanting to hurt her as he was hurt. "Little innocent, must I spell it all out for you? Your dear wonderful papa was my lover!"

It was what her mind had tried to tell her earlier. It was the thought that she had struck away. There were no shields to protect her. She felt the dawn but it was not bright; it was dark, treacherous and filled with slime. She felt the black gushes of algae reach for her with their undefined, shapeless mounds, and she wrenched free with all her might. "Liar!" she screamed, her pain filling the room, tearing at her body. She took the door and threw it open, running, her sobs wasting her mind. She cried with the aching, bent over as she ran with the ineffable pain of a truth that destroyed all in its path. The cool evening air found her, and she sped down the steps unseeing, tears smudging her cheeks. Her world had suddenly collapsed beneath her feet. There was nought but sludge all around. No where to step, nothing left to take hold, nothing . . . for all had been wrenched from her! She had left her island shell and slowly, each day, a layer and then another layer of life's frosting had been viciously vandalized from her. It left her with the stench of malodorous mold. Its worms worked their white bodies, wiggling as they gorged themselves, and she flung herself away from the sight!

She ran blindly, hysterically, not knowing where she ran, only aware that she must escape the horror, and then suddenly she found herself held tightly in a pair of strong arms. She beat at her prison, for she wanted only to run and keep running, and then through the delirium she saw a pair of green eyes and they stroked her. She needed a buoy and he was there, and his eyes spoke of strength. She threw herself into his chest and gave free vent to her emotions. She cared not who saw, indeed she had no control to care. The Earl scooped her up in his arms and hailed a passing hack, directing him the short distance to his own lodgings.

He had just left Sir Wilson's house and had seen with no little surprise, and much concern, Kate come bowling wildly out of the small residence across the street. With an easy speed he made for her, catching her trembling body in his arms. She was in no state to take to Sarah, and in no state to question. Without a word he made the decision to carry her to his home, calm her, and discover the cause of her misery.

29

In the seclusion of the closed carriage, the Earl hugged Kate's shaking form to him. He stroked her weeping head soothingly. Her distress pierced his breast sharply, and though he knew not why she sobbed, his words spoke of strength. Through her agony, she heard his voice, full and tender with concern, and she hugged him with all her might, lest he too crumble before her. She only knew that all she had believed in, all that was, had dissipated into less than nothing and more than she could bear! Yet this man, the very man who had represented the rakish, heartless side of life, had become for her a pillar and she held onto him. His voice threatened the engulfing horrors reaching for her. His austere power beat the slime down. His magic gave her earth!

She buried her face into his chest and her sobbing quieted. She felt herself carried again into the cool night air, up the steps of his house and into his hall.

The Earl's butler came forward, and he was unable to cover his amazement at the Earl's startling entrance; however, his employer gave him no time to wonder. "I am not at home to anyone," ordered the Earl as he swept past him, carrying the trembling bundle in his arms. "And I am not to be disturbed under any circumstances!"

"Very good, m'Lord," said the awed Kirkly, watching the Earl disappear with the young woman into his library. The Earl carried Kate to his sofa facing the fire and placed her gently into its crook. She turned from him and hid her tearstained face in her hands. Silently the Earl poured a stiff mummer of brandy and brought it to her, placing it in her hands and saying in a tone that would brook no argument, "Drink!"

"I . . . I . . . can't . . ." faltered Kate, unable to bring her eyes to his.

"Drink it and don't argue with me, girl!" he snapped with quiet authority. "For if you find you cannot do the thing on your own, I am afraid that I shall have no alternative but to administer the libation to you myself. You would not enjoy that, I do assure you!"

His tone teased for a smile, but she could not give it, and her lips trembled pitifully as she put the warm liquid to her lips. She sipped and stopped but he pushed it toward her mouth, and at length after several such repetitions the brandy was downed.

Oddly enough, she felt better. Her mind felt not so very heavy, but the tears were still there at the rim of her large child-like eyes. He sat beside her on the sofa, his hat and coat having been discarded; he felt it time to do the same with hers and proceeded to remove her hooded cloak. She allowed this but avoided his eye. The job done, he turned to her and took up her hand, patting it consolingly and subjecting her to a penetrating eye.

"Now, Cousin Kate, do you think you can tell me what has occurred to upset you?"

"No," she whispered. "Oh, how can I tell you? Indeed, you, Aunt Sarah, Nell, you must already know." Once again she turned her face away into her hands.

"May I ask . . . whose house it was that you came stampeding out of?" pursued the Earl.

"It was Perry's," said Kate, not looking up from her hand.

"I see," said the Earl, stung with a sharp sensation of jealousy.

She laughed bitterly. "You see? Have you not seen all along? You and the woman I call aunt, even Nell." She felt a spasm of that first overwhelming pain she had experienced when she first discovered the truth.

The Earl heard the hysterical note in her voice and saw a look in the chit's eyes that he could not like. She had sustained a shock, and he was almost certain what that shock had been.

"So, you learned the truth about Perry?" he said softly, watching every flicker of her eyes, every pulsating movement beneath the skin of her temple.

She laughed, and it was a wild, clipped sound. He heard the hurt and all he wanted to do was hold her and make it go away. But he waited, cautiously; whatever he did, it would have to be the right thing! "Truth? I have Perry's truths. Pretty young Perry, offering me marriage and truths. Have you ever seen a man make love to another man? 'Tis all very well to whisper about such things; have you ever seen it?" she screamed, very near the edge of trauma.

He winced inwardly, but his voice assuaged her. "Yes, fondling, 'tis a startling thing, indeed; but it is a part of life . . ."

She rounded on him. "A part of life? Very well . . . why then did you not tell me? Why did you let me discover it for myself? Why?"

"We thought to spare you," he said gently.

"Spare me? In defending himself, do you know what

Perry accused my father of? Do you know what he said?" shrieked Kate, beating at the Earl's mighty chest.

He held her then, allowing her pounding to subside within the tight embrace of his arms, allowing her sobs to drain into his heart, softly saying her name, stroking her long black hair.

"My papa, oh Branwell, my papa was diseased!" she faltered at last, saying the words, hearing the words, and shrinking into herself at their sound.

"No, darling, no, your papa was a good father. That is all you ever needed to know. Now that he is gone, 'tis still all you have to know."

"I wish I didn't know anything else. Oh Branwell, why did you lie to me? Perhaps if you had told me about Perry from the start, perhaps then I should never have known about Papa."

"There was no way to tell you about Perry without involving your father. You would have probed until you had it all."

"So you resorted to subterfuge, lies, and pretending a passion for me. Oh God, I am my father's child! Am I diseased as well? Did it curdle your blood to have to kiss such as me?" she cried.

He shook her by the shoulders roughly. "Kate! Kate, stop it! Oh my lovely fondling, do you remember the first time I ever saw your glorious face? 'Twas on board the *Bermudian*. Since that moment I have been wanting to hold you, caress you. What is this nonsensical talk of yours?"

"I am the daughter of a sodomite. How can you bear to touch me?" she whispered, shame engulfing her pride.

"Hush now! What have your father's tastes to do with you? Can you not remember Sir Horace as he was *to you* . . . a good man? That is all you ever have to remember. What he did in his bedroom, that was his own affair. It had nought to do with the man you knew and loved, the man who raised you into the lovely and wondrous creature that you are."

"Wondrous?" she challenged, wanting him to convince

her. "I am nought but an accident, indeed!"

"Stop it!" he ordered. "Sir Horace adored your mother and you." He had to do something. Her pain was etching itself in her tortured mind, and its lashings were cutting through his heart. He had to wipe it all away, somehow. His hold around her tightened and his head lowered as his hand gently turned her chin, and his mouth took hers sweetly, tenderly, with a passion that knew only the touch of featherdown.

She stiffened beneath his touch, but there was a magic in his lips, and it drove some of the hurt away. She felt it fade, felt herself drawn into another realm, and the constriction in her throat ebbed. She needed to be free of her father's sin. She needed to be free of her own thoughts, and the Earl's touch freed her. Her arms went around his neck and she pressed herself into his kiss, giving more than he wanted to take!

He was surprised by her response, surprised by the tumultuous awakening in his own breast and by the feel of her arms holding him! But this was not the time! He put her from him. He was not about to seduce the poor child. One trauma a night was far too many! She was, after all, an innocent.

"Come, I'll take you home," he said, beginning to rise.

She felt her heart sink into shame. He did not want her. He found her undesirable; her father's sins *did* carry over onto her! Oh God, Branwell was repelled by her! This stud of a man, this lover of women, this strong man with the glinting green eyes could have any beautiful woman. Why would he want the daughter of a homosexual? She looked up at him, a sad quiet to her voice. "You don't want me?"

He stopped on the edge of the sofa and faced her fully again. "Not want you? Are you daft, child? I have wanted you longer than I can now remember, but . . ."

"But I am not good enough," she faltered, avoiding his eye, wanting him to love her, suddenly desperate for him. He alone had the power to wipe her miserable thoughts away, and she wanted him to use that power now!

"Damnation! You are too good for me."

"You say that simply because you are a gentleman," she accused.

He grinned and tried to win a smile from her. "You once said I was no such thing." He won no response. He put his arm around her, burning at the touch of her. "No, I am no gentleman," he whispered before taking her fully against him and rediscovering her lips.

His kiss turned into many, and they covered her eyes, her cheeks and ears, returned to her cherry mouth, separating the lips, tantalizing her with his expertise. He was in need of her and she was a wild young thing, a hot-blooded woman-child, responding to his every move. She pressed herself willingly into his hard body, her own pleading for more. His virility pulsated throbbingly, demanding release as his hands worked at the back of her gown. He stood up, pulling her to her feet before him, and she trembled within his circle as her clothing dropped to the floor.

His eyes swept over her body hungrily, glorying in the sight of her perfection, and his hands took heated appraisal of her velvet flesh. "Oh God, you are beautiful, you sweetings, you lovely little thing," he whispered, his hands fondling her voluptuous breasts, cupping them, delighting in the sensation they aroused. His hands wandered lingering over the curves of her slender hips and found the small but tantalizing fullness of her buttocks and he grabbed, pulling her yet closer, holding her from beneath their bewitching form. The movement caused her to arch beneath his towering body and he groaned. His hand reluctantly left its treasure to find yet more in the sleekness of her thighs and as he separated her legs, his mouth burned her taut ripe nipples with his frenzied kisses.

She trembled hungrily in his hands, groaning with pleasure, lost to his trespassing. All thoughts were flown before this ecstasy. She need only feel and what she was feeling was wild desire. His fingers teased her as they worked at the apex of her thighs, entering between the lips of her honeycomb, yet not thrusting. He worked as though to gather her honey and she contorted her body with the need for more. He had been holding her up, for indeed had his bent arm loosed her she would have fallen, so weak were her knees. She gasped at the mesmerizing workings of his fingers, and felt herself lowered to the hearth rug; she felt him shrug off his waistcoat and work the buttons of his breeches, but all she could do was thrust herself with groaning excitement into his touch.

"Oh God, Kate, I can't stop. I am sorry, sweetings, for I should, but damn if I will," he whispered, kissing her ears and throat, for he had freed the swollen muscle from his breeches and held it poised ready as he mounted her.

He was on fire and as he wedged the tuberant muscle in his hand between her legs, found there the small, tight opening and demanded his entrance, he felt a hard triumphant surging within him. He entered her as slowly as he could control himself, at first, taming his propulsion, but she was no tame creature, willing to take it slow! She threw herself into his thrust and he found himself tearing through her virginity, groaning with wild pleasure as he made her his! He whispered his delight with her, whispered his ecstasy, bit gently at her lips, parted them to give her more of himself, and poured words of glory into her ears. His lusty hands instructed her as he plunged deeper into her womb, caressing away her fear.

His hands aroused her wildly, and her response had been to meet his body with her own beating fire. She bowed her body, taking him fully; but his thrust, his deep plunging thrust, had hurt, and though that sudden hurt was gone, she felt a dull soreness, but, oh, his movements aroused a tenseness in her loins, and she gave of herself.

"Sweet fondling, you are mine, your virginity is forever mine," he whispered across her mouth. The thought of this frenzied his passion, sending his sensual pitchings into wild rotating surges. He was intoxicated with her sweetness, and as his fever mounted steadily, so did its rhythm. His large deft hands moved to her hips and then slid beneath her well-rounded butt, forcing her up to meet his hungry plunges. It was good, damn, it was good, and it was right, thought he almost violently, in defiance of conscience.

She was conveyed into untraveled depths, carried away by his passion for her. She felt engulfed in a new and hidden domain where only sensations ruled! And as her body heat mounted, blacking out all else, Kate learned of fulfillment. In a moment of intense life, she learned of satisfaction as a swift, uninhibited tenseness surged through her erotic body. It took her breath, flying with her spirit, giving her glory, unfolding its secrets and departing with a force that left her limbs relaxed beneath his own!

Branwell felt the pitch of her climax and exulted in his heart. Never before had it been so wondrous, so perfect, so pure—and it was pure! He gave her his seed in the last of their rapturous dance, kissing her mouth full and with a tenderness he had never before known himself capable of feeling. And she, child of innocence? She delighted in his caress, in his scent, in his power. For indeed, thought she, as he had, was it not good? Was it not right? Immoral? Such a question, had it found its way, would have been spurned. What had she to do with such evil thoughts? She loved! And loving made it all quite beautiful, and here Perry's words flickered across her mind. What had he said about love, no matter with whom? Was it not, in the end, love that was the conqueror, the equilibrator, and the answer?

She lay in Branwell's arms and they cherished her. His breath near her ears, his hands were lovingly stroking, adoring, massaging away the soreness between her thighs. She felt thankful for the darkness, grateful that the candles had nearly burned themselves out. She was too shy to meet his glance fully and his words, passionate still, admiring, praising, fanned her shyness. She knew her cheeks were raw, for she burned with the earth-shattering memory of her feverish abandonment. How could she have done all the things her mind's eye had recorded? It shamed her pride into mute silence, and she felt unable to look at the man that had claimed her bounty. There, too, was an insistent ache in her loins, a dull pain, and she had the worried suspicion that she was bleeding. At last she found her voice, though in truth it was hardly audible. "I . . . I think, Branwell, that I bleed."

He raised himself on one arm and leaned over to examine her legs, there finding a trickle of warm blood. "My poor fondling, it will not always be so, come," he said, taking her hand and pulling her to her feet. She colored, for she was all too aware of her nakedness before his admiring eye. He was charged with a glorious sensation of fulfillment. He felt it steal into his heart and tickle his soul. Lord, but she had satisfied him, this little virgin queen with her innocent movements and her warm response. He wrapped her in her cloak, and then swung her like a babe into his large and capable arms, leaving the remainder of her clothes where they had fallen.

"Bran," objected Kate. "Where, where do you take me?" Then observing that he made for the door, "The servants, they will see us. . . ."

He laughed at her distress. "Poor fondling. No one will dare to cast a glance this way, but if you like, you may hide your face in my shirt."

She did, wondering how she could ever face anyone again. She was no longer a maid, but this man's mistress. She had been possessed, totally in body, and she knew from the very first in heart. But he loved her, he must love her! He could not have taken her with such tenderness if he did not love her. She had given herself freely without ever first wondering if he loved her. The question loomed now in her mind. He must love her? And want to marry her? He simply must!

He took her above to his bedchamber and there laid her gently upon his massive four-poster bed. A moment later he returned with a dampened warm cloth. His ministrations were tender, loving, but Kate was hesitant to speak of the thing that now nagged at her mind. She lay back when he finished his repairs and watched him undress, wondering worriedly if he meant to keep her here all night, yet unable to leave him. She would have to, though, no matter their future; she would have to keep up appearances, for they were not married yet! She sighed happily over the thought of being his wife. He glanced her way, enjoying the sound of her contentment, anxious to be rid of his clothes, anxious to feel her naked beauty beneath his flesh. And she, in her love, in her newfound wonder, watched him, as Eve must have watched Adam when they first learned of each other.

He moved toward her, and she found his broad chest with its soft unconfined mass of dark curling hair. Then her eyes wandered to his flat narrow belly and his lines spoke of a strength not yet revealed. Then he was dropping his breeches to the floor and Kate's gray eyes opened wide, for she had never before seen a nude man!

He laughed heartily at her expression, loving her delectable innocence, refreshed by its glitter. He boarded the bed, straddling her with his arms, grinning as he brushed a warm kiss to her nose. She cast him a reproachful look. "Lud, Branwell, no wonder I ache so." She had little time for further comment, as his hands had already slipped around her and his mouth came down, demanding her nectar.

"No, Branwell, you can't mean to . . ." she whispered when she was finally able to wrench her lips from his. But his hands were already teasing, tantalizing, insisting.

"Please, Branwell, I shall never again be able to walk. Bran . . ." she pleaded half-heartedly, almost simultaneously pressing herself against his hardness, thrilling to his educated and seductive fingers.

He brought his head up, facing her, looking long into her eyes, his own alight with mischief, and something else, something he would have scoffed to own. "Shall I stop then, my fondling?" he teased, before tasting her ears and neck.

She groaned, and had he taken the sound to mean she wished a halt to the proceedings, he would have been sadly out. Her groan was followed by another, and she offered him her circulating, haunching hips, tempting him further, tempting him beyond, and now he groaned, for at this point, he could not stop!

30

"Stand aside, I said. I am his Lordship's fiancée!" blasted Lady Claire.

"But, madam, his Lordship is not at home," pleaded the butler, much vexed and at a quandary as to how he could possibly use force to detain the Lady Claire Rathborne.

"Not at home! Then you will have no objection to my waiting for him in the study!" snapped she. The Earl had missed the little dinner arrangement her father had ordered him to attend. Lady Haverly had been there and much shocked she was when her nephew had not arrived. It was past ten, and Lady Claire meant to do battle!

"Oh, you cannot wait. His Lordship left strict instructions that he was not to be disturbed," cried the harassed fellow.

"Aha!" ejaculated Claire, narrowing her eyes. "Then he is at home, and you needn't show me the way. I know it well!" said she, taking the stairs, her skirts held high, her complexion heated. The Earl had probably imbibed a cognac too many, but she would see him and make certain he was aware that there was no way out of his predicament!

In his room the Earl lay on his side, his handsome head held up by his hand, and he was indeed intoxicated. But it was an intoxication of the spirit and the heart, and it was due to the gray-eyed vision before him. He had been teasing her, kissing the tip of her nose, nibbling at her neck, and all of it seemed not enough.

"What I should now do is prepare a steaming hot hip bath for you, fondling," he said, brushing her lip tenderly with his finger, contemplating the fullness of its ripe curves, loving the fresh unpainted cherriness of its hue, becoming aroused as her lips parted to answer him.

"Hip bath? Branwell, I must leave," she said objecting, attempting to disengage herself from him.

He prohibited any such action. "Not yet, no, first the hip bath, and with my own hands I shall send your virgin soreness away to other realms. We want none of it here to interfere with our pleasures," he teased audaciously.

She blushed and felt her cheeks hot as she turned her face away, leaving him her exquisite profile. She spoke in a low whisper, a tinge of fear touching her. "You mean, our sins."

He crooked an arched look at her. "Sins? No, my treasure, never say such thoughts dwell in that pretty head of yours. 'Tis not sin, 'tis . . ."

At this interesting juncture the door to his room flew open with some force, and the dim light from the hall struck their faces.

"What the devil?" expostulated Branwell, as his eyes focused and found Lady Claire hovering witchlike at the threshold. He heard Kate whimper and felt her dive behind him, and he knew an urge to rise up and strike the life from Claire's prying eyes. Then her words and Kate's body stiffening beside his own made him realize he would have to deal with her, immediately!

"I might have known!" exclaimed Claire, unabashed with the scene before her. "You miserable rutting stud! Well, don't think that I will release you from our engagement simply because you are incapable of being faithful. I don't care how many whores you bed; by the end of the week I will be Lady Mannering!"

"Damn your spiked tongue, you bitch!" shouted the Earl, jumping out of bed and taking the floor, heedless of his nakedness. He grabbed Claire by the arm, but she wrenched free and entered the room, eyeing the bed. He saw her purpose and headed her off, taking hold of her this time in a grip she could not loose. A moment later the door to his dressing room was opened and she was flung inside. He closed the door behind him and turned to face Claire in the darkness. "What do you think you are doing here?"

"You were supposed to have been at my home tonight, to arrange the marriage settlement with Father. Your aunt was most surprised by your absence and my father was outraged. You bastard, don't think that your Sarah with her honeyed mouth can keep my father at bay forever! She may have calmed him down tonight, but it won't serve!"

The marriage settlement! It came back to him in a flood, it was to have been for tonight! Even the sight of Claire at his door had not brought it home. He was, unless his plan was successful, to be married to the doxy standing before him. Lord, but he felt a new revulsion for her! And Kate, Kate in the next room, what would she be thinking? Damn, what would she be feeling? "You can't mean to go through with this scheme of yours, Claire?"

"Are you crazed? Do you think I would let you, your money, and your title slip through my fingers after having gone to so much effort?" she countered, contemptuous of his question.

"Bitch!" he said softly. "Cunning little bitch, you've worked it all out rather well!" He wanted to slap the smugness from her face, but he had never before hit a woman, and though his hands itched, he maintained control of himself. He said, instead, "Very well then, shall we make the best of it? I don't believe it necessary to be at one another's throats as long as we do not interfere with each other's pleasures."

"Exactly, Bran," she said, sweetly attempting to entwine his neck with her arms. He held her at bay, his disgust of her showing in his eyes.

"Look Claire, I make no lie of it. I have no interest in you or your feelings; however, I have no wish to further distress your father. You may tell him that I was in my cups tonight. He will understand, under the circumstances. I will compose a letter to that effect and have it sent around tomorrow. You may tell him to show my acceptance of the situation I am dispatching you off with Sarah to my jewelers on Friday to choose a diamond ring to honor the occasion of our forthcoming engagement."

"A ring, oh Branwell, how very generous," breathed Claire.

He pulled a face, "Sarah will not be pleased, but I shall have her call for you promptly at eleven, Friday morning. Do not keep her waiting. Look for her arrival!"

"Of course, darling. See how complacent I can be?" she said, hoping she appeared alluring in such a role.

He ignored her remark, but strode across the room, silently complimenting himself on not bumping into any furniture, and opened the door to the hall. "Good night, Claire."

"Do you not see me out?" she pouted.

"You know the way," he said curtly. She brushed past him, and he stood at the second floor landing watching her departure before turning back to his own room. He opened his door, noting that the fire was nearly burned out, and a chill swept his naked form. "Kate, Kate I am sorry," he started as he moved toward the bed. But even before he reached it, he knew. Without seeing, without feeling the covers, he knew she was gone!

"Hell and damnation!" he screamed in the empty room as he flung on his clothes. Where had she gone? Deuce take it all, why was she running from him?

Kate had seen Lady Claire, tall, hovering like some great female predator, and she felt shame fill her veins. Then the woman's words flooded her mind, making her aware what depths hell could still offer. Was the creature indeed a demon, a witch? No, she was Branwell's betrothed!

It stung her in a multitude of waspish bites. Attacking mind, body, and spirit all at once. Branwell had a life she knew nothing about. He had a love, a love he was going to make his bride. This was not his fault. Immediately, she excused him. She had never allowed him much opportunity to confide in her. She had gone from despising him to adoring him in one plunge. She had given him her love with her chastity and assumed that he too gave. She had wanted him. She had been the one to ask, and oh, God—she loved him! The dawning of such intelligence should be accompanied with the clamor of spring songs and church bells, but her dawning coincided with the revelation that he was engaged to marry another woman!

Her pride was struck a blow. She would never let him know how she felt. He could take her while he loved another, without the least show of guilt. He could caress without his heart being in it. He felt nothing for her. She heard very little of their conversation in the adjoining room. Hurriedly she found her cloak and wrapped it around her, stealing down the stairs and slipping unseen into the library. Here she hastily donned her stockings, gown, and shoes before quietly and unobtrusively making her exit. This had been possible, for the butler, foreseeing uncomfortable proceedings with the emergence of Lady Claire, decided the expedient thing would be to remove himself to his own quarters for the night. So it was that Kate met the night alone, disillusioned, and with barely enough coins in her cloak pocket to see her home.

She walked some distance before she spotted an empty hack and hailed its driver. A few minutes later, she was letting herself into her aunt's residence through the rear with her key and rushing up the back stairs to her room. There she found her bed, and with little left of hope, threw herself into her pillows. Oh Lud, Kate Newbury, who are you? She thought desperately. She had to sort out the threads of her disorganized life. She had to measure their lengths and take account. She wanted to feel whole and banish the terror from her heart.

Yet, horror filled her still. Her father had been a homosexual! The word, the detestable word, struck agony. For a time she had been attracted to Perry Banyon, only to discover that he had been her father's lover. Now she had given herself, unrestrained and with little show of pride, to a man who was nought but a rake, and who was engaged to another woman. She loved Branwell Mannering, but he loved—if he could love—someone else. She would never let him know how she felt. He would laugh at her foolishness. He had taken her, just as he probably took scores of other willing females. His heart had nought to do with it, and she would show herself every bit as worldly as he! Hadn't he said once that she was hot-blooded? Well she would let him think so! This decision, so far from easing her maddened brain, swept her with self-pity and further cause for tears. Indeed, she felt the spite in her heart as a wedge, a sharp pointed wedge, and it soothed not at all!

In the meantime, the Earl had discovered that Kate had managed to retrieve her clothes and vanish into the streets. His first thought, his first worry was for her safety. London was not the place for a young and beautiful woman to walk about unescorted at night. He left his lodgings abruptly, walking swiftly to his stables, and ordered his horse to be saddled. First, he would go to Sarah's, and if she was not there, he would comb the streets; but he would find her!

He reached Lady Haverly's within a matter of minutes, sweeping Travis with but one roughly-thrown question, "Has Miss Newbury arrived?"

"Miss Newbury?" said the butler puzzled. "I don't believe she has gone out this evening, my lord. Indeed, I heard Miss Premble clucking her tongue that miss slept without dinner."

Dinner, thought the Earl; neither he nor Kate had eaten this evening. He took the stairs, two steps at a time, for he was impatient to see her, wondering how she could have returned without being seen. Yet she had left without being seen; therefore it was possible. When he reached the second floor, it occurred to him that he was not in possession of the direction of her room.

Therefore he put up a shout. "Kate?" thundered the Earl. "Kate?"

The lady answering to that name cringed on her bed. He was here! It was most gratifying, yet she was not ready to face him. She buried her face in her pillows and was unsure whether she wanted him to go, or find her.

"Kate, for God's sake, do I have to break down every door up here, or will you answer?" shouted the Earl, slamming the first door handy into its adjoining wall.

"Branwell!" cried Lady Haverly, emerging into the hall, her hair tucked beneath a lace cap, her tall figure swathed in a dark silk banyan of Indian design. "Whatever are you shouting about? And do stop crashing my doors about. I won't have it! Really, what a scamp you are, to be sure, and I am most put out with you, so you shan't get around me tonight!"

"Sarah, which is Kate's bedchamber?" said the Earl shortly, ignoring her remarks to him.

"Don't try and change the subject, Branwell. Really, I am most miffed with you. First you send me that perfectly odious little note, telling me that you are to be married to that . . . that creature, when you know I don't like the chit. Insist that I break all other engagements, and let me tell you that Sir Francis was taking me to dinner tonight and I rather fancied he wanted to propose. Not that I would accept, but it certainly would have been most enjoyable to hear the old codger come up to scratch. And then you, wretched nephew that you are, you don't come up to scratch. Well, and I say really!"

He could see that explanations were in order, but at the moment he had a pressing need. "Which is Kate's room?"

"But why?"

"Is she in her room?"

"Of course she is in her room," snapped his aunt, going across the hall and knocking softly. "Kate darling, here is Branwell making such a commotion that I am certain he has startled you from your sleep, but he seems determined to know where you are."

"I am here, Auntie," answered Kate in a small voice, thinking it best to announce her presence.

The Earl's relief was too evident for him to hide and his aunt's gaze narrowed. "Branwell," she said intimidatingly. "What is toward?"

For answer he brushed gently past her and tried the knob; it was locked. "Kate, Kate, I would like a few minutes with you."

"Go away," she said, keeping the trembling of her voice down.

"Will you not see me?" he pursued.

"No," she answered, wishing she could say more, but aware that her voice would betray her.

"Very well, but I shall return in the morning, at which time I will insist on an interview," he said grimly. She did not respond to this and he turned to find his aunt's astonished gaze upon him.

"Branwell?"

"Now, my aunt, I find that I am quite hungry, and if you will be so kind as to send to your kitchen for some light cold collation, we may retire to the parlor and discuss the events of my day."

"Very well, dear, though cook is bound to be most put out, for it is quite late. However, perhaps Travis can smooth it out. Come along," she said, linking her arms through his.

The Earl poured himself a brandy and sat back in his chair, his hunger having been assuaged with bread and cheese. His aunt was now in the possession of most of the day's events (though he had said nothing of Kate), and it was left only to describe her part in his well-laid scheme to free himself of Lady Claire.

"But Branwell, it would appear that Rathborne has us rather boxed. It would not do to displease the Queen," said Sarah, frowning.

"We won't displease her. In fact, I doubt very much that any of this will ever reach her ears."

"But never say you mean to flee the country? Oh, Branwell, think of the scandal. No do not. I shall stand buff for you, but how I shall miss you," said his aunt unhappily.

"I do not intend to flee the country." He smiled fondly at her. "I had an interesting afternoon with the Beau and Willy. If all goes according to plan, we just may get through this."

"But how?"

"First, we shall compose an eloquent note to Rathborne regarding my inability to make his dinner party this evening. Secondly, you will ask him to visit with you tomorrow and convince him that a slight delay will not be harmful; in fact, you will show him that rushing his daughter into marriage would only serve to give the gossip-mongers meat to tear into. He will perceive your sound judgment in the matter and you will insist that he come to you for breakfast on Friday at ten sharp. Tell him that I will be present at that time to discuss the marriage settlement, and so I shall. I will be here with Willy; then you will say that you do not feel well and will retire to your room. However, in reality you will be off to fetch Lady Claire, without the Viscount's knowledge. You will go to collect her in a common hack."

"A common hack?" frowned Sarah disapprovingly. "I cannot like that. What is all this? I don't believe I understand what you are about. Though I am quite certain it is most wicked. In truth, both Claire and Rathborne deserve it, for he is not wholly ignorant of what his daughter is, yet he would hold you at gunpoint."

"Precisely my thoughts on the subject. Now, if you will but pay close attention, love, you shall understand," said the Earl, leaning toward her in order to illuminate her horizon with the edifying details of his design!

31

The morning light brought consciousness to Kate and with it came the convulsion of pain. Ah pain! It is, when sprung from the mainstream of the mind, an invisible force, yet as real as the aftermath of the whip's lashings. She had in one night sustained the bitterness of realities, and such realities! She could not now think of her father without visualizing him with Perry and it sickened her. They were ghostly figures, deformed, worth only pity, yet one had been her father! Her father, whose sexual nature had been perverted. And Perry had been the object of his perversion. She felt a broken lady, and she needed repairs, and her mind offered them. Who was she to judge the needs of others? Who was she to judge love's wanderings? She berated herself for judging her father, yet still she felt her soul scattered in a myriad of unmatching pieces, too delicate to forge together as a whole, for even her own beliefs, her own hopes had received a death blow!

Always, she had trusted herself to save her love for the man she would marry. It had sustained her many frustrated hours, knowing that somewhere, perhaps soon, she would marry for love, and be loved! Last night, she thought her heart fulfilled. She had trusted her instincts and she gave to the Earl because her spirit called for him . . . only him! It would seem that all the men in her young life were betraying her images of them. Her walls, walls she thought indestructible, crumbled, and she had felt her heart mourning as she had listened to Lady Claire and knew the Earl belonged to another!

Kate sat atop her funeral pile and surveyed its wreckage, but an insistent knocking at her door brought her head around.

"What is it?" asked Kate.

" 'Tis me darlin', 'tis Nell. I've brought you some coffee and biscuits and there is a tart, a strawberry tart, made fresh with hothouse strawberries just this morning. Do open the door."

Food, thought Kate, yes, food; I haven't eaten since yesterday afternoon. She rose and went to the door, opening it and finding the aroma of coffee tantalizing in spite of her melancholy.

"There now," said Nell cheerfully as she placed the tray upon the window table. "Shall I have a cup with you? Indeed, I think I will," said Nell pouring, but eyeing Kate from the corner of her eye.

Kate took the cup and sat upon the edge of her bed sipping slowly, coming to a decision. "Nell, I know about Perry . . . about Papa."

Nell nearly dropped her cup as she moved forward on her seat.

"Know? What do you know?"

"Please, Nell, don't make me explain. I know what his nightmares meant. Please don't question me, just accept it. I know."

Nell crossed to her and stroked her head consolingly. "My poor girl."

"No, don't coddle me, Nell; it won't serve. I would have the whole truth now, if you please."

"Let it rest, child," said Nell, moving away.

Kate sipped her coffee, keeping her hand steady, finding this next to impossible. She put the cup down on a nearby stool and continued, "It matters, Nell. I don't know why, I only know that I must have all of it now. I want no more surprises."

"What would you have from me?" cried Nell, wringing her hands.

"I want to know about my mother. Did she know about Papa?"

"Oh faith, Kate. I can't be sure. I didn't know then, you see. I never suspected, but I think she did."

"How did she find out? For she did find out. Papa said

that she forgave him, so she must have found out."

"She was carrying you, and it was near the time. She went for a walk. I know not what took her to the stables."

"What happened in the stables?" asked Kate, feeling a constriction in her throat.

"She saw your father with . . . It was a shock. . . . And in her delicate . . ."

"It killed her," said Kate softly.

"No, no, you don't understand. She loved him. She told me he was good to her, that it didn't matter . . . his sickness. For he did, in his way, love her. It wasn't that, and it wasn't you coming early that took her. Lord knows she wasn't strong enough to bear a child. That was what took her, only that," cried Nell agitatedly.

"I see," said Kate.

"Oh my darlin'," said Nell, returning her hands to the girl's head, stroking the long black tresses lovingly. "It doesn't matter. You've got your whole life ahead. What have such things to do with you?"

"Will it not haunt me into society, Nell? Will not some point and say, 'Her father was a . . .'"

"Stop it! Away with such things. You be better than that," said Nell angrily. "And if it's worrying you, it needn't, for none ever knew. Only the family knows."

"Oh, so I am protected by secrecy?" mocked Kate. "I hate that. I hate having a skeleton in my closet. I would rather bare it to the world and tell them all to go to the devil!"

"You can't do that, child; society ain't prepared for such openness of manners."

"Why? My father was a good man, a loving father . . . a . . . Oh Nell, I loved him so," cried Kate, suddenly sinking into her sadness. A torrent of cleansing sobs racked her body, but left her feeling somehow better, relieved.

A knock sounded at her door and Nell called out impatiently. A young lackey's voice filtered through the door. "Sorry to disturb you, but the Earl of Mannering be wishing a word with miss."

Kate's hand went up almost automatically to her face

to brush at the wet tears, and she whispered to her governess, "Tell him to go away, Nell."

"Are you certain, love?" asked Nell hesitatingly, for personally she felt the Earl was just the sort of catalyst Kate needed.

"Yes." Then, as her heart reacted: "No, no, I shall be ready in twenty minutes, if he will wait in the parlor."

Nell relayed her message to the lackey and turned to assist her charge with her toilette.

When they had finished, Nell stood above Kate who sat quietly upon her vanity swivel chair, combing and pinning the last of Kate's curls. She had gathered the long flowing black silk at the top of her head and tied it with a pale green velvet ribbon, allowing it to cascade in thick torrents about her head, before twisting them and pinning them in place. Short wispy curls framed her forehead and dangled bewitchingly about her dainty ears. She wore a high-waisted day dress of pale green velvet, trimmed only with a tuft of ivory lace at the wide scoop neckline, and again at the cuff of the tight-fitting sleeves. She looked enchanting, and the gravity of her gray eyes gave her a hint of sophistication.

"There, a picture you are, my pet," exclaimed Nell, much pleased with the result.

"Thank you, Nell," said Kate, feeling a twinge of excitement in spite of herself.

They made their way to the stairs and down its wide carpeted length to the hall and across to the parlor, and though Kate prepared and cautioned herself, when Nell opened the door and Kate saw the Earl standing there, her heart flew to her eyes!

Branwell Mannering stood at a distance from them, his hands clasped behind his back. He was tall, swarthy, devilishly handsome, imperious to all but his own machinations and arrogant enough to allow it to show. But he was no God! He was man. Man, true, and not demon, and not God. Only man, and what was even more disconcerting was the fact that he represented, The Man to Kate. He was the only man she wanted. His dress was

superb, she liked the deep richness of his brown velvet
coat and the soft contrast of his buff-colored waistcoat
and breeches. His hessians shone with a light of their own
and sported gold tassels. He was wondrous to behold, and
her honest gray eyes betrayed the coolness of her countenance and he was alive to their light!

The Earl smiled, bowing peremptorily to Nell. "Miss
Premble, how rosy-cheeked and bright you do look. I
wonder if it has ought to do with that dratted fellow of
mine, Hatch?" he asked, teasing her.

She blushed and knew not where to cast her eyes, and
he laughed at her discomfort. "He bids me advise you
that he awaits your pleasure in the kitchen, should you be
able to get away. I assured him, for I could see nothing
else would serve, that you would go to him at once. I do
hope I have not overstepped?"

Miss Premble sent the Earl a haughty look. "Your
Lordship sports with me, but if it is your Lordship's wish
that I do what I can to humor his first mate, I would
have no objection," said she.

"Ho! And it is my wish. A happy first mate is always
my aim," said the Earl, much amused.

Miss Premble turned to Kate. "With your permission,
Miss Kathleen?" she said, formally.

A broad grin attempted to lodge itself in Kate's mouth,
and nearly succeeded in spreading wide her lips. However, she mastered it, merely replacing it with a gentle
smile. "Of course, Nell, do what you can for the poor
bemused fellow."

Much embarrassed, Miss Premble took her leave of
them and then green eyes met and engulfed gray. Even
from across the room, they sent a burning message to
each other. It was a moment indeed, and neither wanted
to break it with words. They touched not, yet every fiber
felt sensations. They spoke not, yet their minds were
alive and in total harmony. Alas, memories, bitter
memories, have no place at moments like this, but they do
force their path in spite of will. Kate remembered. This

man, The Man, he belonged to another. She turned away and the moment was gone.

"Kate, you left me last night, before I could explain," said the Earl, coming toward her.

"Explain?" She turned to find him towering above her, and she wished he would keep his distance, for she found it difficult to think with him so close. "What is there to explain? Are you not engaged to that woman?"

He could not call himself a man of honor if he were now to lay Claire open before Kate. Though Lady Claire greatly deserved her defamation, he could not do it. His codes were strong. He therefore could not deny that he was engaged to Claire, for in truth, if he did not extricate himself, he certainly would be. Too, he could not offer Kate what she obviously expected—marriage—even if he were free to do so. He did not at this moment wish to engage upon the holy state! The gentleman seemed to be in a bit of a mess, for while he felt that these things were the case, he also felt an inexplicable need to comfort Kate. However, she had asked the question and he had to be honest. "Yes, Kate, at the moment it would appear that way, but it is not what you think."

She gave him her back, attempting with all her strength, and she was finding that she had much, to regain control of herself. She would not humble her pride before him. She would rather he thought her a lady of pleasure than pity her! Such was her pride.

"It matters not. Really, after all, my undoing was not your fault. I forced myself upon you. You must not feel any guilt simply because you were my first," said she with some sangfroid.

The reaction she received was not what she expected, for she expected him to be relieved. The Earl's green eyes took on flames of fire and his face grew grim. There was a turbulence within his chest, and he knew a wild urge to shake her. Damn such words, he thought viciously, how dare she speak such things to him? Why to hear her, you would think she meant there to be others! Such an idea had never entered his mind before. She was his virgin queen, his, no one else's, and he had never entertained any doubt that this was how it would remain. She had sent bubbles of anger through his veins and he took her arm, forcing her around. His lips were nearly upon her own, and his eyes poured lava into hers.

"Your first . . and your last, sweetings!"

"Oh?" she mocked. "How so, my lord? You are to wed another, are you not?"

"That has nought to do with you," he ejaculated irrationally.

She laughed mockingly and for the first time in his life he struck a woman. His hand left its mark across her soft cheek and would have sent her flying had he not retained his hold upon her arm. She gasped and brought her head up, her face smarting with the insult, yet she stared hard at him, defiantly, demanding his shame, but he felt none at that moment. He was in a rage, an uncontrolled rage, and why? Simply because this little lush creature had intimated that another man might make love to her.

"No other will touch you, Kate, depend upon it!" he hissed before flinging her arm from his hand and turning to stalk out of the room.

Kate watched his retreating form with indignation and some surprise. How dare he? Did he think because he had taken her, he had the right to abuse her? Well, she would soon show him the error of such thoughts. She flung herself into the sofa and gave vent to her fury. No tears, this was no time for that. She sat plotting her revenge, devising his end. She loved, but now she hated as well, and the two engendered a bevy of formidable plans. However, at length her cogitations quieted and her thoughts assembled themselves for her inspection. It happened that it came to her that she was a woman, fully grown, and quite on her own. She had a sizable inheritance, a lovely home, some intelligence, and a great deal of will. It also came to her, sadly, forcefully, that no longer would there be always someone to care for her needs; such times were past. There was no one whom she knew who would not at one time in her life leave her alone.

People rarely, if ever, find a "once and for always" as they do in the fairy tales!

It came, this understanding, not as a bright dawning light, but a slow dark realization. Life, a constant mystery, a series of events was there to be survived, and damnation, thought Kate defiantly, she would survive!

Travis broke in on her thoughts, for he opened the door and announced, "Mr. Daniel Ludlow."

Kate jumped to her feet and stared with total disbelief. Danny? Danny here? Then there he stood, tall, gangly, absurdly youthful in his fashionable garb, his pale hair flowing freely, fringing his forehead and framing his lean face and his eyes. Kate found his beloved light eyes and they were brimming over with glee. "Kate, hang me if you ain't a sight," he said, coming forward and taking her in his lanky arms to swing her around.

Kate took Danny as a wilting flower takes on rain. She held him, for he was a part of her lost childhood. "Danny, you've come, and just when I need you. Oh, Danny, they would destroy me if they could, but they shan't. Oh, now you are here they shan't!" she sobbed, tears of joy streaming her cheeks.

Danny looked startled, but was staunch to the challenge. "Destroy you? The devil you say. I'll plant a face he won't forget on the first one who tries."

She laughed shakily and hugged him again. "My fierce loyal friend. Thank God you are here! But tell me, how did it come about?" she asked, changing the subject.

"Eh? We'll get to that in a moment. Now what I want to know is what the deuce do you mean about someone destroying you? What's toward, Kate?" he asked, looking ominous.

"Oh, just a bit of depression talking. Now come and tell me how you happen to be here and what it means," urged Kate, leading him to the sofa.

He pounced upon the sofa eagerly, in a way that was all his. It sent a flood of happy memories to balm her nerves, and she smiled lovingly at his boyish face. " 'Tis that famous, Kate. You'll never guess, but m'father suggested it. And I'll be studying at Cambridge."

"Oh, Danny, that is wonderful! But I thought he wouldn't hear of you studying in England . . . wanted you home."

"He changed his mind. It was after we got your letter about your father . . . I am sorry, Kate," he said, lowering his voice. "Well, it was then that he said I should come here and have a look in on you and then take up my studies at Trinity. It was on my turning eighteen—and I do thank you for the neckcloth; it came just before I left Bermuda. And here I am!" he ended merrily.

"And here you are," she repeated contentedly.

They spoke at length about all their mutual friends and acquaintances back on their isle and then Kate settled back upon the sofa with a sad sigh. He eyed her a moment before venturing, "What's wrong, Kate? Something is; you've changed."

"Indeed I have. It is impossible not to change! You probably will, too, after living in London."

"No, there is something you are not telling me, something more, Kate. A man. Is it a man?" he asked pointedly.

"Oh, Danny, since coming to England my life has gone topsy-turvy, and I have done something awful!" she confessed agitatedly.

He laughed. "Nothing you could do would be awful. Perhaps irregular, though."

"Oh, I wish it were just irregular, but it is not. It is far, far worse than that."

"My shoulder came with me," said Danny, grinning widely.

"Oh, and it is a dear sweet shoulder. Do you remember I wrote to you about the Earl of Mannering, how he was a privateer and my Aunt Sarah's nephew?"

"Yes, I recall. You called him a pirate; it rather annoyed me, for you haven't the grasp of it at all."

"Never mind that, Danny. You see, I seduced him!" said Kate, gray eyes wide at her confession.

He took her blunt statement very well, considering that it hit him flush, unaware, and most squarely. "What?

The devil you say?" He shook his head over it. " 'Tis impossible. You didn't even like the fellow!"

"I didn't at first. I still don't, but, well, love is a strange sort of thing."

"But I don't believe it. You don't mean that you really—You didn't . . . I mean . . . he didn't . . . Everything?" he said at last and received the answer from her eyes. He shouted, "Damn the swine!" He had imagined himself in love with Kate when she dwelt in his domain. When she left, he found himself lonely, but not for a lover, for a friend. His joy at anticipating his career at Cambridge had sent all thoughts of marriage to the winds, yet now, knowing some unknown conquering hero had mastered his Kate, he felt a pang of jealousy and, too, a sweeping sense of guardianship over her. He cast his glance over her figure. "Are you with child?"

She stared at him, startled, "With child?" She had never even thought of this possibility. "I . . . I don't know. I mean, I think 'tis too soon to tell . . . and, oh Lud, Danny, I never thought of *that!*" said Kate in a note of dismay.

"Never mind that. Has he asked you to marry him?" asked Danny with some show of authority.

"He can't. He is engaged to another woman," said Kate in a small voice.

"Oh, Kate, how could you let yourself get into such a scrape?" he asked with some tartness.

"Well, I didn't know he was engaged at the time," snapped the lady in defense.

"The cad! You mean he did not tell you?" thundered Danny. "Upon my honor, 'tis beneath contempt!"

"The circumstances were unusual, Danny, and at any rate, it matters not," said Kate.

"It will when your belly starts puffing up." The notion struck him suddenly as ludicrous and he began to laugh.

She glared. "Danny Ludlow, it is not funny, and there is no saying that I am with child."

"I'd swear to it that you are, in fact, willing to lay you a monkey that you are," said Danny unabashed.

"Oh no, Danny, do not say so, for if I am, the babe and I are undone," cried Kate, thoroughly distressed now.

Danny saw the error of his ways and coughed. "No need to fret it, Kate. I'll marry you myself. Have always wanted to. Still do."

"Don't be silly. You will be starting university life."

"What has that to do with anything?" He interrupted her. "You wouldn't be in the way, never have been before. You are a good sport and we have money enough. Would be jolly good fun," said Danny with more confidence than he felt.

"But Danny, if I *were* with child, it would not be yours," she pointed out unrelentlessly.

"What has that to do with anything? A babe is a babe. I like the little brats—that is, when they don't drool on me. And you could see to it that it wouldn't do that, so where is the issue?"

"The issue is that I love you, but not in the way needed to be your wife, and you, my friend, do not love me."

"We could learn the knack of it. After all, we are comfortable together."

"No, Danny."

"I leave for Cambridge on Friday the twentieth at eleven. When I go, you shall go with me. Only thing to do."

"No, Danny. I may not be with child."

"Doesn't matter."

"But it does, and my answer is no."

"To what, dear?" asked Aunt Sarah, coming into the room, a lovely smile glowing on her face.

Introductions were made and an invitation to dinner extended to Mr. Ludlow before he was allowed to depart, and as he did, he turned to Kate. "Set your mind to it, Kate, for I don't mean to leave go."

She stared after him, wishing she could go with him—but as his friend, not his wife!

32

Dinner at Lady Haverly's was proving to be an ordeal for all involved. Kate was astonished when the Earl arrived, for she had never imagined he would be present this evening. Her feelings upon seeing him in his elegant black superfine were mixed, and she avoided his eye. Danny seemed determined to loathe him and make his contempt apparent, much to the Earl's amusement and amicable exasperation.

Kate often tried to catch Danny's eye, for he would not refrain from sending the Earl the most murderous glances, and she was acutely aware of them. There, too, when he wasn't glaring like a demon at the Earl, he was emitting the oddest spiked repartees. The Earl gazed speculatively at the lad, who was in many ways much like his own brother Matthew, and he found he liked him in spite of his barbs, and he wondered just how much Kate confided in him.

They had retired after dinner to the parlor for their tea. The Earl poured glasses of port for himself and Danny, handing it to the boy with a friendly grin. "Peculiar how this particular port is favored above all others," said the Earl in way of mild conversation.

"It is Portuguese, is it not?" said Danny politely.

"Indeed. There are few ports to rival those of Portugal."

"I suppose all places must in the end have something special to recommend them," said Sarah lightly. "I have often wondered, what is there about Bermuda, Mr. Ludlow, that you would call special?"

"Everything. Its lime waters, its cedars—native only to my isle—its passion flowers."

"Of that we have an example in Kate," said the Earl, raising his glass to her.

Danny took exception and rounded on him. "You raise your glass, yet Kate is no passion flower. She is a rose! The passion flower cannot compare to her, for it is wild, flamboyant, to be picked and used, as they do to make perfume. Now a rose, that is a wondrous thing, a thing apart from all others; there is an intricacy in the folds of its petals. It is a flower to treasure, *untouched*. I can look at the rose, but I would not pick it if I knew myself incapable of nurturing it and prolonging its life," said Danny meaningfully.

"So you believe in leaving it there for another to pick, eh lad?" teased the Earl, knowing well the boy's meaning and finding his gravity lightly amusing.

"Yes . . . no . . . what I mean is that I would leave it there for someone who *cared* more than I," said Danny frowning, for what he felt had been a classic allegory was not turning out quite as he planned.

"Ah, but in leaving it, you take the risk of losing it to someone far less worthy of appreciating its beauty. You could in fact lose it to someone who would perhaps crush it in his grasp!" pursued the Earl.

Danny frowned darkly over this, but Kate, angry with them both, interrupted. "Women are not flowers. And Danny, though he uses roses to explain his point, does in fact refer to women. I think this line of conversation needs a new direction, such as your upcoming marriage, my lord. When do you expect it to take place?" asked Kate, facing him boldly.

Aunt Sarah, on whom the above illusions had been totally lost, found something at last that she understood, and she groaned, "Never. I hope it will never take place, not with that creature."

"But Kate asks a question that must be answered. If it takes place, fondling, which I doubt, it will be next week."

"If?" said Danny frowning.

"If," reiterated the Earl. "It is my hope that it shall not take place."

"Why?" asked Kate, barely able to keep the hope from her tone.

"Because I don't wish to get married. It is not the sort of thing that would sit well on my shoulders," said the Earl gently, aware that he was letting her down.

"I see," said Kate, turning away.

He regarded her for a long calculating moment, but decided to remain silent. Kate took his silence as further evidence of his lack of regard. She felt hurt, weaponless, piqued, and she burned with something more: a sudden urge to spite him. He had said no other would touch her; the notion seemed to disturb him; perhaps here was her weapon!

She turned to Danny and began a furious flirtation. Danny saw her game and played, whispering in her ear, "He is wild with jealousy but, Kate, what's the use? You heard him. If he don't marry the other wench, he won't marry at all. You'll come with me to Cambridge on Friday, and I'll make you my wife. We will be right and tight. See if we won't."

"No, Danny."

"Must. Nothing for it, m'girl. Don't want to wait till you are too far gone, you know. Wouldn't like to see you wearing a scarlet cloak."

"Stop it!" said Kate.

"I know. It's a dastardly dirty situation, but nothing for it, Kate, won't have you pointed at. Won't have you wearing a scarlet cloak and shamed. Dash it, Kate, can't think I'd let you suffer that!"

"Please stop, Danny, I must think," cried Kate, moving away only to find herself face to face with the Earl. God, she suddenly felt suffocated. He took hold of her arm and held it vicelike, leading her apart from Danny and Sarah.

"Have a care, my lord; I am not yours to handle!" warned Kate.

"Then whose, my pretty, if not mine?"

She wanted to answer him. She wanted to hurt him, to get a response from him, and her only way out came before she could stop it. "Mr. Ludlow's, my lord. I am thinking of becoming his wife."

The Earl laughed; he threw back his head and laughed

with total disbelief. He was no fledgling to be taken in by her games.

"You won't marry him, my fondling; you don't love him."

"I love him far more steadily than you can imagine," she retorted, stomping away from him, so that she didn't catch the glitter in his angry green eyes.

33

The Viscount of Rathborne entered Sarah's elegant parlor, very much like the unsuspecting fly, and he smiled upon her good spirits. She was an excellent woman, this Sarah Haverly, and indeed lovely to look upon. Many was the time he wondered what she would be like in his bed, but, alas, she had never shown any inclination of finding her way there! However, her notes to him in these last two days displayed a change of heart. He fancied that he might use the situation at hand to further his cause with the attractive widow.

"Rathborne, you rogue, I never suspected that yours was a prompt nature," said Sarah, giving him her hand.

"Your note called for Friday, April 20, 1805, at precisely ten o'clock. I could do hardly less than obey the ruler of my heart," said he, placing his kiss warmly upon her wrist.

"Charmer, come sit by me while I pour our tea," said Sarah, with a flash of her bright eyes. "I do wish you were not so fastidious about your diet. My cook has a way with bacon . . ."

"Bacon? Heigh-ho, Sarah, I have m'figure to think about."

"Why, I rather think you should think about mine," said Sarah audaciously, hoping she wasn't overdoing it.

His eyes wandered over her hungrily. "I have been

thinking of nought else, and save my appetite for tonight, my Juno."

The door opened and emitted the Earl of Mannering and Sir Wilson Malmsey, and Sarah smiled gratefully up at her nephew.

"La, darlings, you are early. We didn't expect you until later, but come in," said Sarah smiling. "Sit, you may have tea with the Viscount while you go over the marriage settlements."

"Indeed," said Rathborne, pulling out an official-looking document and handing it to the Earl. "I acquired this yesterday afternoon. No time for a posting of the banns; it's a Special License. Had to use m'influence to get it so fast, let me tell you."

The Earl pocketed it. "Indeed most clever, Viscount; you do think of everything."

Eventually, Lady Haverly wandered away from them and stood by the fire, putting a hand to her forehead, and then, when she was certain that the Earl's eyes were upon her, she went into a swoon! A moment later she would most certainly have fallen in a faint upon the floor had not the Earl jumped up hastily to catch her, saying,

"Sarah, what is it?" and whispering, "Nice touch, ole girl."

"La, but my head is spinning."

"Perhaps you had better retire. Shall I see you to your room?" asked the Earl.

She held his arm for strength. "No, no, I think I can manage it."

The Viscount had come forward, as had Willy, and she placed her hand into Rathborne's. "Do excuse me?"

"Indeed, I hope it is nothing that will interfere with our plans for this evening," he remarked, his eyes narrowing.

She felt a wave of annoyance that his concern was a selfish one, and her brow went up in spite of her failing spirits. "Do not distress yourself; a few hours rest is all I need. The thought that we meet tonight speeds away all my ills," she said, smiling sweetly, wanting to box his ears.

Sarah was seen languishing toward the door, waving them to their seats before she vanished and went into action in the hall!

"Travis . . . Travis," she whispered, "does the hackney I requested wait outdoors?"

"Indeed, madam, he has been waiting since the Earl's arrival."

"Quick then, Travis. Help me with my cloak," said Sarah, diving into a black hooded velvet cloak of voluminous proportions. A moment later she sat comfortably, if somewhat nervously, back in a common hack that made its way toward the Rathborne residence. Here a street urchin was dispatched with the message that Lady Claire was being awaited outdoors.

The butler demanded to know who awaited his mistress, but Claire, who was ready for Lady Haverly, threw on her redingote of blue velvet and remarked that she knew very well who it was and he needn't bother about it.

Lady Claire made her way to the waiting hackney, one brow up as she stepped inside. "Lady Haverly, good morning, but is something wrong with your coach?"

"It has a broken axle, I believe my groom said, and 'tis a bit too cool for me, so I did not take out my phaeton, though I daresay you would have preferred that to this. But never mind; 'tis only temporary."

Lady Claire surveyed her surroundings with distaste, but put it aside. She was about to choose her engagement ring. It was a victory, indeed.

Sarah put a black-gloved finger to her lips as a thought struck her. "I have just had a splendid notion, Lady Claire. What say you to stopping by and fetching the Beau? His taste is exceptional in all such matters of elegance, and I for one would welcome any notions he may have toward the design of your ring."

Claire contemplated this a moment; indeed, the Beau's presence at such an outing would further solidify her victory over the Earl.

"I should like that very much, Lady Haverly. 'Tis a

splendid notion." Sarah indicated the Beau's direction and a few minutes later, they were standing before the fashionable lodging of Mr. George (Beau) Brummell, arbiter of fashion. They were shown into the parlor, which was richly furnished and displayed many intricacies of art. Every piece, every facet, seemed designed to enhance yet another creation. Nothing was overdone and yet every inch spoke of elegance.

The valet stood before Lady Claire and offered to bring refreshment, but she declined the treat, moving to where Lady Haverly had gone to stand near the window overlooking the street. At this point the Beau entered the room and captured their attention.

As always he was the epitome of fashion and good taste. His dark blue superfine was molded to his slim form. His neckcloth was tied in the Brummell fall; his waistcoat, a soft shade of blue, was intricately embroidered with dark threads; his breeches appeared painted to his slender legs and were pale enough in color to be taken as such. His hessians were as ever glittering in their shine, and his movement was superior, as was his demeanor. All clamored after the Beau, who insisted that men, for the first time in fashion's history, take a hip bath each day, change their linens at least twice a day, and wear little or no colognes. Gone were the pink, yellow and gold satins that men had sported in the past, and in its place came tailoring, wide shoulders, slim waists, Corinthian bodies, and hairstyles to win many a maid's heart!

Claire was not the first to lose what little heart she had to such as he, and hers fluttered at his entrance. "Beau, we have come to fetch you."

"Indeed?" said the Beau, bringing up his gold-rimmed quizzing glass.

"Put that odious thing down," snapped Sarah. "You shan't play off your tricks with me. The very idea."

He smiled winningly. "I wasn't leveling my glass at you, Sarah, so don't pucker up at me."

"Well then, at whom? Me?" said Claire, arching her brow.

He glanced over her gown, for the ladies had shed their outerwear, and he found her revealing satin gown of little style. "How you manage to ignore my advice and still find favor in my eyes never ceases to amaze me, Claire," said the Beau languidly.

"Don't be horrid. If I find favor, you can't really dislike my style of dress," she said, pouting.

"But I do. You should follow Lady Hester's example. Now there is a woman of style," said he sharply.

"You never cease to tell me so," said Claire. "But that is not why we came. We are on our way to the jeweler's to choose my engagement ring."

"Engagement ring?" queried the Beau, surprised.

"Yes, I am to marry the Earl of Mannering," said Claire, watching his reaction.

"Are you? My congratulations," said the Beau blandly.

Suddenly their attention was arrested by Lady Haverly, who apparently fainted, falling quite fortunately onto the sofa at her back.

"Sarah," said the Beau going to her at once, slipping his arm beneath her shoulders, and gazing in her eyes.

"Oh, George, I feel quite unwell."

"Shall I send for the doctor?"

"No, perhaps a bit of brandy."

Lady Claire hurriedly went to a sideboard and poured a sampling, bringing it to the Beau and placing it in his hands, saying, "Oh dear, Lady Haverly, if you are not feeling well, perhaps we had best leave our excursion for another day," her tone clearly indicating how shabby a notion she felt this to be.

"Oh no, my dear. I shall be quite all right," said Sarah, sipping the brandy. "Perhaps if I just rested here a while we could proceed."

"If you really think you shall feel up to it," said Claire hopefully.

"Indeed yes, you two children have a spot of tea while I just rest a bit," said Lady Haverly, closing her eyes.

The Beau rose and took Claire by the hand, leading her

out of the room. "Let us retire to my study so that we won't disturb her," he said, crossing the hall and opening his study door.

Once safely inside, Claire turned an angry face upon the Beau. "The old witch, she don't wish me to marry him. She probably isn't ill at all, just wants to foil my plans. But she shan't!"

The Beau's brow went up. "Rather unjust, don't you think, my love? And don't you think it a bit incongruous to have your lover help design a ring that will bind you to another man?"

"Oh now, Beau, don't be stuffy," snapped Claire.

"Stuffy? Indeed, I rather think I am very broad-minded. I don't think it odd at all, though it does strike *me* as humorous, but I was curious to ascertain your feelings on the matter."

"And now that you have that tucked away, does your opinion of me change?"

"Not in the least, Claire," he answered cryptically.

She shot him a quick look but decided to let it pass. Instead she moved toward him, wrapping her arms around his waist and leaning her head back. "Kiss me, Beau."

He gave her a peck upon the lips and she pouted, putting her hand into his hair. "I said, kiss me."

"No, it would wrinkle my coat," he answered glibly.

"May the devil and all his attendants trample the damn thing," she snapped, pulling at its sleeves. He allowed her to remove it and fling it into a nearby chair, and he smiled, touching her lips with his fingers. "It always strikes me, how very much I can still want you, in spite of what you are." And this as his mouth tooks hers, parting it, working it so that she pressed herself wildly against him.

He moved backward, finding the sofa and pulling her across his lap. "But, sir, will I not damage the smoothness of your breeches?" taunted the lady.

"Indeed, I suppose I shall have to remove them in the end," said the gentleman as he sent his hand down the front of her gown to find and fondle the youthful firmness of her breast. His mouth took hers passionately and he whispered, "Claire, you don't love him. Why do you marry him and not me?"

" 'Tis impossible, Beau; you know it. Your fortune is nearly gone, and you may be king of the ton, but your background is humble and . . . and . . ."

"You needn't enumerate my failings. I am quite aware of them. Never mind, dear, I merely wanted to banish a sudden fancy I had," he said, taking her lips again.

"Certes!" ejaculated the Earl from the threshold of the room. "I never would have thought it!"

Claire jumped out of the Beau's arms and attempted to straighten her gown. "Branwell, Papa!"

"What is the meaning of this?" demanded the Earl, for apparently the Viscount Rathborne was speechless.

Willy fumbled uncomfortably with the fobs at his waist and objected to his friend's question. "Dash it, Bran, can't really mean to ask such a thing. You can see what the meaning is for yourself. The Beau, here, nearly got caught with his pants down!"

The Viscount blubbered something at Sir Wilson, who thought it expedient to retreat a few steps. The Earl nearly lost his composure, but remembered the stakes and regained it at once. "What are you doing here, Claire?" He glared at Willy, lest his friend think it timely to put in another such remark.

"What are *you* doing here?" she countered.

"We came by to collect the Beau on our way to the *Gazette,*" offered Willy helpfully. "Didn't know he was . . . occupied. . . . So sorry."

She cast Sir Wilson a killing glance before sending pleading eyes to her parent. "Papa, you misread the situation. I came with Lady Haverly to ask the Beau to join us on our expedition to Branwell's jeweler."

"Sarah is here?" said the Viscount, his brow clearing perceptibly.

"Of course. She is in the next room resting, for she was not feeling well," said Claire hopefully.

"You say my aunt is here?" asked the Earl, turning on

his heel and disappearing into the hall, his retinue following close behind. The parlor door swung wide at his touch and his eyes scanned the room; however, Aunt Sarah was nowhere to be found!

The Earl turned to find Claire's brows drawn in a "V," her agitation visible. "Here, you say?"

"But, but she was here! Was she not, George?" asked Claire, turning to the Beau for help.

He looked away from her, his expression grave and his silence most deafening.

"George!" she demanded with utter disbelief.

"I am afraid that anything I might say would only further damage your reputation, Lady Claire," said Beau Brummell, looking her directly in the eye.

She sent him daggers of fury and stalked into the hall and shouted imperiously to his gentleman's gentleman, who appeared immediately upon the scene. "Where is Lady Haverly? Has she retired to one of the bedrooms?" demanded Lady Claire.

"Lady Haverly?" repeated the small man, much surprised.

"Yes, damn you, Lady Haverly! Where is she?"

"I am sure I don't know," said the man.

"Well then! Did she leave?" asked the exasperated woman.

"Leave, m'lady?"

"Yes, leave! Really, you saw us in, you offered us both refreshment."

"I offered *you* refreshment m'lady, none other," said the man carefully.

Lady Claire sent her eyes to the Beau with sudden understanding. They were in it together; it was a trap! The servant was dismissed and Claire barely waited for him to leave before rounding on her flushed parent. "Papa, this is a hoax. I have been trapped, you must see that."

The Viscount opened his mouth to speak, but he could not. He sensed that all was not what it appeared. There were too many coincidences. Yet he had seen his daughter in Beau Brummell's arms. He knew what his daughter was, yet he had hoped to marry her off to the Earl and wash his hands of her escapades. He now saw that at an end and closed his weary lids. However, the Earl felt it incumbent upon himself to see the thing through.

"Lady Claire, you forget that I witnessed *you* in the Beau's arms, as did your father and my friend Sir Wilson. Unfortunate, but there it is, and there you were neatly ensconced, giving no indication that you were held against your will. Where then is the trap?" asked the Earl quietly.

"You tricked me," shouted the lady.

"Into revealing yourself," replied the Earl. He turned toward the Viscount. "I regret, sir, that under these circumstances, I do not feel Lady Claire and I would suit, and therefore request that you withdraw the offer of her hand."

The Viscount regarded the Earl calculatingly. He was a worthy opponent. "And if I do not? After all, there is a doubt as to what we really saw here, and Mr. Brummell is too much the gentleman to speak about it."

"Upon my honor!" ejaculated Sir Wilson, outraged. "You are a scoundrel. I don't doubt you were in on your daughter's scheme to trap Branwell. Well, make no mistake, he was right for having me along, for while the Beau, being *the* gentleman involved, can't go about with the story, it don't stop me none. Juicy piece of gossip, and being an outsider there is no code that would expect me not to entertain m'friends with the news!"

"I see," said the Viscount. "Very well then, her hand is not available to you. I am certain you will understand," said he dryly.

"Papa!" exclaimed his daughter. But he was already facing Brummell, looking at him with much loathing. "I could make you suffer for this turn."

"Could you? I think not. I have offered marriage to your daughter who, quite thankfully I might add, has refused me, as her competence is greater than mine. I rather think you would also find the match disagreeable for similar reasons," said the Beau urbanely, taking out his snuff box, flicking it open with a graceful wrist movement, and taking an infinitesimal pinch of snuff.

The Viscount noted that the Earl was making good his escape and detained him. "A moment, Branwell, if you would. I should like to know about your aunt, for as you may have heard, we had some plans of our own and I am curious as to what to expect. How much was she a part of all this?"

The Earl's countenance was grave. "My aunt Sarah is an integral part of my life, sir, and I am certain she would have me apologize for having had to dupe you, but you did leave us little choice."

"I see," said the Viscount Rathborne, mourning the loss, for he had looked forward to romping with the merry widow. He sighed his defeat and turned to his thwarted daughter. "Come, Claire."

She cast the assembled men a scalding look and said, "Branwell, do not think this over! Oh no, my handsome buck, you have gained yourself an enemy." She then turned to the Beau. "And you, sir, have lost yourself a lover. Perhaps Lady Hester will have to do?"

"If Lady Hester would have had me, Claire, I never would have glanced your way," said the Beau dryly.

She chose to ignore Sir Wilson and he breathed a sigh of relief to see her go, turning to the Earl and saying thankfully, "Damn glad she didn't threaten me, don't like females to do that. It rather gives me a crawly sensation. Don't like crawly sensations."

The Earl laughed and turned to shake the Beau's hand. "You were stupendous, George. Damn but you were, and freedom tastes sweet."

"Didn't like it, Branwell," offered Willy, crossly pouring himself a stiff drink. "Didn't like barging in here on the Beau with his breeches nearly down. Not the thing, you know. Didn't like the Viscount's attitude and don't like Lady Claire's threats," said Willy, evidently much distressed over the proceedings.

"But Willy . . ." began the Earl.

"Don't want to hear it! Much put out with you, Branwell; mustn't get yourself in such a scrape again, for depend upon it, you shall be calling on me and I won't like it!"

34

The Earl had one more stop before he would be able to make his eager path to Kate. Ah Kate! Little minx, working her wiles to make him jealous with that puppy Ludlow! Why would she do such a thing but to get him to declare himself, and he had no intention of doing that! She inspired new emotions within his hardened breast and to be sure, he was wildly possessive of her. But love, marriage? Ah, bah! He had not extricated himself from one unwanted marriage just to plunge himself into another. That had never been his intent. Marriage, his thoughts were that it but ends in clawing at one another. That was not what he wanted for Kate and himself! He needed Kate and his needs regarding her were totally irrational yet still, if he could help it, he would not commit himself to marriage.

What then? 'Twas a sticky affair, indeed, that he was involving himself within. She was no shopkeeper's daughter to be set up in her own establishment as his mistress. Good Lord, Sarah would have his skin! Furthermore, he frowned over this; he could not subject Kate to such a life, to the snubs and ridicule of society. And Kate, his intuition told him she would not readily accept such a situation. Therefore, there would have to be stolen meetings and under the guise of their relationship as cousins, such could be arranged. Still, he anticipated problems, and there was something else nagging at his spirits. He had when he was still a youth made up his mind never to father any bastards; he had seen the pain it brought to all concerned; yet, for the first time in many years, he had given a woman his seed. What if Kate were with child?

254

Damn, he would have to control himself in the future if they had escaped such a thing now!

Kate hugged Nell to her fiercely. "Oh, Nell, I do love you."

"Bless me, child, what is all this? You are only going for a turn about Hyde Park," exclaimed her governess, with some surprise.

Danny stepped hastily in between. " 'Tis the excitement of my being here. Has her all feathery; pay it no mind, Nell."

Miss Premble cast him an affectionate look. " 'Tis that good to have you with us again, Daniel. You'll have my Kathleen herself in no time at all," she said with a sigh, brushing Kate's long black hair lovingly. Then giving her charge a gentle push: "Now off with you two. We'll expect you back by lunch."

Kate blushed and pulled the hood of her blue velvet cloak up and around her head, hiding her guilty eyes. Danny coughed and put his top hat on his head, following Kate out the door and to the curbing, where a hired postchaise and pair awaited them. Kate sucked in a long breath and allowed Danny to help her climb in, settling back on the worn upholstery while he climbed in beside her.

"Whew!" exclaimed he, making himself comfortable. "Devilishly glad your aunt wasn't about."

"Oh, Danny, I feel so wicked running off like this. Nell will be so hurt."

"There was nothing else for it! Must see that," said Danny.

"Well, I don't know. We could have waited."

"You're talking like a noddy!" said Danny. " 'Tis true Nell wouldn't have objected to our making a match of it, but even if your aunt agreed, she'd be bound to insist we wait until you were presented to society, and by that time, m'girl, you would have been showing!"

"Oh, Danny, stop it! You are being most vexing. There is no reason to suppose that I am with child."

"No reason?" expostulated the young man. "There is every reason in the world. I mean you did . . ."

"Take a damper, my friend, or I shall let some of that excellent red blood of yours," threatened the lady, blushing.

He patted her gloved hand. "Don't get into a miff, ole girl, not with me."

"And, Danny, I don't know very much about getting married. How does one go about it?" asked Kate, worrying anew.

"I'd rather you leave such things to me," said he, in a worldly tone.

"Yes, but do you know how 'tis done?" asked she, persistent to the last.

"Getting married is the simplest thing in the world . . . 'tis the divorce that's the devil of a kick!" He grinned.

"Do be serious, oaf! How shall we go about the thing?" He frowned over the problem. "First thing, we'll get a room. Then we'll get a vicar. . . ." He smiled, pleased with himself. "That's it, get a vicar; he'll do the thing right and tight. See if he don't!"

"I do hope so," said Kate doubtfully, the Earl's green eyes flashing through her mind and a heavy sensation of emptiness sweeping her withered heart.

"There now!" exclaimed Danny, spreading a heavy blanket between them and producing a pack of cards from his greatcoat pocket. "We'll pass the time with a round of piquet."

"I don't feel very much like it, Dan."

"Nonsense, just what we need to calm our nerves. Do cheer up, Kate, everything will be quite all right. I left a note, you know . . ." he said, springing the last on her suddenly.

"What?" shrieked the lady.

"Yes, left it with Travis. He is to present it to Nell just about noon," grinned Danny, a secret light playing about his eyes.

"But, Danny, that barely gives us an hour or so before they will know."

"I wouldn't worry about it."

"But what if the Earl arrives to find my aunt in a state about me?" said Kate, much distressed. Somehow she didn't want the Earl to know she had departed with Danny. What about his warning that no other would have her? What if he tried to stop them? He might kill Danny.

"Oh, Danny, 'twas the worst possible thing you could have done."

"I am certain you think that now, Kate, but you won't always, I hope," he said, casting his mind over his plans, hoping he had done the right thing, hoping he had not misread the Earl's character or the fact that the Earl felt more for Kate than he was willing to admit. The truth was that he didn't want to get married, though he intended to, if all didn't go according to his plan. So, like Kate, he had his worries.

Noon arrived, and with it the Earl of Mannering. He was shown into the dining room where Miss Premble and Aunt Sarah sat at a cold collation of various thinly sliced meats, lobster salad, and hot turtle soup.

"Ah, Branwell," smiled Lady Haverly. "I received your note and was most pleased that all went according to plan. But, where did you go? Why did you not come straight here, for I wanted to hear all the details."

"I am sorry, Sarah, but I had a meeting with Pitt that couldn't be postponed. Where is your niece?"

Sarah turned to Miss Premble. "Indeed, Elllen, where is she? Not out with that nice young man Ludlow still, for I thought you said she would be back by lunch?"

"Perhaps she came in without our noticing. I'll just have a run upstairs and see," said Nell, smiling and slipping out, hopeful of catching a glance of Master Hatch. But as she left the Earl whispered, "Sorry, Nell, Hatch isn't with me this trip."

She blushed, kept her eyes lowered, and rushed from the room, and the Earl laughed heartily after her. He liked Miss Premble.

"Really, Branwell, you shouldn't tease her so," chuckled Sarah. "She is such a dear. Now tell me everything!"

"It was as I thought. Had Sir Wilson not been there as witness, Rathborne would still have attempted to hold me to the engagement."

"No! Why, the wicked man! And I must send him a note breaking our assignation for tonight," said she, frowning slightly.

"No need. I have already advised him of that little fact," grinned the Earl, pleased with himself.

"Have you indeed?" said Sarah, raising a brow, her tone indicating less than total approval.

"You can't mean to imply that you meant to keep that assignation?" said the Earl, surprised.

"No, no! I don't care for Rathborne. But 'twas not your place to end it, young man!"

He laughed and tweaked her nose. "Don't be put out with me, love."

However, they were interrupted at that moment by Nell, who came in waving a note. "Lady Haverly, I know not what to say. Oh, Lady Haverly, Travis just gave me this note; 'tis from Daniel!"

The Earl moved away from the sideboard, where he was helping himself to a generous portion of cold sirloin, and brought his plate to the table, frowning across at Nell as he sat down and waited for her hysteria to end.

"Now, Ellen, I can't and will not attend you if you insist on waving that piece of notepaper in my face whilst I am at my turtle soup. Either give it to me to read or tell me what it is that has you so vexed," said Sarah authoritatively.

Miss Premble put a hand to her heart, evidently in an attempt to still its wayward beating. "It's Kate! Oh, perhaps you should read it for yourself," said she, sinking into a chair and handing the note over to Lady Haverly.

Aunt Sarah read it through and closed her eyes. "Good God!"

Now the Earl's attention was aroused, and he put down his fork, no longer interested in his food. "Very well, what is it?"

"Kate. She has run off with that young man Ludlow," said his aunt, giving it to him rather bluntly.

His jaw dropped and then set as his eyes took on an icy lining. "I don't believe it . . ."

Lady Haverly pointed to a line in the letter. "He says, here, that there are reasons—*excellent reasons*—why he felt they could no longer wait to culminate a marriage he has long hoped for." She sent her disturbed expression across at her nephew. "Branwell, they are nought but children. Why, the boy is but eighteen. 'Tis absurd!"

"Give it here," demanded the Earl, reaching for the paper. He read it through and then rose abruptly.

"What are you going to do?" cried Sarah. Nell, too, sent him a questioning look.

"The boy has made the mistake of giving us his direction. Mark me, Sarah, they shan't marry and your niece will be returned by tonight," said the Earl, stalking out of the room and bellowing for his greatcoat.

A few moments later the Earl of Mannering, his dark top hat planted firmly and angularly over his black tresses, his eyes two slits of green ice beneath his drawn dark brows, wielded his horse through the heavy London traffic. He was a hunter, and he knew this particular game well. The creatures he pursued had more than an hour's start on him, but they were hampered with a hired post-chaise, whose horses would be slow, and whose carriage would be heavy. An hour's gain in such as that against his sleek bay was nought. However, the Earl's thoughts were not calmed with such knowledge. In spite of his assurances to himself, he was still edgy, he was still wild with the inevitable, "what-if?" that plagues the most knowledgeable at times. He was at the moment insanely jealous . . . of a slip of a boy! Yes, Daniel Ludlow was but a young lad, and one that the Earl had felt he liked, but now he was the enemy, for he traveled with Kate. He traveled with Kate and would make her his if he could and . . . and . . . hell and damnation, thought the Earl wildly, he'd not let the boy have her! If by some unaccountable circumstance, Daniel Ludlow managed to pull this escapade off, then nightfall would see his Kate a widow! This bloody notion gave the Earl little satisfaction and sent his determination to stop them soaring. Then a thought struck him. Daniel Ludlow was but eighteen. He was under age. How could he have possibly procured a special license without a guardian's signature?

"Oh, Danny, go tell the driver to hurry; surely he must have finished his meal by now?" Kate fretted, for it was well past noon, and by now her aunt would have Danny's odious letter in hand.

Danny grinned. "Seems to me that you got your bristles up, little girl. What are you so fidgety about? Let the man finish his ale, and we'll be off. You finish your dessert. Come on, Kate, 'tis another two hours to Cambridge."

She sighed, wondering how he could be so placid over the entire affair. However, fifteen minutes later they were on their way. The time dragged and Kate was unable to enjoy the passing scenery though its quaintness struck her eye. She felt she could not breathe. She didn't want to marry Danny Ludlow. She wished now that she hadn't been so impulsive to accept, but at the time she had wanted to teach the Earl a lesson, though now the entire thing struck her as ludicrous. Oh, Kate, you are a fool, she chided herself. Danny had curled up his lanky form in a corner of their tight-fitting carriage and was sleeping like a lamb. A lamb, she thought ruefully, and she was taking him to the slaughter! She couldn't marry him. She would tell him when they reached Cambridge, and she would take the next mail coach back. Oh, she dreaded that. How ashamed she would feel, and how could she ever explain? She was worried, too, lest the Earl discover them gone and come after her. He was a fiend, a bully! Hadn't he struck her? Hadn't he said no other would have her? Why, she did not understand, for he meant to marry another, but believe him she most certainly did. Oh, God, if he came after them, he might injure poor Danny.

The time dragged, and such cogitations aided not its

passing. Then Danny was stretching and smiling and forcing the smile from her as she watched him. "How long have I been out?" he asked, rubbing his eyes very much like the little boy she remembered.

"A while. Do you know, I think we are nearing the village," said Kate, suddenly excited. "And there, Danny, that looks like a very nice inn."

He stretched his head out the window. "Dash it, Kate, it is a bit away from town. Think we had better continue more into its heart," he said, frowning.

"No, this is perfect," she said thoughtfully. "If we are followed, they wouldn't think to look for us on the outskirts. Tell the driver to stop here."

"We'll only have to move into town tomorrow. Want to be near Trinity, you know," he said.

"And so you shall, after you see me on the mail coach. I am not going to marry you, Danny," said Kate, looking at him full.

"Damn, Kate, you can't be going back 'n' forth like that. Why it's . . . it's . . ."

"It's my decision. But for now we'll stop at . . . what is its name?

"The Red Bull," he grumbled.

"The Red Bull. Then, we'll spend the night . . . separately . . . and in the morning you'll put me on a mail coach to London."

"You've got maggots in your head!" he snapped, as he leaned over and bade the driver pull into the Red Bull, then returned his attention to her. "You can't spend the night with me and then return home. You'll be a fallen lady!"

"Who is to know? My aunt won't tell anyone, and I am not really spending the night with you. We'll have separate rooms."

"I am getting a vicar and that is that!" he said, taking charge.

"But . . ."

"I won't hear another word. You have gone daft, but I haven't!" he said, interrupting her with some asperity.

Ten minutes later saw Kate situated in a private dining room alone. Her companion had gone in search of the local vicar. However, he returned sooner than she expected, and at his heels was a somber-clad individual introduced to her as Parson Stone. She observed that his name suited him well, and the light in her gray eyes began to dance in spite of her distress.

"I understand, young woman, that you and this young gentleman wish to be wed," said Parson Stone, pulling at his lower lip.

"I am sorry that you have been fetched here on a . . ."

"I didn't fetch him here, Kate. He was here, staying at the Red Bull. So it was a good thing you chose this place after all. Now I won't have to go searching about town for a vicar. He is a parson, but I don't think it makes a hound of difference, do you?"

"It doesn't make any difference because, Danny, I am not going to marry you," snapped the lady.

The parson looked very surprised, and somewhat ill-at-ease, and began to back away. "Well then . . ."

Danny detained him by holding his elbow, to which the parson took strong exception.

Just about this time, the Earl's horse rounded the curve in the road and his keen eyes wandered over the courtyard of the Red Bull. On an impulse he turned his horse into its drive and there questioned the numerous ostlers that came running out to take charge of his steed. Satisfied with their answers, he dismounted and gave up his bay to their keeping. He was tired from the day's ride and he was out of temper! He entered the main dining room, where he was met by the innkeeper. That worthy opened his eyes wide upon receiving a half-crown and hastened to give the noble gentleman anything he wanted. What the noble gentleman wanted was answers. Pleased to oblige, the innkeeper pointed the way to the object of the Earl's search, also adding that a parson had now joined the group.

The Earl's strides were hard and they were quick, and he burst the door open with a force that sent it convulsively against the wall. Naturally this brought around the heads of the three startled occupants of the room.

"What is the meaning of this outrage?" gushed Parson Stone.

Kate jumped up from her seat, and the Earl's eyes swept over her. She was exquisite and the sight of her satisfied one of his many needs, but her words were to singe. "Branwell, I know why you have come, but you are too late. I am already Mr. Ludlow's wife, and therefore you can do nought!"

The Earl sent her a murderous glance. "That, my dear, is regrettable. I had liked your young man and had no wish to injure him; however, under the circumstances . . ." He began to take off his gloves and Kate's eyes opened wide as she saw that he meant to challenge poor Danny to a duel. This is not what she wanted. She thought by saying the thing was already done she could send him on his way. She ran in between them. "Stop it, stop it! Have you no honor? He is but a boy."

Danny, somewhat pale but nonetheless game, took umbrage. "Take a damper, Kate." He met the Earl's hard gaze.

"I know not what all this is about," said Parson Stone, "and, I want none of it. I am here with my family on our way to Scotland for we are on holiday. First this young man asks that I marry him to this woman, and then she says she will not marry him; now she says she is already married to him. Really, it is most confusing, and who the deuce are you?" said he, staring at the Earl.

The Earl digested the parson's words, and then a slow smile worked its path across his face. "Then you have not performed the ceremony yet?"

"Ceremony? Mr. Ludlow has not yet given me the special license. How can I have performed the ceremony?" answered the parson testily.

"Special license?" asked Mr. Ludlow, blankly.

"Have you it?" asked Parson Stone.

"No, but 'tis of no matter. Marry us and then you may rest assured I shall set about the thing."

The parson laughed without humor. "You are wasting my time, Mr. Ludlow. The thing cannot be done without a special license."

"But you do not understand," said Mr. Ludlow, lowering his voice. "This young woman and I must get married at once!"

"Eh, but why?" asked Parson Stone.

The Earl glanced penetratingly at Danny as Danny moved closer to Kate and put his arm protectively around her shoulders. He had a sudden urge to grab Kate away from the lad's touch.

"There are extenuating circumstances, Parson, that make it necessary for us to marry immediately. Plainer than that I cannot make it."

The Earl took a step forward. "You will have to be a sight more plain for me."

Danny faced him, "I should think *you* would need the least explanation, Lord Mannering." He sighed. "Parson, do you take my meaning yet? Do you understand why we must go ahead with the marriage?"

The put-upon parson gasped and sent Kate a look of disapproval.

"I see. However, there is little I can do for you without the special license."

Danny turned his gaze to Kate, who looked murderously up at him. "Come then, love; there is nothing for it but to go and procure one."

"Get your hands off Miss Newbury," thundered the Earl, suddenly.

Danny, so far from removing his arm, brought up his hand and began fingering her lips, while Kate, too stunned by the proceedings to move, stood rigidly within his ministrations. As he played with her lip, looking into her angry gray eyes, he smiled, but managed to turn his attention to the Earl. "Eh, what was that you said?"

"Damn it, lad, do you want me to kill you? For I swear you are but begging for it," said the Earl, his voice now dangerously low. "Get your hands off her this instant."

"She is mine, Lord Mannering," said Danny, equally as quiet, returning his attention to Kate's lips.

He was taken by the shoulder and flung across the room. "Damn it, lad, but you've tried my patience long enough," swore the Earl, taking an ominous step toward him.

"Really, gentlemen. Gentlemen!" objected the parson.

Danny was still quite calm as he stood to his full height, ready to engage with the Earl. "Your patience? What have you to do with ought, barring the fact that you have fathered Kate's babe?"

"What was that you said?" asked the parson, much struck, looking at Kate with new wonder.

"What are you about, Danny? How can you say such a thing?" cried Kate. She was upset, angry and at a total loss to understand her friend's temporary madness. Her cheeks burned and she detested the manner in which the parson was now regarding her.

"So, that is it?" breathed the Earl, his green eyes glinting angrily. "She is with child! Did you think me a knave, to let another man parent my spawn? Oh no, my young bucko, you'll not buy her at such a price! Marriage? Damn, but I wanted none of it; but I'm not about to shirk my duty as a gentleman. No other will call my child his own!" snapped the Earl, much frenzied at being so caught.

Kate heard him, felt her heart sink at his words and knew an urge to throw the vase at her fingertips at him. He would marry her simply to prevent his honor from being questioned. And this, all because Danny must needs speak about a child. What child? 'Twas too soon for her to know. "But no, Branwell, you mistake and have no cause to concern yourself over your honor. I am not with child," said Kate.

Danny coughed and put his arm around her, chucking her beneath the chin. "Never mind the parson, Kate; you need feel no shame! You were an innocent, seduced by *this* villian," said he, indicating the Earl with his extended chin.

She yanked herself from him. "Oh Danny, I could pink you! Go away, all of you. I am not going to marry anyone!"

The Earl chose to ignore her and turned on the parson, who was listening to the proceedings with the air of one who has the finest location at an intriguing play. The special license the Viscount of Rathborne had delivered to him that very morning was produced from his inside pocket and slapped forcefully into the parson's hand.

"There is the license, my friend. Kindly perform the necessary at once!"

"But this is preposterous!" blubbered the parson.

"I think you will find it in order," returned the Earl with his usual air of self-assurance.

"I won't marry you!" snapped Miss Newbury.

The parson spun around and stared with bulging eyes at the lady. "My dear young woman. I am most shocked. I should think a woman in your position should be grateful to have anyone wed her, considering she does not even know who the father of her child is," said Parson Stone priggishly. All sense of the proprieties had been offended, and he felt most gravely over the entire affair.

Kate's color increased and she opened her mouth to stammer her denial; however the Earl cut her off. "I wish you'd hurry, sir; you will find my name already listed on the document, and Miss Newbury's you have but to fill in."

"Very well," said the parson, producing his spectacles.

Kate stood silent, furious, and yet not totally willing to withdraw. She wanted to marry the Earl. Even now, knowing he loved another woman and was marrying her under false pretenses, she still wanted him for her own. She glanced toward Danny and saw there a hint of glee about his eyes and the suspicion rippled through her that her sweet, simple Danny had somehow engineered this affair. But no, that was impossible. She attempted once more to extricate herself.

"But Branwell, you are engaged to another woman,

surely?" she began timidly, hoping his words would ease her conscience.

"Engaged? Oh to be sure I was, but that was a thing I managed to forgo! It would appear, however, that I shall not now be so fortunate," he said irritably, for he was out of temper. He did not like having his hand forced and he was entering this marriage unwillingly. His code of honor demanded it, for Kate had been an innocent and the babe was his, but how the devil did she know so soon?

Kate bit her lip and turned to Danny for help. He came forward and whispered in her ears, "There is nothing for it, Kate. 'Tis the Earl or me, and we both know who it is you want."

"Mr. Ludlow, if you don't mind," said the Earl, eyeing Danny's hand upon Miss Newbury's shoulder.

Danny removed his hand and stood back to witness his friend's wedding. It went rather quickly and rather well, a problem arising only when the parson asked for the ring to be produced. However, though the Earl's forehead seemed damp through the ceremony, he managed to think with some speed and produced his signet ring from off his finger. It was too large and directly after the ceremony, Kate returned it to him, but, nevertheless, thus it was that on Friday, April 20, 1805, she became Lady Mannering and Branwell's countess!

35

Kate adjusted the hood of her cloak, for a wind had picked up and was playing with her hair. She glared at the Earl's back some twenty feet in the lead and urged her horse into a trot, bringing her abreast. "Could no better nag be found or did you do this to punish me?" snapped Kate. She was sadly uncomfortable and put out with her husband, who had refused to hire a post-chaise, but chose to ride horseback the distance back to London.

"It was the best I could do under the circumstances. There were no others to be had at the inn and I wanted to waste no more time," said he curtly. "Besides, you needn't worry that I shall leave you behind; my poor bay is tired to death!"

She threw him a defiant look. "*I* did not make you come all this way, my lord, so don't be pitching your little taunts at me. Nor did I ask that we return to London in the same day!"

"I daresay you would have been happy to have married your suckling?" he mocked.

"A good deal happier than it has made me to marry you!" she returned.

He sent her a sharp look. "Really, madam? And the babe you carry, would it not have wanted its real father? Or did that not matter?"

"Everyone keeps speaking of a child. How is it such an issue?" she asked irritably.

He opened his eyes wide. "It is why I married you, madam! It is the reason that young fool felt it necessary to run off with you in such haste. The child must be fathered!"

His words stung. He had said much like it in the inn, but something inside had hoped that his pride had spoken, giving him an excuse to marry her. She had hoped for more. She felt the words like a shaft of sharp pointed metal and she felt her blood ooze slowly to the surface. She stared at the road ahead of her and said quietly, "Well then, you have tied yourself to me in vain!"

"What do you mean?" he asked, his eyes narrowing.

"I have no notion whether or not I am at this moment carrying a child. How could I possible know? 'Tis too soon!"

"But your Mr. Ludlow . . . he said . . ." faltered the Earl, genuinely astonished.

"I know not where Danny got his wild notion, but he did have it and it is impossible to shake him of something once he has it firmly in his mind. It was not, however, from me that he formed his opinion. How could I possibly know?"

The Earl's seething was seen in his eyes and in the setting of his jaw. "Why did you not speak up?"

"I did . . . if you would but recall . . . but no one paid me any heed."

"Damnation!" swore the Earl. Then a thought lodged itself. Perhaps this thing had been contrived. After all, Danny had left a note, stating exactly where they were going, and he had made no attempt to gain his way once the Earl had made his intention to marry Kate known. He stopped his horse and pulled on Kate's reins, staring hard into her eyes. "Well, my girl, you have had one day's work!"

"What do you mean?" she asked, frowning.

"I mean this entire scheme. Who thought of it? Your simple friend or you? It must have been you; women are always more cunning!" he snapped, furious with her, with himself for having fallen into yet another trap.

"You mistake, my lord," she said quietly, another hurt thrusting its way. "Neither Danny nor I would stoop to such a thing."

"No? Very well, you may or may not be with child, but depend upon it. You soon will be!"

This so infuriated Kate that she yanked her reins from him and threw over her shoulder, "Not by you, my lord; never by you!"

He was upon her in a moment; he held her reins and her arm, nearly pulling her out of her saddle. "Don't think I married you just to allow another to share your favors and fruits, my sweetings! 'Tis the last time you shall infer such a thing. Mark me, you will learn to rue such words! Now ride, madam, for I mean to reach London without further delay!"

She had no choice but to follow him, as it was growing dark, but she felt a hatred stir in her breast. She knew him not at all, and he knew little of her. The remainder of the journey was passed in silence, even when they stopped for dinner some forty minutes later; not a word was spoken and she avoided his eye.

It was well into the evening when they dismounted before the curbing at the Earl's town house. They were obliged to leave the horses standing, as it was late and his livery boys were not about. Kate mounted the steps in his wake and watched silently as he produced a key and inserted it. However, before the door was thus unlocked, it opened wide and a tall, staunch individual, whom Kate recognized as the Earl's butler, stood before them.

"My Lord, good evening," he said, attempting to hide his surprise at finding his lordship again in the company of a young woman.

"Good evening, Kirkly. Would you send a lackey to stable my horses? And Kirkly, this is Lady Kathleen Mannering, my wife."

The butler was unable to extinguish his astonishment, though he did hasten to offer the Earl and his lady his deepest congratulations.

"Would you like me to summon the staff, my Lord?" he continued, still in the throes of curious bewilderment.

"That is unnecessary, considering the hour. You may announce the news and have them ready for madam in the morning. After the boy returns from the stables, send him into the study to me. I know it is late, but I shall have a note I want him to take around to Lady Haverly."

"Very good, my lord," said Kirkly, who had by now regained his composure.

Kate had stood mutely by, blushing profusely, unable to look at either her husband or her butler. Because she knew not what else to do, she followed the Earl to his study.

This room stirred a memory she did not at this moment wish to recall, and she moved to the fire, giving the Earl her back. However, he seemed unaware of her presence as he sat at his desk and drew forth paper. A knock sounded at the door and he glanced up to find Kirkly at the doorway. "I beg your pardon, my lord. I wonder if I might inquire whether or not her ladyship is in need of refreshment after your journey?"

The Earl frowned and glanced toward Kate, who still kept her countenance veiled and averted. "Indeed, Kirkly, have a tray of tea sent up to my . . . to our . . . room, and hot wash water as well. I trust the fire will be lit?"

"Indeed yes, my lord, thank you," said the butler, closing the door behind him.

The Earl returned to his paper and Kate—suddenly tired, disappointed and temporarily drained of emotion—said in a quiet voice, "If you will excuse me, I think I should like to retire."

He looked up and there was a coldness in his eyes. "Would you? Very well, I think you know the way."

She found an emotion returning, and it was that of violent dislike. Though her cheeks were aflame, she put up her chin, turned on her boot heel and took her leave. The steps to the second floor were taken at great speed and the large master chamber reached soon after. She slammed the door, flung off her cloak and landed it on a nearby chair and stalked to and fro a moment seething with rage! The brute, the cruel, heartless cur. . . .

A knock sounded and a young lackey appeared with a tray. He was shy of meeting her gaze, unused to serving ladies, for this had for many years now been a bachelor's residence. She indicated the window table with her hand and waited for him to leave before inspecting it. How nice of him, she thought sardonically, to order her tea. She would have none of it, the unfeeling swine that he was!

She went to the wash basin and poured herself some clean water, scrubbing her hands and face with renewed vigor, toweling dry and then flopping unladylike into a nearby chair. She had not even a brush to untangle her locks, and, faith, she had no nightdress! The door to the room opened and Kate's mouth dropped as she watched Branwell enter and it suddenly occurred to her that he meant to sleep with her in this room!

She rose and backed away from him, a frown covering

her lovely features. "What do you think you are doing?" she hissed venomously, as she watched him shrug out of his brown superfine.

"Do? What should I be doing, my bride, but preparing for bed," he said in a tone that frightened her.

"You don't mean to sleep here, with me?" she asked defiantly.

"I most certainly do, though sleep was but a later intention of mine," he said, coming toward her, his waistcoat having been deposited upon the floor. There was a glint in his eyes and a sensuous smile about his mouth that made her take another step backward.

"Don't you come near me, Branwell!" she warned.

He stopped and his eyes narrowed angrily. "Again tell me that you would have preferred to marry your suckling; try and convince me, my fondling!"

"I would have!"

"And how far would you have gone? Would you have prevented him from coming near you? I still remember how his fingers caressed your lips. I could have killed you both at that moment." He had his hands around her slim arms and he pulled her roughly to him. She was furious and powerless in his grip and she loathed him all the more for making her so. "Better his touch than yours!"

He shook her, for she had aroused his temper. "Well then, my sweetings, you have married the wrong man, for it's my touch you shall have to endure! I mean to consummate this marriage, Kate, now!" His lips took hers hungrily, but they were rough in his anger. He was in a rage, a rage of her making, and he took no time for tenderness. He had never kissed a woman with such force, or such brutality before, and Kate felt her lips seared beneath his. His arms went around her back and she felt his hand press at the back of her waist, holding her to his hard muscular body as his lips burned her cheek and neck, and she hissed, "You brute . . . I hate you! You are no better than I first thought you. A pirate reigning on those who are unarmed!"

One of his hands flew to her long black hair and caught

it pitilessly, forcing her head back, forcing her eyes up. "I remember a far different reaction the last time I held you, madam!" he sneered. She gasped, but had little time for words as his mouth, spurred on by the memory of what pleasure she had once given, met hers. Her lips were forced apart by his and she struggled vainly to turn her head away. His touch was no longer that of a gentle, patient lover. He felt that he had been tricked into marrying her and as long as he had himself neatly tied to her, he would enjoy what pleasures she could give.

Kate beat at his chest, pushed against him ineffectually, wanting him in spite of her pride, despising herself for wanting him and forcing her will to fight him!

One of his hands held her by her hair, the other moved from her back to her trim muslin bodice, and she felt his fingers between her breasts just as she heard the rendering tear of the material. The gown gave way from the shoulders as he tore it viciously from her flesh, exposing the beauty of her lush feminine form. Her hands flew up to cover her naked breasts and she took a step in her attempt to escape him. He made as though he were a wild untamed animal, the growl deep in his throat as he reached out and held her arm, yanking her to him. "Would you have let him touch you like this," he said disdainfully, his hand covering her breast, fondling, his thumb working at her taut nipple. "Would you have let him, Kate?" His question now was a shout, a wild angry shout, an accusation! She glared at him. "Let me go! Do you hear me! Let me go, I hate you!"

This served to send her flying backward and she landed on the huge four-poster bed, flat on her back. She gasped and scrambled to her feet, but he was there towering above her and one shove of his hand landed her on her back again. She tucked her legs beneath her and attempted to scurry over to the other side, but his ubiquitous hands were there again pulling her back, holding her by her wrist, simultaneously undoing his breeches. She clawed at him, beat at him, kicked, and cried, but he held her fast. She bit nearly through his hand until he did indeed take notice. "Damnation!" he thundered, as he mounted the bed and pulled her beneath him. "What sharp teeth you have, my fondling. Now, now, madam, let us see how long you will still wish to use them," he said, and his body covered hers. His mouth found her breasts and took the nipples, playing, teasing, sucking, taunting her into submission. But she was obsessed with fighting him off. He had hurt her pride, and her pride demanded payment. She was no match for his strength, but she struggled beneath him, cursing him as he tore away the last shred of her muslin gown. His knees separated her own and his hand slid over her thighs to the mound they sought. But this time there was no cosseting, no caressing, as his finger dived into the regions of his desire. She felt him probing her, felt him arch his back as he prepared to replace his finger with that larger, harder muscle, and she cried, "Please, Branwell. Do not, not like this; it is against my will!"

"What, against your will, as this marriage was against mine," he said, unmercifully.

He plunged with a fierceness that sent wild rivulets of ecstasy through his limbs and she stiffened beneath him. She felt his hard pulsating muscle rotate sensually within her and her body betrayed her, for it responded. It responded to his scent, to the feel of his power and the erotic touch of him. Her mind though was possessed with a different will and that will would have fought him still. It won the battle momentarily, and she contained her own ardent needs. She lay beneath him, inert and unresponsive to his wild grindings. She forced herself to lay impassive, unfeeling, cold to his words, his magic words that had the power to send hot blood stinging through her veins!

He raised his head back, this man, the man her heart had cried for, and she could see in the way that his jaw worked that his anger was present still. "So, sweetings, cold against me? I can change that, you know." Even as he spoke his hands had altered their position. They moved from her buttocks to her knees. Suddenly he was bending her legs, forcing them away from the mattress, leaving her legs bent in the air, her calves folded in upon her thighs and he was plunging further into her and his mouth was at her ear, "You needn't move for me now, my beauty, all you need do is feel. Do you feel?"

And she felt! She felt the walls of her honeycomb hold and pulsate his throbbing manhood, taking even as she would expunge him. Her body called her a liar and she felt herself on fire as he moved. He groaned at her ear, "Damn, but you are so tight, and your body is perfect, perfect." Then his mouth took hers again, parting her lips, his tongue finding and making love to her own, and Kate was lost!

His every move engendered a response in her, and she found her arms going round his neck. She clung to him as she met his hungry dives, she felt him urge her calves round his back and she objected not. She heard his passionate encouragements and gloried in them, feeling whole beneath him, feeling whole enjoined to him. She had to move with him, for there was a wild symphony in her ears and in her body. She had to take what he was giving and she gave in return and gave, until both were lost to all but their own new realm!

When they had done, they lay enervated beside one another and he would have slept, contented. But Kate, not so! Complicated is the female mind, especially when it has been abused, and Kate felt herself abused, violated, forced into shaming herself! She was a victim of this man and herself, and she would punish both! He had married her to save honor. He didn't love her, and tonight he had raped her. Well, she would never let him touch her again, not without love!

She yanked away the coverlet and wrapped it round her naked body as she slid off the bed. The Earl's brow went up and he propped himself on his elbow to watch her. "Where the deuce do you think you are going?"

"To the daybed in your dressing room. Until a room can be prepared for me that will have to do," she answered coldly. "And, my lord, if you ever come near me again I swear I shall take a knife if not to you then to myself. For you shall not lower me into the role of common slut again!"

He frowned, for she confused him. He knew in the end she had responded to him, and he remembered that first night with her and how different, how fulfilling it had been. He wanted her, but in truth he was ashamed of having forced her, and he was hurt by her continued coldness. He slid his legs out of bed. She backed away, her gray eyes shining with her fear and again this made him feel a wince of shame. "You needn't cower, madam. I shall not touch you again tonight." He looked her over regretfully. "The sad truth is I want no unwilling female in my arms. So consider yourself safe from my hands, until you ask for it." He rose and moved toward his dressing room, and she watched his naked retreating form, inwardly marveling at his powerful lines. He turned at his dressing room door. "Good night, Kate."

She said nothing but turned her head against him and crept into her bed. As she pulled the covers round her, she received a whiff of his scent and in spite of herself, her heart and body reacted warmly!

36

Kate opened her eyes with a start, and, as her mind cleared away the haze of drifting dreams, she remembered! It was morning, and she was the Countess of Mannering. Her room was shrouded in gray dullness, for her drapes had not yet been drawn, but there was a crack of light peeping from its center folds. The fire in the hearth had been lit as well, and she wondered if the Earl had gone to the trouble for her. She yawned and propped herself upon her pillow, pulling the covers around her and grimacing as she remembered the fate of her gown.

She had absolutely no clothes, no hairbrush, no toothbrush. A fine state you've got yourself into, Kathleen New . . . Mannering, she corrected with a sigh. Well, there was nothing for it. She would have to ask the Earl to procure her these things.

She put her naked feet upon the wooden floor and found it cold in spite of the fire. With a shiver, she wrapped the coverlet completely about her shoulders and ran to the dressing-room door. A knock produced only silence. Another, more of the same. Boldly she turned the knob and found it unlocked. The door opened inwardly and she peeped her head around its edge and found there an empty room. She sighed and padded back to her bed and noticed the folded envelope upon her nightstand. With a sudden frown daunting her spirits she picked the envelope up and slit it open with her finger. Her frown buried itself as she read:

Good morning, my Lady Mannering,

I felt, after your ordeal, you needed sleep more than you needed a parting kiss, so I chose not to wake you.

I trust the fire I started for you will keep you warm until your Miss Premble arrives with your things. As my staff is comprised entirely of males, I have ordered none to disturb you until she comes.

You have said that you hate me. Very well, it will not greatly disturb you to have our *honeymoon* cut short by my return to the sea. For it is to the sea that I go and know not when I shall return.

Sarah will guide you, and you have in Miss Premble an excellent companion, so I know I leave you in good hands.

There is one thing more, madam. I have said I shall not again touch you until *you* will it. So be it! However, I trust you will honor our marriage vows in my absence, for if you would rather put the knife to yourself than let me near your bed, so would *I* rather put the knife to you rather than let another near your bed. I trust I am fully understood!

Your fond husband,
Branwell

Such was the note she crumpled in her hand. She flung it to the flames and then dove after it, retrieving it from its deathbed and holding it against her heart. A tear flowed inexplicably, and all she could think was that he was gone! She had anticipated and planned many things; this was not one of them.

After a time, the tears were replaced with indignation. How could he leave her? How would it appear to Aunt Sarah, to Nell, and to his own servants . . . ? He had left her alone to face them all. Marriage? She had not even his wedding ring. Well, she thought defiantly, she would show him! She would teach him that her pride was not to be trifled with. But then a knock sounded at her door and Nell's voice was calling for admittance. "Nell, oh Nell!" she cried, holding the coverlet to her and rushing to fling the door open and throw her free arm around her former governess's neck.

"Wish't, child," said Miss Premble, lovingly. "Now then, let me pass, child, for I've brought a portmanteau with some things you'll be needing. Indeed, I see that you need them badly, for your hair is that tangled!" She went to the bellrope and gave it a hard yank before turning to Kate, who had dived into her portmanteau to investigate its contents.

"The rest of your things will be sent over later in the day, Kathleen." She stopped to face Kirkly, who had come in answer to the bell. "Oh thank you, sir, for being so prompt, but my lady will be wanting a bath. In the meantime, if you would be so good as to send up coffee."

"Very good, but until Lady Mannering's dressing room can be aired, I'll have her bath prepared in his lordship's dressing room," said Kirkly, unsure whether he liked receiving orders from this woman. However, the Earl had advised him that Miss Premble would be coming to serve as his lady's companion-housekeeper, and after all it would be nice to have the house fully staffed and led by a fashionable hostess again.

Kate slipped into a wrapper Nell had been foresighted

enough to pack and crawled back into bed, avoiding Miss Premble's penetrating eye. "Now, Nell 'tis no use looking so prudishly at me."

"How so, my Lady? 'Twould be presumptuous of me to do any such thing. You are no longer my charge, but Lady Mannering; 'tis not for me to be saying when you have misbehaved or not," said Nell primly, sitting on a chair and folding her hands in her lap.

"Are you pleased to be here, Nell? Now you will be near your Master Hatch," teased Kate, feeling more in spirits now that Nell was at hand.

"Never you mind! But Master Hatch has gone off with his Lordship, and I don't expect they will return for weeks and weeks."

"How did you know? I didn't tell you Lord Mannering had gone," said Kate frowning.

"Why, Master Hatch came by yesterday, and he mentioned that he was off to sea with the Earl. Though, 'tis not me that should be answering questions, my lady," said Miss Premble, remembering the scrape Kate had plunged herself into.

"Now, Nell, you said it wasn't your place," bantered Kate.

Nell felt hurt, and it showed in her eyes and the fading of her full-bodied cheeks, but Kate jumped from her bed and took the woman's hand. "Oh darling Nell, don't look like that. I'm a spoiled thoughtless creature to speak so. I was but jesting, really."

"Then, Kathleen, will you not confide in me and tell me how all this came about?"

Kate could not bring herself to lay her wounds bare to Nell; she looked away and said idly, "The Earl and I married because . . ." She hesitated. What could she say, what could she possibly say?

"Oh Nell, it was all so complicated and Danny thought he wanted to marry me, you see, but I could see that he didn't, and I wanted to return home, but he and the Earl thought that my reputation, and theirs for clouding mine, was tarnished. It was decided that marriage was the only buff for the situation, so here I am, Countess of Mannering!"

"That is the strangest round tale I ever have heard, my lady," said Miss Premble, rising and going to the door that had opened to emit a lackey with a tray of steaming hot coffee. She relieved him of his burden and brought it to the nightstand, where she busied herself with pouring, saying slowly, "Lady Haverly was in ecstasy when she read the Earl's note advising her that he had wed you. She sends a notice to the *Gazette* this morning and wishes me to extend her most loving felicitations. She expects to call on you later in the day, and my Lady . . ."

"Yes, and do stop calling me 'my Lady,' Nell. It sounds absurd!"

"Why it should, I have no idea, and as it is your title you had better get acquainted with the sound. But what I was about to say was that Lady Haverly has no notion that the Earl has departed for the sea. She will be most surprised," said Nell, in way of a warning.

"I see . . . thank you, Nell. I suppose I had better think of a feasible tale to tell, then."

"Perhaps if you explained that this time 'twas not privateering that called him, but his country's needs," Nell offered carefully.

"What mean you, Nell?" asked Kate eyeing her with some astonishment.

"Well, Master Hatch did give me his confidence, but I don't think I'd be breaking it to tell you. For you are his mistress now, after all," said Nell more to herself than to Kate. " 'Tis this, my lady, though this you mustn't repeat. Prime Minister Pitt has asked the Earl to carry out a mission for him."

"What?" shrieked Kate. "What sort of mission?"

"Hatch didn't tell me that, and it's just as well that we don't know, but I don't suppose it would hurt for you to let on that the Earl was asked by someone of great importance to carry out his country's call."

"No, that is perfect," said Kate, deep in thought, marveling to herself. She had found her opinion of her husband fluctuating from low to high and down again. Suddenly she saw a new facet to his life, and it filled her with curiosity. However, she put it aside. Her hurts were still raw, and her need for revenge burned too deeply for any other considerations to weigh. She had found a way in which to save face; she would use it for that, not to feather new interest in the man she was determined to despise!

Sails billowed smoothly in the wind as the *Gypsy* cut its path through the dark blue waters! Master Hatch was busy at his post, his large form looming predatorily on the horizon. His thoughts were of his full-bodied woman, Nell, but he put them aside for there was work to be done, if he were to get the crew into shape! He shouted his orders to the men, and the men worked happily, their song in the air, for were they not at sea? Yea! They were at sea and it was good to have their mistress rolling lewdly beneath their legs!

Their captain was at the helm, setting their course and attempting to set his mind. But his thoughts wandered. He looked at the variegated sky, the clouds shaping before his eyes into white blankets, and he could see Kate. She was a transparent figure before his gaze, yet she was real, with the power to pull at his heart. She floated there, her tantalizing black hair dancing in the wind, her exquisite little face beguiling him with its charms, and her gray eyes taunting him with their sudden coldness! There was an accusation on her lips and on her countenance, and he felt it pierce his chest. When he had bent over her a few days ago, to leave his note beside her bed, he had wanted to wake her, kiss her, but he knew it was impossible. Something had set them miles apart. She said she hated him! Well, she would wake to find herself abandoned; 'twas what she wanted, after all! There was a dry taste in his mouth from such a victory. It was a winning he derived little pleasure from. He would have rather had her here at his side, and later in his bed. He would rather hear her laugh and see her smile than see the fear and the sadness creep into her eyes. *Bah!* Such was marriage that it drove two people into barren fields. Without it they had loved. Oh God, he could still remember her responses of that first night. It was wondrous. Even when he had taken her against her will, it had been better than it ever was with any other. Well, such thoughts were doing him little good. They were now, in many ways, an ocean apart, and at the moment he had not the power to close the gap!

Prime Minister Pitt had said he was needed, and Branwell had plunged into the affair most willingly, but then he had not realized he would soon be a groom! However, there was nothing for it. His course had been set. Admiral Nelson was stationed off Tetuán Bay and he needed word of the French fleet. How were their numbers? Where were they destined? To date, none of the admiralty had been able to discover these answers, and without them the English colonies were in danger!

Then, too, there was talk of a French invasion. It was said, and with reason, that Boney was about to cross the channel and send his armies into England. Pitt had to make England master of the seas in order to dispel this possibility.

Wisely the Earl had set his route for the coast of Portugal, for there he had friends and there he received answers. The French fleet was comprised of twelve French warships, eight French frigates, and eight Spanish frigates and they had left Cadiz on April 9! There was nothing for it; the Earl would have to make a calculated guess and set his course if he was to come across them and get word to Nelson!

37

A week had brought many changes to Lord Mannering's former bachelor residence. Indeed, it had once been, under his mother's influence, one of the most fashionable residences in all of London society. Under its former hostess's patronage it had held the wittiest, the loveliest the ton had to offer. Its new lady seemed determined to revive its glory. It had all started quite simply enough. Kate had donned the one gown Nell had brought her that first morning and it was a simple but elegant day dress of gold velvet, trimmed with wide brown satin striping. When she had had it made, her aunt assured her it was bound to be the highest kick of fashion. She dressed her long shining black hair à la Grecque and with Miss Premble in attendance meandered downstairs to her absent husband's study. Here it was she received her first morning caller.

Sir Wilson Malmsey appeared at what he felt was a bright and early hour of the morning at his friend's lodgings. Kirkly opened the door to receive Sir Wilson's hat, coat, and walking stick. "Hello, ole boy. The Earl up?"

"I am afraid the Earl has already left and is not expected for some time to come," said Kirkly, formally.

"Dash it! Never say he has gone to sea again. Devil of a man to hold down. Very well." He started to relieve the butler of his things but was stayed by that worthy's offer. "However, Sir, Lady Mannering is in the study, should you wish to see her."

Sir Wilson's eyes showed promise of exploding from his face. "What's that you say? Lady Mannering? But that is impossible, I tell you. Why, we got rid of her yesterday, with m'own eyes!"

The butler cleared his throat. "Lady Mannering is in the study," he repeated. "Shall I announce you?"

"You'll do no such thing!" said Sir Wilson, much frightened at such a prospect and quite ready to bolt. However, the knocker sounded at this precise moment and the door was opened to allow Lady Haverly entrance. She perceived Sir Wilson, blew him a kiss, and dropped off her bonnet, cloak, and gloves on top of Sir Wilson's things, which were still held by Kirkly. Kirkly in turn dropped his burden into a waiting lackey's hands.

"Where is my darling Kate?" asked Sarah merrily. "And how nice of you to come to pay your respects so early. Though I daresay we are intruding on the honeymooners. But never mind, they shall go off together presently and be alone," said she to Sir Wilson.

"Kate? Thought the woman's name was Claire. And thought you didn't find it to your liking. Good morning, Lady Haverly," said Sir Wilson, beginning to think he should have stayed at home.

"Claire? No, no, you silly boy! He has married my niece, Kate." She turned to Kirkly. "Where are they . . . still abed I suppose?" She giggled much like a school girl.

"Lady Mannering is in the study, but his lordship has left early this morning for his ship," said Kirkly, pleased to find her as much in awe of this circumstance as he was himself.

"What?" shrieked Sarah. "Well, I shall get to the bottom of this. Come along, Willy," she said, taking him by the arm and dragging him with her.

"No wish to intrude," said Sir Wilson, hopeful of getting away.

He was, however, magisterially ushered into the room across the hall to find there one of the loveliest creatures he had ever before clapped eyes on. These were in fact his very first words, which in turn served to bring the smile back to Kate's eyes.

"You mustn't mind Sir Wilson; he is a bit odd, but very dear," offered Sarah, giving her niece a warm hug. "Now, you poor little thing, what can this mean, Branwell's running off to sea and leaving you so soon after the wedding? Did you have a spat?"

"Oh, Aunt Sarah, you must not mind. I assure you I do not; t'was not his choice, after all."

"Oh, how so?" asked Lady Haverly, eyes narrowing.

"It seems he has been asked, by someone very important, to go on government business," said Kate portentously.

"By jove," ejaculated Sir Wilson. "Dash it, should like to know what is afoot."

This was a question that was tossed about a great deal before it was finally allowed to rest; however at the end of an hour's visit, Sir Wilson declared himself madly in love with his best friend's wife and invited her to the theater that very evening. Lady Haverly sent him an eye that was loaded with meaning and he hastened to include her in the invitation, which she graciously accepted. Thus it was that Kate had her first formal introduction into society as Lady Mannering. It was to prove to be the fall of the first domino!

She sat in their box, a flower encased in red soft petals. Her winged brows moved expressively over her bright gray eyes and her head, a shower of black gleaming curls, moved this way and that as she found new objects to gaze upon. She had been here before, but everything seemed so different now. Now she was really a part of this glittering world of fashionables! Elegantly dressed gentlemen in other boxes nodded to Sir Wilson and allowed their roving eyes to devour her. Whispers went around as people discovered she was Lady Mannering, and the interest was rampant. And then her world spiraled, for she was accosted by a man whose honey curls twirled around a handsome head, and she looked up into the bright eyes of Tom Moore.

"Mr. Moore!" exclaimed Kate, nearly jumping out of her seat. "I have been so hoping I would see you in London!"

"My little Kate. Can it be? . . . Is the Nea of my thoughts really here?" he asked quietly, putting her small white gloved hand to his lips.

"I don't really know, sir, am I?" she countered, allowing him to gaze into her warm gray eyes. He sucked in his breath and had not Sir Wilson returned at that moment with refreshments, most certainly would have taken up a chair beside the lady. Willy put the lemonade down and clapped the poet's back, for he was universally liked by the ton. "Tom, old boy, how are you and your rhymes?"

"As buoyant as ever, Willy, but why did you not tell me my Nea had arrived from my fairy isle?"

"Nea? You mean to tell me that Lady Mannering here is the Nea of your poems?" said Sir Wilson, much struck.

"None other, though when I wrote my poems in her honor she was not Lady Mannering."

"Tom darling, la, but it has been an age!" exclaimed Lady Haverly, who had just entered the box. She had been off gossiping with her friends.

"Why, Sarah, as beautiful as ever," said Tom Moore, ever gallant.

"Have you been meeting my niece?" asked Sarah, smiling happily.

"Your niece? Good Lord, the night is full of surprises," said Tom, chuckling ruefully.

"Never say then that you know each other?" said Sarah.

"Of course, Aunt Sarah. Do you not remember my mentioning that Mr. Moore was in Bermuda last year? He left just about this time, in fact," said Kate, smiling sweetly up at him, remembering their innocent flirtation and thinking it had been more like centuries ago.

"Indeed, I left last April with your niece's sweet beauty firmly implanted in my mind, but I fear I have lost my Nea to another," said Moore sadly.

"Nea?" said Kate with a frown. "What does such a word mean?"

"It means lovie or some such nonsense," offered Willy, wishing Tom Moore would take himself off.

"It means sweetheart," said Tom Moore, his eyes caressing her face.

"Oh," said Kate in a small voice, her eyes flying to her lap.

"I believe the first act is about to begin," said Lady Haverly, giving Tom Moore her hand and his dismissal. He smiled, well aware what she was about, and he took his leave. More than one pair of eyes in the crowded boxes had witnessed Tom Moore's interest in the new beauty. The owner of a pair of dark bright eyes studied Kate long and leisurely before leaning on her velvet cushioned chair and touching her stepbrother's white gloved hand. "Alban, they say she is Lord Mannering's bride, but that he has managed to tear himself away to go to sea." There was an underlining to her words.

Count Alban Mirabel's brown eyes followed the line of his sister's gaze and appraised Kate's figure with a trenchancy that caught Kate's attention. She glanced up, feeling a peculiar sensation, and found the Count's bright eyes upon her. He blew her a kiss and she turned her face away from him, but was nonetheless flattered.

Lady Moravia jealously followed her stepbrother's admiring eyes and felt a pang of unlabeled emotions sweep through her. It was always so whenever he chose to flirt with women in her presence. She said nothing to deter his hungry eyes, but waited for him to turn his mind to her words.

"You say the Earl has left his bride? Really, he struck me not a fool, yet such a move was most certainly folly."

"Nay, my love, he goes for Pitt!"

"Ah, and how came you by this?" he asked, his attention suddenly sharp, his eyes still devouring Kate.

"I overheard Lady Haverly earlier, and Lady Hester was most upset that such news was repeated. She denied it far too much."

"So, the *Gypsy* goes to find the French fleet. We will need to get this to the coast as soon as possible." He turned, alert to the drop of Lady Moravia's lower lip, and found a toadlike man of repellent address.

"How dare you approach us here?" hissed Lady Moravia.

Jack Walepole tipped his hat and sidled near the hangings of their box. "It was necessary, my lady. I have located an individual who has knowledge of the powder you require, and he is willing to mix a small amount for you; however, he wants much more than you authorized me to pay, and as he leaves tonight . . ."

Lady Moravia made an impatient gesture, but her brother's hand calmed her. He turned to the small ugly man and said quietly, "It is just as well you are here."

He took out several notes from his inner pocket. "That should do to buy us the drug, and the rest will see you to the coast tonight, eh Jack?"

Jack Walepole narrowed his small pinlike eyes. "For what purpose?"

"I have a piece of information I want you to convey to our contact, yes?"

"For the right price, Count; anything for the right price."

"Good! We will not quibble now, not here," he said, rising to lead Jack Walepole into the hall. "I shall return presently, Mora. I must get pen and paper."

As Mr. Walepole turned to leave, the lights from the wall sconces hit his face and Kate caught the movement and glanced his way. She gasped and her face drained of color. Jack Walepole! She hadn't thought of him or the night he had tried to violate her for months now. It had been an incident she had blotted out from her mind, firmly refusing it memory. The sight of him brought back the horror of how close he had come to . . . Oh God! He was in London! The knowledge sent a chill up her spine, and she sat rigid and white, unable to tear her eyes away.

"What is it, dear?" inquired Sarah, noting Kate's expression.

" 'Tis nothing, really," said Kate, watching Walepole's retreating form. It *was* him! She was not mistaken. He walked freely about, unfettered by his crimes.

She found herself still watching the box after he had gone, and only when the Count returned alone and looked her way, was she able to tear her eyes away.

Sir Wilson noted the Count's continued inspection of Lady Mannering and felt it incumbent upon himself to comment, "Don't like that Count! If he keeps staring at Lady Mannering, I believe I'll go bend his bone box for him!"

Lady Haverly laughed, and Kate offered him a sweet smile. "Never mind him, Willy," said Aunt Sarah comfortingly. "The play is about to begin."

Midsummer Night's Dream was continued without

further incident to warp Kate's pleasure. Indeed, the naïve remarks Sir Wilson let fall at various intervals regarding the interaction of the players was nearly as hilarious as the show, and Kate found herself much at ease with this, the first of what would soon be a host of escorts at her side. By the time he had escorted Kate home, he was her 'Silly-Willy' and seemed most pleased with his new title.

His carriage continued to Lady Haverly's and as he saw her to the front door and bent low over her hand, she gave his a rap. "Remember, Willy, my Kate may be admired, but I won't have any talk. You will see to that?" warned Sarah.

"Sarah! I am shocked. Do you think *I* would overstep?"

She laughed. "Indeed no. Still people can draw the wrong inference from perfectly innocent situations, and Branwell is away; so make your visits circumspect!"

"Upon my honor! Indeed, I had very little else in mind," said Sir Wilson, really disturbed that he could be thought of in any other light than the one in which he always saw himself, and that was one sporting a perfect halo!

At home Kate sat upon her bed while Nell fussed about her. "Oh Nell, darling, you needn't have waited up for me."

"And how would you have unbuttoned your gown, my lady?" countered Miss Premble.

"Well, then, that settles it. I have done without Eliza long enough, and as I miss her and obviously need her, for such things are not for *you* to do, I shall send for her tomorrow. And her Johnny! For I am certain they are married by now. He may be my groom, for tomorrow I go with Sir Wilson to choose my very own phaeton!" announced Kate.

"Don't you think that is something you should wait for your husband to come home and do for you?" asked Nell reproachfully.

"No! It is something *I* shall do. After all, it will be my phaeton, not his."

She was thinking about this and her day, long after Nell had left her, but it only served to put off other thoughts. Thoughts of Branwell! His face with his black billowing hair flowing wildly around his head, his green eyes glinting with their own special dance, would not be banished. In all her unguarded moments his image taunted her, and now in bed, the memory of his embraces aroused her. She buried her face into her pillow and told the quiet of the room that she hated him. Again and again she said it, as though repetition would prove it; and her heart whispered, "Liar."

38

The information Captain Branwell had received from his Portuguese friends had led them safely astern the French fleet's wake. They took it like a tiger, stealthily, slow, manuevering through the deep indigo water, following the signs of the fleet's leavings and never allowing themselves a moment's lapse where they might be seen.

Decision time had come, for April was gone and Nelson awaited word. Captain Branwell stared hard into the sky and screwed up his mouth, for Hatch was waiting by his side, waiting for direction. "They make for the West Indies, Hatch! I much fear it, 'tis the sugar they want! There is no time to lose if we're to get to Nelson and our fleet."

"Aye, you be in the right of it there, Capt'n. 'Tis the sugar, for the route spells it out, don't it?"

"That it does, Hatch! All sails, my friend. I mean to tread water!"

So it was that the *Gypsy* came about, all hands ready and eager. For there would be a night in port soon and the boredom of the last few days had them all on edge.

Admiral Nelson's fleet lay anchored in Tetuán Bay. They had done taking in their provisions and water and sat waiting, idle, ready for a fight. Nelson fidgeted in his quarters, writing to his beloved Emma and sending to Lisbon for word of the French fleet's whereabouts. His agents had nothing to report and he waited, champing at his bit.

It was but a few days into May that a bright sun and a friendly wind brought Tetuán Bay a gift. The *Gypsy* sailed into port, her British flag rolling, her sails billowing, as her crew clewed up and shouted greetings to their fellow Englishmen. There was much glee and merriment as the *Gypsy* docked, and Admiral Nelson appeared topside to greet his visitor.

Nelson was a small man who had given his country an arm and an eye, and who was willing to give what he had left. The Earl towered above him, yet was always struck by the smaller man's powerful presence.

"Eh, Branwell, what word have you for me?" said Nelson, leading the Earl into his dining quarters.

"They make for the West Indies: twelve French of the line, eight of their own frigates and eight Spanish."

"Ah, but for what purpose? Not another Rochefort incident! Damnation! But why don't they open up and fight?"

"I suspect they want the sugar, and there is barely enough time to stop them if that is their purpose."

"Stop them? Ha! I warrant you, Branwell, do but let me have at them. That is all I ask." He played with the beef in his plate. "Devil a bit, but salt beef and the French fleet is far preferable to roast beef and champagne without them. May God prosper my exertions!"

"I rather think he will, Admiral," said Branwell smiling. "Do we leave in the morning?"

"Aye, I do, but you have done your part. There is no need . . ."

"On the contrary, the islands are tricky; you will need my *Gypsy* to get you their exact direction."

"So be it then, if you are game," Nelson smiled.

While the Earl and Nelson tackled their problems at sea, Kate did pleasant battle with London and became all the crack in an exceptionally short space of time. She was hailed in many of the clubs along St. James Street and her name appeared on all the guest lists of the careening ton. For was she not the new Countess of Mannering . . . and was she not rich, beautiful, charming, and amusingly naïve? Yes indeed, Kate made a refreshing new entrée into the beau monde, much to her surprise and her aunt's pleasure.

The Earl had not been gone a week when she had selected, with Sir Wilson's help, a smart looking open phaeton and a pair of dappling grays of prime blood to lead it. Then, too, Beau Brummell had singled her out, and this was enough to insure her future. He had returned from Oatlands to discover that the Earl had managed to get himself married on the very day he had shrugged off Claire. This amusing circumstance sent the Beau to Sir Wilson, who declared his undying devotion to Kate and took the Beau to Mannering House. Mr. George Brummell found there a childlike woman with open gray eyes, forthright speech, and a great deal of countenance. He admitted himself to her realm, thoroughly enchanted.

Kate should have had her head turned by her growing list of admirers. She did not. She was tense, irritable, restless, and in need of many things, none of which were supplied by her successful debut into society. She needed Branwell. She wanted him to see what a sensation she had become. She wanted him jealous, though she knew not why. She wanted him with her! She wanted! All her newfound interests did not serve to banish this need.

She had found herself introduced to a Venetian couple at a rout some nights ago. Though she had no great liking for the cold Lady Moravia, she found she was amused by the woman's stepbrother, Count Alban Mirabel. She had recognized him, instantly, as the man who had blown her a kiss in the box opposite hers . . . and the man who had spoken to Jack Walepole. She had questioned him about Mr. Walepole, but the Count had answered that he was but a chance acquaintance who constantly attempted to ingratiate himself with them. She had let it pass.

She entered her aunt's drawing room on Sir Wilson's arm to find it already inundated with glittering fashionables. Lady Haverly was entertaining a select few, but the room was nearly overflowing with her selection. Sarah glided toward her, her pale mauve satin rustling about her stately form as she engulfed Kate with her affection. "There, Kate, how grand you look! Why have you never worn silver before? My, it suits you. 'Tis a new gown, for I'll swear it was not one of the ones we chose together."

Kate's white gloved hand touched the silver ribbon of her sleeveless gown. "Of course it is new. Those others were for a maid, not a married woman. Do you think it too daring?" she asked, frowning.

Sarah surveyed the silver sarcenet's lines. The bodice was low and Kate's voluptuous breasts billowed above the confines. Its waist was banded beneath the bosom and it clung in a tight line to the ankle. "I daresay, child, with a figure like yours you would look daring in a sack!" teased Sarah. "Now come."

Kate wandered with Sarah from one fashionable to another but her interests lay in the conversation of the men. Here she found Lady Hester, who squeezed her hand. "Hello, Kate. You will never credit it, but they would condemn Pitt to me!"

"Oh, that is really too bad!" Kate laughed. "No, I must say, gentlemen, that such action warrants severe punishment!"

"I do not condemn Pitt, and he is a kinsman of mine as well, at any rate!" remarked Lord Grenville. " 'Tis not I that cry out, but the people. Here," he said, pointing to an article in the *Chronicle*. "Look what it says here: "The state of anxiety and suspense respecting the enemy cannot long be protracted!" He shoved the paper to the nearest of his audience, who happened to be Beau Brummell.

Mr. Brummell took up his quizzing glass and surveyed

Grenville deprecatingly. "Does *their* so printing . . . make it so?" asked the Beau, pushing the newspaper back at Grenville.

"Now, George, don't get snide with me. 'Tis no use, for in truth you know as well as I that Nelson is out on this, as is Pitt!"

"Not so!" snapped Sir Wilson flushing. "What the deuce do you expect of them? They ain't gods to be whipping up instant answers for your delectation! Lord, if you want to put blame on someone, blame that fool Orde. Egad! When I think of how he sat with five warships and two frigates, dancing up a dust, while the frogs slipped past his nose. 'Tis enough to steep me in maudlin tears, I tell you."

"He wasn't dancing, he was at a dinner. I mean after all . . . they must eat!" said Grenville in way of defense. "'Tis Nelson that is at fault, for he should get word to us what he is about."

"Perhaps he has," said the Count, idly playing with the fobs at his waist. "Do you always know everything your Prime Minister knows, as soon as he knows it?"

Grenville narrowed his eyes. "Eh? But damn, Parliament had better know whatever he knows or I shan't be a part of it!"

"And why should Parliament know what he and Nelson are about?" snapped Lady Hester with a shake of her fair head. "When you can do nought but flap your mouths in criticisms that say little regarding what he should do. Only what he shouldn't!"

Beau Brummell smiled at her but said nothing. Lady Hester was one who could defend herself as well as her uncle. His eyes had always found satisfaction in her form. Kate noted the look in his eyes as they rested on Lady Hester. She was not a beauty, but she was a fine figure of a woman. It occurred to her that the Beau was smitten, but oh how sad, for it was obvious that Lady Hester looked at him as a dear friend. Unrequited love! How terribly, terribly sad, thought Kate.

"You are even more exquisite tonight, *anima mia*," said

the Count, coming up close to her.

"Ah, Count Mirabel, you are nought but a flatterer, I fear. Last evening you told me that I could be no more beautiful than I was . . . a perfect angel, I think, was your description," laughed Kate.

"You see, then, how you continue to astound me. Come, we shall discuss this in private, this ability of yours," said he, putting his hand beneath her bare elbow.

She laughed and gently withdrew her arm. "I think not, for this conversation regarding Nelson intrigues me."

"As it should, since your husband has gone in hot pursuit of the French in order that he may warn your faithful Admiral Nelson."

She raised a brow. "How do you know this?"

"I do not, I only speculate," said he carefully, watching her eyes. "Why else would he have left his young and beautiful bride, if not for his country?"

"Why indeed?" said she smiling, but she had the feeling that all was not right. She could not pinpoint her feeling to anything specific, yet it was there in the air and she found the Count less amusing thereafter.

At home, Eliza helped her undress, rattling in her old gay fashion, pleased with her position as Lady Mannering's personal maid. "Oh, m'lady, John be that puffed up with pride to be your groom."

"And how are your rooms upstairs? Adequate, Eliza?"

"Oh yes, m'lady, and the lovely china tea set! Well we treasure it, m'lady; I can't thank ye enough."

"Oh yes you can, and you have," laughed Kate. "There, now off with you. I can brush my own hair and it's late."

"I can't let you do that. 'Tis m'job."

"Not tonight. I want to do it, really; it will tire me enough for sleep."

Eliza bobbed her way out and Kate fell into long thoughtful strokes with her brush. There was danger for Branwell out there. She had never thought of that before tonight and this new revelation made her ill with worry!

39

The *Gypsy* made its clean path to the islands, unhampered by storms. The moody blue seemed pleased as it caressed the schooner's sides, lovingly favoring the *Gypsy* with its gentle spirit. The trip to the West Indies took them less than twenty days, but they seemed a veritable year to Captain Branwell. His heart and thoughts were elsewhere, though his duty was here. Off the coast of Martinique they spotted the French fleet and were nearly themselves lost. However, Branwell's crew was well trained for tight situations and they were soon out of range. Their discovery was taken to Admiral Nelson's squadron, still out at sea. The *Gypsy* saw Nelson take on some two thousand troops at Barbados before they sailed southward. The English were itching to do battle with the French and had the French surrendered, there would have been many a sorry man.

However, the French learned of Nelson's coming and, though they were twice the English fleet in size, they chose to run rather than meet him in combat!

"Damn, why won't they stand still and put up arms?" cried Nelson to Branwell as they made their farewells.

"It would gain them little; they would lose and so they know," said Branwell, grinning at Nelson's frustration. "But you have won, Admiral. It is because of your coming that two hundred English ships full with sugar are saved from their greedy hands!"

"Aye, but it won't end here, Branwell. I shall give chase. And you, lad, you return to London and have the Admiralty send a squadron to meet them, eh?"

"Aye!" grinned Branwell.

Thus it was that on June 6, 1805, Captain Branwell Mannering set the *Gypsy* pointing homeward. Nelson would hound the French back to Europe and with any luck perhaps a fleet could be put out to welcome them. But it was not these thoughts that drove Branwell. His mind was racked with visions of Kate. He felt a hunger in his heart and an ache in his groin and a doubt as to whether or not these pains would be alleviated upon his return.

Kate's time had come and passed and she knew herself free of a child in her womb. No longer would this worry nag at her. She didn't want a baby now. Not with Branwell and her relationship so black. It was one more thing to flaunt at Branwell Mannering! For the longer he was gone, the more she wanted to abuse him. Her indignation grew with each passing day and her pride felt the blows. She would start each day by wondering if he were safe, instantly telling herself that he had to be. From there she would wonder if he had docked his ship somewhere, and whether or not he had found a woman with which to pass his days, a woman more pliable than she had been.

She had not expected him in early May, but when June passed its middle she could no longer believe he was still at sea! As June drew near its end, she grew all the more restless, all the more anxious. She kept expecting him to walk swaggeringly into his home. She would sit and imagine the look of his astonishment to find his home much altered. For she had opened the dusty ballroom and had the Windsor chairs redone in gold satin. Gold satin hung from the windows and everywhere there were plants! She had brought in hothouse greens and placed them in every niche and corner, wherever the light was enough to sustain them. She had redone the tearoom in red velvet and her dressing room in pink and silver.

The months of May and June had been one party after another, and she had been a part of the social round—Lady Mansfield's small party, Lady Bush's ball—and tonight there was Lady Barrymore's masquerade. Still she was restless, and everyone was leaving with the Prince next week for Brighton!

Even Aunt Sarah talked of swooping her up and taking her to Branwell's Brighton house. "For, darling, Bran can always join us whenever he returns from his jaunt!" said Aunt Sarah merrily. Kate was sorely tempted to go, but she would wait one more week! Why she was waiting she knew not, yet she knew herself reluctant to leave Mannering House.

She paced to and fro in the drawing room, unsettled and frustrated, when her thoughts were interrupted by a small commotion at the door. It flew open and a gay young man's voice called out, "Good Lord, trust me! Your lady and I are old friends," said Danny Ludlow, beaming and motioning with his head at Kirkly. "Kate, tell your man to stand aside!"

Kate's heart leaped and she felt a wondrous joy at finding Danny before her. However, she had a past grievance and remembering it, put her arms akimbo. "Oh, I don't know. I think I should ask Kirkly to throw you out on your ear, my friend."

"Kate!" ejaculated Mr. Ludlow, attempting to shrug off Kirkly's hold.

She laughed to see that her butler had evidently taken her literally. "Very well, Kirkly, you may release him. I was really only jesting." Then to Danny, "You may enter, Mr. Ludlow."

He came forward, his blond hair streaking his forehead, his vague blue eyes bright, his hands outstretched. "Kate, never say you are put out with me?"

"Traitor!" accused the lady.

"Oh no, Kate, I but did the best thing for you."

"Ha!"

He got on the knees of his gray knit breeches and put up his folded hands. "I beg thy forgiveness, beloved, on m'hands and knees. Truly I do."

She laughed and took his fists in her hands. "Oh, Danny, get up, do!"

Sir Wilson had by this time found his way to the drawing room, having the advantage of being well known to Kirkly as well as a household favorite. He stopped short on the threshold, taking in this scene with growing astonishment.

Unaware of his presence, Danny Ludlow tugged at Kate's white muslin.

"Have I won it then?" cried Danny, dramatically referring to her forgiveness.

"I'll be hanged if you have!" said Sir Wilson vehemently. "What, Kate, shall I throw the impudent puppy out then?"

Kate burst into a gurgle of mirth. "Oh my Silly-Willy, come in and meet a very dear friend of mine."

Mr. Ludlow hastened to his feet and straightened his gray superfine coat, pulling at the sleeves and attempting to banish the flush from his cheeks. He saw at a glance that the gentleman who had entered the drawing room to find him at a disadvantage was nattily attired in the very latest kick of fashion, being a bright green superfine coat and yellow pantaloons and, therefore, was one to hold with some esteem.

The necessary introductions were made, after which both gentlemen stood eyeing one another. This state of affairs was not broken until it chanced into the conversation that the Earl had not yet returned from sea.

"What! Gone to sea? But when?" cried Danny, much struck.

"Oh Danny, you would never credit it, but the dashing blade you saw me married to took off the very next morning!" said Kate, sardonically.

"No!" exclaimed Danny, apparently feeling this was not in keeping with the norm. "Must have been too much for him, Kate!" At which he burst into hilarious laughter.

Kate glared, finding very little to laugh at. Sir Wilson, much struck with this, allowed a glimmer of a smile to bend his mouth, but found himself so out of favor with his adored one that this quickly vanished.

"You are horrid, Danny; and indeed, I am getting worried, for it has been more than two months now."

"*Hmmm.* Seems a mite longer than his usual runs, but then it isn't one of his usual runs," offered Sir Wilson, who had himself been fretting over the Earl's prolonged absence.

"Well then, Kate, nothing for it, now that I'm released for the summer. Shall be happy to escort you about town," said Danny, containing his mirth.

"Thank you for your kind offices, but Lady Mannering shan't be in need of them," said Sir Wilson, once more glaring.

"I daresay you may think so," said Danny dangerously.

"Stop it!" interrupted Kate. "Come now, we can all be friends."

Mr. Ludlow and Sir Wilson made no comment regarding this. However, they seemed not to disagree with it either. Kate attempted to find another line. "So Danny, you are about town. Where do you stay?"

"At Claridge's, which reminds me. Some friends of mine have told me about a fair near Charing Cross. Came to escort you there!" said he, throwing a defiant look at Sir Wilson.

"A fair you say?" asked Sir Wilson, his interest aroused. "At Charing Cross?"

"Lord yes! I am told that for only a shilling one may have a look at a three-year-old heifer with two distinct heads!" said Danny, with no little excitement.

"Really? Hang me if I haven't been wanting a look at such a thing!" exclaimed Sir Wilson, fully intrigued. "Have you seen it already?"

"No, though my friends have and say 'tis worth every penny!"

"Wondrous phenomena these things," agreed Sir Wilson. "You know the last fair I attended, they had this strange fellow who took vipers out of a bag, and hang me if he didn't play with the slippery things, ending it all by stuffing them in his mouth!"

"Oh faith!" ejaculated Kate. "Never say he ate them?"

"Oh no, pulled them out again," said Sir Wilson blandly. "I tell you what. Get your cloak, Kate, and Mr. Ludlow and I shall be happy to take you."

"Indeed!" said Danny.

"I have no wish to see men stuff their mouths with vipers," cried Kate.

"No?" said Danny, surprised. "But there are scads of things I daresay you will like to see. Come on then, girl."

Kate laughed and pulled her bellrope, asking the lackey that appeared to fetch her jacket from Eliza. A few moments later, Kate, her black curls gathered beneath a white straw bonnet banded with red velvet, enwrapped in her white muslin spencer jacket fitted at the waist and flaring at the hip over her white muslin gown, found herself seated beside Mr. Ludlow and facing Sir Wilson as they made they way to Charing Cross.

It was a beautiful day. The breeze was comfortable, the sky blue, and the sun bright but not burning. Kate put aside her frustrations and began to enjoy herself between her two gallants. The fair grounds were reached in good time and Kate found herself wandering about what seemed a smoking, ill-smelling maze of tents, people, and animals.

Crowds consisting of peasants and gentry alike, meandered, laughing, jesting, throwing coins, and throwing jibs. Kate's large gray eyes were enthralled. Tents of every color and size loomed on her horizon, with their owners beckoning to her to sample their wares, and she would have stopped at several had not Danny and Willy urged her on to the point of their object. They had received direction toward the tent housing the two-headed heifer and were intent on making their way.

"Why, Lady Mannering," said a lazy female voice, catching Kate's attention. Kate turned around, pulling Mr. Ludlow and Sir Wilson to a stop, and found herself gazing up into the dark eyes of Lady Moravia. The woman was indeed a beauty, with her short dark curls and her tall buxom figure. She wore a bright muslin gown of yellow, and her chip hat was tilted at an attractive angle. Kate noted Danny's mouth dropping in delighted awe!

"Oh, Lady Moravia, how nice! Are you also intent on seeing the two-headed heifer?" asked Kate.

Lady Moravia laughed and her dark eyes swept Sir Wilson a charming smile before resting on Danny's youthful countenance. "La, but it seems I have misplaced my brother, or he me, and daren't attend such a spectacle alone."

"We should be delighted to give you company," offered Sir Wilson at once, and Danny stammered his agreement to such a worthy notion.

Kate realized that Lady Moravia awaited an introduction to Mr. Ludlow and reluctantly gave it. For some reason she liked not that the sophisticated lady's eyes should encompass her simple Danny. However, there was nothing for it. Danny had gallantly offered Lady Moravia his arm, which she gratefully took possession of, giving him a sultry smile that left his heart palpitating at a severe rate.

Some time later, the heifer left behind them, the Count of Mirabel discovered and asked to join their little party, Kate found herself once again in a state of restlessness. She was listening to Sir Wilson and Danny give a dissertation regarding the heifer's heads to a passing acquaintance, with Moravia helpfully adding whatever they chanced to omit, when she sighed and moved away. The Count moved with her, smiling in some amusement. "The two-headed heifer seems not to hold your attention?"

She laughed. "No, we have seen that it has the right number of eyes, ears, horns, and mouths and that it chewed the cud in both mouths and ate with both at the same time! I found it pitiful!"

"Come then, shall we have our fortune read?" he asked, taking her elbow.

She glanced up at him, finding him floridly handsome in his white suit. "Yes, yes, I should like that."

"Ah, tarot has a fascination for you?"

"Let us say rather that I find it amusing to compare the truth of the cards with what actually does happen," laughed Kate.

"Ah, a skeptic?" he asked, one thin dark brow going upward.

"Most definitely."

"Then why bother?"

"Because there is a mystery about card reading, fortune telling that intrigues me. And you?"

"I am no skeptic. I believe!"

"Really? I would not have thought so."

"But why? Do I look so pragmatic?" he asked, slightly offended.

"Oh no, not at all. You, Count, definitely have an aura about you, but those who do usually are the cause of their own fate. I would not have thought you would believe in predestiny."

"There now you have a point, but I do not say that by learning the future, we cannot change it. Quite the contrary."

She laughed. "This grows over my head, Count."

They laughed together as they entered Madame Zenith's tent, unaware that a honey-haired woman stopped her companion to gaze sardonically at them. Lady Claire sneered and said to the uniformed Hussar at her side, "The Earl of Mannering's new bride pleasures herself in his absence."

The *Gypsy* had docked in Brighton early that morning and such was the Earl's temper that he found he could not wait to see his ship batted down. He left it to Hatch, disembarked with his horse and made the journey to London in less than five hours. There was a broad smile on his bronzed face as he swept into his house and greeted Kirkly. His dark thick brows went up as he noted that his bride had evidently imported some of her island into his home, but he liked the effect. "Have her ladyship join me in the dining room; I am ravenous," said he, crossing the hall.

Kirkly took a step after him. "My lord."

"Yes?" said the Earl, turning round.

"Lady Mannering is not at home."

"Oh? Where is she? At Lady Haverly's?"

"No, my lord."

"Well then?" said the Earl, a frown beginning to mar his brow.

"Her ladyship has gone to the fair with Sir Wilson and a Mr. Daniel Ludlow," said the butler, somehow sure that his lordship would not be pleased.

"A fair, with Sir Wilson and Ludlow? Which fair?"

"I believe it is the one taking place at Charing Cross."

"Thank you, Kirkly. Have my lunch served to me at once and a fresh horse brought to me from the stables."

"Very good, sir," said Kirkly, noting that the smile had left the Earl's eyes.

Half an hour later, the Earl was managing his horse through the London bustle on his way to Charing Cross. It was ridiculous, for how he was to find her at a fair was beyond him, but he had to try. He had this absurd notion of finding her immediately and taking her in his arms.

Kate was seated before a woman wearing gypsy's garb. She had a leathery look to her skin, but her eyes were sharp and bright. Her voice held a tired quality and Kate felt a pang of pity for her, realizing the hardness of the woman's life. The Count stood at Kate's side with an interested expression as he watched the woman shuffle her cards. She placed the deck of cards on the center of her cloth-covered table. "There, my lady, lay your right hand upon the cards, ah, just so," she said, smiling. "Now, tell me, where is your husband?"

Kate's eyes opened wide and she wondered how the woman knew that her husband was gone. "He is, I believe, at sea."

The woman seemed to go into a trance and her words were such that Kate could not understand them. Then the bright eyes were flashing once again and the woman was separating the cards into three piles. The cards from the top of the deck were then turned over by the gypsy with her left hand and arranged in a diagram. "Ah, you worry about his absence, and your court card is that of the Queen. You are loving, you are fruitful, and he, yes, he is the King of Swords! Is he not a man of power, strength, perhaps military intelligence?"

"Why . . . he is a man of power . . . yes . . ." said Kate, surprised.

"You come to me for your future, yes?"

"Well, yes, I suppose," said Kate, somewhat embarrassed before the Count.

A dark ugly looking card was overturned. "Ah, it is the devil, my lady; there are bad times ahead. You are to beware." She turned up yet another of a blindfolded woman holding two swords and she clucked her tongue. "You meet stalemate with your loved one. I foresee misunderstandings." She sat back, with a weary sigh.

"The cards have given what they can."

Kate stood up, a frown covering her pretty face. "Thank you, Madame Zenith, you have been most kind."

The Count took her arm and she smiled at him. "I see *you* are taking no chances."

The Earl stabled his horse at the fair grounds and meandered through the maze of people. The stench of tobacco and food was almost overpowering when it first met his nostrils and it says something about the human ability to adapt that after a few moments he was able able to adjust and forget. His name was hailed by a few chance acquaintances and he stopped to chat and ask whether Sir Wilson had been spotted. He was in luck, as they happened to be the very gentlemen Danny and Willy had stopped earlier to give a full description of the two-headed heifer. He followed their directions and heard his name once again, but this time it was on the lips of a female and one that he grimaced to recognize. "Claire, what a charming setting in which to find you," he said, urbanely.

"I had no idea you had returned," said Claire. "Just in time, my lord," said she, provocatively.

"Oh?"

"Why, haven't you heard about your wife?" taunted Claire.

"My wife?" he asked, for she had hit a vulnerable spot.

"Lud, but Papa tells me she is hailed as the Incomparable at Watiers, and they are taking bets as to who will next replace Sir Wilson as her cavalier! *I* am prone to think the Count Mirabel will fill that post."

"You evil-mouthed bitch! Shut your lying tongue," snapped the Earl, heedless of the soldier at Lady Claire's side. The soldier thought it best to intercede on his lady's behalf and stepped forward. "I say, sir, that is no way to speak to a lady."

"Indeed, I heartily agree with you," said the Earl, turning his back to leave the soldier speechless, the lady seething. She shouted after him, "At this very moment, she is in the fortune teller's tent with the Count."

However, Claire had no need to further lower the vision of herself before her soldier's eye. Kate, smiling brightly, and her hand reposing gently on the Count's bent arm, came prancing out of Madame Zenith's tent to find the Earl towering above her. His face was a mask of hidden emotions and hers drained of color as her gray eyes discovered that his green ones were the only ones with the power to leave her limbs weak!

40

There he stood, this man, the very one she had been dreaming of, hating, wanting, and raging against. He stood before her, and he was but a man, not so very better looking than the Count at her side, and certainly not half as gallant, yet every fiber of her being melted beneath his glance. Her spirit soared and he brought a new light to her gray eyes. There was an explosion within her chest, an upheaval within her belly, and she knew herself a coward before her emotions. "Branwell," she breathed, unable to move, unable to take her eyes from his face.

"Madam," he said, taking her hand to his lips and

placing a controlled kiss upon the cloth of her glove. She felt his lips through the material and they singed her flesh.

He tore his gaze away and studied the Count. "Count Mirabel, how nice of you to show my wife about," he said carefully.

"Good to see you, Lord Mannering. But please, no thanks are needed; it has been a pleasure to take Lady Mannering beneath my wing."

"The Count was kind enough to introduce me to the mysteries of tarot," said Kate, finding her voice.

"Ah, have you lost Mr. Ludlow and Sir Wilson then?" asked the Earl blandly, showing not his emotions.

The Count laughed. "It seems their talk of two-headed cows depressed your lady. I left them with my sister, whom I should be getting back to. If you will excuse me?" he said lightly, bowing to Kate and vanishing in the crowd.

The Earl took up Kate's arm and began steering her away. "Where are you taking me?" said she with some surprise.

"Home, madam. This is not the sort of place I wish my wife to explore, nor is the Count proper escort!" he snapped.

"Oh, why that is beyond everything," countered the lady, putting a hand to her hips and turning around to face him. "You vanish for more than two months and then come back here to tell me what I may and may not do? You may go to the devil!"

"So shall we both, but now we are going home," he said, taking up her arm once again.

"Touch me and I shall scream," said his wife sweetly, unmovable.

"Would you subject yourself to the tattle-mongers, Kate?" he asked, frowning.

"Would *you* subject me to them, Branwell?"

"Don't try me, Kate."

"Branwell, you dog!" ejaculated Willy coming up to slap his friend on his shoulder. "When did you get back? What's to do with Nelson?"

The Earl grinned at his friend. "Ho there, Willy, one at a time. I put into Brighton this morning and rode home."

"In what time?" demanded Willy interrupting.

"I didn't time myself, but I think it was under five hours," said the Earl, laughing.

"Bad. Prinny has done it in just a wee bit over four," he sighed. "Well, perhaps next time."

"Look, Willy, would you mind if I left you? I should like to see Kate home."

"Right, of course you would, honeymoon and all that. You dog," winked Willy, then turned to Kate. "Come for you at eight, love."

She smiled sweetly, "Yes do, and ask Danny along, won't you?"

"*Hmmm*, yes; very well, might as well, bound to come anyway; might as well be at m'invitation!"

"Hold there. What are you two talking about?" asked the Earl.

"We are going to a masquerade tonight," said Kate curtly.

"Why then does Willy come for you, when you both can see that I am home and perfectly capable of escorting my own wife?" asked the Earl, dangerously.

"Dash it, Bran. You can't come, must see that!" said Willy.

"No, Sir Wilson, I do not see that!" said the Earl, glaring.

"You don't have a costume," explained Willy.

"Willy, don't worry your head over such trifles. I shall have one by this evening," said the Earl with some exasperation.

"Well then, if you must come, do. It has nought to do with me. I shall still come for Kate. Have been doing so while you were gone. Like to, won't give up m'plans simply because you decide to pop in on us. Come if you must, but don't interfere!" said Willy much vexed.

The Earl might have lost his temper, but this was his Willy and he was well acquainted with Sir Wilson's flow of mind. He studied him a moment and suddenly gave vent to a chuckle. "Very well, Willy, you may escort us both. Do I take it that young Ludlow joins us?"

"Yes he does, Branwell," said Kate, the anger still kindling in her eyes.

"Then we shall see you later this evening, Willy," he said, leading Kate away. There was little she could now do without making a scene. She had no wish to do this and walked quietly beside her husband as he wound through the labyrinth of vibrating life, now and then shielding his bride from its spontaneous zealousness!

Kate's fulminating eye wandered over the Earl's broad back as he fetched his horse and tethered it at the back of a waiting hackney. He pulled open the cab's door and turned to her, his own gaze no less angry. "Get in, madam."

She put up her chin, but allowed him to assist her and settled back in her seat, staring hard out of her window. Questions trilled at her mind, demanding answers. Where had he been for two months? Why had he gone? Who had he seen? The questions were left unasked and they passed a good part of the journey in silence. However, he chose to break the thick air with a sharp "I know I interrupt your pleasures, madam, but I shouldn't think it too much to give up for your husband's homecoming."

She whirled on him, her gray eyes lit with yellow flames. "My husband's homecoming? You choose your words well, Branwell, very much in the way of your kind."

"Am I not your husband, Kate?" growled the Earl.

"In fact you are, though I have had cause to wonder. You left me in your home to face your servants alone! You left me to Aunt Sarah, who very kindly introduced me to your friends, and had it not been for them I should have been quite miserable. But heigh-ho you have returned!" she said, sarcastically.

"Cool your tongue, Kate; your face was not formed for a shrew," he said, suddenly grinning, loving the sight of her.

She felt a flow of warmth surge through her. Not yet,

she would not warm to him so quickly. He could not get away with all he had done and come home to conquer her as well. He would find she was no easy petticoat! She returned her attention to the passing streets, and he made no attempt to engage her further.

Mannering House was soon reached, and Kate swept past him on her way upstairs, when she stopped to watch her traitorous Nell cavort for the Earl.

"My lord, they said you were come home! 'Tis that good it is to see you here and well," cried Nell, coming forward from the recesses of the back hall. "I am sorry I wasn't here earlier, but I was running an errand."

"Hello, Miss Premble," hailed the Earl, grinning. "Master Hatch fared poorly without you, but he should be here by tonight and I trust you will find him as bonny as ever!" He saw the flush steal into her cheeks and laughed, before lightly taking the steps in Kate's wake.

She found her way to her room, slammed her door closed behind her, and threw off her jacket and bonnet, pacing all the while. She heard the Earl moving in his dressing room and dared him to attempt her door. When he knocked a moment later, she was only surprised that he had not just come barging in his usual manner!

"Yes?" she answered.

He opened the door to her room from his dressing room. "May I enter, Kate?"

"Truly, are you asking? Pray, your manners have been altered by your voyage!" she mocked.

He felt his temper rise, but he was a man of self-discipline and had a purpose in mind. "It occurred to me that among my other crimes against you, I neglected to present you with a proper wedding ring."

"Oh pray, Branwell, 'tis not needed," said Kate glibly.

Again he controlled himself, coming forward, holding a wide antique gold band in his hand. He held it out to her and she could see emblazoned in the center two hearts of diamond clusters. It was very simple and very lovely. "This was my mother's," he said.

Her expression changed at once and she reached for it,

"Oh, Branwell, it is quite . . . quite beautiful."

"I believe it will fit you; my mother was just such a small thing as you," he said, slipping it on her finger. A knock on her hall door broke the moment.

"Yes?" called Branwell irritably.

"I am sorry to interrupt, my lord. I have here something for madam," said Kirkly. "I thought perhaps she might wish to have it immediately."

"Indeed?" said the Earl.

"Come in," said his lady.

Kirkly entered the room holding a huge arrangement of hothouse flowers. It was stunning, and Kate exclaimed as he set it on the vanity. "Why, how lovely. Who sent them, Kirkly?"

"I don't know, madam; however, there is a card, addressed to you," he said, taking the card from the vase and handing it to her.

She took it up and slit the envelope:

Anima mia,
You are as wild as the lily and as exquisite as the rose.
                                                    Alban

Kate blushed over the note's contents, so intent upon it she hadn't realized that the Earl had meandered to her side.

"*Anima mia*? My soul? Why should the Count, whom you have only recently met, refer to you as his soul?" said the Earl, his tone hinting of repressed passion.

"Oh, now you are reading *my* letters?" snapped Kate, her cheeks red.

The Earl misread the blush to mean guilt and his agitation mounted. "I will have my answer, madam!"

"How should I know? I did not even know what it meant. I don't understand Italian," said Kate, exasperated as all innocence is when wrongly accused.

"He signs his name Alban," further attacked the Earl.

"He may sign his name Herbert for all I care," countered the lady. "And, I shall befriend whom I wish, and use first names when *I* deem it proper to do so!"

"You think so, madam?" asked the Earl ominously.

"Indeed I do," said Kate, throwing down the gauntlet.

"Then you have much to learn, innocent! These tricks may have worked behind my back, but they shall not now!" With which he turned on his heel and stalked from her presence.

She stood in vengeful indignation, thinking. These tricks? Behind his back? The man is a devil, an arrogant bully, a brute! She heard the front door bang shut and knew a sudden urge to cry.

The Earl's hat sat jauntily on his head as he stomped down the street, turned the corner, and made for Beau Brummell's lodgings.

Was he going mad? What was wrong with him? Kate. Kate was what was wrong with him! He ached for her. All he wanted to do was catch her up in his arms, hold her, touch her, and all he kept doing was ranting at her. He knew that he had almost hit her. He had wanted to hit her when he saw her at the fair grounds on the Count's arm, and then again when he read the Count's little love note! Damnation! He wanted to hit somebody! He had never been so irrational before. It was not at all what he planned; nothing he had done since he arrived in London had been near to what he planned. Even when he presented her with the wedding ring. He had devised words in his mind with which to melt her, and they had stuck in his throat. Tongue-tied, he? Tongue-tied with a woman? Impossible, yet he had been. Her mocking had thrown him off key! Why could she not love him as she did that first night? It had been the finest, freest moment of his life, their first joining. Could marriage so change a woman?

The door to Brummell's residence opened to emit the Earl and he was shown into the study. The Beau glanced up from his writing desk. "Egad!" ejaculated the Beau. "What the devil are you wearing?"

The Earl glanced down, impatiently, at his clothes, remembering suddenly that he still wore the riding buckskins he had traveled to London in this morning. "Oh never mind, George, I have a problem!"

"Indeed you do, daring to come into my home. Take them off and wear my robe if you must, but take those dreadful things off!"

"Never mind m'clothes, Beau, need your insight!" said the Earl, dropping into a nearby sofa.

"If you soil my Chippendale, you shall pay for its reupholstery!" threatened the Beau with a wagging finger.

"Damn if I will," grinned the Earl.

"You'll be damned if you don't. Now, what is your problem, though I can probably guess."

"Can you? Very well then, my omniscient friend. What is my problem?"

"Your wife, of course. What man's isn't? Precisely why I don't indulge in the sport m'self!"

"Yes, will you kindly tell me what has been happening to change the sweet, innocent girl I married into a shrew?"

"You have a duncelike mind," said the Beau.

"I beg your pardon," said the Earl.

"It isn't mine you should be begging for, but your wife's, Branwell. I mean, really, one doesn't up and go to sea the morning after. It isn't the thing!"

"It was necessary."

"And about your marriage, how came you to get caught so soon after your escape from Claire?"

"It doesn't matter. I did."

"No comparison between them. Your Kate is quite the rage, you know."

"And how came that about?" asked the Earl suspiciously.

"Oh you needn't thank me; she was well on her way to the top when I came on the scene, though I do admit my approval helped."

"I don't want her all the crack!"

"Pity. For she is bound to be, somewhat strong-minded. Says whatever pops into her head."

"I met Claire today, at the fair in Charing Cross. She says that my lady and Count Mirabel are seen together," said the Earl, cautiously.

"Did she? Just the sort of thing Claire would say. Well,

as to that, your Kate never has yet stepped over. Sarah is always with her whenever Willy escorts her home, and she has never gone off alone with the Count. However, the Count is a charming blade; no saying that she wouldn't have, had you been gone longer."

"I see. So much for a woman's marriage vows," said the Earl dryly.

"Look here, Branwell, you ain't seeing clearly," said the Beau frowning, for his remark had not produced the effect he had looked to.

The Earl was already getting up. "I trust you will find your upholstery as free from dust now as it was before I planted m'self there. Do I see you at the masquerade to-night?"

"Only a man who would enter my abode dressed as you are would dare put such a question to me!" sighed the Beau. "Do you think that Beau Brummell would attend such a thing?"

"You might enjoy it," chuckled the Earl.

"I would detest it, as you will, but then it is just the sort of nonsense women will like and create," said the Beau, waving farewell to his friend.

The Earl then made his way to his tailor's, for he had little time to have a costume thrown together, for he had every intention of attending this affair with his wife!

41

Lady Moravia paced the flowered carpet of her hotel suite, glancing nervously at her stepbrother, who was smoking a pipe near the window overlooking the street. Her eyes swept his face as she shook her dark bobbing curls. "I am worried, Alban; what if the powder works too quickly? It has a reputation for doing just that. Oh good God, what if he were to be affected before I had time to move away from him?"

"Mora, darling, you worry so," said Alban, turning toward her, reaching for her arm and pulling her close to him. His lips took hers as they had countless other times, and she felt as wondrous as she had that first time, so many years ago. "*Amico ed ámante*," he breathed into her ear. "Would I endanger you? No, 'tis for you, for us, we take this path that neither be forced to marry for wealth that we may live our lives together in our home! The Austrians take much, but soon Napoleon will be pleased, eh? We will have gained. Tonight is right, *ámante*, for we will be disguised. It will not be remembered who was near him when he fell. Perhaps evil will not be suspected. Walepole tells us he has been ill with the gout as of late."

"I love you, Alban. I would give my all for you."

"And I you, Mora, you know that," he said, his hand finding its way down the bodice of her gown, clutching her large overflowing breast with a sudden frantic need. It had always been this way between them, this wild surging passion, but he could make her doubt when his eyes followed others, as they often did.

"How can I be sure when you take other women?" she cried, pulling away.

He laughed and called her back to his arms, gently, cajolingly. "Mora, our parents did us an injustice when they married. We love, but we dare not declare it. We are not blood, yet they would call it incest. I am a man, but it would be doubted if I didn't play the gallant. It is enough that I take no bride. Do not ask me not to play my role as a man! All other women are meaningless. I share nothing with them, nothing! It is you that holds my mind, my life."

She knew in his own way he meant it. He did love her; theirs was a relationship that could never go asunder. Their ties were deep-rooted. "Ah yes, my love," she said, surrendering herself to his embrace.

Kate donned her shoulder-length black wig. It was banged and clipped and called 'the Cleopatra', as indeed the Egyptian Queen was the woman whom she was representing this evening. With her gold silk gown, one shoulder of which had a trail of pleated gold cascading at the back, she looked very much the part. She donned her gold mask and with a sigh surveyed herself.

" 'Tis magnificent ye look!" exclaimed Eliza.

"Indeed you do, my love," agreed Nell, who had come to Kate's room to have a look.

"Thank you," said Kate quietly. Her spirits had lost their reviving anger and had narrowed into melancholy. Everything was wrong. Just everything. She picked up her black velvet cloak and strolled out of her room to wait for Sir Wilson's arrival in the parlor.

Nell and Eliza exchanged glances, "I thought she'd be feeling more the thing once his lordship come home," said Eliza, shaking her head.

"She will, they have but to understand one another first."

"What's to understand? They be noddy on each other. Any fool can see that."

"They have too much pride. But here, now, we shouldn't be discussing them in such a way," chided Miss Premble, moving out of the room.

Downstairs, Kate opened the parlor door and nearly retreated when she found the Earl standing near the window sipping port. They had taken their dinners in separate rooms and she hadn't seen him since he had stepped out earlier that day! She was surprised and taken with his costume. He had chosen a red bandana for his head, a red wide-sleeved, open-necked shirt, black vest, black breeches, and black flap-top boots. His black glistening waves stroked his forehead and waved about his head, and he looked the fierce pirate he portrayed. He saw her and held up his glass. "My queen, join me."

She hesitated, "Indeed, I rarely take the invitation of a pirate."

"Then make this a rare occasion, Kate," he said softly.

His tone reminded her of another night, so long ago, when he had been all and everything to her. She entered the room and closed the door behind her. He poured another glass of brandy and strode easily toward her to place the drink in her ungloved hand. Having done it, he noted the ring on her left hand and stroked it tenderly. "Kate?"

"Yes, Branwell?" she said, almost hopefully.

"I make you my apologies about the Count, that is. My accusations were unjust."

"Thank you," said Kate, brightening. He was constantly surprising her.

"You look superb as Cleopatra."

"Thank you again, Branwell," she said, a smile lighting her features.

"Indeed, your figure is most alluring," he said, his voice lowering a note, his green eyes warming her with a deep fire. She felt herself slipping, felt herself moving toward him, but she checked such action.

"Do you think so? I thought I had put on a little weight," she said at an attempt to turn the conversation.

"Eh?" he said picking up new interest, appraising her with a new notion. She saw it and was shaken by an illogical irritation. Her gray eyes went cold.

"No, Branwell, I am not pregnant," she said bitingly.

He frowned at her tone, "Why fling it at me? Are you trying to annoy me, Kate? Have I indeed married a shrewish female whose fancy it is to provoke her husband?"

His accusation stung, and she was caught by it, unable to answer and saved the necessity of doing so by Kirkly's announcement, which was followed by the appearance of a devil and a highwayman!

Kate turned round and burst into a relief of mirth. "Danny, which are you?"

"Why he is the devil, of course!" said Sir Wilson, with a show of indignation. "Never think I'd go out dressed like that! Not I! A dashing highwayman is what was needed!"

"Take a damper, Willy," said Danny, by now on the best of amiable terms with his older friend. "Everyone knows it's the Devil that's the charmer. All the ladies love a devil!"

"I say!" said Sir Wilson gazing at Kate. "I say, dash it, Kate! If you had told me you were going as Cleopatra, I would have come as Caesar!"

"And I, Mark Anthony!" supplied Danny.

"Then it is just as well she didn't tell either of you, for we would then have been deprived of your spectacle," said the Earl.

Sir Wilson then gave the Earl his penetrating scrutiny, "A pirate? Damn good notion, Branwell. I'm inclined to think it a shade more dashing than a highwayman."

"No!" mocked the Earl. "Nothing could beat the high toby!"

"Do you really think so?" said Sir Wilson, pleased.

"Well, perhaps a devil might oust you," said the Earl thoughtfully, his eyes dancing.

It was in such high spirits that the party started for Lady Barrymore's masquerade. Their positions in Sir Wilson's coach were rather cramped; however, the distance was not far and they survived the journey, still in spirits. Lady Barrymore's rooms were spacious. It was a warm night, made warmer still by the press of people she had invited. It was possibly the last rout of the London season, for the Prince had already departed for Brighton. It was known that Brummell would follow him on the morrow, and hither would the ton follow!

Lady Haverly was discovered by the Earl, who laughed uproariously at her costume. "Sarah, a peasant?"

"A Neapolitan peasant, you wretch! And do keep your voice down. I want no one else to know."

"But your voice gives you away. There is not another earthly being with a voice like yours." He laughed.

"No? Oh thank you, love, for now I shall disguise it," she said, altering its tone. This sent her nephew off into a new spasm, and he found himself deserted by his loving aunt. He glanced around the room and discovered there to be at least four red devils and three highwaymen, which sent another ripple of chuckles through him. However, what he next saw, set the muscles in his jaw working, for there was indeed a Caesar, and the Earl was certain it was none other than the Count Mirabel. Had Kate planned it with him? Something in his heart pained and the pain brought on his displeasure. He sought Kate with his eyes, watching as the Count made his way to her. He could not see her eyes, he could not tell whether or not she evinced surprise at the Count's costume, but her conversation seemed as though she did not! He made his way to them when a heavy hand on his shoulder detained him:

"Branwell, would know the set of your shoulders anywhere, you old sea dog!" said Prime Minister Pitt.

Beside the Prime Minister, who had not bothered to wear a costume, was a tall full-bodied gypsy woman, whom the Earl had trouble putting a name to, until she spoke. "So, my darling Pitt, you give away the Earl's disguise. Fie on you, sir," she said, belieing her words with her bantering tone.

"I haven't given him away. He dresses much as he is," laughed the Prime Minister. He had imbibed enough drink to make him forget the pain in his foot.

The Earl was smiling, but his mind was busy studying Lady Moravia. She and her brother were a mystery. Venetians were under Austrian rule while most of the remainder of Italy was under Napoleon. So then, what was their purpose here in England? Why was she always flirting with Pitt? And the Count, what was his connection with Walepole? Jack Walepole was under suspicion. His name had cropped up at the Horse Guards before the Earl had gone to sea. What was it all about? She smiled invitingly at the Earl, and he put out his arm. "I believe, my lady, this dance was promised to me," he said gallantly.

"Pirate!" Pitt laughed. "Stealing my treasure from under m'nose! If I were a younger man I would have at you."

"Please, sir, if you did I would be felled instantly," grinned the Earl.

He led her onto the dance floor and his fingers brushed against hers, discovering there an unusual ring. It was rectangular shaped, very similar to a flat box, and reminded him of something he couldn't quite remember. Moravia's eyes flirted with him and he returned the compliment.

Kate saw her husband, and she flinched as though pricked by some malicious force. She watched them from the corner of her eye, for she had no trouble in recognizing Lady Moravia at all. Her eyes followed her husband's gaze where it rested on the bosom of Mora's low cut gown and she turned away, furious and determined to revenge her honor! It hurt to see him flirt with another woman. She felt the agony anyone who has battled with jealousy would know. And, too, she felt the anguish of flaunted pride. How dare he? In front of all the beau monde, show himself indifferent to his wife and enamored of another? She had but one weapon left to her and it was to show herself equally as faithless!

"*Anima mia*," murmured the Count. "Come, let us steal away outdoors; the air stifles us here."

"I do feel warm, thank you, Count Mirabel."

"My small one, will you not call me Alban?"

"No, I cannot do that," said Kate dimpling, taking his arm, trying to forget that her husband careened about the dance floor with the Count's sister.

"Do try. I should so love to hear my name on your lips."

"Why?"

He looked taken aback. "Why? What a very odd question, to be sure," he chuckled. "You puzzle me, *anima mia*."

"I do? I can't imagine why, but I do wish you would not call me 'your soul.' It is most improper."

"Improper? Nay! Truth is never improper. You are my soul, though in Italian it is more."

"But I don't wish it to be more. I am married," said Kate.

He stopped beside a patch of evergreens. "You are also a woman! Why do you deny yourself the pleasures your husband obviously does not deny to himself? You are wasted on such as he. I think him blind!" said the Count, slipping his arm around Kate's small waist.

"Stop it, Count," she said suddenly, finding herself locked in his embrace. She was hungry for affection, and she gazed up at him. Was he not handsome, was he not tempting? Then why could she not feel desire? She pushed at his chest. "Please, it is beginning to get warmer out here than it was inside; let us return."

He threw his head back and laughed. "You amuse me, little beauty." He dropped his hands, releasing her, and gave her his arm. She liked him for not pursuing further, and was well disposed to him as they strolled back to the house and reentered the drawing room.

The Earl's eyes had left Moravia's and followed his wife and the Count to the garden doors. He itched with irritation during the remainder of the dance, and when it was at an end was heartily thankful that Danny came up to claim Moravia's hand. He started for the garden door but was detained by Lady Barrymore, who suffered him to listen to an account of her trouble over the masquerade. Just as he was finding an opening to make good his escape and pursue his wife, Kate, holding the Count's arm, came sauntering into the room. He watched the Count's predatory hand take up Kate's and put it to his lips, and his eyes fulminated as he watched the Count make his way to Moravia.

Kate was engrossed in a lively banter with Lady Hester when the Earl finally approached her. They were standing beside the pianoforte and arguing the lyrics of "Barbara Allen." "But she was hard-hearted, Kate, admit it!"

"I shall not! Really, Hester, how can you say so? You are taking the story out of context. Your Sweet William played with every wench in the village when she gave him her heart. It was only when he knew himself to be dying that he called to her. And then afterward she was so morose that she died of a heart too soft for her own good!"

Hester laughed and rapped Kate's hand. "But Kate, you are a veritable tigress! Branwell, here you are; tell her Barbara Allen was wrong!"

"Indeed she was. William wanted to make amends but

she was set on revenge and in the end it did her no good," said the Earl.

"There, you see!" cried Hester.

"Revenge? It was not revenge; it was justice. The only injustice was that by doling it out, she must again suffer."

"You are impossible." Hester laughed, turning to answer a question put to her by another friend.

It left Kate suddenly staring up into the Earl's green glinting eyes, and she thought, *he* looks angry! He goes about openly flirting with Lady Moravia and then glints his eyes at me!

"Did you enjoy the fresh air with Count Mirabel—or is it Alban?"

"I enjoyed the fresh air very much, thank you. Did you enjoy your dance with Lady Moravia—or is it Mora?" she countered, her cheeks flushed.

He frowned, wondering if that was what sent her out with the Count, the Count who was dressed as Caesar. "How did he know you were coming as Cleopatra?"

"Tarot!" she said sardonically.

"What?" frowned the Earl.

"He learned it from the cards, or the stars, or from his gypsy sister. He was most mysterious about it when I inquired," said Kate, defiantly.

"Ho there, Branwell," said the Prime Minister. "I have not yet met your bride, and I am told that Cleopatra is Lady Mannering," said Pitt, coming upon them, Lady Moravia on his arm.

Kate smiled and gave her hand into that of the Prime Minister's.

"Charmed, charmed. I should love to have a look at you when you are not so decked. Hester tells me you are a beauty."

"Hester is very kind," said Kate sweetly.

The Earl's eyes were elsewhere; he was watching Lady Moravia out of the corner of his eye. Kate saw him and inwardly fumed. Dash it, she thought, he can't keep his eyes off her. Then suddenly the Prime Minister was coughing. She felt a wet sensation flowing down the front of her gown, causing the thin material to flatten to her form, and the Earl was apologizing.

"So sorry, Pitt, I am a clumsy fool," said Branwell, patting the Prime Minister's back.

"Good Lord, don't bother about me. 'Tis your poor wife, she has received my champagne on her gown!" said Pitt, much distressed.

Lady Moravia was frightened. She stepped backward and found her stepbrother's arms. His hand patted her shoulder, and she whispered.

"We are undone. The Earl must have seen me open my ring. That little thing was contrived."

"Yes, I observed. He nearly pushed you out of the way to manuever that. However, he has only his suspicions. Hush now," said the Count.

The Earl glanced across at his bride. "I am sorry, Kate."

"Indeed, how can I expect that you should have watched what you were about; your eyes were elsewhere!" snapped his lady.

Lady Hester took her by the shoulders and led her out of the room, but she stopped Hester in the hall. "Do you know, I am not feeling quite the thing. If you would make my apologies to Lady Barrymore, I think I will just sneak off."

"You can't mean to go by yourself, Kate?" said Lady Hester surprised.

Kate sighed, "Can't I?"

"No Kate. It would not do. Let me call Branwell."

"There is no need to call him," said the Earl coming upon them, his lady's cloak in his hands. He dropped it around her shoulders. "I have asked that a hackney be hailed for us, so that Danny and Willy may continue to enjoy themselves." He turned to Hester and took up her hand. "Good night, Hester, take care that you get the Prime Minister home soon."

She studied him a moment. "I see; very well, Branwell. I do believe he is looking a bit fagged."

This brought the frown to Kate's brow. What was all this over the Prime Minister? Something was afoot, yet she did not know what. At any rate, overriding her sixth sense was her jealousy of Lady Moravia and it prevailed on their way home.

Later, she lay awake in her bed. She heard the rustling of his, and for an instant almost wished he would storm in upon her as he had on their wedding night! That would be better than his cold indifference.

"Between Heaven and Hell *mia* Mora, the third coalition must be broken!" said the Count, rising from the bed.

Mora watched him, taking in the lines of his slender form, loving the look of him. She was tired. She didn't want to think about it anymore. "I have still some powder left."

"Ah yes, the powder. But the Earl knows! I cannot risk you. No, there must be another way. If only we could learn whether or not Nelson will go to Trafalgar, then we could choose that time to strike at Austria."

"Does not Napoleon want us to do away with Pitt? Will he not be angry?"

"No, he cares not how we aid him to break the third coalition; he only wishes it broken. It was my notion to throw England into a frenzy with Pitt's death. Who would they have? A mad King? A prancing Prince who cares more for the cut of his coat than the lines of Europe? No, but the Earl would see to it that we would not escape if Pitt were to die. We must discover Nelson's plans. The Earl will not tell you, Mora, now that he knows you are for the French. But perhaps his little bride may give away that which she does not understand."

"I do not like that," said Mora, pouting.

He returned to the bed. "*Mia* Mora, you have nought to fear from her. She is nothing to me," he said, covering Mora's face with his kisses. Her mind wandered back, back some eight years. She had been fourteen and a woman fully formed when his father had married her mother and she had come to Mirabel to live. Alban had been seventeen and, la, she had loved him at first glance. It was summer and warm and they would go to the lake together. Were they not brother and sister? And they would swim. She remembered how his eyes had wandered over her naked body before he touched her, before he led her hand to him, begging her to touch him. She had become his and they loved! Then she was with child and she was sent to the convent. But she had lost it, and she had been ill for months. And Alban, he had come to her. None had known it was his. The doctor said she would never bear children again, and all worries fled.

"Mora, Mora, what is wrong, love?" he cooed, bringing her back to the present.

"Nothing. We will never have children, Alban. Your name will not be carried on," she said sadly.

"Children? We are free. What do we want with children?"

"I am being foolish. Never mind," she said, snuggling into his arms.

"We will leave for Brighton in the morning. Let us sleep," he said, rolling over to his side. She molded herself against his back, holding him. Fiercely holding him to her. He was all that mattered.

"Let go, Mora. I would sleep now," he said, stretching himself out.

42

Kate folded her arms and gave her back to the group occupying her drawing room. There was a lively discussion ensuing, whether or not a closed carriage would be needed in Brighton and, if so, who would travel the distance in it!

"I shan't!" said Sir Wilson firmly. "Mean to drive m'phaeton."

"So do I," agreed Kate from across the room.

"I mean to ride with Willy," offered Danny.

"I shall be taking my horse. So you must see, Kate, that you and Sarah should go in her carriage. I can have a groom take your phaeton," said the Earl.

"No you shan't!" cried Kate. "I won't have any ham-handed groom take on my grays! Sarah, tell him you would much rather ride in an open phaeton than a stuffy old carriage."

"I can't do that, dear, for it will be most dusty in your phaeton; the roads always are at this time of year when there is so much bustle and traffic. It will be far more comfortable in my carriage."

"Then you take Nell in your carriage."

"Er, she can't do that," said the Earl.

"Why can she not?" demanded his lady.

"Master Hatch and Miss Premble have left us for a time. To get married," said the Earl, springing it on her.

"What? But she didn't even tell me," said Kate, a sad look coming over her, though she was not surprised.

"She didn't quite know how," said the Earl. "She asked Hatch to give me the news. I gave them a month's leave, so Nell will not be available to accompany us to Brighton."

"Well, Aunt Sarah, you may take your maid up with you."

"And so I shall, but I don't think you should drive in an open phaeton."

"I shall have Eliza and John with me. It will be perfectly acceptable even to the sternest matron!"

"I suppose," said Aunt Sarah, doubtfully. "Very well, we set out tomorrow then?"

"Tomorrow," agreed one and all. However, the Earl was most unhappy regarding his wife's choice of conveyance. He would have preferred her to ride horseback with him, or in a closed carriage with his aunt. It would now appear that he would have to act as an outrider for Kate!

The trip had turned out to be too dusty, dry, and hot to be enjoyable, especially because Eliza and John had a lover's quarrel, and neither one made good company for Kate. The Earl kept her in view but was too far ahead to afford them conversation, and the inn too crowded to pass a leisurely lunch! When they had finally reached the coast and Kate felt the salt air, she was near to swooning.

Kate drove her team easily through the streets. They were well paved and in good repair. The houses were modern and bright, touched with romanticism in their structure. But what caught the eye from afar was the Royal Pavilion. It was a piece of architecture that stood out alone, surrounded by its well-laid-out grounds. The divergency of its design was both bewildering and magnificent, predominated by its Oriental plan and its rich glory. Kate stopped the phaeton to allow Eliza and John to ogle its lines, during which time they discovered themselves quite ready to kiss and make up and would have carried the entire transaction out had not Kate felt it imprudent to do so in the back of her open carriage on the open road!

They arrived at Steine Street and looked up at an impressive red-brick building of some three stories in height. As their luggage had been sent on ahead earlier that day in a gig, with Cook, Kirkly and two of the Mannering lackeys, John had nought to do but see the phaeton and the grays stabled. Kate sighed and led Eliza up the steps of the covered portico and pulled the knocker. She was greeted by Kirkly, which made her feel quite at home.

"A hot bath has been prepared for you in your suite, madam," said Kirkly. "One of the boys will show you the way."

"Why how thoughtful, Kirkly." Kate smiled.

"Indeed, madam, it was his lordship's orders."

"Oh. Of course," said Kate. "Come, Eliza," she added, following the young lackey up the narrow flight of stairs to the second floor. There was no sign of the Earl anywhere about, and she wondered where he might be as she followed the boy down the hall to a gold framed door. It opened onto a bright lovely room of grand proportions where a marble bath had been set before an unlit fireplace. The room opened onto a terrace that overlooked the rear grounds; other than this Kate saw but one door and imagined this to be the dressing room.

"You must be tired, Eliza; if you will but help me with my buttons, you may go discover which is to be your quarters and have a bit of a rest."

"Oh thank you, my lady," said Eliza gratefully.

A few moments later the yellow brocade drapes had been drawn and Kate was neck high in bubbles. She put her head back and closed her eyes and her mind found the Earl. His eyes were glinting at her, and his lips were smiling. Then there he was, standing over her! "Branwell, what are you doing here?" she demanded, sitting up with indignation, remembering where she was and sinking back down again.

He grinned. "I regret having to disturb you, Kate, but I am using our dressing room as my bedroom. However, the servants are not aware of our arrangement and have left your toiletries in my room. I thought you might need them," he said, placing the articles in question on her vanity table. He lingered and she watched him warily, thinking how masculine he looked in his open-necked white shirt.

"Was your drive very fatiguing?" he asked idly.

"Yes. Sarah was right there, for it was dusty and slow-going."

"You would have preferred riding. I shall have to acquire a suitable mount for your pleasure."

"Thank you, though I didn't enjoy riding four hours the last time we did it," said Kate, remembering their journey from Cambridge to London.

"Those were different circumstances."

"Nevertheless, I was saddle-sore a week after you left for the seas," said Kate, pulling a face.

"Were you?" laughed the Earl. "I had no idea."

"It is not funny," said Kate, smiling.

His eyes wandered over her face and neck and down farther, where the bubbles were dissipating, separating, and he moved toward her.

"What do you think you are doing?" asked Kate, startled by his move.

"You cannot reach your back, and as you have dismissed your maid, I thought I'd lend a hand," said the Earl, picking up the washcloth and getting to his knees.

"No thank you, my lord. I can manage," said his lady.

"Don't call me 'my lord'; it is ridiculous," he said, dipping the washcloth and applying it to the small of her back, working it around in sweeps, massaging rather than washing!

"No more ridiculous than this marriage," said she, trying to keep herself aloof to his ministrations, yet feeling her blood take off like wildfire!

"It needn't be, Kate," he whispered, kissing her neck tenderly, reaching around her, pulling her flat against the marble tub with his arm across her chest, taking her mouth hungrily, urgently, almost begging her not to resist. She wanted to give in to him. She wanted to banish all her anger, all her jealousy and doubts, and give herself to him. She wanted his hand to wander over her body, she wished for it as she allowed him the nectar of her mouth. He felt her response and his hand moved into the water, cupping her breast, fondling it, reaching out and touching both nipples with his fingers at once, sending her into an uncontrollable frenzy. "Let me, Kate. Tell me you want me. Tell me," he demanded, his voice hard with his need.

"No!" she whispered, almost wishing he would take her against her will. She couldn't say yes, she just couldn't let him take her so easily. Not after all he had done. Oh, but she wanted him.

"You want me, you know you want me," he pleaded. "Please, Kate, say you do; admit it."

They were the wrong words. He was a lover of women, a glorious man with magic in his hands and in his voice, but they were the wrong words for Kate. She took the challenge and pulled out of his embrace. "Don't flatter yourself, my lord," said she, feeling wicked, feeling cheap, and, what was more, feeling she was betraying him! Yet she couldn't help herself.

She saw the rigid set of his jaw. She saw the hurt flash through his eyes, and watched him draw coldly away from her, no longer wanting her, and knew she had gone too far. "It seems I have. I shan't make that mistake in the future," he said, turning and leaving the room. She wanted to call after him. She wanted to stay him, but she could not. She had not yet learned how to overcome herself. She rose from her bath and wrapped herself in a towel, sank down upon the massive bed and allowed her tears to flow.

Her husband found relief in stomping down the stairs, where he found Willy and Danny entering the house in a heated argument.

"Damn, but if you had kept to the fingerposts we wouldn't have missed that last turn off!" shouted Danny.

"It wasn't m'job to keep to them! You were supposed to watch for 'em."

"I did, until you decided to take the short-cut. Then there were none!" returned Danny.

"Come on, you two. What we want is brandy!" said the Earl, smiling ruefully.

"Eh, brandy. That's it!" agreed Sir Wilson.

"Where is Kate?" asked Danny, looking around.

"Resting," said the Earl quietly.

". . . and Sarah?" added Sir Wilson.

"Not arrived yet, but have no fear. By tonight we shall have a houseful. Have your servants been taken to their rooms?" asked the Earl.

"Just m'valet and groom, didn't bring any others, and Danny here don't use a valet. But you can see that, can't you?" laughed Willy.

"*Certes!* Are you casting a disparagement on my clothes?" asked Danny, suspiciously.

"Am I doing that?" asked Willy, innocently.

But the Earl had lapsed into deep thought in his seat by the bow window overlooking the street. Danny followed what he thought to be the line of his eye, and discovered Lady Moravia in lively conversation with another pretty young woman across the street.

Danny's brow went up; perhaps that was what was bothering Kate. Was the Earl a chaser? He cleared his throat and said lightly, "It seems the Earl don't hear you, Willy; his eyes and mind be on Lady Moravia."

"Eh?" said Willy, coming forward. "Ay, lovely piece that one, though not in my style. Too large, don't go for the Junos, you know. And something else I can't like about her, can't put m'finger on it, but there you are!"

The Earl's thoughts switched from Kate to Moravia. Here was a partial puzzle solved. She and her brother were here to do what they could to break up the third coalition. There was no other reason for wanting Pitt out of the way. Pitt had organized and managed the third coalition. It was his, and it was unlikely any other would be able to pick up the seeds should Pitt be lost to the country. The King was half-mad and Prinny . . . was Prinny! But why would the Lady Moravia and her brother side with the French? Venice was under Austrian rule, and though the Italians hated the Austrians, what would they gain by a French takeover? They had no hope of ousting them both. No, the end of the third coalition would only mean the French would have a foothold on Venice. Well, special guards had been arranged for Pitt, though the Earl doubted any further attempt would be made against him. He would have to keep his eyes upon the Italians and discover what new thing they plotted!

He looked up at Danny. "What, Lady Moravia? She holds little attraction for me. 'Tis her political position that intrigues me."

"Political? What mean you by that?" asked Willy, interested.

"What a dreadful drive that was!" exclaimed Lady Haverly bursting into the room, her blue muslin crumpled and her bonnet askew. "I need a glass of lemonade and then I plan to soak for hours."

"You look as though you have already soaked for hours," said Willy unthinkingly.

He received a rap across his arm from Aunt Sarah's already-abused bonnet. "Odious boy!"

43

The Pump Room at Brighton was overflowing with the fashionables. Kate, prettily attired in pink muslin, was at the country dance with Willy. Lady Haverly had discovered her dearest friends and sat in happy conversation, whilst the Earl and Danny paid court to Lady Moravia. Watching Danny's antics it was questionable whether his desire to find favor in the lady's eyes was as great as his desire that the Earl should not!

The conversation spreading around the room was all of Nelson! It was now known that he had received, mysteriously, word that the French had made for the West Indies and that his many months at sea had been pursuing them and saving the sugar!

"God preserve the fellow, for a better admiral never lived!" remarked Lord Grenville. "Why, he has chased those blasted Frogs clear back to France! The cowards won't stand and fight."

"Was it not you that only a week or so ago were hammering at Nelson's name?" asked Lady Haverly sweetly. "Indeed, I am quite certain it was."

"Never mind that now, Sarah, and don't pick at me!" muttered Grenville.

"But indeed," said the Count, keeping this line of conversation open, "it would appear that the good admiral has saved Jamaica from French hands. The West Indies merchants will praise him to the heavens. I wonder where next he will go?"

"Why, he comes home to Merton and Emma," said Sarah, surprised. "Did you not know? He is expected quite soon."

"He has no business living with that woman! 'Tis outrageous, their open affair. Why, his wife still lives!" said a dowager, sitting beside Sarah.

"Most inconsiderate of Lady Nelson, don't you think? After all, Lord Hamilton popped off; 'tis the least she could do, or give poor Nelson a divorce," said Sarah, sweetly.

The dowager found this mode of conversation not to her liking and gave Sarah her shoulder much to Sarah's open amusement.

"So then, he goes to Merton. I wonder for how long?" continued the Count.

"Why Emma writes me that she hopes to keep him until the fall, unless Napoleon alters his plans," returned Sarah. "I do wish we would have peace again. It was so delightful when we were in Paris in 1802; 'twas such a gay time," Sarah sighed.

"Indeed, my sister and I had the opportunity to spend some few months there . . . we too found Paris enchanting," said the Count. Then thinking he had, perhaps, said too much, he excused himself and made his way to the dance floor, cutting in on Sir Wilson. Willy took it badly, for he had been enjoying himself and was in no mood to give over. However, he soon realized to persist would be to make a cake of himself, and so he backed away with a sigh of regret.

"That was not nice!" teased Kate. "He will now have to seek out a dancing partner and he so hates having the young fledgings thrown at him."

"No doubt why he chooses your company so much. You are safe as well as beautiful," said the Count.

Kate glanced at him sharply. "I am not certain I like that, though it rather sums it up."

"I have missed you, my beauty. Why do you keep your distance from me?" he asked warmly.

She watched the Earl and his flirtation with Moravia irked her beyond belief, but she had found flirting with the Count could be dangerous. She had no wish to lead him to think she would bestow her favors upon him. Therefore she restrained herself, saying lightly, "I have not been keeping my distance."

"Then you do not wish to avoid me?" he pursued.

"But why should I?"

"Because, perhaps, you are a little bit afraid of what may occur between us," he said, audaciously.

"Am I? I had not realized that." Kate laughed, making light of it.

"But of course, my beauty, of course. Why else do you refuse to be alone with me? Why else do you avoid my eye?"

Now this was getting out of hand. If the Count's stepsister didn't keep her hands off Branwell, she might very well cross the room and tear the creature apart. Her irritation showed in her response. "Because, Count, you are too forward, too aggressive."

"No. It is because I make your blood beat."

"You take a great deal upon yourself. Make my blood beat, indeed! I am not a heroine in a romantic novel, and you, sir, are not my hero!" snapped the lady.

"I could be, if you would but give me the chance," said the Count, at his most seductive. He was piqued. Very few women had ever resisted him. He had started with but a mild interest, but the more he heard *no* from her lips, the more he wanted. Often he had found wanting far more exciting than having, but he imagined that Kate, once aroused, would be quite pleasing.

Kate's cheeks were on fire. She knew not where to look, because whenever she looked away from the Count, it was to find Moravia, far too close to the Earl. Yet she had to get away or she would scream. She excused herself and nearly flew from the room, making her way to the garden.

The Earl had not been blind to all of this. He could not hear what was being said, but he noted the hue of his wife's cheeks, and he noted too that her gray eyes sparkled with anger! He watched her take flight, and he saw the Count's troubled expression follow her and the thought presented itself, with an accompanying sting, that the two had had a lover's quarrel. Blind are the eyes of people in love; at least it has been so written and would in many instances prove true. It was indeed the case here.

Branwell excused himself from Lady Moravia and meandered toward Kate, following her outside to the terrace. It was a warm summer night. July was upon them, giving them heat, and very little breeze to carry the fragrance of flowers in bloom. He watched Kate as she leaned against the railing and came to stand behind her. "Are you all right, madam?"

She turned around at the sound of his voice and had an absurd urge to fling herself into his arms. She wanted to cry. She wanted to say how much she loved him and hated him for looking at Moravia. She wanted to tell him that she needed him, would always need him, wanted him. She said, instead, "Quite, thank you."

"You appeared somewhat flushed," he said, giving himself an excuse to stay.

"It is far too hot for dancing. I would, in fact, like to go home," she said sadly.

"As you wish," he said, giving her his arm. She placed her hand gingerly upon it, too aware of him to do more.

"Should we not tell Aunt Sarah that we leave?" she asked, doubtfully.

"No. They will all come home when they have had enough," he said, leading her out through the terrace steps to the garden. They walked leisurely, silently, each too conscious of the other, each full with the other and unable to overcome the thin, gauzy veil separating them.

"Willy was full of talk of Nelson's latest exploit," said Kate, breaking the stillness. "He would have it that it was you who gave Nelson the information he needed to go after the French."

"Is that what he was telling you earlier?" grinned the Earl.

"Indeed, he has it all worked out systematically. When you left, when the despatches from Nelson arrived. Is it true, Branwell?" she asked curiously, looking up at his rugged profile.

"And if it were?"

"I would be most surprised," said she.

"Would you? Why?"

"Because I once said that my eyes could not lie, yet they must, for when I looked upon you, I saw not that sort of man."

"I see," he said quietly.

"Is it true?" she continued.

"How would you know if I spoke the truth or not? I could just admit to it to win your approval."

"Then you would have already done so. You hesitate; do you not trust me?"

He laughed. "No."

"Oh, I never thought that you wouldn't trust me," said Kate, surprised.

"I would have trusted Kate Newbury; that little love had all my trust, all my heart." It slipped out before he could recall it.

"And as Kate Mannering, she lost it?" she asked, feeling breathless. He had said that he loved her. Was that not what he was saying?

They had reached their lodgings and for answer he pulled the knocker. She was still looking doubtfully at him when Kirkly opened the door. He stood aside to let her pass and as she started for the stairs he stopped and bid her good night. She looked surprised.

"Do you not come up?"

"Not yet," he said quietly.

"Oh, then would you mind just undoing my buttons? I told Eliza not to wait up for me."

He worked at them and as the gown parted down the center of her back he felt his insides stirring. Damnation! Didn't she know what she was doing to him? His tone was curt. "There, the blasted things are done!"

She thanked him and rushed up the stairs and flung herself into her room. She had killed his love! He didn't even want her anymore! This was terrible, terrible. It wasn't what she wanted. She wanted to bring him down, make him hers, make him wild with jealousy, desire, until he cried out his love for her to her, to the world! All she achieved was an ache in her gut and a coldness in his! Her tears flowed as she disrobed. She caught the reflection of herself in the mirror and stood naked, moving her hands to her hips. Was she lovely? Was her form enough to please him? Her breasts were not as large as Moravia's, and she was not so tall. She brushed her long black hair and spread it over her shoulders, allowing the curls to wind themselves around her breasts. Was she not pretty? she asked herself. Suddenly she was filled with a perverse notion of seducing the Earl. Now that he no longer wanted her, had shown himself immune to her charms. Hadn't she tried to flaunt them at him tonight? Hadn't she bent low over him, pressing herself against him on their way to the ball. Hadn't he behaved as though she didn't exist? And now, that she would give him what he wanted, where was he? Downstairs, he was downstairs. Even as she answered her own question, she heard the hall door to the small dressing room he was using as a bedroom open and close. She paced across her room, hoping he would come in and find her naked; maybe then he would not be able to help himself. He would take her and fall in love with her again. Oh dash it, Branwell, come in, do!

Branwell Mannering, his manhood bulging at his breeches, demanding its needs, calling for an end to his celibacy, shrugged off his vest and threw it with some force into a nearby chair. His shirt followed and then he turned to Kate's door. He would have her, to hell with his promise! She was his wife, and he would have her. He walked to the door and stopped. Fiend seize his promise, open the door! He turned and made for the small window. He stuck his head into the night air, for he couldn't breathe. There had to be an answer, he couldn't go on like this! The door between the two rooms opened and Kate stood like a fruit-filled goddess, on the threshold. He stood rigid, unable to move, unable to go to her, afraid that she would retreat. His eyes traveled over her full round breasts high above her incredibly small waist, and they pointed at him, beckoned to him, but he stood like a pillar of stone!

Her cheeks were on fire, but then so was her blood. She was shocked by her own daring, and she was aroused by it as well. She moved into the room, determined to tease him into taking her. She said nothing as she glided toward him, emboldened by the glazed desire in his eyes. She was there before him, her nipples against his bare skin, lightly brushing him beneath his chest. He made no move to take her into his arms. She wanted him! It was all he could think. Oh God, she was here, wanting him and he had the unholy desire to hear it from her. He wanted to wrap his hands in her tantalizing hair and hear her cry out her love of him! So he stood, cold marble, making her go the full length. Tonight it would be no rape!

She was vexed that her body had not stirred him enough to take her. She had hoped the sight of her thus would have made him rush at her, but he made no move. He didn't want her! It was an awful feeling. She had to make him want her. What was it Eliza had once said about touching a man? She reached out timidly and let her hand find his thigh. Gingerly she moved her fingers upward until they discovered the long hardness of pulsating masculinity. She felt him react to her touch and, encouraged, she went further, unbuttoning his pants and releasing the dark pink muscle. Her hands went around it, moving as she had moved her body when it had lodged there. She was on fire now, rallied by the wildness she felt racing through him to her. She went on her knees, suddenly taking his hardness into her mouth, wondering if she were doing it right, sure that she was from his reaction. Then she felt herself lifted by her arms, felt his go around her fiercely, pressing her into his firm hot body. "You hot-blooded woman, where did you learn that little trick?" he asked, his voice hoarse, his body in ecstasy, yet needing answer to his question.

"Girls do talk, my lord," she answered sweetly and felt herself scooped up by his strong muscular arms. His eyes glinted down at her as he carried her into their room and laid her down against the mattress. She watched him hungrily, anticipatingly as he flung off his breeches and climbed onto the bed beside her, and as his mouth met hers, she drew his body to her with her arms. His hands caressed her sensually, parting her legs and his finger teased the lips contained therein. His mouth wandered over her neck and found her breasts, pushing them together with his hands, burying his face in their lush beauty, caressing her waist. She was on fire with his erotic handling, and she wanted him. She couldn't wait any longer. "Take me, Branwell; take me, please," she whispered, no longer caring about her pride.

"It is my intention, fondling," he said, rolling over on

his back. "But, you first," he said, pulling her on top of him.

She was surprised, unsure, but he soon laid such thoughts away. He slipped himself into her, pulling her down to his mouth, his hands wrapped in her hair, moving to her butt, instructing her, encouraging her, biting at her neck, whispering his delight in her ears, moving her in a new and wild motion. "Ride, fondling, ride . . . harder, girl. Oh God . . . but you're good . . . so good," he said, passionately taking her mouth. She climaxed over and over again, each time thinking she couldn't possibly again, until their joining had given them all it could and then she lay in his arms listening with joy to his words. He loved her! Was it possible? Was all the misery at an end? But what of Moravia? But she didn't want to ask, she didn't want to bring another woman's name and image here at such a moment!

Tightly held in his arms she drifted off to sleep, awakening slowly, pleasurably, to the feel of him between her legs. She opened her eyes to find his dancing. " 'Tis *my* turn, sweetings . . . one seduction deserves another. . . ."

"Oh no, Branwell, later. I am sleeping."

"You *were* sleeping," he said, turning her over onto her stomach, and pulling her up by her hips. His hands came around and clutched at her breasts. "Oh faith, girl, but you were formed for this!" he said, plunging into her hungrily. She gasped as he entered her, moving with him, surprised by the new position, aroused by it. She gave until she could only groan, full with love of him, worship of him. His hands were all over her, pleasuring her, teasing her, praising her and they met their joy together. He pulled her back down onto the mattress, holding her around the waist, loving her with his every breath.

"I love you, Branwell," she said, quietly. "I love you." She waited for his response, hurt by his silence.

His thoughts were many as he held back, but he was overcome with her, knew himself a slave to her. "I love you, Kate," he said.

Yet she thought not of his words, but of the delay. She frowned as she slept and she dreamed and the dreams turned into nightmares, and she awoke with a start! But he was there beside her, sleeping contentedly, and as she pressed herself to him, he stirred and smiled in his sleep.

44

"Lordy, ye be still abed, m'lady; 'tis that bright outside! I brung yer coffee. Don't it smell that sweet!" said Eliza, cheerfully, as she placed the tray upon the round tea table near the window. She continued in her busy movements, drawing back the yellow hangings and fixing them with their ropings before turning to find that her lady was not alone! The smile vanished from her countenance and was replaced with astonishment as she beheld the Earl's naked chest and grinning face, noting that his lady was hiding at his back. She bobbed a curtsy and cast her eyes downward. "Oh! Good morning, m'Lord."

"I think you had better knock in the future, Eliza. And Eliza, fetch another cup," said the Earl, still grinning.

Pleased to escape, Eliza scurried out of the room to do his bidding, but as soon as she was out of sight her smile returned. It would appear that all would now be well with her mistress, and this pleased her much.

The Earl turned to his bride and gathered her to him. "You have no idea how delectable you look first thing in the morning, fondling," he said, kissing her nose.

This brought contentment, and he was rewarded with a bear hug. He groaned with pleasurable delight at the feel of her against him and began lowering her back onto the mattress. "Stop it, Bran; Eliza will be here in a moment and our coffee will get cold."

Eliza did indeed return, knocking for admission first. She was allowed to enter with the Earl's cup and speedily dismissed. As it happened, the cups were never used and the coffee was allowed to get cold.

Much later Kate rose from the bed and the Earl watched her gently swinging hips as she went to the washstand. She was everything to him, but it was not this that predominated his thoughts yet. At this time he could only think how much she satisfied him, how much he wanted her, and how different it was with her. He wanted to be alone with her and his face took on a youthful smile. "Kate, wear something simple, and easy to remove. We go on a picnic, you and I!"

"A picnic. Oh, I should love it," cried she delighted, turning to face him, her expression of happiness glowing all around her.

He sucked in breath. God, but she was perfect, and he found himself aroused again, wanting her again. Her breasts taunted him as she moved about the room and he called her name softly, "Kate."

She turned, holding a yellow muslin in her hands. "Yes, Bran? No, Branwell!" she said firmly, stepping back. "I have not had my coffee, and it is too late for breakfast, but I do intend to have my lunch, and if we are to go on this picnic I shall have to get ready and tell Cook to prepare us a boxed meal. So keep your distance, sir!"

He sighed and allowed her to have her way, making designs on her for later. She hummed a tune as she dressed and he listened happily to her as he went about his business in the dressing room. He was ready first and came up behind her while she dressed her hair, kissing her on the top of her head. "Don't put it up, Kate. I like it this way," he said, fingering its smooth length.

She smiled. "Very well, but I shall tie it back for the drive." She took a survey of him in her mirror, noting how bold he looked in his vest and shirtsleeves. He wore buckskins and topboots, and his hair was arranged lazily about his face. Oh, God, how she loved him, and the thought made her tremble.

"I shall take over your duty, slug-a-mine, and have Cook prepare us lunch while you fiddle at your finery," he teased, traversing the room and throwing a kiss at her from the doorway. It was an odd thing for him to do; he could not remember ever having honored a female with such a silly thing before. Yet, it left him feeling good, really good! He whistled as he skipped lightly down the stairs, and Kirkly and his young lackey exchanged glances.

"Ah, there you are, Kirkly ole boy. I have a message for Cook, if you would be so good."

"Of course, my lord."

"Madam and I are going on a picnic."

"A picnic?" exclaimed Willy, who had appeared from the drawing room door. "Splendid notion!"

"You are not invited, Willy," said the Earl amiably.

"Not invited? Devil you say," said Willy, much hurt.

"Sorry Willy, you know, honeymoon and all that," said the Earl, grinning.

"Honeymoon? Egad, almost forgot, know what else, never got you a wedding present. Shall do so today, go with Sarah and do the thing."

"Where is our young Danny?"

"Off to Dymchurch," said Willy.

"Dymchurch? Whatever for?" asked the Earl, surprised.

"Some friend from Cambridge has a home there. Visiting. Which reminds me. Where is that scamp? Why ain't he here?"

"If you are referring to my brother," grinned the Earl, "he is spending the holidays in Cornwall with some cousins of ours."

"Devilish place Cornwall, surprised you have cousins there. Though not really surprised. After all, you ain't your average fellow, are you?" said Willy, apparently making sense to himself.

Kate apppeared on the stairs, much taking away their breath and receiving many compliments.

Just about this time, Jack Walepole, wiping the sweat from his brow, waited for the knocker to be answered at the Count's small but cozy cottage. A day maid of considerable proportions answered it, her eyes opening wide at the sight of the repulsive little man, but she stood aside and allowed him to enter, taking his card and asking him to wait while she informed her master of his arrival.

The Count, clothed in a pale blue lightweight coat of superfine, over a white linen shirt, open at the neck, and a pale blue silk vest, looked up from his reading. "Walepole, you say?" he asked the maid, thinking Moravia had chosen a particularly unattractive female in this specimen.

"Yes, Count," she said, handing him the card.

"Have him come in at once. Go quickly," said the Count, not wanting Walepole standing about in the hall where any chance visitor might drop in to find him.

Jack Walepole appeared and closed the door behind him. "Good morning, Count Mirabel."

"Is it?"

"Indeed, it will be, for I have some information that should fetch us both a handsome fee," said Walepole, rubbing his short-fingered hands together.

The Count regarded him with distaste. "I shall be the only judge of that, Walepole."

"Of course you shall," said Walepole, his expression unreadable.

The door opened once again, this time to emit Lady Moravia. She glided into the room, her gauzy gown of white floating about her well-proportioned form, and the Count's eyebrow went up as he found the toadish man's eyes devouring the sight of her full bosom.

"Mora!" he snapped. "Sit here," he ordered sharply, pointing to a high-backed chair away from Walepole's scrutiny. He would have no such man look at what was his, unless it served his purpose!

"I've come from the Horse Guards, made contact, finally. But he was a greedy fellow, had to pay more than I thought," said Walepole.

"It seems, Walepole, that you are ever paying far more than you believed necessary. Lamentable, and a dangerous habit to fall into," said the Count dryly.

"Er, I see your point, but I think when you hear what I've brought you, you will agree that it is worth it."

"Then let us hear it."

"Prussia has refused to join the third coalition, though Frederick William III has agreed not to make it known yet, while the coalition regroups its forces."

"That is it? That is all?" cried Lady Moravia.

"No, Mora, you do not realize. It is much, very very much!" breathed the Count excitedly. "Pitt was hoping, praying; only the devil and God know how much he needed Prussia's troops. If they do not join he will not have enough to strike! Napoleon must know of this at once. I will prepare a despatch, and yes, Walepole, this will see us well paid."

Jack Walepole smiled. "I thought so, Count. Will you be wanting me to ride to Dymchurch?"

"Indeed yes," cried the Count, who had already gone to his desk.

"And so I shall, but first we shall partake of some luncheon, for it was a long hot ride from London and I am parched and hungry," said Walepole boldly.

The Count stopped and gazed at Walepole. He detested the little man. He had political reasons as well as personal ones for spying, and indeed, he betrayed not his own country but worked toward Venetian freedom. First they would oust the Austrians, and then the French, but of the two the French were the lesser evil! But Walepole was a traitor to his own kind. However, he needed him.

"Yes, yes, of course. Mora, have that silly wench bring Mr. Walepole some luncheon. We will not be taking lunch ourselves, but we shall be happy to see you satisfied," said the Count, not altogether graciously.

The glen the Earl chose for an outing with his lady was well secluded, adorned with wildflowers for Kate to exclaim over, birds to serenade them and a stream to lull them with its refreshing song. They had devoured the tasty cold pigeons and muffins Cook had prepared and Kate was sipping her lemonade, the Earl his wine, whilst she watched a busy squirrel and he watched her. She sighed and turned to him, her gray eyes full with happiness, and he reached out to stroke her face, thinking, This was glory. He downed his wine and put away his glass with a show of emphasis. "And now, madam, for dessert," he said, reaching for her. She screeched and jumped to her feet and began running, turning her head to find him at her heels, whereupon she screeched again. He had caught her a moment later round the waist, and she panted, out of breath, her breasts heaving above her gown. He grew suddenly intent on his purpose as he pressed her against the evergreen tree at her back.

He pulled the ribbon from her hair, releasing its luxurious lengths, entwining his hands in its silky texture, as his mouth came down to meet hers. She wrapped her arms round his neck, lifting herself to him, pressing into him, thinking he was her all! His kisses toured her face, explored the garden sweetness of her, while one hand hiked up the skirts of her muslin gown.

"What . . . what are you doing?" she gasped, excited and shocked all at once.

"Guess, my fondling!"

"But, you can not . . . someone might come upon us," she objected. Even as she did, his hand discovered that which it sought.

"There are no cottages about for miles, Kate, and I want you," he said huskily, his lips brushing against hers but not taking, for he had further things to say. "Now, Kate, now . . . here in the open with the breeze to blanket us."

The thought was sensual and titillating but she had to think of the proprieties. "No! You monstrous thing! It's . . . indecent."

" 'Tis necessary, my love," he said, forcing her back against the tree, lifting her up into its heights, miraculously unbuttoning his breeches at the same time.

"What are you doing?" she asked again, surprised to find herself somewhat off the ground in an upright position. It seemed improbable that he could take her thusly.

She held onto his neck for support while his hands undid the buttons of her bodice, exposing her breasts to his mouth, while she rode his raised knee. Then he held her with both hands, replacing his knee with the hard projectile of his muscle free now from his breeches. He didn't enter her, though; he played, moving the pulsating dark pink between the threshold of her honeybun. He was sending her into a frenzy as he played, moving himself round and up and down its tender length, slowly, teasingly, tempting her to ask for more. As he pressed the peak of his muscle between those tantalizing lips, Kate groaned with fever and felt herself lifted to new heights. He was verdure to her soul, this man. He was a sorcerer, with a skill, with his own power and scent, and he caused her to drift into erotic pleasure. He was wild for her, hungry for her, loving this foreplay, for he was lust when near her. The mere thought that she was his and his alone sent him into a passion, but he was ever surprised by his own reaction to her. Surprised that he could think of no other woman, want no other woman. Surprised that only Kate had the power to alter his moods out of control. He wanted Kate to need everything he had to give her. He loved hearing her moans of pleasure; it delighted his senses and fulfilled a need within him to satisfy her!

"Branwell, please, take me," she cried, begging him with her body. She was arching herself, throwing herself into him with a wild grace.

God, he thought, no other had ever pleased him this way. Never before had he known what satisfaction truly was. All other times had been but a body function, but this . . . this was the workings of the soul! He took her then, lowering her to the ground, placing her upon her back and taking her with wild untamed pride, exulting in their dance and thinking he would see the world damned before he would give her up!

"Now, Walepole, that you have rested and refreshed yourself, here is the despatch. You will tell him I expect a reply!" said Count Mirabel, getting to his feet and crossing to where Walepole sat before an empty plate.

"That I will, that I will," said Walepole, picking at his teeth noisily. "But, you've forgotten somethin', haven't you?"

"Not at all," said the Count, taking out a small leather pouch from his inner pocket. "I think you will find enough here to satisfy you, and pay our agent."

"Agents be damned! The cutthroats ain't nought but a pack of smugglers, making the trip for brandy, making it whether we give 'em a packet or no. And that Frenchie on the other side, he gets his pay from Boney. There is danger for only one cove, and that's me!"

"What are you saying?" asked the Count, narrowing his eyes.

"I'm saying," said Walepole, playing with the leather pouch in his hand, "that this ain't weighty enough. I'll have two!"

"You will go to the devil!" spit the Count.

"Mayhap I will, but when I go, I will still have had two bags, Count!" said Walepole, levelly.

The Count made an oath as he glared at him, but he had no other choice. It was too late a date to try and find another contact on this side of the Channel, and this piece of news had to go immediately. Besides, Walepole had proved himself useful in many directions.

He released another curse, but he went to the desk, took out a key from the ring at his waist and opened one of the desk drawers. A similar bag was produced and he slid it over the desk top at Walepole, who walked leisurely toward it and picked it up, dangling it before the Count's eyes, as though to dig in his victory. He thought himself a clever fellow, indeed.

Lady Moravia appeared in the room at this moment and came forward, passing Walepole, who turned to her, took off his hat, sweeping it across his chest with a smile as he sauntered out. He made his way to the stables down the street from the Mirabel cottage, where those locals who had not stables of their own leased space. He paid for his time and led out his horse.

The Earl drove his lady's team around the corner, driving to an inch and drawing a pretty compliment from his wife. They laughed over the sight of two dogs playing on the walk, when Kate suddenly gasped and dived at the Earl, fearfully holding his arm to her chest.

He stopped the team and took her to his breast, a worried look coming over him. "My God, Kate, what is it, love?"

"That man," gasped Kate, staring at Jack Walepole as he rode his horse toward them.

Jack Walepole had by now reached them and was about to pass when he saw and recognized Kate. He tipped his hat to her and his smile was wicked upon his lips as well as in his dark pinlike eyes. The Earl noted this and nearly jumped from the phaeton with every intention of pulling the foul creature off his horse and making him answer for his lewd behavior to Kate. However, Kate was in a terror and would not let go of his arm.

He turned to her. "Who is he, Kate?"

"Jack Walepole," she whispered.

The Earl remembered the name. The Horse Guards were interested in him, for the toadlike man was under suspicion, but what had Kate to do with him, how did she know him? These questions were asked and duly answered, and the Earl felt a sudden soaring mind-bending urge to kill! Jack Walepole had tried to rape Kate! He made a mental note to find the evil man and break his neck!

45

July progressed in a froth of joy! Each day brought Kate and Branwell closer to one another. They had eyes and soul only for one another, they sought only each other and were contented only within each other's circle. This was a fact bound to interest their well-wishers and give rise to much loving and amiable jesting amongst the Earl's household. Danny and Willy congratulated themselves soundly, each believing that he was responsible in some mysterious way for the blossoming love taking place before them. Aunt Sarah, her hopes realized, floated about in a trancelike state of jubilation. This, to be honest, was due to two facts. One, we already have taken note of above; the other was due to a certain distinguished country squire she had met one evening at the Pump Room and who had since become a daily visitor at the Earl's Brighton home!

Squire John, a man of many excellent traits, the best of these being that he found Lady Haverly perfect in every way, had much to recommend him. He was tall enough, built well for a man of some odd fifty years. These years, twenty of which were spent as a happy widower, had left him well disposed and quite ready to bestow his steady heart upon Sarah. He was attempting to do so in the Earl's drawing room, when Danny and Willy burst forth, arms linked, the laugh in their eyes and still on their lips. Totally unaware that they had broken up with some force a romantic tête-à-tête, they proceeded to relay the latest on-dit. That being that an acquaintance of theirs, whom, Danny added to Willy's dissertation, had not a sou to his name, was chasing after the Clifford heiress, and had until moments ago been gaining points.

"However, what did the noddy do but try to outshine his blond rival by standing on his head."

"Good Lord!" ejaculated Sarah, growing interested. "Whyever would he think such a stunt would impress the silly girl?"

"Oh, as to that, you know there is this dashing colonel whom the girl claims is her cousin, and she mentioned admiring his expertise at such acrobatics," explained Danny.

"Yes, so Felix," put in Willy, taking over, "ups and claims that he can top the fellow's antics by standing on his head on a ledge. Well, there was no ledge but that around the fountain."

"And what must Felix do, but lose his balance and fall in," put in Danny. This so vividly brought back the scene to them that they once more fell into wicked mirth, which in turn tickled the Squire's sense of humor, for he remembered his youth. Sarah, much amused and much delighted with her sweet John, sighed!

August came and there was nothing to disturb the universal bliss of such a household. Indeed, the Earl's absorption in his wife forbade all interest in Moravia's political intentions, and though he put about discreet inquiry, Jack Walepole seemed to have vanished. However, the first week ended with a letter to the Earl from Admiral Nelson!

Branwell sat in his study, Kate playing idly with the hair at the nape of his neck, frowning over the letter, whilst he stroked her bare arm. She peeped over his shoulder to look at Admiral Nelson's scribbling and wrinkled her pert nose. "What is it that he says to make you look so black?"

"Something is afoot! It appears he has arranged a meeting for Monday of next week with Pitt, and he wants me there."

"No!" cried Kate. "You can't mean to go. I . . . I won't let you."

He smiled. "Believe me, fondling, though I am persuaded a man should do more than wallow in lust of his wife, I have no wish to go."

"Then you will take me," demanded Kate.

"No. It is not a comfortable trip at this time of year, and there would be nought for you to do alone in London. No. But I will make the trip in one day."

"You mean you will ride there and back in one day? Oh, 'tis too much for you and your poor horse."

"Goose!" he grinned. "It certainly is not too much for me. All this soft living makes you forget that I am a pirate and as such am quite used to hard hours!"

She pouted. "Oh what a fool I was, Branwell. A pirate indeed! You are noble and brave and good and handsome."

He laughed. "Stop, stop or I shall be unable to leave your side for even a few hours."

She kissed him long and sweetly and he pulled her down into his lap, letting Nelson's letter slip to the floor.

It was of course natural that within a few hours the entire household, a close-knit group, totally engrossed with each other's doings, became acquainted with the news of the Earl's projected outing. However, the reasons for his journey were left in obscurity, lending those with imagination much for conjecture.

"Meeting with Pitt and Nelson, you know," nodded Willy knowingly to Danny.

"Yes. But why?" asked his companion, frowning.

"Haven't the slightest, and tell you what, lad, don't want to know. Stay out of the Earl's way in case he tries to tell us."

"But why?" repeated Danny.

"Why? Dash it, boy, if the Earl opens his mummer it's to inveigle us into his doings, depend upon it."

"I should like that," said Danny with gumption.

"Should you?" asked Willy, surprised.

"Of course. What a rare dust we could kick up!" said Danny, wistfully.

Sir Wilson said nothing to this but he frowned, silently wondering whether he was getting old. He would soon embark upon his twenty-eighth year. Hang it, he was getting old, thought he with a weary sigh!

Danny rose from his seat and announced his intentions of going out. "Coming?" he asked.

"Where to, lad?"

"Anywhere, take a run to the sea, exercise the horses."

Willy mulled over this a bit; it was sultry, he was feeling lazy, but he was also feeling bored. "Very well," he said, getting up slowly to join his young friend.

They had not gone very far when they found the Count and his sister turning up the street and Danny, still somewhat lightly infatuated with the older beauty, waved them to a halt. "*Certes!* But I say, Lady Moravia, I haven't seen you about in an age."

She smiled, for she liked the young boy, and was amused with his boyish show of favor. "Indeed, Mr. Ludlow, that has been a regret of mine, but I have not been about very much as of late."

"I thought not, for I have looked for you at all the routs," declared Danny.

"And how is Lady Mannering?" asked the Count. "Though my sister has been unwell recently, she insisted I attend some of the dinners given, but I saw not her ladyship there."

Sir Wilson had never liked the Count and his sister, and took umbrage that the Count should inquire after Kate and not Branwell, too.

"Lady Mannering and her husband have been keeping to themselves. Honeymoon, you know," said Willy.

"Oh yes, I suppose to make up for his lordship's absconding to the sea after the wedding," said the Count.

It was Danny's turn to take affront on behalf of Kate. "That was unavoidable, Count. Why, the Earl can't bear to be parted with Kate; he is even making the trip to London in one day in order that they do not spend a night apart!"

"Trip to London?" asked Lady Moravia.

Sir Wilson tried to catch Danny's eye, but was unsuccessful.

"Yes, he goes on Monday to meet with Pitt and Nelson," said Danny portentously.

"Really?" said the Count. "This sounds intriguing. Why would the big whigs choose this time of year for such a strange meeting?"

"Don't know. Must be getting along now. Late for an appointment," said Sir Wilson, linking Danny's arm and dragging him away rather abruptly.

When they were out of hearing, Danny turned wrathfully upon Willy. "Why did you do that?"

"Got to keep your mummer shut, lad. Said too much, didn't want you to say any more. Though you really said everything, glad you didn't know anything more. Would have spilled that, too, I suppose," said Willy, shaking his head.

"What do you mean?" asked Danny, blushing hotly.

"Can't trust them. But even if we could, that was privileged information. As guests of Branwell's we get news that others don't. There is an impropriety in spreading such news about. Not the thing. You're young, you'll learn," said Willy, feeling wise.

Danny said nothing as he walked beside Sir Wilson, but he digested his friend's words, and after a bit said, "You are right, Willy, indeed you are. But do you think, in this case, I have done harm?"

"Want the truth or want to be coddled?"

"I think I want to be coddled."

"In that case here is the truth. Don't trust the Count and his sister. Strange couple; perhaps we should mention the matter to the Earl."

"Willy . . . you make me feel like a school boy. I should die of shame," whined Danny.

Willy snorted, "I wouldn't do such a paltry thing as to lay the blame at your door. Hang it, lad, what sort of a man do you take me for? Should say *I* let it slip out."

"And what sort of a man do you take me for?" thundered Danny, much incensed. "Is my credit as a gentleman such that you would offer me such a shabby insult? I shall tell the Earl, and I shall tell him exactly as it was. Let you take the blame, indeed!"

That agreed upon, they went on their way and found some friends collecting seaweed, which Willy declared to be singularly odd behavior on the part of his friends, but which Danny seemed to take great interest in, thus whiling away the hours!

46

A small frail man in half dress, with an armless sleeve to his dark coat, squinted the one eye left to him and stretched in impatience, moving his hand as he spoke. "But you realize, Prime Minister, that my time and movement must depend upon Bonaparte."

"Our information is that Napoleon is at Boulogne with the Imperial Guard and one hundred twenty thousand soldiers, Admiral. If the French fleets combine, there will be an armada of sixty-two ships of the line," said Pitt, with a shake of his head. "Admiral Cornwallis drew up broadsides with the enemy at Brest and fought them back, but they are getting information and have a plan. My agents tell me they think to take their squadrons for a sweep up the Channel to Ireland, the devils!"

Branwell Mannering laughed. "With admirals whose spirits and bravery sink each time they are faced with force? Napoleon stands no chance, and well he knows it. As to his getting information, I have a notion that there is a leak at the Horse Guards that should be corked."

"Nevertheless, I must hold that we shall have to keep Boney busy, and we must hold the Straits!" said Pitt resolutely.

"Indeed, but how may we engage, if the French won't fight?" asked Nelson with some exasperation. "I have been chasing the damn Frogs all over the Atlantic, and they won't face me!"

"That is where you come in, Branwell, though you may decline this, for I must own it to be dangerous and you are not, after all, part of the Admiralty."

"In what way may I serve?" asked Branwell at once.

"I have it that the combined fleet will be on the move, and depend upon it, Mannering, if you are spotted, your only chance for survival will be speed. For I am asking you to try and discover their destination."

"Consider it done," said Branwell, at once.

"It is your duty if you accept to keep this confidential. Much depends on it," said Pitt gravely. "Yet you have a young bride. She will not be pleased. What will you tell her?"

"Then you are saying I am honor bound to lie to my wife?" asked the Earl, dryly.

Pitt laughed. Admiral Nelson, much in sympathy for he had his Emma to deal with, did not; neither did Branwell. Pitt's laughter ceased and he coughed into his hand. "Eh, yes, sticky to be sure. But women tend to prattle."

"Lady Hester does not," said the Earl, quietly.

"No, no, she does not. Very well, then, you may give her surface information only."

"And, you wish me to leave?"

"Immediately," said Pitt.

The Earl rose. "Then if you will excuse me, I have a long ride back."

Several hours later Jack Walepole sidled to the back door of the Prime Minister's abode. A lackey appeared, and raised a brow.

"I'm to bring this 'ere to your Prime Minister Pitt, I am," said Jack Walepole shoving past the man into the kitchen, putting on a cockney dialect.

"Eh, what ye got there, covey?" asked the lackey curiously.

"Aw now, it's a gift; china, I was told. Ye look like a fellow I can trust. I'll jest leave it wit ye, right?"

"Don't make no ha'porth a difference to me if ye want to leave it wit me or no. 'Taint me ye got to trust . . . 'tis the butler, but he be a right 'un."

"Good. Mind if I has me a glass of water? Devilish hot out there," said Walepole, stretching his arms out.

"It's over there," said the lackey, indicating with a throw of his chin.

Walepole crossed the floor leisurely. "Rich home this, eh?"

"I don't know about that, but the master he be a fair man."

"Heard Nelson was here today; sure would like to get a look at sech a hero."

"I seen him!" said the lackey proudly. "Served him coffee and cakes I did."

"Heard tell how he be going after the Frogs. Chase 'em away from the Channel?"

"No, he don't move yet, he be waiting on some information," said the lackey portentously.

"Gawd, how de ye know that?" marveled Walepole, scratching his scraggly dark hair.

"Heard 'em while I was setting out the tray."

"How is he going to find out where the French be heading?"

"Don't know, didn't get anymore. Why ye asking?" said the lackey, screwing up his mouth.

"Curious, ain't ye?"

"No, what can I do about any of it? 'Taint no good worrying whether they be right or wrong. They ain't gonna listen to the likes of me," said the fellow, philosophically.

"Ain't that the truth though!" Walepole grinned. He made a smacking noise of appreciation for the water, and waved himself out, smiling to himself all the while.

Sunset brought the Earl home, and his arms went around Kate hungrily. He was road weary and not looking forward to telling her he was off with the *Gypsy*. His ship was docked in Brighton Harbor and he would be leaving in the morning, and he would be leaving without Master Hatch. He was not in good temper. She saw it at once and cooed to him softly, as though he were a babe, and found her methods strangely satisfying.

"You are displeased with today's work?" she asked, pulling off his green riding jacket, unbuttoning the waistcoat, sending her gentle hands up his chest. He caught them and held them with his own. "Kate. I will be leaving for the *Gypsy* in the morning."

"No, no," she cried.

"I must, but I don't expect to be gone very long, two or three days, maybe four. 'Tis only to Boulogne and down to Cadiz."

"Then I shall come."

"You may not. It will be no place for a woman."

"I don't care. I am coming."

"I said no, and I won't discuss it."

"If you go, I go. And, Branwell, I will not discuss it."

"Kate, I have no wish to put you under lock and key, and please, sweetings, I am too tired to pursue this nonsensical line of conversation."

She thought for a moment, devised her plan and planted a kiss upon his cheek. "You are right, my lord, and I am most thoughtless."

He eyed her suspiciously but said nothing more, for his dinner was brought to him and Kate chose to delight him with a diatribe of anecdotes whilst he consumed his meal.

He awoke the next morning, placed a kiss upon her sleeping forehead, and proceeded to dress. It was 5:00 A.M. by the time he had completed his dressing, and though he dearly wished to wake her and to hold her, he allowed her to continue sleeping, for he was afraid she might decide to badger him about accompanying him.

A moment after he stepped out the door, Kate was up and diving into the breeches she had borrowed from Danny. She tucked in his shirt, buttoned a buckskin vest which was far too large for her, slid into his brown buckskin riding jacket, grimaced at the image she presented and pulled on her riding boots. She pinned her hair atop her head and put on a riding hat, slung long over her forehead, before she scurried out of the house and made for the stables. Here she had a horse saddled, not minding that it was Willy's; she ordered John to follow as best he could, for she would leave it tethered at the shipyard for him to retrieve. And then she was on her way.

The *Gypsy* had orders to always be ready to sail at a moment's notice. However, there were some provisions that needed to be taken on. Captain Branwell's crew was busy at these when Kate arrived at the docks some twenty minutes after she had left her stables.

No one noticed the small young lad who sneaked on board, for the men were distracted with the joy of their anticipated sail, and the loss of Mr. Hatch! His command went to a Mr. Hardy, who was sorely unable to fill the space. No help from Captain Branwell, as he was in his cabin, plotting their course. Kate slinked to the stern and found an open storage hatch. She jumped down into its hold and found the compartment hot, dusty, and dark. As she made herself comfortable on a sack of grain, she wondered if there might be mice about, and one very amiably gave her the answer! This nearly drew a screech from her but she restrained herself. However, when the trap door of the hatch was shut and her hole was devoid of light, she felt herself go rigid with apprehension. After a time, she fell asleep for lack of anything better to do and was not roused until she felt the swaying of the ship.

It rolled beneath her, and she heard lapping at its sides. She struggled with her legs, and finally got them to work before she attempted to remove the door of the hatch! This was no easy task in the dark. It took all of ten minutes and much ingenuity, but at last she had the sacks of grain piled in a pyramid. She scampered from her hiding place, removed the door, and pulled herself up by her arms directly into the paunch of one seaworthy individual! Startled, he jumped with as much surprise as she, before recovering himself and noting that she was a figure worth some mirth!

"Lookee 'ere, lads . . . vast there, mates . . . lookee 'ere at whot oi 'ave! Tis a present from the hold!"

Kate found herself the object of much ridicule as a few sailors took time out from their chores to fall into hearty laughter. "Aim ye to be a sailor?" asked another burly individual.

Kate had had enough. Where was Branwell, anyway, she thought with some irritation. She pulled off her cap and allowed her long waist-length hair to come cascading down her back, and received the expected results!

"Hang me, mates! It's a hell-pucking woman!" said the man who had discovered her.

"Now, gentlemen . . . if you will be so kind as to show me to your Captain?" said Kate, a light dancing in her eyes at their expressions.

However, there was no need to search out the Captain; he had found her. His hat was removed and slapped against his knee before he flung it at the first man's head he happened to see!

"You sightless buzzards! You dupes. How did you allow my wife to board this ship?" The Earl rounded on Kate and took hold of her arm. "You have cost me a serious delay, madam, and I am not pleased. I am used to having my orders obeyed."

"Never say so? Orders, indeed?" said Kate, dangerously.

"I should take you over my knee and . . ." He caught the expressions of his interested men and stopped himself. "Turn about, lads!"

"Oh, Branwell, no, then you will make me feel awful . . . is that your purpose?"

The men delayed responding to his order, awaiting the outcome of this.

"Kate . . . Kate! You don't understand; there is a great deal of danger, and in our case they will take no prisoners! If we are spotted they will see this ship down, and we have not the sort of weapons to fight off a warship."

"If you go down, then so shall I; therefore, I would prefer it to be together for I would not be half as brave dying all by myself."

He looked at her a long moment and then hugged her to him, miserable and happy all at once. "So be it, fondling." He shouted to his men, "Steady as she goes!"

Surprisingly enough, this set up a cheer! As a rule sailors didn't care for females on board their ship; it spelled bad luck, but they saw Kate in a different light. She had outwitted them and found her way on board. Then she had dazzled them and won over their captain, whom they trusted. Indeed, they liked the new addition!

Boulogne was reached an hour later, and it was discovered that the French fleet had already left for the south. The wind was fair, both anchors were at the bows, and the sails were filled as they followed. They were making good time. It was to St. Vincent at the southwest end of Portugal they headed for there they would discover what it was they needed to know.

Kate moved about her husband's stateroom. It was small, yet it housed a large chest, a washstand, and a rather larger bed than she had expected. She was feeling good and giddy and victorious, and she pounced on the bed very much like a child who has gained against all odds. The Earl entered his cabin in time to witness this and so far from being vexed, he chuckled at her antics.

"Come here, naughty puss."

She went to him on her knees at once, and put her

arms around his neck, attempting to pull him onto the bed with her. The firmer he stood, teasing her, the harder she pulled, until he allowed her to have her way. She covered his face with kisses, traversed his chest with many more, went further down, and stopped, for the cabin door opened. She jumped and move away, blushing profusely.

"Gawd! Sorry, Capt'n. Forgot about your Lady," said the steward, who had wheeled in their dinner.

"That's quite all right, Zach, and I will serve her Ladyship tonight. You may go," he said lightly, throwing Kate a meaningful glance. But the entrance of food upon the scene banished all thought of romance in Kate, for she recalled with a shriek that she hadn't eaten anything all day. She pushed the Earl's probing hands away, admonishing him severely. He laughed and watched her as she uncovered plates, nibbled, and groaned. However, they had not eaten very much when a bell sounded and the Captain stood up sharply. "Stay here, Kate!" he shouted, vanishing with some speed into the companionway.

She heard his voice thundering above her. She heard the men running about and then she heard the hard shattering of air. It was an explosion, the explosion of cannons! She looked out her porthole but could see nought, for it was as black as coal.

She had to see what was happening. She ran out of the cabin and up the companion stairs to the poop. She saw Branwell at the helm, steering, and he was shouting orders to his men, calling to Mr. Hardy to look sharp. She watched them, marveling at their speed, at their uniform grace, when another deafening roar burst the air and its ball fell short, hitting water and splashing the *Gypsy* with its force, soaking Kate, who stood in its path. My God! thought Kate; this is war. One unknown man shooting against another unknown man! The water, soaking her—it could have been death! She peered at the openness, looking for the French sails, barely making them out, for the sky and sea met as one in the blackness.

Suddenly the *Gypsy* swerved as the Earl turned into the wind, tacking into it, zigzag fashion, and she took a pride in his skill. They were passing out of range, yet the huge French warship kept up a continuous fire of cannon and cannonade, and the air was dotted gray with smoke and dust!

The wind blew fresh and thick, and as the *Gypsy* passed out of range, the French hurled musket fire upon them, ramming shots off their deck, shattering the wood and sending it hurtling about. A flying splinter tore off the buckle of Mr. Hardy's shoe and as he shook his fist at the French warship, his fellow crew groaned with laughter.

"This is getting a bit too warm, eh, Mr. Hardy?" bantered the Captain. "That's the spirit, lads, keep a cool head and we'll see Portugal yet, and may Nelson send the Frogs to perdition for this night's work!"

The next shot fell short, as did the others that followed and soon the French craft was left astern. Kate sighed with relief when she realized they were out of range. The *Gypsy* was built for just such a run. The heavy warship with its twenty-four cannons and five decks had virtually no chance to catch up to them. Such was her relief that a gurgle of laughter at the memory of Mr. Hardy shaking his burly fist over the loss of his buckle tickled through Kate. The captain of the *Gypsy* heard and turned around on her like a fury, for he had not seen her during the commotion. "Kate! I told you to stay below!"

"Yes, but . . ."

He grabbed her by the arm, for this was something he would not tolerate, and he shook her angrily. She could have been injured if a cannon shot had hit a mast. Hell, she had been standing directly in the line of fire! *Certes*, but she was a child! She would have to learn that there were some things she would not be able to talk or caress her way out of!

He shouted at her, "Enough, Kate!" Then he dragged her roughly to the companion stairway and down into his cabin. Once behind closed doors he turned around, her arm still in his grasp. "If you wish to remain on board my ship, madam, you will obey my commands, as do my crew. Not only your safety depends upon it but theirs, those men up there! They trust me and well they should, for we have been to Hades and back together, but damn it, Kate, you distract me with your tricks, and then what good will I be to them? You could have been hurt." He reached for her face with his free hand and stroked it, suddenly tender, surprised at his own emotions. "And then, my fondling, I would be no good to those men up there. So if you think yourself on a lark, next time think of that and put your tricks away!"

She felt foolish and contrite and a tear formed. "I . . . I didn't realize, Bran."

"Oh, Kate," he said, taking her into his arms.

"Branwell, I am sorry, indeed I am." She purred against his ear, softening in his arms, like a kitten warm and pettable. His lips took hers gently, assuaging his irritation, and the thought that each day saw new horizons to his love for her presented itself with no little force. This small pliant woman-child with her large gray eyes was exacting a toll from him. She had taken his soul; he knew it lost to her, and he rejoiced in the knowledge.

He sighed and put her from him. "Now get some rest, darling. I've got to get back on deck!"

She would have stayed him but he was gone, and she felt suddenly weary. She dropped her wet clothes upon the floor and without bothering to brush her winded, salted locks, she crept beneath the covers of the damp sheets and fell asleep. It was hours later when she felt him beside her. She felt the weight of him and reached out to stroke his back, coming alive with the touch of him. She pressed her naked body to his but he did not respond, and she propped herself up to have a look at his face. Was he angry still? She did not find anger; he was a man exhausted and quite deeply asleep. She sighed and snuggled herself against him, pleased that even in his sleep his hand reached for her.

When next she awoke, it was nearly daylight, but it

was not the brightening room that tingled her senses to wakefulness! She felt a hot gushing race through her limbs, and she felt a pleasurable sensation surging through her loins. She opened her eyes to find Branwell's body stretched out beside her, his head between her legs, his mouth at the apex of her thighs, and she groaned. Reaching for his arm, whispering his name, she called him to a halt, for she was somewhat frightened by this new sensation.

His hands spread her legs farther, and his voice came wild and urgent. "You are delicious, madam." His hands redirected hers, until he built her pitch to new heights, until her hands worked him to a climax at which point he controlled himself, turned, and mounted her. He took hold of her butt, raising it up to him. "Now, my love," he said, fiercely plunging into her, hard, taking her with a sensual roughness that turned her into a hungry untamed woman. He soared within her, teaching her the steps to his new dance, taking her with him to explore the tantalizing summit of their wondrous love. For indeed, it was love at its purest. It could not have been finer, for they were two beings joined and vowing their troth to one another. They were two creatures willing to be one, willing to blend into a new single being, willing to give that creation life!

47

The Earl had asked his household to keep an eye out for Jack Walepole. All they knew was that he posed a threat to Kate. It was all they needed to know. But until the second week in August none had seen him in Brighton. However, it was on the third day of the *Gypsy*'s mission that Danny and Willy were strolling home from the Pump Room and noticed a toadlike man with a bush of wayward black hair and a dark shadow covering his cheeks and chin come sauntering out of the Count's cottage.

"Damn, but he fits the description, don't he?" said Willy, touching Danny's arm in a way that halted him from further approach.

"*Certes,* but he does! Can't be two such creatures walking the earth; it wouldn't be fair," said Danny.

Willy cast him an odd look, but said simply, "Quite."

"What do you think we should do?" asked Danny.

"Follow him. Nothing else for it. Told you, didn't I? Said if Branwell gives us any information it will end in our having to get involved. See where this has led us."

"No," said Danny.

"You will, and it won't be anywhere you want to go."

"But we must, you know."

"Indeed, nothing for it. Must, but there you are," said Willy.

They proceeded their reconnaissance with much stealth, and it says much to their credit that Jack Walepole noted them not. He was an unpleasant and vile man, but he was cunning and not without sense.

Soon they took to horse, which was not easy as they had to manage the affair of leasing two horses in whispers and attempt to watch Walepole's movements down the road.

Some two hours later they lost him in Romney Marsh near the village of Dymchurch. "Don't like this area, liable to get bludgeoned by a smuggler," said Willy, looking warily about him.

"Eh? Are we in the marshes?" asked Danny, suddenly surprised.

"Been in for some miles past. Don't like it, could be taken for revenuers. They don't like the revenuers here, you know. I don't like the revenuers, why should they? And damn if I want to be taken for one," said Willy, distressed over the notion.

"Well, perhaps we had better turn back. It is pretty obvious he has gone into Dymchurch."

"We could have a look in at the tavern, though it ain't a good idea."

"Why isn't it a good idea?" asked Danny, fascinated with this mode of thought.

"Well, stands to reason, the smugglers will be about . . . might not like us drinking in their tavern! I wouldn't like a revenuer drinking in *my* tavern!" said Willy reasonably.

"But we aren't revenuers!" said Danny.

"They don't know that."

"Then shall we return?"

"Hang me if I will! Poor spirited not to see the thing through. Told you Branwell would have us involved. Warned you, but you wouldn't listen. Now see where he has us, drinking ale with smugglers and being murdered as revenuers!"

The tavern known as the White Hart was reached some twenty-five minutes after this discussion, and our gallants strode bravely to its doors. It was at this particular moment that an unfortunate individual wrongly suspected of being an exciseman was given a facer by one of the tavern's regular patrons. The poor fellow's dazed expression as he lunged backward told a story regarding the strength of the man who had landed him the one blow. Willy and Danny stepped aside, took pity, and held up their hands to receive the unconscious man. He was helped by them into an upright position and placed against the wall of the tavern. However, this availed not, for the poor man then slid to the floor with a heavy thud.

Danny and Willy stared for a moment and gave the fellow a sympathetic shake of their heads, and Willy added, "So sorry, ole boy." Upon which they braced themselves and entered the tavern. The place consisted of a rough set of men and women alike, any of which could indeed have been engaged in the questionable activity of smuggling. They looked around, smiling when they thought it would help, but saw no sign of Walepole. The tavernkeeper suggested rather strenuously that they enjoy a bumper of ale, which they thought it wise to do. However, after another bumper of ale apiece, the prospect of remaining at the tavern a bit longer weighed not as sadly, and it was quite soon after that they found themselves readily accepted. Willy and Danny found themselves being heartily slapped on the back as being right 'uns, received a wench each to enliven their spirits, and gave thanks that they were not revenuers!

Portugal proved once more to be fruitful, and the *Gypsy*'s sails were full as she traveled northward, making record time. The news that Branwell had to report was grave, for the French fleet had moved and it had stationed itself at Cadiz. This could only mean that they meant to attack and take Trafalgar! It was certain now that what Branwell had to relate would send Admiral Nelson and his ship the *Victory* to collect his fleet and meet Monsieur Villeneuve! Damn, thought Branwell with determination, they would give the Frogs a drubbing!

Just as the *Gypsy*'s watch spotted English soil, Willy and Danny awoke to find themselves beneath a table on the hard wooden floor of the White Hart. The sun was shining brightly, but they were spared its rays as they groaned into consciousness.

Danny blinked and said, "Oh God!"

"Daniel, must you shout?" complained Willy, putting a hand to his forehead. "You see what comes of listening to Branwell?" he added as an afterthought.

"Morning, gents!" said the tavernkeeper cheerfully. "We didn't want to disturb you! Thought it best to let ye sleep it off."

"Eh, oh quite," said Willy.

"Do ye still want it delivered?" asked the tavernkeeper.

"Want . . . what . . . delivered?" asked Willy. Danny was still only capable of uttering two words, those being "Oh God."

"Why, the brandy. Bought two kegs, asked if m'men would deliver it. We struck a deal," said the tavernkeeper suspiciously.

"I purchased French brandy?"

"Aye, 'tis that which landed ye under the table. Tasted it, and wouldn't let go of the bottle, the lad, too. Bought and paid for yer kegs ye did."

"Oh, I remember now," said Willy. "I think you must deliver it . . . don't have a wagon, you see."

"Well, me and the lads, we been thinking it be safer fer ye to carry it, less chance of ye being stopped."

Willy wanted now to be rid of this burly man with the loud voice. He agreed, and then proceeded to run outdoors and be very sick. Danny, one might think in sympathy, followed suit.

"Sarah, Danny, Willy!" exclaimed Kate, running hoydenishly across the hall to the drawing room. "We are back. . . ."

"Good Lord, Branwell!" said Sarah, rising from the sofa. "Never say she went out on the streets like that?"

"Out in the streets and into my hatch, where she was not discovered until she made herself known several hours later," said Branwell, a light dancing in his eyes.

"Where are Willy and Danny?" asked Kate, disappointed that they weren't present to hear her tales.

"They haven't returned since yesterday. Out on some lark, I imagine."

"Well then, Sarah, I leave my Kate to you. See to it that she stays out of mischief," smiled Branwell.

"But where are you going?" demanded Sarah, astonished.

"To London. And I have no time to waste," said he, turning to flick his wife's nose. He bent low and whispered something in her ear, and it was significant to Sarah that a blush stole onto her niece's cheek!

A few hours later and near to dinner, two young gentlemen found their way into the Mannering residence and were immediately pounced upon by Kate.

"Where have you two been? You look dreadful. Have you been foxed, you horrid boys? Why should you do such a thing to yourselves? And oh wait till you hear," exclaimed Kate.

"We have been to Dymchurch, where we drank brandy with smugglers, who thankfully did not think we were revenuers and left us undead, though I hesitate to call our state of existence, at the moment, living. Wait till we hear what?" asked Willy, receiving an admiring glance from Danny, who thought his lucidity under their present circumstances quite exceptional!

"We have found the French, and they are at Cadiz, and we were fired upon, and I could have been killed but was only splashed, you see. And Branwell has gone to London to tell Pitt!"

"Dash it, Kate, I wish I had been with you instead of with Willy, here."

"Well, I like that!" exclaimed Willy, thinking this was an unjust thing to say.

"Not that I don't like your company, Willy, but to be fired upon, I mean really. One rarely gets the chance," explained Danny.

Sir Wilson Malmsey sighed, much in accord with this line of thought. However, he retaliated after a moment, "We *could have* been fired upon!"

"It's not the same thing."

Kate held her stomach and roared with amusement as the conversation continued, expanded, and became increasingly ludicrous. Then with a sigh she thought of Branwell. He would not be returning until tomorrow evening, and oh! she was already missing him more than she thought possible!

48

Kate strolled leisurely down the street on her way home from the dressmaker's shop. It was well into the late afternoon and she was sure to receive a scolding from Sarah for having gone off without her maid in attendance, but she so liked being free. It gave her leisure to think and enjoy the salt air. She sighed, wondering if Branwell would be able to keep his promise and return before dinner. The wind had picked up and caught her yellow straw bonnet, causing it to flap, and, as she reached up to settle it upon her head once again, her shawl slipped from her arm. With a sigh of exasperation she pulled the yellow muslin shawl around her and brought her eyes back to the walk. This, in time to view two young people meandering slowly toward her, both of whom she knew.

The young woman was the Clifford heiress, whom Sarah had pointed out to her on occasion, and the other creature was one that caused her heart to bend in on itself! She hadn't thought of Perry Banyon in months. It was not her way to dwell on thoughts that pained. She had blocked him from her mind. She had warded off thoughts that reminded and she had banished his name from her consciousness. It gave her a start to see him strolling toward her, smiling intimately at the unsuspecting girl batting her dull eyes at him. So, he was a determined fellow, it would appear, and had set his sights at yet another wealthy female! He had not the power to wring more pain from Kate, for her life and heart were full, but she had no wish to encounter him. They saw her, he saw her, but she didn't care; she darted down the narrow drive of a small but quaint cottage at her right.

She reached the front doors and realized it was the Count Mirabel's cottage and nearly cursed herself for a nodcock. She couldn't stay here lest they see her and ask her in, which Branwell would dislike excessively. Then, too, she couldn't go back to the walk, for she could see Perry and the Clifford girl just above the yew hedge. With a quick movement she circled the house, hugging the bushes and darting away from both the cottage windows and Perry's vision!

"There is nothing for it, Mora, *mia damma* . . . you must not fear! All will be well. Have we not come this far?" said the Count, taking his stepsister into his embrace.

"But Napoleon! You say that the message he sends us makes it dangerous for us to remain, yet we do not go," cried Moravia.

"Indeed, for he plans a land attack at Ulm and Austerlitz, and the coalition stands no chance. He knows it. They cannot group army enough until December, not without

Prussia, and Prussia has shown itself a coward! But he strikes not until October; we have time. Next week we leave, leisurely, and no one will suspect or try to detain us."

"Oh, Alban! We go to Venice, to Mirabel. I do so miss it. These English are not in my style with their cold eyes. Their blood is ice and ours bubbles with the Po!"

"Yes, we go to Venice, but first, my love, first we go to Paris and collect our prize, yes!" He kissed her long and tenderly. He was always tender when pleased. "*Mia* Mora, come, we shall go inside."

Kate gasped, and put a hand to her mouth. The Count and his sister? But how could she be his sister? His touch had not been that of a brother . . . and they were spies! So involved was she with this new development that she never heard the rustle of a bush behind her. She stepped backward, thinking to make her retreat, when she stepped directly into the hold of Jack Walepole. His hand went over her mouth, muffling her scream, and his other hand took her wrist, bending her arm backward against her spine. It happened so swiftly that she didn't realize what was toward, didn't realize her danger until she heard his voice at her ear. "So, my little virgin! But you ain't no virgin any longer. You be Lady Mannering, and a spy to boot!"

He dragged her into the open, displaying his catch to the Count's startled eyes. "Look'ee what I found slinking about, listening to our business. Think her lord set her to it?"

"Oh my God, Alban, she has heard us. She knows," said Moravia.

The Count's eyes reflected his irritation. "It appears we shall have to alter our plans. We leave for Paris, immediately, and Lady Mannering will honor our expedition with her company!"

"But why?" cried Moravia.

"Because, *mia* Mora, she has learned more than we want her lord to know just yet! We should never make the coast if we were to let her go, and as our game is not murder, we cannot silence her in that way either. Unless we are left no choice! As of now, we have the choice. She will afford us safe passage, should anyone attempt to deter our progress," said the Count.

He turned to Walepole. "Bring her inside, quickly, before someone observes us out here," he said, taking his sister by the arm and leading them all into the drawing room. He moved quickly and locked the doors to the hallway, insuring their privacy, and then he turned to survey Lady Mannering in the toad's grasp. He hated Walepole and he had long wanted Kate. He had no liking for seeing such a pretty in such an ugly's rough hands. He went to the cabinet at his back and produced a powder from a small envelope. This was transferred to a glass and mixed with brandy, barely a jiggerful.

"Mora, you will assist me! Walepole, place Her Ladyship on her back."

Kate was a fighter, and in her effort overturned a table and gave Mora a kick that caused the woman to pinch at Kate's arm. In the end, Kate found herself on her back, her head held roughly back, her mouth forced open, and small bits of the brandy and powder mixture were being poured down her throat. Oh God, she thought, why can I not prevent myself from swallowing? Well, I shall not let it affect me. I shall not . . . oh Lord, I feel dizzy . . . .

She was rearranged. She felt herself lifted, but it was not Walepole who lifted her. She saw the Count's face above hers, saw his smile, and it frightened her as much as Walepole's. But she couldn't move her lips. She could feel, she could see, though things were becoming vague, but she couldn't speak. And still she was thinking, I shan't let it affect me. . . .

"There, she is nearly out Mora, go pack. Take only what we shall need for a few days. We will buy what we need in Paris." He turned to Walepole. "You may come with us to Dymchurch and arrange our passage; you will receive your final payment there."

"Very well, I'll go hire a post-chaise and drive it up to the gate, but how do you mean to get her into it without being seen?"

"Leave that to me!" The Count turned to find Mora

still there, and she was looking sulky. "Hurry up, *mia damma*; there is no time!"

"You call me your dove, but your eyes are on her!" she said accusingly.

"Don't be a fool; now hurry! Walepole gets our carriage, and you will have to help me with our baggage here," he said, curtly.

She swirled in her skirts and left the room, and the Count turned his eyes to Kate, traversing her body and wondering what it would be like to take her. But now, now there was no time. Later, when they were on the boat.

"Hang it, Willy, We should have sent Kate's groom. I feel ridiculous sitting in this wagon," snapped Danny.

Willy maneuvered the horse and sighed, "Stupid! This is smuggled brandy; can't have a groom with a loose mouth knowing about it."

"Well, who says his mouth is loose?"

"Who says it ain't?" countered Willy.

"Devilish way to spend a day, tramping to and fro from Dymchurch with two kegs of brandy!"

"Stop nagging at me! You sound like an old woman!" returned Willy.

"Old woman?" ejaculated Danny. "An old woman would be out bathing in the sea and *not* smuggling brandy into the Earl of Mannering's home!"

This rather caught Willy as just, and he allowed the matter to drop. However, by the time they reached and passed Hastings, another topic of disagreement had crept up, and they were well in its midst when a carriage passed them on the road. Oddly enough, though both had been speaking at once, and neither had shown signs of ceasing, they did so most abruptly.

"That blasted fellow again, damn if it wasn't that blasted fellow again!" said Willy, much upset.

"Had to be! Branwell said he looked like a toad with a mop of dark hair, and so he does. Besides, he is the same fellow we followed into the marshes the other night."

"Think we ought to follow him?" asked Willy.

But Danny didn't hear him. He was frowning severely. "Know what, Willy? That was Lady Moravia and the Count inside that carriage."

"I know," said Willy placidly.

"You know and you ain't surprised?"

"Told you, rum 'uns."

"Did no such thing. You never called them that; you said you didn't trust them. But . . ."

"Well, now that I've seen them with that blasted fellow I'm calling them rum 'uns!"

Danny frowned again. "Know what, Willy? There was someone else in the coach with them, slumped over. A woman I think, with black hair, and if I didn't know better—But that's silly! Come on, Willy, let's spring 'em. I have a notion to get home now!" said Danny on impulse.

The Earl's meeting had gone well. The third coalition was indeed in danger. Without Prussia's forces, they stood little chance against Boney on the eastern front. Their only chance would be to gain control of the seas! Now with the knowledge that the French fleet was grouping at Cadiz, preparing to take Trafalgar, Nelson would be able to corner them and force them into battle. Branwell reached Brighton in good time and, smiling, strode past Kirkly, who held the door open. However, he caught himself up short when Sarah charged down upon him in the hall.

"Oh Branwell, Kate . . . Kate is missing!" cried Sarah wretchedly.

The Earl's green eyes lost their color as did his cheeks, and he felt an odd rendition of fear pierce his flesh. "What do you mean, Sarah?"

"She went to her dressmaker for a fitting, but she was due here an hour ago, and what I find most disconcerting is . . ."

The door knocker sounded and, their faces pulled with anxiety, they rushed at the door—Kirkly, Branwell, and Sarah—almost fighting for the right to open it. However, dignity won over, and Kirkly was allowed to perform his duty. Willy and Danny stood before them, smiling idiotically and feeling a twinge of umbrage at the oaths they received. Then Danny frowned and stepped into the house. "Where is Kate?" he demanded, apprehension shooting through him. He had felt this way once before when he and Kate had gone exploring and she had gone off away from him. She had fallen through an opening in the coral cave they were exploring and lay unconscious in its pit. They had been children, and he was then not old enough to know how to get her out, and the tide was coming in. He had run all the way home to his father and together they had managed to pull Kate out, but he had been sick inside during the entire ordeal. For some inexplicable reason, he felt very much the same now.

"I don't know, Danny. Have you not seen her then?" cried Sarah.

"Indeed no," said Willy. "We have only just now returned from Dymchurch. What's toward?"

Branwell, every muscle pulsing, every nerve ending on fire, turned to his aunt. "At once, Sarah, what was disconcerting?"

"Yes, yes! You see . . . I met the Clifford girl . . . and, well, Perry Banyon was with her. I would have cut him dead, but you see, I could not be rude to her, so I stopped to chat, and Perry mentioned seeing Kate just around the corner!"

"What more is there?" he demanded.

"They said she darted down the drive of that quaint cottage, the one the Count has leased, and they supposed her to have gone inside. Well, naturally, when I came home and found that she had not yet arrived I despatched a lackey to see after her, but there' was no one about except some servant girl and she in a huff! Said the Count had dismissed her and . . ."

"Devil a bit!" exploded Danny, interrupting. "But it can't be. . . . Why would Kate go off with them and not tell you?"

"Go off with them?" asked the Earl, rounding on him.

"Yes, I thought I saw her, but then thought it couldn't be, for she was slumped over, and it was the toad . . .

that Walepole fellow driving the coach . . . toward Dymchurch," said Danny, feeling worse with each word.

The Earl started for the door, shouting over his shoulder, "I'll be taking your horse, Willy; mine is done in."

"We'll be after you in Kate's phaeton," called Willy after him, but the Earl had already vanished from their view. His mind and body had turned into a perfect working machine, intent on one thing, getting to his Kate. It dawned on him that she was the essence of his being. She was that which gave him life. He had lived twenty-eight years without her, but now, now he was very certain he could not live one day into the future without her! At all cost he would reach her, and the Devil or God help any that tried to prevent him. And Walepole was one he intended to tear into threads of flesh with his own hands.

Kate awoke to find herself in a small attic room. It was not very bright, for the sun was setting, and it was dirty and smelled of mildew. She was dizzy and the objects swimming around the room seemed twice their normal size and stretched out of shape. No one was with her! It was the very next thing that came to mind. Oh, thank God! Was she free of them? If only she could raise her arms and pull herself up, but they were like dead weights. Her legs, too, they were numb and she felt a cripple. Her body was crippled! Oh God, what had they done to her? She was terrified. Then she saw the Count come into the room. His figure was distorted, as was his smile as he stood over her.

He reached down and stroked her silky black hair. It had tumbled around her shoulders, and he liked the feel of its flowing lengths. His hand traveled to her shoulder and moved farther downward, sucking in his breath at the feel of her alluring figure. The door burst open and he spun around to face Mora's livid countenance.

"Alban! How can you?" she cried.

He rose at once and went to her, scooping her in his arms. "It is nothing, nothing, *mia* Mora; she is nothing to me!"

"But you would take her, even lifeless as she is; you

would take her! Why?" pleaded Mora.

He frowned. "I don't know! Perhaps because she rejected me. Come, you have nought to fear; she is nothing beside you."

"I don't believe you!"

"Go downstairs, Mora, and leave me be. I have asked you before not to do this. You interrupt my pleasures and that must not be!" he said cruelly, his patience running out.

Walepole appeared at that moment and surveyed the situation. His tongue darted out, licking his lower lip. "You be wanted, Count. All that's needed is to set the price, and since you don't care for my way of bargaining, you best be doing it yourself."

The Count made an exasperated sound and brushed past him, stopping to turn to Mora. "Be ready to leave, Moravia; it will be soon."

She watched him go, thinking he had never flaunted his desire for another woman before her. This one, this Lady Mannering, intrigued him too much! She represented a danger. Jack Walepole watched Moravia's expression and said slowly, "If I were you, I wouldn't take the little doxy along."

"It is only to the coast of France; he sends her back when we disembark!" snapped Moravia.

"He might not. He might wish to keep her longer, if she is as enjoyable as she looks," taunted Walepole.

"Shut up!"

"Now, now, no need to get your bristles aired! Have a notion! I could relieve you of your problem, for a fee."

"How?"

"I could take her, now, while he is with the men, fixing a price. It gives me just enough time to ride off with her. I have the horse all ready in the stable."

"You would see to it that she is returned to her home, after we have landed in France?" asked Moravia, excitedly.

"Of course," said Walepole.

"But Alban, he will be so angry with me," said Mora, doubtfully.

"You couldn't stop me . . . you were in your room. I ran off with her. Not your fault," said Walepole suggestively.

Moravia thought quickly and made up her mind. "Take her to your horse. I will bring you the money."

Kate heard all this and tried to scream, but nothing happened. She couldn't make a sound as he lifted her into his arms. Oh God, she was sick all over. The touch of him, the ugly scent of him, sent waves of nausea through her. She felt herself slung over the horse's back. She felt the hard leather's curving rim cut into her flat belly and saw the ground beneath her head and again tried to scream. Only this time she heard her voice; it was weak and hoarse and her mouth was dry, but she could hear her voice.

"So, you be getting back to your senses, m'proud lady. Well, well, just in time," said Walepole thickly. He was seated behind her on the saddle, waiting for Moravia.

Mora appeared with a small handkerchief and she offered it up to Walepole. He sneered, "What . . . for a pittance?"

" 'Tis all I have; he has all the money, you know that."

He thought quickly. There would be ransom enough for Lady Mannering after he had finished with her. He took the handkerchief and stuffed it into his pocket and gave his horse a nasty kick, sending them bounding forward!

Lady Moravia returned to the White Hart and encountered Alban on the stairs. "Alban, Alban, I tried to stop him. Walepole. He has absconded with Lady Mannering."

"What, the devil! No doubt he plans to ransom her for a fee! May he rot in perdition. Well, there is no time; we are to get our things and go now!"

Quietly, Lady Moravia followed him, smiling contentedly to herself.

Jack Walepole made for the open glen, bypassing the Dymchurch road. He wanted to find a nice secluded spot, for soon it would be dark enough for him to exact his pleasure without fear of interruption!

It was wearing off! She could feel a tingling sensation in her limbs. Her legs, though strangely stiff, were jiggling against the horse's motion, and she moved them experimentally. Now for her hands, for her arms. Oh God, she could move them. She touched the horse's side, pressing her hand into its muscle, closing and opening her hand. She wiggled her toes inside her shoes, and she waited. She waited for the right moment! It came soon enough. Walepole began slowing his horse, and she felt the canter subside and bounce into a trot, and she heard his malicious voice. "Aye there, m'proud wench, we'll see how proud ye be. We'll see how you writhe beneath me, and then I'll sell you back to that lord of yours!"

Kate saw the ground bouncing beneath her chin, and she slid unobtrusively backward, waiting for the right speed. Walepole looked around and discovered he liked his whereabouts, a small patch of glen surrounded by thick green swatches of woods. Indeed, it would do. He slowed into a walk. All at once Kate gave herself a push, falling backwards off the horse, but landing on her butt. She was filled with desperation and it lifted her to her feet and took her running to the thick of the woods. She could feel the horse at her back. Any moment Walepole would run her down. But she couldn't . . . wouldn't look back! She tore madly into the forest; her gown was shredded as she dove through the brambles, and her bare arms were bleeding within seconds. But she ran on and on, never once looking back! She didn't have to. She could hear him, winding his horse through the thicket, crashing through the bush, screeching out his filth at her, threatening his evil at her, and she ran, dived, and ran again. Her heart beat at her chest wall, crying for relief, but her mind silenced it! It cried, I shall burst, Kate, I shall burst! But she ran, for her mind screamed of terror!

Then the protection of the woods left her, and once again she was in an open field with the danger just behind her. There was a road a hundred yards away, and past it another patch of trees. Could she make it? Oh God, let me make it, let me gain time. Time for Branwell to come, for he *would* come. Her heart called for him, and she knew he would hear!

She darted into the open glen, racing through its tall grass, her body on fire with pain, her lungs demanding respite, and her ears full with Walepole's laugh! It echoed and surrounded her as though a devil were looming into giant proportions, leaving hell to take over the skies! Was she mad? Was this all part of a nightmare? It couldn't be real! Could this be real? But she didn't stop, she couldn't stop; just as the graceful deer runs to escape the hunter's bullet, she ran and had even less chance!

She felt the earth reverberate with the beat of the horse's galloping. Then pain went seering through her flesh, grazing her spirit, and sending her sprawling to the ground!

Walepole had laughed with the chase! Indeed it was no nightmare, but real, and it filled him with glory! The glory of power, and how he loved it! She was a wild gazelle, and he the master, and he took off his buckled belt and swung it around his head, a war cry filling the air as he aimed his weapon. It landed with force across Kate's soft back. It tore through her thin muslin, making its bloody track across her back, sending her down, and he laughed at his victory. God, this was life, he thought, this made it worth the while, this! It made it for him, and he went off his horse, forgetting it, forgetting thoughts of preserving her flesh for ransom! Lashing followed lashing as Kate got to her knees, crying but refusing to be buckled down! Her body writhed spasmodically with each blow but she ran, no longer sure of what she was doing.

Walepole went after her. He was half-crazed. He thought only of torture, he thought only of paying back . . . of killing! But before killing, he would take her, and take her, that's what he would do. So he told her as he lunged for her legs. He missed his target as she dashed sideways and he fell to the ground. He picked himself up with renewed fury and was after her in a moment, but Kate had already made the road. She was no longer in a state to realize its significance, but he was! He saw the road and there saw a danger to his plans! He was obsessed with the need to expunge his evil upon her. And was it not glory? Did she not bleed, and at his hands? Was he not mighty? He lunged at her again, spurred on by his thoughts, and he caught her long flowing hair, pulling at it unmercifully. Twisting it around his wrist, he yanked her down onto the ground, then he dragged her. She cried out and heard herself, for she cried Branwell's name. She felt herself brought low, yet she clawed at Walepole's hands with her nails, and she pulled her head against the pain, biting into his arm, and he slapped her across her face.

He pulled her into the woods adjacent to the road. He thought of how he would take her, there in the woods. Yes, better than the glen, and there he would leave her broken body when he had done. For in the woods she might not be found for months, and her death would not be traced to him!

Kate screamed and screamed, and she called down her curse upon him. "Mannering will know. He will know . . . and there is nowhere, nowhere you will be able to hide. He will kill you, Walepole. If you touch me, he will kill you. . . ."

"I have already touched you," he said, stopping to dig his nails across the bleeding welts at her back. "Here . . . and here . . . and here," he said, scratching through the blood into what was left of her flesh. She cried out in agony, and not twenty yards down the road to Dymchurch the Earl of Mannering heard her! It took Branwell less than a thought to fathom the direction of her scream, and then but a moment to reach her. Walepole had dragged Kate farther into the woods, and his cruel hands had torn away what was left of the bodice of her gown, and he was lost to his blood lust. He never heard the Earl coming down upon him until Branwell's growl, which was the sound of Zeus's thunder, and Branwell's hands, those of Mars, had taken him in tow!

Jack Walepole's deformed body was raised into the air and flung onto the ground. The Earl had seen him, but what he saw was a wild ugly animal whose teeth were bared over Kate, and he lunged with but one intent and that was to destroy! Walepole's head struck a rock and his eyes glazed as the blood gushed, and he saw the Earl reach down for him again and put up his hands to ward off the blow. It was useless! The Earl took him up again, raising him high enough to smash him forcefully to earth! And again, and again!

Kate heard Branwell. She whispered his name, and then she sobbed. It was a heartbreaking sound that shook her whole body. She had known he would come. She knew it, yet she cried. And the sobs were not of pain, not physical pain. She cried because she had doubted, she cried because she saw his rage, and knew *him* to be in pain, and she cried because her heart was filled with the realization that she had been the object of hatred! It was a disquieting thought to discover someone had wanted to kill her, to hurt her and then kill her! She watched in tearful awe as the Earl hurled the broken body of Jack Walepole into a heap upon the ground, and she knew that Walepole was dead. She called Branwell's name. He turned at once and went to her, taking her in his arms, seeing her blood all about him, and the tears came to his eyes and spilled over. She reached out hesitatingly, for she was dizzy and unsure, and she gingerly touched the rolling tear, saying wondrously, "I didn't know gods had tears." Then Kate felt herself slip away.

He caught her limp body to him, rocking her in his arms, crying with a violence, saying her name over and over. Thanking God for bringing him in time, and sobbing over the thought that he might have lost her.

Kate's eyelids fluttered and her gray eyes smiled, for the first things she saw were the Earl's green eyes, shining down at her. He had soaked his handkerchief in the stream and put its coolness to her head, bringing her round to him. He made a strange sound much between a sob and a laugh, and kissed the hand he clasped fervently in his own. "Fondling, you gave me a fright," he said softly.

"I want to go home, Branwell," said Kate, suddenly remembering.

"We will, darling. I expect Willy and Danny will be along any moment with the phaeton, and I'll take you home."

She looked down to find the Earl had covered her with his riding coat, and she sighed, "It was a favorite dress of mine."

He laughed. "No doubt I shall be made to pay for another."

She didn't smile and there was a sadness in her she couldn't shake. "He hated me, Branwell, he really hated me. He *wanted* to *hurt* me . . . and then to kill me! Why? I must have wounded him terribly to have instilled in him such a need for revenge. How could I have been so cruel, and never have realized it? How many people have I done that to?"

"No sweetings, no. Hush! *You* wound anyone? The fault was not with you, but with him. He was malformed and it twisted his mind. He didn't hate *you*, he hated all mankind. His hating is over."

"I know, I saw. Oh Branwell, I don't like killing."

"It was necessary."

"I want to go home," said Kate in answer to this. She reminded him of a small child seeking security and reassurance. He soothed and he coddled. He had to get her home and attend her wounds . . . the mental as well as the physical ones.

Danny and Willy arrived shortly thereafter. There was much distress at Kate's condition, and it is necessary to note that both Danny and Willy, neither of whom had ever before thought of killing, did so now! However, Walepole was dead, and though Danny had the urge to kick the dead man's body, he controlled himself. He watched the Earl put Kate in the phaeton, watched Willy add his jacket to that of the Earl's, draping it over Kate's knees, and he sighed!

Walepole's and the Earl's horses were fetched, but Danny and Willy stood silent a long while before meeting one another's glance. It was Danny who broke the silence. "Do you know what, Willy?"

"I certainly do. We now have a body, a dead body on our hands." He sighed. "We shall have to go into Dymchurch and report it to the magistrate."

"Well, we can't, must see that," said Danny practically.

"Oh, why not?" asked Willy surprised, but hopeful.

"Well, plain as pikestaff!" exclaimed Danny, pleased to be taking the lead. "You gave your coat to Kate, you are standing in your waistcoat and shirtsleeves. Can't go calling on a magistrate in your shirtsleeves!"

Willy turned a beaming eye upon Danny. "Indeed, lad, you have learned a great deal. There is much hope for you! Very well, nothing for it, we must leave the scoundrel to the buzzards. At least for tonight. In the morning Branwell will know what to do."

Danny mounted Walepole's horse. "I'd rather the buzzards do it all," said he with some venom.

"Hold a moment, we are forgetting about the Count and his sister," said Willy. "Shouldn't we ride into Dymchurch and discover their lay?"

"They are probably half-way across the Channel by now, Willy."

"I am so glad, for the truth is, shouldn't know what to do with them once we got 'em. Would you?"

Danny screwed up his mouth. "Would have been only one thing to do! Take 'em to the Earl."

Willy opened his eyes wide. "Excellent notion. Think we should?"

Danny interrupted him, "Let's go home, Willy."

"Precisely what I was going to say," said Willy, taking umbrage.

Epilogue

October saw changes! Danny was once again at Cambridge and getting himself involved in every imaginable lark. The Mannerings were once again installed in London. Nell and Master Hatch found comfort and pleasure in their marriage. Aunt Sarah, whose mind was as ever unfathomable, kept her Squire John dangling and none knew whether she meant to end her widowhood. Mr. Perry Banyon acquired as wife the Clifford heiress, and one may only speculate regarding their future. The Count and his stepsister reached Bonaparte and Paris safely and were amply rewarded. Pleased with their deeds, and who is to say they should not be, for politics is a relative item, they continued to Venice and their Villa Mirabel. It is to be supposed they may continue much in the same manner.

They were to see the fruits of their political endeavors, for though it may be considered regrettable, the third coalition saw its death on October 20, 1805! Boney marched upon the Austrian army, too weak and unprepared to fend him off! He won his battle at Austerlitz and the road to Venice was open. Austria withdrew from the third coalition and from Italy!

However, England and Prime Minister Pitt were compensated the loss of the third coalition by a battle that made England the master of the seas! On October 21, 1805, just one day after the French battle with Austria, Nelson, his ship *Victory* and the combined fleet met that of the French at Trafalgar! Once again Admiral Nelson gave unflinchingly for his country! He won the battle, saving the Straits, giving England control of the seas, and losing his life in the achievement of his goals!

The news of Nelson's death was a blow to England.

He was beloved by all and no less so by Branwell Mannering! Some days afterward Branwell sat in his study at Mannering House in London, sadly pondering the fates, when Kate skipped into the room and climbed upon his lap.

"Would you like to name him Nelson?" she asked joyfully.

"What? What are you jabbering about, fondling?" he asked her absently, coming out of his reverie. "Name whom?"

"Our son, of course. Who else would we have the naming of?" She glanced over the desk. "Weren't you supposed to give a speech at Parliament tomorrow? Your paper is blank, and do hurry, for Willy and Brummell will be here soon. They dine with us tonight."

"Our son?" interrupted the Earl, blankly. "Kate, Kate . . . are you with child?" he asked with some excitement.

"How could I not be?" she retorted, nuzzling him.

His hand traveled to her flat belly, marveling that his child, his very own child, was lodged within this small being, and then his lips sought her own, and his kiss was, as always, like their very first!